WATERSHED

✦ HN DEEB ✦

WATERSHED

Copyright © 2019 by HN Deeb

ISBN 978-1-7336848-0-4 (ebook)
ISBN 978-1-7336848-1-1 (paperback)

Fruitstone Press, Los Angeles
fruitstonepress.com
info@fruitstonepress.com

Cover design and layout by Damonza, damonza.com

"Cassie's gift" design by HN Deeb

Author photograph by David Carlson, davidcarlsonphotography.com

This is a work of fiction. The future it depicts is not (yet) real, and all names, characters, places, entities, and events portrayed are either products of the author's imagination or used fictitiously. Any resemblance to actual persons, living or dead, or to actual events, is coincidental.

For Tom

PART 1

—As friction frees the sacred element from bonds,
does injustice spur the seeker from chains.

—Catechism of Transcendence,
Renunciation

CHAPTER 1
CASSIE

CASSIE FROZE MID-CRAWL. The joist above her head had creaked ominously. She was too far in by now to do anything about it if the tunnel collapsed. She tapped the two-by-four with her lump hammer anyway, if only for reassurance. Inhaling as deeply as the subterranean chamber allowed and puffing a strand of mousy hair away from her eyes, she pointed her headlamp in front of her and slunk forward like—like whatever she hoped was not slinking along behind her. Only a few more yards to go.

Cassie hated tunnel jobs. Added blindness and added work for no more pay. Almost every job took place at night for obvious reasons—better cover and less risk of evaporation—but a tunnel shrugged off the beam of light she carried even more than a sewer did. Thankfully, this one had shoring. The smuggler bosses often relied on simple stand-up time (aka fingers crossed) before a shorter tunnel caved. Once a team of children jacked the shield, picked and chiseled the earth, and bucketed spoil out from hand to hand, the bosses had no more patience to build and space timber frames and usually sent the thief in with only a rope and a prayer.

A sharp pain broke her renewed concentration. Cassie touched her bony shoulder and felt her dusty fingertips moisten. A rock or root protruding from the tunnel face had sliced the skin right across the freckle in that spot. She cussed the diggers but it wasn't really their fault. The job was quick and dirty. She used to slither easily through the two-foot wormholes. Since a growth spurt in the spring, though, she got tangled by legs too long and arms too unwieldy. She shouldn't complain, especially because she hadn't had to dig at all this time. It was the bosses' birthday present to her, their graduation gift to the best water thief in the city.

The shadows ahead suddenly gained texture in the head-lamp's ray. Cassie had reached the end of the tunnel. She wiped away a thin layer of soil and felt the sheer angle of a manmade wall. This part of the job made it worthwhile. Private cisterns were illegal but plenty of rich families kept one buried politely out of sight. A foot away lay a tub of water big enough to splash around in. The illicit, luxurious thought was intoxicating.

A foot was as close as she would get. Cassie pulled the drill from her tool harness and fit the forty-gauge bit and extension. If the engineer had calibrated correctly, she would pierce the casing near the top. If not, she would cause a leak and hope the walls didn't shatter under tons of pressure and flood the tunnel.

She spit on the auger and pointed it at the wall. The motor whirred and the bit whined as it cut through cement plaster. She felt it slog through concrete smoothly, missing any steel reinforcement bars, then crack the interior plastic lining.

She withdrew the machine and held her breath. Silence. Cassie shivered. Once, she had done a job further east, near the mountains, where the tank had been made of redwood. The sawdust scent had made her feel warmly cocooned even though she was in a pocket six feet under.

A whisper of cool, damp air reached her. Cassie exhaled. Quickly, she pulled the larger auger from the harness and bored through the wall, this time at an upward angle. It wasn't the only way to crack a cistern, only the hardest. She knew from experience that a cistern seemed like a safe but really was full of holes. It had intake points from the catchment system, pumps and pipes into the building it served, a manhole cover and screened vents on the surface. All would be heavily guarded by people, dogs, alarms, razor wire, triple locks, you name it.

But she also knew that a cistern had a soft underbelly, buried out of sight and mind for most owners. They forgot about pipes for overflow—who could even imagine that these days? Older units had cleanout drains. Drains were the best as long as you could get down the hatch into the access pit and piggyback on the existing piping. With drains, you could collect almost every drop. But they were mostly obsolete because no one would dream of draining water except in the dead of night, under armed guard, and with a re-collection plan. Even then, most people with cisterns were too paranoid to risk it and rich enough to afford maintenance by other means.

The drill broke through and Cassie retrieved and disassembled it. Her Killian fingers were one reason she was the best. Killians had nimble fingers, her godmother Inma told her once. Inma wasn't a Killian. She'd said it offhand with a bittersweet snicker but the rest of that day it had seemed like Cassie's hands belonged to someone else. To ghosts.

She unstrapped the eighteen-inch pipe from her vest—the one advantage to the growth spurt was that she could heft the kit more easily—and threaded it into the tank. When it was through, she pressed the button on the end she still held and heard the extra tubing telescope out. The flex joint would make it pivot downward. If she had drilled to the right height, the other end now dipped below the water's surface inside the cistern.

Her arms ached. A chilly sweat dribbled down her forehead. Her scratchy tank top clung irritatingly to the spot between her shoulder blades. Pins and needles crept through the hip she had been leaning on while she worked. She tried to shift position to relieve the numbness and smacked her head against the cave wall. A vision of entombment rushed into her mind. She pictured her dying body curled in this forgotten cavity until the worms nibbled it to nothing. Impossibly, the tunnel went even blacker. She gasped the thin air, which only made the panic grow and the sweat trickle faster into her eyes.

Cassie closed her throat mid-breath, trapping a gulp of air that squeezed painfully down her esophagus. She focused on controlling the muscles below her ribs like her mentor May had taught her. Eyes clenched, she counted to ten, resisting the urgent flurry of worries warning her that she was taking too long, she would be caught, the bosses would be angry, the lamp would burn out, the siphon would fail, the tunnel would cave.

She shook her head, opened her eyes, and breathed again. She wiped her palms on her pants and, moving even faster than before, unhooked the small pump from her belt as well as the hose she had dragged behind her the whole way. It doubled as a guide rope in case…she buried the thought.

She screwed a valve on one end of the pump onto the pipe sticking out of the cistern wall. She flipped a switch. The pump's battery power wasn't much but it would be enough to prime the siphon. She would attach the hose to the valve on the other side of the pump as soon as the water approached. The temptation was strong to let it spill a little and drink. But you never knew how clean the water was. Most people waited to purify it through filters on the way into their houses. Two water thieves Cassie grew up with had drunk in a moment of weakness and died. Even if you didn't get sick, the bosses would withhold pay—or do worse—if they suspected a cheat. Once they started swigging, most people couldn't stop and spilled wildly, wastefully, making a muddy mess. You wouldn't need a boss's keen eye to spot the telltale streaks.

A line followed by a filmy sheen crossed into view beneath the plastic window of the pump housing, telling Cassie that the water had come through, pushing ahead of it the air in the piping. She secured the hose and that was it. Job done. The water would flow toward the tunnel entrance, where a stronger pump installed near the vertical shaft would draw it faster, up into barrels waiting on the surface. From there, who knew what the bosses did with it, other than slip it into the smugglers' black market. "More liquid than money," Boss Whittier always guffawed, whatever that joke meant.

Trying not to scramble too fast from sheer relief, Cassie made her way back the way she'd come. The way out always began scarier than the way in because the tunnel sloped downward from the cistern wall to allow gravity to work its physical magic on the siphon.

Crack! Ahead of her, wood snapped—the weak joist. Panic shot up her spine again. She surged forward carelessly and ran face first into the splintered timber. Without thinking, she smacked it out of the way. The dirt it held back came loose. Soil rained onto her.

The tunnel was caving. All the earlier hypothetical catastrophes were suddenly clear and present. She inhaled and got a mouthful of musty crumbs. She spat them out and scrabbled and kicked, desperate to reach the next support beam before the earth fell too fast to scoop it behind her.

The tool belt snagged, slowing her down in the narrowing space. She reached a hand to unhook it, but even drowning in dirt she knew the math. If she survived, there was no way she could repay the bosses for the lost kit. She'd be as dead without it up there as with it down here.

Which was looking certain now. Her legs got nowhere churning against the avalanche. She lunged, screaming, reaching for anything—and her fingertips grazed the smooth edge of the next two-by-four. She gripped and pulled with both hands. If it snapped, too, this was the end.

The beam slipped, shifted, but held. Cassie heaved herself forward. Her body free, she flew on until she reached the right angle where the tunnel shot up and opened onto the floor of a room in the abandoned building that served as a staging post. As her colleagues pulled her out of the ground, a huge grin spread across her face. Way too close a call. But she did it. Sixty-four and O. Still the best.

ᗰᗰ

"It's alive!" Teddy greeted Cassie with wide open arms as she limboed under the skewed planks that served as a doorway to what had been a college field house a long time ago. Now it was the water thieves' hangout.

Cassie noticed that Teddy had gotten bigger this year, too. She could feel his biceps flex against her ribcage as she hugged him and he held on a moment longer than normal. He must have heard about her trouble on the job and come to wait for her. It was nice. A little surprising, but nice.

But she didn't want to think about the tunnel anymore. She broke away and strode into the hangout. The walls more or less still stood, though most of the roof had fallen in. Where it hadn't, chipped beams and rusty vent pipes hung like the burned-up space capsules suspended from the ceiling of the science museum. Pieces of giant panels and twisted girders sprinkled the ground, which was a mosaic of dirt, concrete, and grubby patches of undegradable artificial turf.

Teddy followed her. "Happy birthday, Cass," he said. "Glad it wasn't your last." So he had heard. It was a weird thing to say, though. Not mean, necessarily, but why was he grinning like that?

"Go soak your head in it, Teddy." Her best friend Mariah hipped him aside and put a half-full glass in Cassie's hand.

Cassie watched Teddy bound away. Mariah's interruption irked unexpectedly. Teddy had been loud and all over the place since they were little, and affectionate with all his friends. But lately it felt like- like in that hug now, she felt her body melt a little as he pressed against her a beat longer than he used to.

She rolled her eyes as much at herself as for Mariah's benefit and sniffed the glass. "Juice?" Fruit was a luxury. Anything sweet was, really.

"Hundred percent," Mariah confirmed proudly. "Everyone saved up for the special occasion." She flourished a flask. "If it's too sweet?"

"No thanks." It would make her even thirstier and, to be

honest, after the sensory fog of the tunnel she wanted to feel buzzless tonight.

Her friend shrugged and grabbed her hand, pulling her along. A few of the more reckless kids perched on strips of teetering second-story walkway. When they were young newbs, Cassie and her friends played hide and seek and king of the mountain amid the debris. She smiled at the memory. It was a good spot. Their place, abandoned when the city shrank, reverting inexorably to scrub, but reclaimed by their little secret society.

She let Mariah drag her toward a knot of teenagers, a few of them Cassie's age, most a bit younger, and one or two former water thieves who still hung around, dispensing advice and demanding respect. They all bounced to music thumping from battery-powered speakers set at the corners of a make-shift dance floor on the clearest strip of ground. Someone had set up a web of laser lights to make a sort of faux ceiling marking off the square from the rest of the field. Another grid a few feet lower lit splotches across the dancers' bodies, splashing color onto their faded clothes. A beam lit up a lipless grin. Cassie jumped back before she realized it was a calavera mask its wearer must have kept after visiting the cemetery that week on Día de Muertos. She noticed others scattered about, which lent the grooving crowd a Dante-esque grace.

Mariah carved out a spot and dived in, her tresses and twins elastic in the effortless way that always enhanced Cassie's own self-consciousness. Teddy was in the mix, too, shaking a booty she couldn't help notice had beefed up like his arms. He needed a haircut. Teddy managed to seem permanently untidy, though not quite in a cultivated way like some of the others. He would retire from thieving in a few weeks, too, and not a moment too soon. If she had trouble in the tunnels by now, he must get stuck.

He caught her looking at him and stunted, almost successfully. As usual, she had no idea if he was seriously trying or pranking. From the sea of bobbing heads, Mariah shot her an "are you coming?" look. Cassie's heels bounced of their own accord. But the rest of her held back.

"Cass." Rescue was at hand. May waved her over from her perch on a mound of frayed pylons. May never danced. She'd been raised in the dustbowl north a ways and considered it absurd to work up a sweat without dire reason.

As Cassie walked up, the older girl adroitly struck a flimsy thumbnail match and lit a puny roll. No longer those of a jobbing thief, May's hands were clean. Only the middle fingernail was painted, the same deep purple as the patch over her bad eye. A swirling tattoo radiated across her dented cheekbone where the force of an exploding pipe had busted it.

"Hey." Cassie looked into May's good eye.

May wore a purple-tipped, jet-black bob flat and close around her face to accentuate both ink and injury. Without them, her pout might have been a tube star's. "Heard you had a close call today."

"I kept it together. Like you taught me. Glad I'm done with tunnels, though."

"About that—nah, don't worry," May headed off Cassie's dismay. "You are totally done. If you wanna be." She pulled a thin plastic strip from the pocket of her extremely vintage leather jacket. A public chip. Given the illegal nature of the business, the bosses always paid in cash.

Cassie looked around. Probably no one here wore a wrist reader.

"It's all there. I checked." May winked her good eyelid, revealing thick kohl lines. "And then some."

"Yeah?" The bosses were fair enough but not known for generosity.

"You're the best." May's tone was matter-of-fact. "Everyone knows it. You're out of the salt mines but they want you as a mentor. You're worth all those dopes put together." She flicked the spent joint toward the edge of the dance floor where a few thieves tripped out moves.

Cassie watched them while she considered the proposal. She would miss the thrill of being so near so much water at once. The giddy, fleeting freedom you felt when you cracked into a cache and the leak sprang that might not be contained. "You can't hold on to water," went the saying. *Not when I'm around*, she thought with a cocky grin.

May seemed to interpret her smirk as rejection. "Yeah, I figured you wouldn't bite. I don't blame you," she sighed, getting up. "You're too good for us." She gave Cassie a friendly pat and sauntered away.

Was May's jibe true? Maybe what kept Cassie from bantering with May, dancing with Mariah, or figuring out Teddy wasn't shyness but snobbishness groomed by Inma's careful, respectable rearing. However much Cassie chafed at it, she knew her godmother had devoted her life—had sacrificed it by choice—to raising Cassie. Cassie couldn't deny her influence and wasn't sure she wanted to. Maybe she really belonged in Inma's above-board world. The one Inma said Cassie's parents would have wanted her to be part of.

She'd find out soon enough. Starting tomorrow, when she registered at the courthouse for her apprenticeship. She knew that in the past, people stayed in school until seventeen or eighteen or longer, but these days an older model applied. At sixteen, you were apprenticed to help meet the needs of an economy with a depleted labor force. Somehow, her aptitude score combining high marks for logical intelligence and initiative with a "serious deficiency" in cooperativeness (highly disputable, in Cassie's opinion) had landed her one with the Judges. She didn't know anyone who knew a Judge. She only did know three things about them: they ruled the country, they traveled a lot, and they sentenced water thieves to death. Her guidance counselor had said it was a high honor, that she might herself become a pillar of national reunity. Cassie had forced a smile and said the travel part sounded great—that much was true—while secretly wondering how she'd ever reconcile her underground past with that bright future.

Someone turned off the music. Teddy leapt onto a slanted beam like a revolutionary at the barricades. He swept a straggling lock from his eyes. His voice boomed across the field. "May I have your—hey, listen up!" Was he slurring? "Tonight, we celebrate the passing on—no, wait, the moving on! The moving on of one of our own." Cassie heard a whoop from the gathering crowd. It sounded like Mariah. She tried to back into the shadows but Teddy had a bead on her. "The all-time best of the best of us." He gestured at her and someone helpfully beamed light at her face. Teddy retrieved something from near his feet and lifted it above his head. "In token of remembrance." He thrust it toward her. "Cassandra Killian, in recognition of your service and noting most adbiram—amiril—dude, your unblemished record in the field...of battle...." His voice cracked and he trailed off without seeming to notice. Someone ululated, probably Mariah again. Cassie slunk out of the spotlight, grabbed the gift with a dismal grin, and backed away hastily. "Yeah!" Teddy tried to encourage a roar from the others. Thankfully, they dispersed with idle shoutouts and a smattering of applause instead.

Left alone, Cassie examined the present. It was like a jewel, though large enough to cradle in both her palms. Made of an almost gossamer resin, it was not quite round but more like a diamond with many triangular facets that each glinted in turn as she rotated it in her hands. Set inside these translucent walls, almost floating, was a model of the same material but with a frosted texture that made it stand out. It was a hand, the fingers curled in a fist around a gush of sculpted water suspended from one corner to its opposite as if frozen in mid-flow. It was beautiful. And must have cost a fortune.

As if reading her mind, Mariah sidled up beside her. "My brother made it from scrap in his spare time."

"Tell him thanks." Cassie couldn't shift her eyes from the sculpture's elegant impossibility. "I love it, actually."

Mariah pondered it, too. "It makes me sad and angry at the same time. Or, not angry, but like I'm a superhero."

"You are. Your power comes from your boobs." Cassie pretended to fire bullets from her own.

"No, they smother you," Mariah giggled as she pulled Cassie's head into her chest.

Cassie ducked her way out. "Do they give this to everyone? I don't remember seeing it before."

"Me neither. When Larissa retired, she got that trophy thing, though."

"Oh yeah. I never got what it was. It looked like a frog... with a hula hoop?"

"Yeah. 'Cause that's what she looked like on a job."

"And they gave Randall that—"

"carving of a—"

"broken-ass pipe—"

"out of dried up dog poo—"

"eww—"

"glazed for posterity, of course—"

"'cause he kept building those hookahs out of scrap—"

"and they never worked—"

"and he'd smoke anything—"

"as long as it had the right 'bouquet!'" They practically collapsed on each other.

"That one was Viv's idea." Mariah wiped her eyes.

Cassie couldn't stop laughing. "Thank God Guillermo was in charge of mine."

Mariah grimaced in thought for a second. "He said it's symbolic. For your sixty-four jobs. Don't ask me how, exactly." She knitted her eyebrows and drew Cassie into a genuine hug this time. Mariah's warm breath whispered through their entangled hair. "Acuérdate de mi, 'mana."

Cassie jerked away. "What do you mean?"

"No, I just, you know," Mariah fumbled. "When you're off becoming a Judge—"

"You hate me—"

"No!"

"I'd hate me. But it wasn't my choice."

"Of course it wasn't. But it will be your choice what to do once you're on the inside. Make it better, you know?"

"As what, an ex-water thief apprentice? And they don't let us actually become one of them—"

"Sometimes they do, and you will because you're a fracking genius and you'll leave this crappy world behind and end up back East at tube star pool parties with actual pools and I'll still…" Mariah trailed off.

"First off, you'll be doing something amazing and have to invite *me* to parties. And we'll holo at each other, and there's gotta be time off when we can come back home and you're my best friend and it's not going to change." She hoped. Although she also hoped Mariah was right. Of course, she'd insist on Mariah joining her eventually. And Teddy, maybe. Inma, too, obviously. Would they let four of them through? A stupid dream. You didn't get through the Fence. Probably not even as a Judge's apprentice.

Mariah sniffed. "Okay." She brushed a hand through her hair and pivoted. "I'll be back." She released Cassie and sped off.

Cassie's juice was gone. She wandered toward the bar nook to see if there was any more. Maybe this time with a little spike. Teddy was there, manning a shift. An older, bigger kid always policed the younger ones with respect to the liquor and everyone with respect to anything. They might be subversives but they weren't careless with liquid.

Cassie caught him rifling through a tub of unsalted potato chips. He pulled one out and ate it.

"That's disgusting."

He looked up, startled. "Huh?"

"Someone else is gonna have to eat the ones you're just fondling."

"Oh. Eh. What they don't know…"

"I don't remember you being so picky. When we were little you ate just about anything we dared you to."

"Only with these. I hate the ones with burned edges or holes with green spots around them or are just little flakes of chip. I don't know why."

"How much have you had to drink, Teddy?" She was teasing, sort of.

He turned to her with a serious look in his eyes. "Almost nothing." They both laughed wryly at the gallows humor. His voice was crisp, his pupils normal, hands steady. His glass held water, probably skimmed from his own thieving job earlier that day. He wasn't drunk. Only Teddy.

"How'd it go today?" she asked.

He fished in the bowl again. "Same old. Tower."

She scrunched her face and nodded to show she was impressed. Tower jobs weren't easy. Reserved for emergencies, military use, and industrial priorities, towers were under government control, which meant tight security. You couldn't dig a secret tunnel to get at their tanks. The bosses had to bribe their way in but if the person you bribed changed her mind or got caught, then the thief going in blind was screwed. Sometimes, they got you in but you had to wait inside the access tube for hours before you could climb and hook up the siphons. It was altogether too iffy. The bosses used to avoid them. Come to think of it, though, there had been two or three since summer. Slimmer pickings elsewhere, she guessed.

Teddy measured her intently. "Let me ask you something, Sixty-four. Do you—did you—enjoy it?"

"I loved it." Her lack of hesitation seemed to surprise him. She tried to explain. "You remember Reunity Day when we were, like, ten?" Teddy nodded. No one could forget the year the citizens were each awarded a bath to celebrate...who cared what? "That feeling—almost floating, and then you lift your hand or foot out and it's freezing and- and raw, almost, and you dunk it back and it's warm and- almost numb, but in the best way, like it's the January storm and you're buried under the covers?" She spoke reverently, savoring the account of that unique occasion.

Teddy watched her with his curious look. Then he frowned wistfully. "Yeah. I guess."

"Anyway," she turned away self-consciously. Her hands absent-mindedly picked at the tatters of a lantern that had been strung across the bar a while back for the moon fest. "Getting close to the tanks makes me feel that way, almost. Like it could happen. Like one day I might magically end up on the other side of the wall, warm and safe." She laughed at herself.

He laughed, too. "You're a mystic, Cassie. I guess that's why you're a natural."

"Don't you like it?" She turned the conversation onto him. "You seem to be working a lot. You've got another one tomorrow night, don't you?"

He snorted. "'Cause I need the money."

Cassie flinched at her insensitivity. Teddy was even poorer than most here. Cassie's pay helped make ends meet for a household of two (of course, Inma thought her odd jobs after school were legit) and she concealed some income Inma didn't have to know about. But Teddy gave all his earnings to help support a large family. If he was working more, things might not be so good on the home front.

He crinkled his eyes and she looked away, behind the bar. "Like your present?" he asked.

She was relieved that he changed the subject. "I should burn it. It's incriminating."

"It'd have to be a pretty hot fire to melt that thing," he replied earnestly.

"Oh, I build 'em pretty hot," she quipped. *Why?*

"Do you?"

She peeked in his direction from the corner of her eye. He was still staring at her with that enigmatic smile. "Maybe I'll throw you in, too," she said. "See if it wipes that stupid grin off your face." It came out too vehemently. Her eyes widened.

Teddy's lip curled in revelation. The look in his eye didn't change but he leaned toward her. She caught her breath and closed her eyes as they found each other. It wasn't her first kiss but she realized it was one she had been waiting for a long time. Even the lingering smell of cooked potato felt comforting rather than off-putting. That thought made her own lip twist.

He drew back. "It's okay?"

She looked up at the night sky that vaulted over the open spaces of the fallen roof. "Yeah." She drew him back to her.

"You're dead, Bergson!" Cassie and Teddy pulled apart and she saw who had called him out: another water thief, Waldo. He emerged from the entryway to the field, scanning the scene, on a mission. Behind him were his friends, Teresa and Marc.

Waldo's stream of curses attracted a crowd as he spotted his target and barreled toward the bar. Teddy stepped out from behind it and planted his feet, knees bent, fists balled, ready to fight. As Waldo marched up to him, Marc boxed him in on one flank and Teresa stepped between him and Cassie on the other.

Waldo rounded on the watchers. "You all wanna know what happened tonight? We just came from Ma'dio." Everyone knew the clinic they used when something went wrong on a job. The staff never asked questions. "Bridget's there." A few sympathetic but unsurprised murmurs floated out. "She's dead." The murmurs intensified. Waldo wheeled back toward Teddy and grabbed the front of his t-shirt. He dropped the other shoe: "He did it."

Cassie looked at Teddy, who shook his head "no." She saw that Waldo was watching them as he continued, breathing hard. "He was prep on the tower job team today."

"Yeah," Teddy admitted, shaking himself loose. "Bridget was fine when I cut out."

"You cut out early."

"I had to get something—" Teddy stopped short but his eyes darted to the glimmering gift in Cassie's hands.

"For your girlfriend?" Waldo sneered. Cassie didn't know whether to protest, shrink, or sock Waldo herself. "While you were conveniently absent, the thing blew up. Bridget was on the ladder."

"Sabotage," Teresa clarified menacingly. Another murmur rumbled through the crowd. A month ago, the accusation would have been unbelievable. That was before the incident when a water thief had almost drowned after a gusher turned a tunnel to mud. That much water, that fast—everyone said it was rigged to burst.

"One of us is working for the Dowsers," Waldo said. His glare worked its way meaningfully around the circle before settling back on Teddy. "Now we know who."

"No way the Dowsers would do that," someone called out. The Dowsers worked for the Judges. They were the pols and cops whose whole point in existing was to find, husband, and distribute water. To control it. They were practically programmed not to waste it. And while the Judges were an aloof and abstract terror, the Dowsers relentlessly hunted water thieves. All of which made Waldo's accusation incredible.

"Think about it." Waldo's stare was still fixed on Teddy. "They want to shut us down. What's a better way to turn everyone against us than if we're dangerous, if we're *wasteful?* All they needed was a mole." His eyes fell on the trophy in Cassie's hand. "Where'd a pauper like you get the money for that, Bergson? Your Dowser friends?"

Teddy found his tongue. "No. No!"

It was too late. The crowd egged on Waldo as his fist struck Teddy's cheek with the sickening sound of bone cracking bone. Teresa and Marc grabbed Teddy's arms. Still reeling from Waldo's mournful news and his unbelievable allegation—not to mention how he had talked about her like she wasn't even there—Cassie jolted alert. Whatever the truth was, Teddy deserved a fair fight. She grabbed Teresa's waist and tossed her into the spectators. As Teddy shook off Marc, she stepped between them. Marc saw the look in her eye and didn't push it.

But before Teddy was totally free, Waldo was already lunging. He slammed a low uppercut into Teddy's belly. Teddy folded and Waldo hammered a fist down on his neck. Teddy was larger, though. He dropped his head and drove into Waldo's chest, knocking them both to the ground. He threw jab after jab at Waldo's face. Lying on his back, Waldo swung wide haymakers, trying to cuff Teddy and roll him off. When that failed, Waldo braced one arm against the blows and tucked the other hand into his pant pocket. He pulled something out.

Teddy lurched. Confusion swept his face. Waldo scrambled free and sprang to his feet, shouting triumphantly and waving a thin blade. But he'd gone too far for the mob. They wanted fun, not more bleak reality. They muttered and melted away to salvage a subdued party. Except Cassie. She met Waldo's eyes. Before either of them could react—before either of them knew how—Teresa tagged his chest and pushed him away. Marc followed.

Cassie rushed to Teddy. A bloodstain patterned stark and wet against the off-white of his undyed t-shirt. She covered the darkening spot with her hand, pressing against his stomach to stanch the flow. The wound was deep.

"Cassie." His eyes leapt back and forth across hers.

"Shh."

"Cassie." Mariah spoke softly behind her. "I'll get help."

Without lifting her gaze from Teddy, Cassie heard her friend sprint away. She tried to appear calm to counter his frantic look, though her own heart spasmed as erratically as his diaphragm beneath her hand. Warmth filled her head to toe. She and Teddy had always been friends, even allies of sorts. But now she felt protective in an all-encompassing way. Her mind divided, half focused on what she could do to slow the bleeding and soothe him, half pondering whether it was only the circumstances that made her compassion so fierce. Would it be the same if Mariah lay wounded in her arms instead?

"Cassie." The timbre of his voice made clear how he would answer that question.

"Mariah's getting help. It's not so bad," she lied. "You'll be okay."

He nodded impatiently. "Okay." He searched for something in her eyes. "But Cassie. I didn't do it. I wouldn't ever do it."

"I believe you." She did. She smiled at him reassuringly. Only when he closed his eyes, satisfied, suffering, did she finally let the frenzy of the day send tears streaming down her cheeks.

CHAPTER 2
INMA

INMACULADA RUIZ STEPPED carefully around the succulents that dotted the roadway median. It was satisfying to feel the pebbles press against her calluses through the cork soles of her flats. On a girlish impulse, she skipped a zigzag to the curb on the south side of the median. The city had squished as much as shrunk, leaving thoroughfares such as this one almost as cramped as in its heyday, at least in this neighborhood. Or so she gathered from the complaints her older colleagues made reliably each morning on entering the office. Inma suspected they rather enjoyed that small continuity. That generation had endured too much change. Then again, so had hers and she was barely on the far side of forty.

Her heart fluttered in protest and sent stars spinning across her vision. Even at this evening hour, the heat made her blood too thick for spontaneous joy. She beat back the bitter thought while the dizziness subsided. Not today. She pinched up her pant legs to check her ankles for biting ants and timed her moment to weave in between the rush-hour cyclists who flitted among the few private cars. Normally, she might return the passengers' sunken-eyed stares from the buses lumbering by. Tonight, however, was one of celebration and anticipation. She was late and still had an errand.

Even through the mask she wore against the ashes blown to town by the wildfires, Inma smelled the sweets shop from outside. She pressed the buzzer beside the iron gate. An incongruously friendly bell tinkled to welcome her inside. Once the door closed behind her, she lowered the gauze, closed her eyes, and filled her lungs with the aroma of sugar and cacao.

"How can I help you?" Inma heard the amusement in the shopkeeper's voice. She'd made herself an easy mark.

Inma opened her eyes and scanned the treats arrayed behind thick glass that extended almost to the ceiling. An armed guard surveyed her drowsily from a stool in a corner. No one ever found her threatening. "A chocolate cake, please," she answered. "A small one."

The proprietor unlocked a section of the case from her own side and pointed at the largest one in it. It was meager—about the size of her hand. Inma read the price labels. The smallest of all would be more prudent yet still enough to give each of them one delicious, indulgent bite. But she already knew she'd pick the happy medium whatever the cost. She shook her head. "That one, please."

The shopkeeper shrugged and huffed like it was a huge mistake, but withdrew one of the medium-sized cakes from the display. She set it on the counter. The glass plate it rested on clinked appetizingly. "Message?" The vendor indicated a row of piping bags. Seeing Inma hesitate, she added, "Only ten percent extra."

It was a special occasion. "Happy Birthday, if it will fit. White icing is cheapest, right?"

"I can fit a name, too."

"Cassandra."

The baker put a hand on her hip and lifted an eyebrow. "A shorter name."

"Cassie."

The shopkeeper selected a bag capped with a fine metal point. She scooped thick icing from a small vat into the open end. It wasn't pure white—even expensive luxuries like sugar and dairy weren't fully processed anymore. With her left hand, she twisted the end and held it closed. With her right, she cupped the narrow end like a gun barrel and pointed it inside the edge of the cake.

Inma watched her spell out the letters in fine, slanting lines, admiring the baker's deft cursive strokes. Every now and then, she embellished with a grace note to finish a letter or start a new one.

"Your daughter?" The shopkeeper spoke without altering her pace.

"Goddaughter."

"Must be a special one."

"Sixteen."

"She'll be transferring, then, too."

"Judge's apprentice."

The baker pouted in admiration or else distaste. She finished the "e" and straightened her back. She put a hand on her hip again. "In that case, you should get another."

Inma chuckled at the opulent suggestion.

The vendor was unfazed. "It's bad luck to serve two occasions with one cake."

Inma laughed again at the folksy sales pitch. Did her own

plainness inspire it or did it work on the well-heeled clientele the baker was more used to flattering? "One will have to do."

The shopkeeper shrugged and set down the piping bag. She took a glass bowl and a bottle of vegetable oil from a cupboard. She dropped a bead into the container and spread it along the curving sides as a backup precaution against sticking. She set the cake plate inside. It rested on a little ledge so as not to slide and let the cake itself bump against the walls of the bowl while Inma carried it. The baker put a rounded lid on top. She snipped a length of hemp twine and swiftly wrapped two loops around the whole package, knotted it, routed a second pass perpendicularly, and tied it off into a slightly saggy four-leaf bow.

Inma gasped at the breathtaking luxury of the final product. The cake itself was an exorbitant treat, made of real chocolate worth its weight in gold—it might as well be for the price—rather than the sausage-factory imitations sold in the drugstores. This particular bakery entailed the added frill of cane sugar, another rarity, which her grandmother had always insisted was the best sweetener for baked goods, if you could find it (and afford it, Inma thought grimly, or the thirst it induced). The presentation, however, was an unexpected bonus. It was like an opal in a fabricated egg, or a ship in a bottle. It made sense; she could hardly have carried the cake home in her burlap shopping bag. And a place that served real chocolate cake wouldn't ruin it by boxing it in flimsy cardboard recycled so many times its fibers probably couldn't support the weight of the dessert. Glass would be cheapest when you totted up all the factors. Still, she had not anticipated that the end result would be as delectable as its parts. She almost reconsidered the recommendation to buy another, then thought better of the extravagance. Too much of a good thing would spoil its splendor, anyway.

Her eyes and lungs had had their fill. She checked her watch: even later now. She had lingered too long. She paid for her prize, exited the shop, and turned the corner heading south to where her eastbound bus would stop.

The pedestrian traffic thickened the closer Inma got to the bus shelter. Eventually, she ran into a wall of backs. She hopped to try to see over them, then settled for rocking side-to-side like a jack-in-the-box to peek between shoulders. Those near her seemed to have glommed onto the crowd like filings onto a magnet. Further ahead, however, enthusiasts waved the Bear Flag and even, unusually, the Stars and Stripes. It could mean a protest—they were becoming more common again after years of quiet—or a political rally for the upcoming elections.

Definitely a rally: she saw now that the glossiest (oh, the expense!) placards bore the green-and-blue seal of the water council against a field of even brighter green above, bright blue below, separated by a curving white wave. Bold black letters proclaimed, "McClarrick." Right—McClarrick was a dark horse contender to be a water councilor. Or, as everyone called them, a Dowser.

A burst of speaker feedback cued the crowd to hush its chants and chatter. Inma couldn't see him but she heard McClarrick's familiar, smiley-voiced baritone on the microphone. She had long ago taken a penitential vow of political abstinence. Still, it wasn't like she could help overhearing as she wormed through the crowd.

"Friends, thank y- thank you, friends, thank you—" Owen McClarrick half-heartedly quelled the whistles and applause.

"Friends, we live in troubled times. Just this morning, we had news of another incident in our city last night." He paused to let the whispers float through the crowd. Inma already knew of the water tower collapse from the gossip at work. Thieves. They were almost caught and, rather than surrender, they tore a hole in the tank. The sabotage caused worse damage than the theft would have. Inma shook her head at the terrible waste of it all.

She reached a spot where she could glimpse McClarrick's lanky frame, thin in the hips and shoulders but taut. His square head with its jutting jaw would have been a little too big for his body if he weren't a politician. He was saying, "A criminal element robs us under cover of night, while we wait for deliverance under cover of law." It sounded to Inma like a subtle jab at the Judges who were the Dowsers' overlords. Dangerous talk.

McClarrick beamed a toothy smile and slicked his forehead sweat back across an ample shock of dark hair. He was handsome, Inma gave him that much. "This election is about a return to true democracy, a return to normalcy. But not complacency. There is work to be done. To control our destiny we must control our most precious resource for communal benefit."

Someone loomed in front of Inma, pulling her attention from the speech. An over-eager campaign volunteer held out his chip, hoping for a donation. Inma ducked away. She wondered how much they would collect. McClarrick was smart to rail against the underworld of water thieves and smugglers, although conditions were such that nobody who wanted to survive could avoid buying black market water altogether.

But he was running to be a Dowser, and it was *de rigueur*

to hate them even more. Their nickname came from the responsibility to find water. But they also held power over its distribution and, therefore, over the thing that preoccupied every person's every waking moment on this side of the Fence. Besides, even if a populist firebrand like McClarrick won a council seat, real power would remain in the hands of the Judges who had imposed martial law fifteen years ago—no, it was Cassie's birthday, so it had to be sixteen. The Dowsers were merely their minions.

She couldn't believe she was thinking it, but the Judges did provide law and order (except this water tower business was another bad sign in a recent string of them). And the smugglers were transparent about their motives. The Dowsers, however, were collaborators at best, crooks at worst. Hypocrites, either way.

An old anger was bubbling up inside her. Inma coaxed herself back into studied apathy. She smiled sourly. In all the years since things fell apart, she still hadn't decided whether the events, and her part in them, made her cynical or clear-eyed. Regardless, she shouldn't have indulged useless old feelings. She broke through the milling bodies and checked her watch. Even later. She had to catch that bus.

CHAPTER 3
CLEMENTINE & SHADOW

THE CHOPPER'S SEARCHLIGHT painted the night desert in grayscale. What angles it illuminated only deepened the shadows that flared like dark flames as the beam passed over. Nocturnal creatures froze, their saucery eyes glistening wetly under the unexpected interrogation.

Though clear of its path, Clementine froze, too, and watched Shadow do the same. She could tell he was fuming. His muscles dimpled with tension. Even the fishhook salt and cocoa hairs of his three-day beard seemed to stand on end. With two other companions, they had eluded their pursuers for hours, but they had not shaken them off entirely. Clementine felt Shadow's anger mounting. When he learned what had happened, it would be directed at her.

The searchlight glittered off a mineral deposit, reminding her of how…

Sunlight glinted off the cap rock above. Gypsum had taken position up there to scout for the target. The flash was Gypsum's first signal. Clementine stepped out from her hiding place and let her pupils adjust. In every direction, forever, parched clay blushed beneath the sun's hard kiss. A dancing devil whirled in the distance. The genuine article, she mused, would feel at home basking on the withered ruins that pocked the dunescape.

From her vantage point beside the decrepit highway, Clementine saw a Jeep with oversized tires limp into the shade of a mesa, trailed by tankers and their sloshing cargo. A parallel ridge rose on the other side to form a canyon. As the path narrowed, the ATV outriders would fold in from the flanks and intersperse among the tankers, out of sight of the Jeep's rearview camera. A blind curve, inclining terrain, and the pitted concrete would slow the convoy considerably.

Gypsum flashed a second signal. Clementine stepped toward the Jeep. She held a reedy length of rusting salvage such as a real beggar might use as a walking stick. The smugglers' convoys attracted many, luring them like ants to honey despite the scorching sun. Some were loners, zealots, and fugitives, phantasmic heirs of the pioneer spirit. Most, though, were simply left behind after the Exod like everyone else. Like Clementine.

She pointed her staff at the Jeep's front tire to make the driver stop. She stretched a tanned, wiry arm toward the passenger window and croaked, "Water."

"You got money?" The driver wasn't old, but exposure had seasoned his face.

She held out a chain strung with punctured coins. Old money. The beggars scavenged them one weather-beaten disc at a time in the ghost towns. Worthless as tender, but she saw the driver mentally assay their melt value. The smugglers would execute him if he traded a drop of their wares but there was no rule against driving a hard bargain for his own stuff. He reached behind his seat with a mottled hand and grabbed a bottle of brackish liquid. It was only half full.

He waggled it at her. "Toss that in, I'll toss this out."

Clementine stared at him hard for a second. Then nodded. Light flashed for a third time from the boulder above. Clementine retracted her arm. Greed turned to fear in the driver's eye. Too late, he grasped for his transmitter. Clementine slung the metal necklace inside the vehicle and lassoed his neck. She tightened the noose and watched him faint.

She swept the hessian hood from her close-cropped curls and climbed into the Jeep beside the driver to check his pulse. Seeing an adult unconscious always repulsed her. She never watched Shadow sleep on those nights when they remained side by side afterwards. It seemed like false modesty, a mask of vulnerability to hide the ugliness of waking humanity. Tender feelings had to be earned in the struggle to love another alert and willful soul.

Besides, she would have preferred to kill this man. But Transcendent protocol forbade unnecessary homicide. No one would die on this raid unless the outriders decided to be heroes. With Gypsum's third signal, Shadow and Truck would have isolated the last tanker and encouraged the outriders to take a lunch break in the lee of the mesa. "No point sweating bullets," Truck would bellow at the guards goodnaturedly. It was his favorite line.

Clementine checked the driver's radio to make sure he hadn't triggered a mayday beacon before she knocked him out. The tankers themselves had trackers but GPS was unreliable. The water merchants had to hack government satellites or bribe someone for access. Remote, cheap security fit their strategy of snaking the convoys lean and sparse through the desert to minimize the risk of theft or confiscation. It also, though, worked to the advantage of a small raiding band that banked on the certainty of surprise thanks to Shadow's old guerrilla habits.

In the Jeep's sideview monitor, she saw Spinney bring the first pickup close to the hindmost tanker. She calculated that he and Laurel had fifty-two minutes to fit a hose to the valve and run the sump pump to drain its precious contents. Twenty more to drive the haul to a rendezvous, distribute the jugs to other Transcendent bands, and watch them evaporate into secret places before abandoning the trucks in plain sight, wiped clean of clues. The six raiders wouldn't take even a sip for themselves. This tribal trust was another Transcendent principle, the wispy, steely spider's silk to bond a scattered people.

The driver stirred. Clementine reapplied the chokehold. There was enough time to fill a hundred plastic barrels the pickups carried. Two thousand gallons but they'd leave ten thousand behind. Seven years of water for a person. Almost a month's worth for a whole Transcendent caravan. It was a goldmine and they could take barely a nugget.

Her chest constricted and a comforting rage swelled across her breast. Why? The most dangerous question boiled up her neck. She thought daggers at the authorities' greed, the merchants' greed, the driver's greed in offering her a dirty pint or two when a lake of cool potable water lapped the smooth lining of the mobile caverns under his care. She saw red.

Then she saw the fourth flash of light. Gypsum's all clear. Clementine shifted to exit the Jeep. Her foot crunched the plastic bottle of brine. She looked at the driver's sleeping face with its cherubic lie. He made a choice when he had the upper hand. Now she had one. In her thirty-five years, in the fifteen—maybe sixteen now—since the Exod went down and the Fence went up, she could never wrap her mind around how the people left out here still accepted to barter for life itself. Maybe her disbelief was the Transcendents' influence, with their mystical reverence for the holiest of elements.

But they wouldn't approve of the decision hardening in her mind, despite their talk of impending war. Even Shadow hinted at war, and would abandon her for it. Well, wars started with an act-of. She gripped her metal stick and pressed its sharp tip against the slouching driver's unshaven throat. She pressed until the skin broke and then pressed harder. He came to, wild-eyed, but she yanked a smile across his gullet and made his sleep everlasting. Let them see red for once.

Clementine took the bottle of water, leapt out of the Jeep, and scrambled up the mesa, her cheeks too flushed to register the whiff of rain, maybe, this year, teased by the early monsoon blowing hotly against her face...

The gust from the helicopter's blades subsided as it veered away from their position. Clementine relaxed. She glanced at Shadow again. He remained coiled with tension. She might have to tell him. But she would not apologize.

Shadow watched the chopper go, knowing it would circle back. Its tenacity troubled him. The getaway had begun smoothly. The short autumn afternoon faded quickly to evening. With Spinney and Laurel off dealing with the trucks, the remaining four raiders stole into the night on foot. The crime scene was a few miles behind them by the time the smugglers could launch a response.

Leaving the broken highway behind, the band had slipped into an arroyo and followed it to the chilly river. Bled almost to extinction, the once-mighty lifeline still flowed this far north, though winter storms—if they came this year—had not yet replenished its measly current. The travelers crossed easily below the weak rapids. They paused for a fireless dinner on the far bank.

While they spooned cold beans from aluminum cans with their pocketknives, Shadow found a stick near the riverbed and drew a squiggle to represent the river and a line west from there. The stick scraped a dented old bottle cap corroding with millenary lassitude in the salt plain. He placed it along the line to mark a spot. A shred of plastic tubing marked another spot farther to the northwest. He brushed a lock behind his ear and looked up to explain.

They would cross the highway one more time where it looped south from Marble Canyon. Then, they would continue as the crow flies into what once had been a wilderness park, according to the time-stained maps the elders kept. It still was, for all intents and purposes. The highways skirted it to the north and south. With luck, they would evade the smugglers' hunters and Spinney and Laurel would meet them with new transportation on the other side.

Such had been the plan. The smugglers ought to have given up chase when dusk fell. But that helicopter had followed their trail north of the highway into the preserve. As it once again swept the vermilion cliffs around them, Shadow wanted to know why it persisted despite the serious risk to flying vehicles posed by the vertiginous landscape.

He was beginning to suspect it had something to do with Clementine. Normally, she was robotically calm throughout a raid. But when they had squatted around the sand map, she bounced excitedly on her heels. Her eyes were lively in the way she usually reserved for private moments between them. Recalling that, the corners of his mouth crinkled in spite of his mood.

The maddening thud of spinning blades faded for a moment as the copter arced away again. Shadow motioned Clementine, Gypsum, and Truck over to him.

"They're not giving up." Truck stated the obvious.

"They're ticked off something more than usual," Gypsum offered.

"They're smart." The others looked at Clementine, unsure what she meant. She pointed a powerful arm below. "They're following the possible trails and ignoring the impasses. They've been going systematically from easy to hard, playing the odds on where we'd be."

"But there's only the one. They don't know where we're at." Gypsum was skeptical.

Clementine shrugged. "They spread the bet. They can't totally discount the possibility that we stuck to the pavement, either."

Shadow pursed his lips. "Think we can get past it?"

"Why not? One bird, we just slip around and by." Truck wiped his hands on his pants, ready to go for it.

Clementine shook her head. "Not from this position. My guess is they have night vision and microphones. If they pick up acoustics that sound like human footfall, they'll home in by sight or heat signals."

Truck and Gypsum looked at her incredulously. These were the merchant-smugglers they were talking about, not elite marshal commandos. Shadow nodded, though. "That's the gear they used last month at Corners. Or so Meskit's team guessed. The search was too...precise." The others glanced around. The circumstances certainly fit that description.

Clementine continued. "They're obviously working with someone." Her voice rose with uncharacteristic lack of caution. "The game's tighter than it used to be." She stared hard at her companions. "Something's changing." Truck looked at the ground. Gypsum tracked the returning searchlight.

Shadow contemplated a point past the tip of his aquiline nose, irked. Clementine insisted on talking openly about things before it was time.

"Alright," he said with finality. "We'll camp in place tonight. Pick spots where the rocks'll block the light." The smugglers couldn't keep choppers in the air indefinitely. Daytime traveling was not his preference but they could still make the rendezvous at a good pace. "Gypsum, first watch." She knew this area best. "If they leave, wake us and we move."

The others nodded. Truck slowly moved a few yards below their position to take a dump then returned to unfurl his second-most-prized possession, a bamboo bedroll. Gypsum leaned against the boulder and half-closed her eyes. Shadow guessed she was counting the intervals between approach and retreat, approach and retreat, trying to plot the pattern Clementine had identified. Clementine herself remained squatting where they had conferenced, watching him.

Shadow turned away and pulled out a shabby case of chipped plastic held together by adhesive and string. Inside was a rare antique: a small transistor radio. A techie—now the head tech, in fact—gave it to him on his first raid as a team leader. The techie had opened the case with a screwdriver and a few delicate pulls on the tape, stretched out the copper coils, and tuned the transformers to extend the range. It could pick up anything transmitted over open analog airwaves. That's what the government and smugglers both used for private communications because everyday digital tuners wouldn't detect the signal.

Its primitiveness was the only thing Shadow liked about the machine. He hated how its static jarred in the natural surroundings as he thumbed the knob. Warily, he clicked the radio on at the lowest volume and held the speaker to his ear, tuning incrementally until he heard voices.

Clementine felt the heat of Shadow staring at her. She looked up. He was still listening to that radio but he was looking at her now. His anger had found its cause.

He came over to her. "You wanna tell me anything?"

Ugh. She hated his paternal mode. "How about you go ahead and say what you want to."

"Did anything happen back there, at the raid?"

Her expression went blank. Let him speak plainly. She wasn't on trial.

Shadow rubbed a thimbleful of sand between his thumb and middle finger. He tried another tack. "You know why they're still on us?"

"Maybe they've had it with us rats gnawing into their silos."

He held out the radio. "That's the word they used: rats."

She tossed her almond eyes skyward. "They call us that all the time."

"And they've sent out three choppers. They wouldn't do that for a regular raid. So I'm asking, as team leader, if you did anything out of the ordinary back there that brought this on."

Not as lover or friend. At least he was being more direct now. But she still didn't feel like playing along. "Did you ask Truck and Gypsum, too? Or only me?"

He ran his fingers through his silvering cowboy hair and down the nape of his weathered neck. It was what he always did to control his temper. "I could see everyone else. You're the only one who'd do- this, without thinking about the rest of us."

A blaze replaced her blank look. He had meant those words to cut deeply. "You forget that I know you have secrets, too, Shadow." She spit flecks with his *nom de guerre*.

He plunged his forefinger at the ground. "I'm talking about now. Today." They were both whisper-shouting now. "And I'm asking you: did you kill the driver?"

Clementine ripped the plastic bottle of dirty water from her pack and threw it at his face, heedless of the noise. "This is the muck those pigs think we're worth."

"You did." He spoke quietly again. "You killed a man. Tell me you had to." His voice was suddenly tender as he pleaded. "Tell me you didn't do it just because he acted like everyone else in this godforsaken country."

"I thought we want a war. A revolution." She sneered the last word.

"The war is coming. And it's not with the smugglers."

"How should I know? No one shares the elders' plans with me." Not that she wanted to be in the Transcendent inner circle.

"So you killed an innocent man to prove a point to me?"

"Innocent."

"He's a parasite, but so are we, if you think about it."

"You might be. I haven't taken anything I don't have a right to."

"Okay, but there's a bigger picture. There are channels open. Or were. After what you did, I don't know."

"Now you tell me."

"Half the smugglers are free thinkers. They ought to be our allies."

"Are they?" He didn't respond, of course. His loyalty was

always to the tribe over her. She leaned back and looked up. "Well, the ones hunting us right now definitely are not."

He tried a different tack. "What about us, the squad? The danger you put us in?"

She rolled her eyes. "Baby—" the sarcasm was meant to sting "—we're already in danger. All we've done on this mission, whatever we gained, doesn't even make up for the sweat we lost." She stuck her tongue in her cheek and looked around. "You don't want to fight the smugglers? Then take it to the Dowsers. They're squeezing everyone dry and we're hustling a couple barrels of water like it'll make a rat's ass of difference."

Shadow exhaled a voiceless whistle. He scratched the stubble above his lip. Clementine didn't meet his eyes again. She had dug in. There was nothing more to say tonight. Soundlessly, he rose and snatched his pack from the ground. He moved to an unclaimed spot and stretched out with nothing but thread-bare clothes between his salty skin and the pebbly earth. He waited for Clementine to lie beside him, waited until fatigue carried him deep into the earth to dream of things he'd buried long ago.

She never did.

CHAPTER 4

CASSIE

CASSIE GROANED AND turned away from the light and draft slipping through the window. Sleep retook her body even as her mind woke. Usually, this tussle ended with three businesslike raps on her door from Inma. That none issued this morning was a bad sign.

She forced herself upright and swung her legs over the edge of the sheetless bed. Her skin pimpled in the chilly air. First thing in the morning, it always blushed with the olive that warmed its pinkish tone. She crossed the corkwood floor and brought down the blanket from her closet. Wrapped in the patchy alpaca fleece, she tiptoed lightly onto the hallway linoleum and into the bathroom, closing the door softly. She needed time to come up with an excuse for sneaking home so late. She hung the blanket on a peg in the wall and shivered again.

The last of last night's events replayed in her mind while she sat on the crapper trying to excrete more than a trickle of goldenrod piss and stared at the ugly floor that hadn't been repaired in her lifetime or even Inma's. As promised, Mariah had returned with help: May, her nonchalance upshifted to a commanding cool. Nudging Cassie aside, May plucked the blood-soaked t-shirt from Teddy's torso, hooked her fingers through the hole in it, and tore the shirt in two, sliding his arms out of the remnant without gentleness. She ripped open a packet of antiseptic gel and squirted it onto the gash in his body. She wrapped the dry part of the shirt rag around the wound and tied it like a sash at his side. Then the three of them lugged Teddy to the Ma'dio clinic, where the impressive flood of blood sped him through triage. Cassie had been the last to say good-bye to him there, while Mariah and May waited outside. That same strange feeling of responsibility for him had surged through her. But he was in the medics' hands now.

She wiped and tossed the paper into the toilet, followed by a scoop of silica mixed with coconut coir from the dry locker. The building was so old the sink sported taps and a pipe underneath rigged to flow to the same place the toilet once did. All long useless objects of her quasi-professional curiosity. She pumped a palmful of gel from a metal canister and coated her hands, then judiciously measured water onto each from the aluminum carafe. Their household was licensed for two gallons of water a day for all personal consumption needs, with one more on Sunday, plus drinking rations at work and school. A municipal truck delivered the quota weekly. Extra occasionally could be found for an extortionary sum from a store. A slightly lower price came with a riskier trip chez the same black market merchants for whom Cassie worked by stealth.

She pulled off the rest of her clothes, squirted a different gel into her palms and lathered, then wiped her body dry with a clean rag. Cleanish but still cold, she scurried back to her room. It would be a scorching hot day this time of year once the sun got warmed up. It was also a day of first impressions when she had to register for the apprenticeship at the courthouse. She pulled on a flowy sundress, unique in her meager wardrobe of plain old because of the cost to dye its multihued print. It was a polyester hand-me-down from one of the Eastern charities and still faintly depicted a natural cliff with a waterfall that began off-center at the bodice and rolled down the pleats into a whitewater illusion of an upswept furl near the hem. She wasn't sure what Judges' apprentices wore but the dress might not fit much longer anyway. She reviewed her reference points in the mirror—hands, neckline, hips, calves—against her vague benchmark of womanliness. Inconclusive. Certainly not the curveball Mariah threw. But she smiled when her wriggling fingers made the tendons on her hands dance and at the knot of muscle that bulged in her calf when she pointed her foot.

In the glass's reflection, her eye fell on Teddy's gift from last night, the sculpted translucent hand grasping a column of water inside its geometric case. It was as beautiful as the actors' trophies ontube. She addressed the awards hall in the mirror like a St. Louis starlet. "Of course, I wouldn't be standing before you tonight if it hadn't been for myself."

The sound of the next-door neighbor, Mrs. Sendhal, haranguing her kids out of bed came through the wall. Cassie gave her gift a last look and stashed it in the locked chest beneath her bed, along with the chip May gave her containing her money from the tunnel job. Would the bosses try to take the bonus back when May told them she refused to stay on? Would they dare, when she worked for a Judge? No point worrying now. Time to face the unpleasantness.

Down the narrow hall toward the front of the apartment, Inma sat at the small table in the tiny kitchen with her back to the entryway. Cassie had once suggested that Inma trim those black locks above her shoulders to cool her down a little—a poor choice of words. Cassie calibrated between sneaking and defiant and headed for the ancient fridge. Opening the door bought her a few more seconds to avoid Inma's disappointment, though it only soured Cassie's own mood to see the temp-cont mods dark and dormant. Dairy: empty. Fruit: empty. Meat: empty. As expected, but her stomach rumbled angrily nonetheless. She'd have to get her usual breakfast barley beanball from the pantry, but it meant turning to speak to Inma.

Inma was gripping a cup of lukewarm water and probably pretending it was coffee. Cassie didn't smell lavender; sometimes, Inma boiled the water and dropped in a few buds. Equally often, though, the morning subscription to private electricity expired while she was still mulling the cost of power. It was also laundry day, Cassie remembered, which meant recharging the batteries on the machine to chill the dry ice. Induction heat for a cup of tea was a drop in that bucket but Inma believed in the penny saved.

Inma slid a glass egg containing chocolate cake across the kitchen table. "Happy birthday," she said evenly. It felt like a trap.

Cassie swallowed whatever she had planned to say. "Thanks?"

"This was to've been dessert last night, but as you weren't here for dinner in the first place—"

"I- they- Mariah..." Cassie stumbled. Genuinely afraid that Inma would suffer either cardiac or Dowser arrest, Cassie had never told her she was a water thief. No way would she spring last night's horror on her now.

"There's no sense wasting this much money, so you can have it for breakfast."

Cassie sat down hesitantly across from her guardian. "It's beautiful," she said honestly. She removed the lid and read the message.

"Enjoy." Inma rose to leave, already dressed for work.

"Thank you, Inma. I'll make it up—"

"Then you can fix the biogas unit. I smell a leak. No sense in wasting that cake on its way out, either."

Cassie's apology withered on her lips. So that was her punishment. The methane digester had been on the fritz for a month. The landlord reduced their rent in exchange for some of the maintenance chores that Cassie had a knack for. Her tinkering solutions had patched the system that converted the tenants' composted waste into cooking fuel. But Inma didn't tolerate half-measures. There were only two more things to try and they both knew it. One meant negotiating the spiders and bird poo on the roof where the solar heater that kept the generator hot enough to process biowaste lived. The other meant opening the hydrolytic chamber or, worse, the slurry pit. There wasn't enough bath gel in the world to make her feel clean afterwards. Cassie felt a swell of fury at the injustice of living in this stupid old house with its outdated everything that never worked and she had to fix.

"Oh." Inma called to her from near the front door. She paced back to the kitchen and held out something unwrapped but tied with twine. "Another gift, this one for graduation. I would've waited in case I saw you tonight—" Inma was a master of the passive-aggressive reproach "—but I should give it to you now if that's what you plan to wear today."

Cassie put a hand to her body self-consciously and took the bundle with the other. Inma continued, "It'll cover those shoulders."

"It's barely November."

"It's not cold I'm worried you'll catch." Inma turned to leave again but paused at the entryway and did an about-face. Her tone lost some of its primness. "I didn't scold you this morning because you're not a child anymore and it's up to you if and when to display the manners I taught you. But you're not out of my care just yet." Without waiting for a reply, she spun back and marched briskly out of the apartment.

Cassie felt the rebuke as intended. Inma was prudish about anything to do with sex. Cassie had a vague sense that it had to do with Cassie's parents who, after all, had her and disappeared. And Inma had seemed anxious about the unknown people and places Cassie would encounter on the apprenticeship. Shame flushed up her throat to her scalp as she watched Inma leave. But resentment, too. A few choice names came to her tongue, which only fueled her guilt. She changed the taste by forking the cake hangrily into her mouth so fast she triggered the health alarm in the utensil. In what flea market Inma found these archaic housewares she had no idea. She rotated the plate and laughed in spite of herself: the cake was missing a huge bite from the bottom on the far side. She slowed down to relish the last bite, already regretting having squandered the first few. She licked every last crumb and drop of icing from the plate and put it in the HE dishwasher (which wouldn't run properly until she fixed the biogas, and even then sputtered for lack of water, which made it barely more useful than the freaking fridge). The sugar left her even thirstier than normal. She gulped down her morning cup of water, wishing there was more of both.

As she walked out of the kitchen, she remembered the unopened gift on the table. It was a sweater. A creamy, clean-dirty natural color. Her fingertips sank into the material and dragged a little as she ran them over it, but in the most luxuriating way, almost like Mrs. Sendhal's baby's hair when Cassie coaxed it to sleep. She had never owned something like this before, though she recognized the fabric. It was cotton. It must have cost Inma a second fortune on top of the cake. Cassie didn't know where in town you even would find cotton clothing.

She untied the string and unfolded the garment. It was thin and light and the sleeves dropped back to reveal a row of chitinous buttons like beetle shells tinged with the faintest blue-green. A small object fell from the folds. Cassie picked it up. It was a box, covered with a wine-colored, velvety material. The pile was stripped in places, exposing a scratched, pliant casing underneath. A tarnished hinge sat midway down one side. On the opposite side, a hook and eye clasped it shut. It was undoubtedly very old.

Cassie gingerly unhooked the lid and opened the box. The velvet continued more plushly on the inside. Resting in a shallow indentation in the bottom half was a silver ring, protected from tarnish by its cocoon or else recently polished. It wasn't exactly beautiful. The band was not round on the outside, but angled, like a screw nut. The silver didn't go all the way around. Instead, a sliver of gemstone completed one of the sides like a belt buckle. Its blood-red color suggested ruby to Cassie, though she wasn't sure, or if it was real. Tilting the ring revealed an inscription along its inner circumference. She caught it in the light from the kitchen window and read: *e pluribus unum.* Whatever that meant.

She tried it on. It fit only her middle finger, and loosely at that. Maybe she could make a chain for it, if the ring had any meaning. Was it another splurge—had Inma caromed from pinchfist to spendthrift? Was it an heirloom? Was it a Killian heirloom? The last possibility made her heart race. She would ask Inma tonight after they made up.

꙲

"Oh, that's a nice one!" The clerk was the first cheerful person Cassie had seen inside the courthouse. The building itself was neoclassical, imposing, a testament to a wealthier, more confident era. Everyone else seemed unhappy: the slovenly security guard who scanned her, the manacled criminals being escorted roughly by Dowser cops, the harried suits whom she assumed were lawyers or officials of some sort. Only the crisply uniformed federales looked immune to the gloom. Why not—they floated above it, elite enforcers of the Judges' "marshal law." If any had been recruited from this city, they'd been shorn of any attachment to it. Cassie hadn't caught sight of a single Judge, so she didn't know what kind of expression they wore. Learned frowns, she imagined.

"Pardon?" she asked the clerk. She was sitting across from him at a desk. He looked like he was slightly cross-eyed, reading something mid-air. Not a holo, she'd have seen that.

"Oh." He pointed at a small grey device on his desk that looked like a multi-sided die. "New AIOS. Photonic hybrid with enhanced retinal visualization." He seemed as proud as if he had invented it. "Not available online," he cracked. "No, seriously, strictly for court business. When you start here, you cannot use it without permission and you cannot take it out of this building."

"Got it." Bureaucratic banality had blunted the fear she'd felt upon entering. "What does it say?"

He rubbed his palms together for a few seconds and wrapped them around the object. When he pulled his hands away it was a deep glowing yellow. "Look."

Cassie stared into the facet facing her and suddenly, instead of the room around her, she was seeing written text. "Meiklejohn. Who's that?"

"The Judge you'll apprentice to. Like I said, a nice one. Not nice, necessarily—well, yeah, actually, he grew up around here so he understands what y'alls lives are like. No offense."

"Uh huh."

"But nice also because he rides circuit."

"What's that?"

"He goes to all different places to sit in judgment. You'll get to see the country, this side of the Fence, anyway, who knows, maybe cross it, even, and you'll do it the—well, the *nice* way. Perqs and such. Starting tomorrow." He seemed almost envious. "You're really lucky."

The clerk went on about what an honor her selection was, how lifting up outstanding local youth such as Cassie was a cornerstone of national reunity. But she barely heard him over a torrent of exhilaration that washed away her remaining animosity toward this place. *See the country. Cross the Fence. Lucky.*

≋

It was Mariah who'd predicted that rising fortune but the person Cassie most wanted to share it with was Teddy. The Ma'dio clinic was crowded. High-efficiency bulbs illuminated every crease of pain on the patients' faces, except for those whimpering in patches of shadow. Some moaned like delirious zombies, a lack of fluid having finally desiccated their minds.

Teddy lay on a cot. He was unconscious. The nurse told her it was septic shock. Waldo's knife had nicked his gut and some nasty bacteria decided to give it a go. The nurse advised Cassie not to stay long.

There was no room to sit beside him so Cassie stood and took Teddy's hand. She had never before touched a person who didn't touch back. A morbid shiver tingled her spine but she held on. There it was again, that strange shift in emphasis, from *caring* for Teddy to caring *for* Teddy. Teddy, who was supposed to do a job tonight but lay here like a log. The bosses wouldn't care that he was incapacitated. If you signed up for a job and bailed, you owed them, period. The last thing the Bergsons needed was more debt, least of all to mobsters.

So the decision came easily. Her new life was still hours away. She had closed the chapter on the old one but she would reopen it tonight. One last water theft, on Teddy's behalf. Piece of cake. She bent to kiss his clammy forehead and tucked an extra protein ration the court clerk had given her under his pillow.

༝༝༝

Even the cocktail of cobwebs, guano, and sludge that coated Cassie's body after fixing the biogas system failed to dampen her spirits, though it took half the gel supply in the house to coax it all off. It was her last time ever doing this chore. Send-hal's eldest next door could deal with it from now on. Cassie was off to a better life. A luxurious life with all the bathing water she could desire.

Inma had not yet returned home by the time Cassie had to leave to make Teddy's rendezvous. She thought about leaving a note but in her magnanimous mood decided that apologizing face-to-face was the adult thing to do. Which she would, as soon as she got back.

She changed into practical clothes: a tank top and capris to protect her knees but allow free movement. On the spur of the moment, she brought along her new sweater against the night chill (but really because it was so soft and singular to her experience that she didn't want to part with it for a moment). On a whim, she tucked her other present, the ring, into her pocket as a good luck charm.

Not that she'd need it. Her old crew better add this one to her pristine all-time record in the books.

CHAPTER 5
CLEMENTINE & SHADOW

THE RAIDERS HIT the road when the morning sun brushed the cliffs. Gypsum, back on watch and honed like a human Doppler receiver, decided the chopper was gone for good. There was no time to lose if they wanted to meet their friends on schedule. The four of them choked down bean paste with a few sips of water and set out across the sandstone as it lit to its full red glory.

Clementine traipsed along behind Gypsum, who took the lead for a while. She knew Gypsum felt something for this land, or wanted to, with its petroglyphs and abandoned pueblos, that the others didn't. Once, while they sheltered from a haboob near Old Salome, Gypsum had explained her theory to Clementine. She said each wave of human settlers came here at their own pace, like hands on a great teleological clock: walkers who fanned out over virgin territory, riders obsessed with God and gold, wagoneers manifesting through the alpine curtain. They all closed in on midnight together, so it struck too loud and broke the clock. Everyone's time was up. Clementine had replied that she didn't believe in fatalism.

Life was a chaotic cage match among gods and nature and humankind. TKO, see you at the rematch.

Behind Clementine walked Truck. Shadow brought up the rear. He hadn't told the others that she killed the convoy driver. Maybe he was avoiding an argument in the middle of a mission, or maybe he was worried they would shrug it off. Tension seethed between Clementine and him. But the day and the hike burned off the last chill of night and they made good time.

The group threaded up the escarpment and onto the plateau, where the elevation kept the temperature comfortable enough to glide swiftly along. The terrain changed to scrubland spotted with Welsh's milkweed and juniper. Once in a while, they passed a cabin or fence or windmill creaking in the breeze. It was almost quaint. Their dereliction preceded the troubles of her lifetime.

The original plan was to follow the winding dirt roads, which would be safer to navigate at night. Given the loss of time and gain in visibility, they beelined northwest instead. The occasional cottontail or spiny lizard darted across the path. All kept an eye out for rattlesnakes.

By mid-afternoon, the drab flatness gave way to russet buttes. The travelers rested amid a landscape of candy-striped fairy chimneys. Clementine felt like Gulliver in the land of giants. What was it called? Borin- Brogging- Brodin- she let her mind turn over on autopilot, as she had all day.

"Clem!" She hadn't heard him calling her name. Shadow was motioning her over. The others sat a few yards away debating geological eras.

She could tell he was still angry beneath his calm exterior.

"We're gonna meet up with the caravan soon." He paused weightily. "I need to know why you did it."

They already had that conversation last night. She tried a different angle. "You brought me into this Transcendent business to make life easier. To be free. But now," she searched for the right term, "now you're a bureaucrat."

"I'm still me," he protested. "I'm fighting for us all to be free. Don't you see that?"

"Don't you see it won't work? Li nan fou—it's bizarre. Let's leave," she pleaded. "We'll survive together, answer to no one but each other. Be the two of us again."

"Clementine, I promise, when this is o—" his sentence failed under a gun blast snapping off the rocks.

Clementine wrinkled her forehead and frowned. Then she buckled.

Shadow dove in front of Clementine, drawing his sidearm before he hit the ground. He scanned for the gunman's position and swore at the quirky landmarks that had seemed ethereal moments before but now trapped him in a giant pinball machine, unable to see around the bumpers. From the corner of his eye, he saw Truck sidle wide to create distance between them. Truck would try to outflank the enemy, though how many there were was impossible to tell.

Shadow lambasted himself for his laxity. He should have expected bounty hunters. Working on contingency, they were cheap backup when the smugglers' hi-tech searches failed. He held no illusion that the driver's life was worth much to the merchants. But maybe Clementine was right that the stakes had risen for everyone. He realized suddenly that he didn't hear her screaming or moaning. He rolled over to check why, more panicked than he wanted to admit.

Two girls chase each other around the growing patch. Martine wields their grandfather's gardening trowel. She swipes at Elita's legs with it, drawing blood. She shoves Elita in the back, hard. Elita falls.... Clementine lurched back to reality. She was on the ground. Something sharp had jabbed her. She craned her neck to see. The back of her left leg was torn up by buckshot.

In her adult life, Clementine had never cried from pain. Nor did she now. The first thing was to apply pressure. Shadow's pack was within reach. She pulled it to her and found a clean hemp towel in which he'd wrapped a few strips of jerky and sorghum crackers tied in bundles. She shook the food carefully into the pack and blew crumbs from the cloth before pressing it against the back of her thigh. She had no idea how large the wound was but didn't sense anything wrong from her buttocks up. The best triage would be to stanch the blood as close to the femoral artery as possible.

Shadow exhaled with relief. Clementine was alive and tending to herself. He heard Gypsum caw. It sounded like it came from a nearby hillock. She was getting a bead on the enemy and relaying it to him and Truck. Gypsum was the best tracker among them. He'd made the mistake of attributing it to her "people" once. "If you mean the specific person who was my grandfather and spent a lifetime honing his ranger skills," she'd shot back, "then you're right."

Shadow angled his body to align with her birdcall. He saw Truck wince as a bullet zinged the cactus next to him. Truck was a large man and an easy target who hated guns. He

viewed the Transcendent restrictions on violence as the thin-
nest red line between human nature and human corpses. Still,
now, he was firing back with his pistol.

Shadow almost laughed aloud. It was an old-timey
shootout. Their foe had squandered the element of surprise,
however. As soon as the slo-mo sensation passed, he realized it
was all over within minutes. They regrouped without bother-
ing to investigate or collect the bounty hunters' bodies. The
more urgent task was to aid Clementine and to elude any
other trackers.

Truck knelt beside her and unclasped the medical kit.
He gently raised Clementine's hand from her thigh. "Gyps:
press here. Hard." He looked up at Shadow, who felt clammy
despite the flush of battle. "How far to rendezvous?"

"Three, four miles."

"And then?"

Shadow breathed hard. "I don't know. Maybe fifty miles
to a doc."

"Okay. Bring me water." To Clementine, he said, "You're
okay, My Darling." He always called her that, and it always
sounded like a capital M and a capital D. She grinned weakly.

Shadow grabbed the first water he saw. It was the plastic
bottle Clementine had flung at him last night. He handed it
to Truck and saw Clementine's expression harden.

Truck pulled a tablet from the kit and dropped it into
the bottle. He waited thirty seconds and plopped in another.
He fished in his own pack for the pump filter, a very small
but hugely expensive piece of equipment that he babied like
a royaling. He poured the bottle's contents into it. Shadow
almost protested. You were supposed to filter first, then disin-
fect. But they didn't have a clean enough receptacle to collect

the purified water. Instead, Truck motioned to Gypsum to remove the towel and then dribbled the liquid directly onto squares of polyester gauze and gently blotted the grit from the worst of Clementine's wounds.

"Those are clean?" Gypsum pointed at the yellowish bandages.

Truck nodded. "Undyed, like God and chemistry intended." He poured the remaining water straight onto the worst gash. From a glass vial, he daubed a clear gel onto the holes.

"Close me up?" Clementine asked feebly.

"No can do, My Darling."

"Why not?" Shadow demanded.

"You don't want rot. She can't walk on it, anyway."

"She won't bleed out?"

"Give me that." Truck gestured to Gypsum to hand him the towel. "We'll have to tie the leg here. I'm not sure how bad the cut is. It could be superficial bleeding."

"Will she lose it?" No matter the situation, Gypsum's spoken words were always soft, silky, and even. Cool or hard as rain, depending on how they struck you.

"Let's take it a step at a time. Sorry, My Darling," he smiled apologetically for the pun.

"Let's go." Clementine and Shadow spoke simultaneously.

Shadow and Truck hoisted Clementine to her feet. "Me first," said Shadow. While Gypsum held Clementine steady, he bowed his back to her and draped her arms around his shoulders. He clasped her hands to his chest with his own and stroked her chapped knuckles lightly with his fingertips before gripping her wrists. Gypsum took his pack and the four hobbled their way out of the desolate fairyland toward help.

Clementine rested her chin in the soft spot behind Shadow's clavicle and closed her eyes. "Ase, Martine! Se pa fòt mwen."

He barely heard the whisper. "What?" he asked automatically.

Her eyelids still drooped but her voice was clear near his ear now. "Enough."

CHAPTER 6
CASSIE

DUSK MUFFLED HER sight but to Cassie's practiced ear the city chattered like a jungle. She hunkered down at the staging point and waited. The place was beyond her normal range—Teddy's need for work seemed to have led him pretty far afield—and it had taken a while to reach it by bus and on foot, although the trip had been uneventful. The neighborhood seemed ordinary, if down at heel. The population had thinned literally and figuratively as she approached it from more central districts. In the last few blocks, she'd seen only a mother begging. The worn woman held a child sick with the poisoning. Cassie had seen many like her before, desperate parents who broke into sealed municipal wells and drew water contaminated by the effluence of long-defunct factories that made weapons for long-forgotten wars.

"Ready?" Cassie didn't recognize the speaker. His hair was crew cut. He wore a simple long-sleeved shirt and loose drawstring pants. "Oh." He seemed surprised to see her.

"What?" she demanded.

"Nothing."

"I'm Cassie. Didn't they tell you I was coming instead?"

"Yeah, uh- yeah. Okay. Ready?"

"You already asked that. Waiting on you." It was best to let these boss's lieutenants know that you were the linchpin of the operation.

"Right. Take your clothes off."

"Uh. Not likely."

"All of them." He thrust a small woven bag toward her. "Put 'em in here." He tossed a piece of clothing at her. "Wear this instead."

"What is it?"

"People used to swim in them. And do sex stuff, I think."

Cassie perked up. If she was getting into a pool of water, she'd wear whatever they told her to. "Turn around. Am I going swimming?"

"Not exactly." He stood with his back to her while she changed.

"You know, I usually get a pretty detailed brief without having to ask for it."

"This isn't usual."

"Okay, I'm done." She stuffed her own clothes in the bag and looked up. Still turned away, he unceremoniously stripped off his shirt and pants so that he stood in tight black shorts of the same material. As she'd guessed when he turned away, his back was strong. He seemed about twenty, a boss in the making.

Without facing her, he ordered, "Let's go. Bring the bag." He folded his clothes and placed them in another small burlap rucksack, then slung it over his shoulder, his lean muscles popping as he moved. He opened the back door of the abandoned house. Cassie followed him into the alley behind it and kept pace. She felt silly wearing this strange garment.

"What's your name, by the way?"

"Gray."

"First or last?"

He looked over his shoulder without slowing down. "Does it matter?"

"Not anymore." She stuck her tongue out at his back. "Seriously, Gray, I've gotta know something about what we're up to."

"First, stop using names as of now. Second, don't talk so loud. Third, it's kind of a dig and drill."

"Tunnel?" She was not getting all scraped up in a tunnel wearing this thing. No more tunnels.

"Not exactly."

"Seriously, Gr- boss junior, stop saying that."

"I'm not a smuggler." His vehemence startled her. He took a breath. "Okay, listen." He still sounded exasperated with her. "There's a factory down the road here." He pointed, but she couldn't see to what in the darkness. "They have a catchment system that filters their wastewater. And I guess theoretically rain." Cassie had trouble hearing his hurried, hushed explanation. "You go in straight down from the surface."

That couldn't be right. "Don't they have guards? Dogs? Alarms?"

"They think bioswales aren't worth our trouble because you can't hit a jackpot all at once. It's just drip, drip, drip as the ditchwater percolates into a sewer or cistern. Makes no sense to spend money guarding it."

"What about the cistern then? Aren't they afraid we'll dig into it?"

"It's too far in. There's just a fence around the whole complex, and that thing is guarded."

"I don't get it then."

He sighed—more audibly, she thought, than he had been speaking. "There used to be a thing called 'need to know.'"

"I need to know. I'm the one thieving."

"Not exactly."

"Next time I scream."

Gray stopped short but spoke at high speed. "Fine. You need to know? The game's changed. The Dowsers are cracking down on the old ways—" she detected condescension pointed at her "—and that requires innovative thinking and more…subtle solutions." The last part exuded pride. "This—" he tilted his chin toward their destination "—is a pilot site. We'll thread fiberoptically mounted capillaries from outside the perimeter, through the geotextile membrane, and into the gravel exfiltration trench. Their consociation with the lapidarious stratum will divert hydration from permeating entirely into the reservoir. You are here to plant a beacon to guide our device to the trench rather than the contaminated detention zone above it."

Cassie had never heard a boss-type or anyone else talk that way. Gray meant to put her in her place. Jargon wasn't going to intimidate her, though. She pieced it together and fudged some conclusions. "It's not a one-off job. You're gonna keep thieving their water drip-drop, automatically." She smiled. "But you still need me to set it up for you."

"Just need a second body." He cut off her protest: "Shh." He halted and crouched. He pointed again. This time she could see the tall fence a few yards away. Too high to climb easily and tipped with barbed wire. Gray pointed to the right. She saw a guardhouse a couple of ball-tosses away.

They moved left along the fence. At a point that seemed arbitrary to Cassie, Gray stopped, cut a gash in the fence, and shoved her through it. "A hundred yards in across the driveway." He gripped her shoulder and pushed her along. They darted quickly across the rubberized asphalt, avoiding illuminated spots. A few huge vehicles were parked here and there. Cassie had no idea what they transported. Where Gray had indicated, they met a knee-high concrete curb twenty or so feet long. A truck-sized gap separated it from another stretch of curb, and so on, it seemed, in a segmented chain beyond her scope of vision.

"Drop your bag here," Gray ordered. "Change back when you resurface and don't forget to put on your shoes so we don't leave tracks." She did as told.

He dipped a shoulder to loose the backpack and pulled out a small shovel. He unfolded and locked its handle and held it out to Cassie.

"I don't dig."

"You do today." Sensing her recalcitrance, he added, "Or you don't get paid. Same arrangement the boy had." She took it from him. "It isn't deep," he said with slight empathy. "Just a few feet of soil. Take this." He handed her a small round object. "Place it once you hit gravel."

For lack of anywhere else, she tucked it down the front of her costume. "What about you?" Her eyebrows indicated his own state of semi-undress.

"Someone has to keep a lookout and pull you out of there. Besides, I have to repack what you dig up so they don't notice.

Don't worry. I'll get as dirty as you do. Start digging at two-point-five feet in or you won't reach the stone layer."

"How do you know?"

He seemed puzzled for the first time since they met. "Go."

Cassie stepped over the curb. Her feet crushed the weedy plants retained behind it and sunk into a goo that oozed up between her toes as she took what she guessed to be two and a half feet's worth of steps, plus a little extra for good measure to get it right the first time. So this was a bioswale. It felt clean compared to what she'd handled at home that afternoon. The plants thickened around her and something skittered up a stem and into the blackness. She pointed the shovel downward. The plants' roots held the swamp together enough to extract sizable chunks without the hole collapsing in on itself. She proceeded at a slight angle and scooped enough at each level to make room for her to stand lower and lower as she progressed. As her shoulders pumped, she mulled her situation. Gray's explanation had taken less than a minute but it all seemed very risky. She felt exposed in the middle of enemy terrain despite the cover of night and the murky earth that was swallowing her legs and torso. The surrounding silence that reasserted itself once they stopped talking only enhanced her unease. At least Gray was a few feet away, even if she didn't especially like him.

After fifty loads the shovel scraped against something. She squatted and felt the stony bed. She cleared away some of the gravel to make a dent into which she dropped the signaling device. Easy enough.

Shouts above thwarted her satisfaction. They'd been discovered. An instinct screamed to dig sideways into the mud around her to get away. It would be futile, she knew. Trying to remember May's advice about breathing, Cassie stood up and kept her grip on the shovel.

She could hear Gray grunt as he scuffled with someone. It sounded too distant and she felt disoriented until she realized that he was on the far side of the bioswale, near the factory rather than the fence where they had entered. She heaved herself out of the pit and scrambled unsteadily to her feet.

She tiptoed toward the sounds but the fighting had stopped. Instead, she heard a thump and Gray cry out in pain. In the beam of a flashlight, she saw him sitting on the ground, arms pinned back by a burly man. Over them stood a woman who held the light in one hand and a baton in the other. She looked ready to strike again.

"Who sent you, thief?" the woman shouted at Gray. Though her back was to Cassie, the light was enough to see the Dowser badge on the shoulder of her shabby uniform. Gray said nothing. The burly man—he seemed to be a factory guard—tightened his hold. Gray winced but held his tongue. "This is just the beginning of your pain. Unless you cooperate with me," the Dowser said. Gray sneered silently at her. She smashed him in the cheekbone with her baton and sneered back when he whimpered. She shined the light back on his bruised face. He looked away, past her—and caught Cassie staring wide-eyed at him from the shadows. His eyes flashed a warning.

"Are you alone?" the Dowser leaned in. "Tell me who you're working with and your cooperation will be duly noted." She flicked a switch on her weapon and it buzzed as if to emphasize the alternative.

Gray kept his gaze fixed on Cassie. Would he give her

up? He shook his head almost imperceptibly as he answered, "Yes."

"'Yes' what?" the Dowser snapped. She backhanded him impatiently and inched the electrified prod toward his neck. Cassie had enough. She stepped forward, shovel at the ready. Gray recovered from the blow and saw her coming. His brow furrowed. The Dowser noticed. She spun around, pointing a blinding beam as Cassie screamed and brought the shovel down on...nothing. The Dowser took advantage of the miss and caught her arm, but her fingers slipped off Cassie's veneer of muck. Now Cassie took advantage and pushed the cop to the ground.

"Run!" Gray yelled as he struggled to hold back the burly man. He jerked his chin upward, indicating the way they had come. The Dowser pinched Cassie's calf. *"Go!"* Gray shouted again. There was a conviction in his voice that was irrefusable. Cassie kicked loose and skidded back toward the swamp. She remembered her bag. It still lay where she had set it next to Gray's pack. His surely held useful items but it felt weird to take it and leave him behind. She grabbed her own bag and sprinted toward the hole in the fence, the Dowser on her heels.

Cassie was young and fast but her pursuer was taller with a longer stride. Her lungs heaved and her feet squished along gracelessly. She panicked on reaching the fence because she didn't see where Gray had rent it open and didn't know whether she had veered too far left or right. She turned right and moved along the chicken wire. The Dowser gained ground by cutting the corner she had traced. Another flashlight came toward her along the fence from the outside. A police dog barked violent intent.

Panting, her sopping hair stinging her face and shoulders and earthy goop flying off her cranking arms and legs, Cassie finally found the way out and charged through it heedless of the shorn metal that slashed at her. Relief flooded her—then she wrenched backwards. Her bag had snagged on the spiky edges, her speed causing the fabric to rip. Her clothes spilled out and hung like fleeing prisoners flung helplessly against the palisade. The Dowsers were closing in. Cassie grabbed as much material as she could and yanked with both fists. Her new sweater and her pants tore, but tore free.

She ran. The direction mattered less than getting caught. Consternated thoughts syncopated with her heaving breath and pounding steps. The punishment itself was one thing. Almost worse was imagining Inma's reaction. Worst of all, she would lose her apprenticeship and the freedom it promised. *Um.* Nothing worse would—could—follow the punishment for thieving water.

The road thinned and deteriorated. She had moved east or north, away from the staging ground, and away from home. Still, she kept going. If she doubled back, she risked capture. If she altered course, she'd end up more lost.

A dark thought spawned. Maybe it was all a set-up. Her mind flickered to Waldo's accusations the previous evening. As the distance grew between her and the disastrous job, so did her suspicions. Why didn't Gray tell her he was moving to the other side of the swale? Why didn't she hear him go? How did Gray know the job site specs so precisely? She'd assumed from the technical skill he flouted but maybe it was inside information. "I'm not a smuggler," he'd said with passion. A Dowser agent, then—how else did a cop get there so quickly? Had they set a deliberate trap for the best water thief?

Yet Gray ordered her to flee and save herself. He looked really hurt. Then again, he didn't sound any alarm. She was almost caught. Maybe he let her escape to report his arrest in the line of duty to the bosses, so that no one would suspect he was a double agent. Maybe he was a saboteur; maybe he set up Teddy at the water tower job, though why would a Dowser agent cause that much damage?

The last thought brought her up short. She was exhausted and not thinking straight. The next mental blip could lead to a mistake. Surging adrenaline gave way to gurgling hunger and even more distracting thirst. She had to formulate a plan. Any chance of returning home demanded caution as well as an explanation.

She looked around for a place to catch her breath. There was little out here but dilapidated buildings overgrown with desert weeds. She ducked into the entryway of an abandoned fourplex and sat on the steps leading to the upstairs apartments. The mud had caked on her but sweat had moistened it again. She regretted not taking Gray's pack. It would have rags to towel off with so they wouldn't leave tracks. Unless he never intended to get away...she stopped the spiraling thought. There was nothing for it but to strip off the suit—she was clean, if damp, underneath it—tuck it into a pile of debris in a corner, and pull on her own ripped clothes. As she did, a little round device like the one he'd given her to plant fell to the floor. A pinprick light in it blinked. *What the....* It blinked again.

A faint bombination reached her ear. Despite its fatigue, her body snapped into a hunter's crouch. Warily, she peered around the jamb of her hideout and swore under her breath.

A drone hovered at the height of the upper windowsills. It floated her way in a waspish wavering line.

Cassie's stomach dropped. Her heart thumped into the extra room. She had never encountered a Dowser drone. May said they were designed for dowsing but later were hacked to hunt thieves quasi-legally under the martial laws. Still, the Dowsers couldn't have many. A lone water thief miles from anywhere made for expensive quarry. Maybe it was the "game" change Gray had asserted.

The drone bobbed closer. Cassie glanced at the blinking device and forced herself to focus. She either stayed put, perhaps entering one of the apartments, or made a run for it. If she stayed, any sound risked confirming her presence to the drone. It would pin her down until its handlers arrived. If she ran, it would latch onto her and pursue—until its handlers arrived. She took May's ten breaths backwards. At five, she made her decision. At three, she ran.

The drone quit its methodical mapping and zoomed after her. No doubt its cameras transmitted her image. Soon the Dowsers would confirm her identity. There was no going back now. She ought to surrender. Instead, Cassie set her teeth and leaned forward, accelerating through the unfamiliar streets. The few people she passed withdrew hastily, whether from the demonic determination in her face or the faceless technology that hounded her.

Futility's cold dread stole into her thoughts. She couldn't outrun the machine and she didn't know her surroundings at all, let alone well enough to outwit it. The road would end when her legs faltered. Somehow, the realization calmed her. She relaxed her brow and jaw and fists and settled into the rhythm of running for the freedom of running. She even stopped feeling the rough road's jabs against her bare feet.

Her zen was so deep she almost didn't notice the drone stop mid-flight as abruptly as if it had smacked into a wall. It spun in wobbly confusion. In the same moment, an ancient troop transport rolled in front of her. Two right arms stretched down from its gate and gripped her by the triceps. Cassie twisted violently to resist as they yanked her into the truck. She tumbled onto its floor and looked up.

Definitely not Dowsers. What she saw instead was the widely grinning face of a boy her own age. Then another, identical to the first. Cassie would never be able to explain why, but on sight of that stupidly smiling pair, her hair-trigger coils of self-protection unwound. Overcome by the eventfulness of her sixty-fifth and truly final job as a water thief, she promptly passed out.

PART 2

—As it coheres even against gravity,
so we unite even against law.

—Catechism of Transcendence,
Dedication

CHAPTER 7
CASSIE

HER LEGS WERE sore, her shoulder was bruised, her neck was cricked, but the hammering headache held her full attention in its vise. Cassie blinked open one eye, then the other. She lay on an uncomfortable grooved floor. Daylight seeped into wherever she was through cracks and seams.

Two identical faces grinned down at her. Alarmed, Cassie sat up, kicked off an unfamiliar blanket, and crabbed away clumsily. Her back struck the inside of...the rear gate of a truck. She cast around frantically for her bag before recalling that she'd abandoned it during the previous evening's flight. It was empty anyway. She patted her body for anything amiss, checking buttons and deciding whether she felt...untouched. Satisfied, she relaxed a little and looked up. One of the twin faces smiled even more broadly. The other's brown eyes looked pained. They seemed about her age.

"We didn't want to disturb you."

"But we didn't want you to catch cold."

Cassie put a hand to her pulsing head.

One of the boys held out a hand with two small white pills. "Aspirin."

"You aren't feverish."

"Just tense."

"I've got something stronger if you want." The second boy, the one who had seemed hurt that she might be suspicious of them, smiled now. His brother smacked him in the head with an open palm, not lightly. Both wore their black hair in the same short cut.

"Aspirin's fine. Thanks." Her voice creaked rustily. She took the pills, dropped them on her tongue, sucked together what saliva she could, and swallowed hard. "I need a bathroom."

The medicine boy stepped nearer. Cassie put her arms up automatically. He gave her a pitying look and leaned over her to lift the flap above the gate. He wore shorts with frayed cuffs and a more discolored t-shirt of the same undyed material. He stood close enough for her to see the hempen cross-hatching, his belly where his shirt lifted, and the tanner skin of his goose-pimpled calf planted next to her. Its boy-hairs and his nonchalant movements reminded her of Teddy. The brother, too, of course.

The boy poked his head out and back in. "We'll be stopping in a few minutes if you can hold it." Cassie shrugged noncommittally. She didn't really have to go. If anything, she needed to rehydrate. She wanted to get out, get her bearings, and get away.

The boy stepped back and sat on the bench along the side of the truck. "My name's Viper." He held out his hand to shake.

"Okay." Her eyebrow scrunched skeptically.

"This is Cake." He cocked his head toward the other one.

She noticed now that Cake was the slightly scrawnier twin. "Why?"

Cake grinned, about to speak, but Viper cut him off. "Never mind."

"I'm Ca—"

"No." Viper cut her off, too. "Only tell the secret-keeper." His tone was matter-of-fact. Sensing her incipient question, he added, "When it's time."

Secrets. Cassie's hand went to her pocket to secure her private chip. Cake smiled apologetically. "We checked. Couldn't have the Dowsers track us, too."

Sure enough, it wasn't there. Thieves usually left them at home on jobs in case they got caught. But Cassie had a nagging feeling she had hers on her when she left the house. Yes, she had brought it because she was going to record something funny to cheer up Teddy. So…these guys had searched her. Her face betrayed revulsion and anger.

Viper nodded calmly to a reader on the floor. "Nobody touched you. Except we had to take the chip." "Light fingers," added Cake. He waggled his as if playing the air and grinned again. Viper walloped him.

Cassie felt something else in her pocket: the ring. Inma. Who might be facing Dowser questioning right now, depending on whether or not Gray was a saboteur. As might Teddy, who also had to answer to the bosses for the incomplete job. She had to get back and sort everything out. So she might have to play nice enough with these two first. They didn't seem dangerous. "Why did you help me?" Her voice was her own again now, though still raspy through her dry vocal cords. "Did you help me?"

"It was Dad's decision." Viper's thumb indicated the

front of the truck where, presumably, his father drove the cab. "He said anyone running that fast against a drone was worth meeting."

"I couldn't outrun it. The drone just…stopped."

Her body leaned out of the curve and pitched forward as the truck made an unexpected turn and braked. The boys, by contrast, rose to their feet instantly and surfed the jarring halt with expert balance.

"M-hm," Viper confirmed. "That's Castle's doing. C'mon, we'll show you."

Cake opened his eyes wide. "Then we'll take you to our leaders." He guffawed and hopped out of the truck.

Cassie followed. The bright morning sun seared her retinas. Theirs was one of a hodgepodge of vehicles that had pulled over. There were trucks, some canvas-covered like theirs, vans, motorcycles, and a few buses, many of them in styles Cassie had never seen in either the up- or downscale parts of the city. They parked on a pitted lot amid a jumble of abandoned buildings in the middle of nowhere. She had never seen a place like it. Maybe it had been a fort or base. A long, low building ranged along one flank. It seemed to end in the tile-roofed remnants of a palace. Across the road, what might have been a barracks or dormitory was guarded by, improbably, a smaller, turreted castle nestled against a hillock. A few large signposts littered the ground, their colors and words too scratched and faded to interpret.

The twins led Cassie through the cluster. Weaving among the vehicles, she had the impression that their arrangement might be designed to seem more casual than it was. Some appeared to ring others. Each had clearance to maneuver. Many of their occupants were busy with sundry chores. They seemed to be of all ages and their quotidian bustle might have been transposed from Cassie's own street, if not for their movable dwellings and open-air lifestyle and the marginally sparer and shabbier condition of their stuff. One group napped on bedrolls angled to catch the right amount of morning shade. Perhaps they, like the twins' father, were drivers, whose turn it was to rest. Everyone ignored the three kids winding through.

Their destination was a large rectangular van at the fringe. Cake rapped on the rear door. Nothing happened. Viper peeked around the side. Two huge bare feet stuck out the driver's side window of the cab. Viper knocked louder on the side of the van. The feet waggled and disappeared. A moment later they reemerged through the open door, accompanied by a hulking, bearded man who hopped to the ground and strode toward the trio.

"I thought you might come by." His bass voice matched his size. He looked at Cassie calmly. "You know she's not permitted."

"She already guessed you did something to the drone. We just want to show her how."

The man stared Cake down sternly, then smiled as if he had made the point expected of him. He extended a bear claw to Cassie. "Castle. Pleased to meet you."

"Ca—" she caught herself and turned it into a repetition of his name "—stle. Likewise."

"Go figure," he winked.

Castle was large enough to grip the handle of the van's rear door and send it sliding upward from where he stood. He let Viper and Cake scramble up before offering Cassie a chivalrous hand. She shook her head and leapt in. The stench almost knocked her back out again.

"Well, that's how," Castle laughed, stepping gigantically up behind them. "Dowser cops and even marshals don't bother to investigate too far past the smell, so I keep it just stinky enough." He pulled the door down and shut behind them.

Cassie narrowed her nostrils and scanned the van's interior. A shivery finger picked its way up her spine as glimpses of the van's contents flickered to sight under the tubular lights strung within. On low shelves near the floor were round baskets filled with what looked like small rodent turds. In others, pale worms writhed amid a pasty mash. Twiggy trellises climbed the walls, forming cubbies that held tightly wound oval cocoons. Fibrous wisps hung between them like cobwebs. Cake poked at one of the cocoons. Viper punched his arm. Toward the back—or rather the front—of the van, skeins of the stuff draped over sawhorses. The van was cluttered with small tables bolted to its floor, on which rested jars filled with powdery substances. It all made Cassie a little squeamish.

"Silkbugs," Castle whispered reverently. He eased past her and tilted one of the lights so it shined directly on a basket of the critters. She saw now that some were tinted in various hues, as were the cocoons above. "A species entirely symbiotic with humankind," the big man continued. "They can't eat unless we feed them, and we—this little tribe—" he smiled at Viper and Cake "—rely on them for camouflage." He gingerly reorganized the furniture to reveal a concealed space behind it where a small tangle of electronic equipment blinked placidly. "Scanning, mapping—and jamming," Castle said. "Hard stuff to come by, hard to keep running, harder were it lost." He restored the arrangement and lowered his face near one of the baskets. "Same with our little friends."

Respect for these people was growing in Cassie. She had

prejudged them as bumpkins for their appearance and lilting speech. Whatever they planned for her, this Castle had helped her once and might be an ally later. She suppressed her instinct and leaned toward his—pets? livestock? "They're... cute."

Castle seemed pleased with the compliment. He pulled down a jar filled with greenish powder. "Dried mulberry leaves. Fresh is what the poor things crave but the trees are extremely rare where we travel." His voice grew even softer. "We suffer and survive the same things together."

"What about the colors?"

Castle smiled. He pointed to the other jars. "Clays I find and mix in with the food." He plucked a strand of ochre woven silk from a hanging line. "Perhaps you have a use for it."

"Thanks."

"I feed them by hand. You're welcome to join me."

"Uh."

"Don't, they're bloodsuckers," Cake warned.

Viper rolled his eyes. "Don't be a jerk." To Cassie he said, "Cool cover, huh?"

She glanced behind the silken wall to what this enterprise protected. "The drone," she said to Castle. "You jammed it, but did you hack it, too?" The Dowser had barely glimpsed her but she needed to know if the drone had gotten a clear shot. If not, maybe she could go back. "Or could you now?"

Too blunt. She saw Viper and Cake exchange a look. Castle sighed and pushed her toward the door. "I think you better take her now."

Outside, the sun beat harder. The brothers led Cassie back into the maze of vehicles. She squinted against the alloys' reflective gleam. "Take me where?" she asked them.

"Why did you ask Castle about the drone?" came Cake's question back.

"I want to go home." Obviously.

"So why not go?" He gestured back down the desert road. Cassie added figuring out how to survive it to her mental list.

"It's- complica—"

"Don't tell us," Viper blurted before she even got the words out. "Tell the secret-keeper." To Cake, he added conspiratorially, "You know she has to anyway." That was the second time he mentioned such a person.

They had arrived near the apparent center of the troop. Three people huddled around a scratched and splintered folding table. The woman among them got up and stepped forward when she saw the kids approach. She was shorter than Cassie, older than Inma by quite a bit. She looked like a grandmother with her wrap despite the heat and her gray braids patterned artistically against her skull.

"Is she the secret-keeper?" Cassie asked.

"More like the tooth-puller," Cake mimed wrenching out a molar.

"She," said Viper, "is Dahlia."

CHAPTER 8
DAHLIA

DAHLIA PULLED HER wrap tighter around her shoulders as she stood up. Not against any chill in the air (if only) but against the dream she couldn't shake. Last night, the road had grown increasingly uneven as the Transcendent caravan passed eastward out of the city. Dahlia had not slept well on the wafer of bedding unrolled on a worktable bolted to the floor of the van that carried her. Her body had splayed across the table like a Renaissance sinner's as a tortured dream unfolded…

She was youthful again, not Dahlia…Melanie.

The high desert grit Dahlia breathed in the van—

Turned into a bucketful that Henry something-or-other threw in Melanie's face at the sandbox in Mac- Mc—

Dahlia's subconscious rifled through folders to find the name of the park but the moment passed.

Melanie hated babysitting the brat but her mother hoped work would channel her mercurial energies, and she loved her mother.

Dahlia's sleeping mouth twisted with satisfaction given

what happened to the boy much later. She curled fetally. Her shoulder and knee breached the table's brink—

Causing Melanie to slip off the edge of the dreamscape and fall down, down.

Dahlia jolted awake and felt the reassurance of solid-ish ground. She settled into a more relaxed posture and drifted off until…

She was Melanie again. The tableau reset. The kettle hissed. Melanie's mother lifted it from the stove and poured three cups of spicy orange tea.

Dahlia's sleeping nose inhaled the tangy steam.

Her parents drank it black but Melanie curbed the tartness with a plop of milk and sugar.

"And how did Zeno advise the dog tethered to a chariot?" her father asked in his taciturn style.

Melanie was prepared. "Keep up." Her father nodded slowly without expression. Her mother, however, smiled and hummed a gentle melody in a minor key. Feeling proud, Melanie helped herself to a butter cookie from the scalloped plate in the center of the dining table. She sometimes resented this Sunday afternoon ritual but she was aware enough of the decaying world around her to appreciate the privilege of weekly tea and cake.

Dahlia's sleeping tongue ran as if over the lightly glazed design imprinted on the cookie.

"Would you?" Her father took no cookie. He carved isometric—

(it helped to be dreaming of the same year as geometry class)

—slices from a peach with glacial precision.

"Until I could bite the driver and escape." Her mother laughed approvingly through closed lips without interrupting

her hum. Her father continued to nod like a bobbing toy she'd seen once...

(Oh yes, in a friend's mother's car.)

"And how would you know your opportunity?"

Melanie hesitated one second, two seconds...

A pothole bounced the van and bumped the plot.

Her mother's mouth turned downward. She restarted her melody. Her father snapped a wedge from the peach.

Dahlia's sleeping eye gauged the fibrous red flesh near its pit.

Three seconds. Melanie bit into the cookie to stall, then regretted not deserving it, though neither parent had spoken or looked away from her.

Four seconds.

A low rumble sounded near the corner of the dining room ceiling. Melanie looked up. Capiz shells rattled on the chandelier. The noise rolled across and down until its vibration shook the room. Melanie looked at her father. He somersaulted away in his chair, yin-yanged with a now giant slice of peach. She looked at her mother. She sat unperturbed amid the tumbling furniture, frowning at Melanie and humming her melancholy tune.

Only it wasn't her mother anymore, it was a woman with blond hair suited in black. She was out of place in this dreamory.

The earthquake sprang Melanie out of her chair...

Dahlia woke with her back jouncing off the table. Her tongue smacked thickly against the roof of her mouth and her hand reached for a glass that wasn't there. Dahlia ached to think of her parents' fondness for each other, he the philosopher activist who said 'Niners always hailed Mary, she the physician who dealt compassionately in broken bodies.

Dahlia sighed. She couldn't recover the dream's thread

in the joggling wagon. What had her father asked? What song did her mother hum? What would she give for a bite of peach now? The last one she saw slid down a socialite's jewel-sheathed gullet twenty years ago.

⁂

Twenty years. Did it seem like yesterday or a lifetime ago? It was more than a lifetime to the children walking toward her. How old she must seem to them. She didn't think she was— her parents would have considered sixty the prime of life—but had to admit (only to herself) that she hadn't been young enough to adapt easily to the nomadic way when things fell apart. Her rank as a doctor and an elder earned her a private car but could not buy a good night's sleep, despite the dried valerian she kept in a thin tin case with a stone-beaded lid and chewed each evening to calm her overburdened mind. To add to which this young stranger whom Meskit's boys were escorting.

"Thank you, boys, we've been waiting." It might have been a schoolteacher's reprimand. "You may go."

"See you later," Viper offered the girl a handshake.

"Probably," Cake added mysteriously with a salute. They jogged away, forward progress impeded by mutual shoving and tripping.

"Come on over here." Dahlia tried to sound encouraging. Her mouth smiled but her gaze was clinical. Word of a new refugee had spread quickly through the early risers of the camp. Dahlia was intensely curious by nature. She also had a job to do. She hadn't expected someone so young. It could complicate matters.

"Sit with us," Harv told the girl with his throaty, quiet

authority. Harv was an elder, like Dahlia. He was the principal leader, though younger than her—something around fifty—and stringy tall with long straight hair pulled into a ponytail. "I'm Harv," he said as he folded cross-legged onto a spot of tarmac shaded by a camper.

"That's not a fake name," the girl said. She was a quick study, Dahlia observed.

"It's a natural one. Short for harvester ant, which admittedly does not trip off the tongue. But I picked it early on for good reason, and before the pattern took shape."

"I'm Dahlia." Dahlia sat down primly on steps that folded out from the camper. "Another natural name." She assumed David, the other, younger man, would say nothing. He rarely did. The pageant of tattoos fanning down his deltoids to his arms and splattering his chest and sides said plenty. Sure enough, David simply crouched his lean, athletic body next to Harv. "This is David."

"That one isn't." The girl chose cross-legged like Harv.

"It's quite appropriate as a *nom de guerre*. And suitable to its bearer." Dahlia tried her smile of encouragement again. "It's necessary to explain your situation to you."

"It is our custom to shelter those in need," Harv elaborated, "but not indefinitely. You came to us in the middle of the night, and so bought a night of concealment."

"Yeah, well, I didn't exactly stow away. I was pulled in."

"Rescued," Dahlia corrected her.

"Or kidnapped," the girl shot back.

"Regardless," Harv continued. "The time has come for you, and we, to choose. You may go." Harv extended an arm toward the expansive desert. "Or you may seek to stay."

Dahlia watched her contemplate the ribbon of asphalt that rippled across the emptiness. "That simple?" the girl asked.

"No, not simple." Harv showed no sign of catching her sarcasm. "To stay is to *stay*. To become one of us."

"Which is who?"

At this, Harv laughed. "Me." He pointed individually at his colleagues in turn, then opened a palm to take in the gathering. "David, Dahlia, the boys who brought you and their father, these others." He dropped his hand to his lap. "And more besides."

"You're...travelers?"

"That word has many meanings. It applies and it doesn't."

Seeing the girl scowl in frustration, Dahlia interceded. "Some call us the Transcendents." She saw no sign of recognition cross the girl's face. Ignorance or else deceit. She made another note on her mental chart.

"If I decide to leave, you'll take me back to the city?"

"No," David of few words finally spoke.

"I'm afraid our itinerary leads onward," Harv said sympathetically. "We offer provisions for three days' journey, if we are satisfied." Dahlia knew three days' journey on foot wouldn't get the girl back to the city. She wondered if the girl did.

"Satisfied with what?"

"You will speak to the secret-keeper."

"And then I can go?"

"If that is what you wish."

"Okay. Lead the way."

"Dahlia, would you?" Harv asked in his grating patrician way and closed his eyes.

"Come, dear." Dahlia stood and adjusted her wrap. She

led Cassie through the unmoving traffic. "Don't worry, the secret-keeper will only ask you questions."

"I have questions, too."

"You're the supplicant here." Still, to know how the girl's mind worked might provide useful data. "Okay. While we walk."

"No offense, but you seem kind of poor." Dahlia stiffened. The girl went on, "I mean, nobody, at least nobody I know, you know, no one who isn't really rich, could afford a car, let alone a truck, so..." she trailed off.

"As you've no doubt noticed in forming your assessment," Dahlia spoke with crisp politeness, "these are the vehicles of poor people, much used, much loved, and much repaired."

"I know, but we must have driven a couple hundred miles overnight and I can't figure out how you get the fuel for it all. Especially 'cause some of these clunkers look like running on gas."

The child was paying attention. Dahlia relaxed and sighed inwardly. People used to travel twice as far on the spur of the moment. "Ah. Well. Surely at your age you know that appearances deceive, all the more so when ingenuity is involved." She saw that the girl wouldn't relent: tenacious. Dahlia made a tactical decision and placed a hand on the girl's forearm to draw her closer. "I'll tell you something I shouldn't if you're not going to become one of us, dear." The girl's body language betrayed her interest: inquisitive. "We have a saying for how we make do, an adage or mnemonic—do you know that word?—to remind ourselves of our options and to select the right one at the right time. If we have a choice. It goes, 'aid, raid, trade.'"

"So you are outlaws."

"There's more to it. The saying, I mean." Dahlia sing-songed hurriedly: *"Aid is easy, earns a debt / Raid is risky, tit for tet / Trade is tricky, mind you net."* She blushed. "So. Anything else?"

"Yeah, I'm starving. Got anything to eat?"

"After the secret-keeper. We're here."

⁂

Having dropped off the girl, Dahlia returned to Harv's camper. He and David—still crouching like a tracker—had been joined by the other four leaders. To David's vigorous nods of agreement, thickset Griz was arguing with the twins' father, Meskit. "She shouldn't be here!"

"Castle picked up a signal, then a drone," Meskit defended himself. "Dahlia said check it out. The kid was running for her life. I wasn't gonna let the Dowsers take her."

"Now isn't the time to call attention to ourselves," objected Lake, the cook. "We'll never make it to the Fence if we're weighed down with every urchin along the way."

"Can she do anything useful?" asked Tesla. The chief technologist favored pragmatism.

"She has filthy nails like a water thief," snorted Griz. "And walks like one, too."

"All the more reason to send her back."

"She won't survive."

"She's probably a Dowser spy."

"Then why were they hunting her?"

"If she's useful—"

"That's not the right criterion. It's too dangerous these days."

"These are the days not to turn our backs. Isn't that the whole point of this insurrection?"

"Not if it stops us from reaching the Fence."

Dahlia absorbed the cacophony. If the girl was a thief… well, time would tell more. Dahlia wanted to buy some. "Let's see what the secret-keeper says."

CHAPTER 9
CASSIE

IT WAS PITCH-BLACK inside the secret-keeper's hut. Hut wasn't the right word, exactly, but Cassie was at a loss to describe the domed metallic structure mounted on a flatbed into which Dahlia shoved her abruptly through a door in its smooth, curved surface. It was cool inside, though current-less. The exterior must reflect sunrays. It also blocked sound, she realized, as she waited a minute, two, five, without hearing anything but the rhythm of her own breath that slowed and slowly filled her awareness.

Eventually, a blue-green glow appeared above her, perhaps near the ceiling, though she was blind to spatial perspective in this chamber. Another disc illuminated in mid-air lower down. Then a third, enough to outline her limbs and texture some shadows.

"Welcome, seeker." The voice was reedier than Cassie had expected, given the shrouded staging. She squelched a snort of surprise. Into the lantern's ambit emerged a man of indeterminate age and average height. His linen suit might have been undyed but gleamed ghoulishly in the turquoise light.

"You were expecting someone more…shamany. I'm afraid I'm not." His voice brightened. "I do have this." He turned his head into the beam and pointed at a black patch slung over his left eye. He peeled it back to reveal an eyelid half torn out and half soldered shut by a thick, pink, slashing scar that disappeared into a hollow eyesocket. He grinned toothily and stepped closer to Cassie. She recoiled instinctively. The phosphorescent air seemed misty even though she knew it wasn't. Fear replaced derision. She tried to count slow breaths.

He laughed tinnily. "I've no inclination to harm you physically. In fact, of anyone in this place, you can trust me. I trained in the law, a profession admittedly mistrusted, but one that nonetheless often carries all hope of earthly restitution. The point is, I know how to keep secrets, and am bound to do so, and so here we are, you and I."

"What's your name?" Cassie asked.

"I'm the secret-keeper. What's yours?"

Viper had said to tell him. And she might learn if they knew more than Castle had let on. "Cassandra. Killian."

Another lamp bloomed close to her face. She could no longer see his, only his suited body from neck to knees. "Yes, I believe you."

"What are these lights?"

"You ask a lot of questions."

"Yeah, I get that a lot lately. I'm a seeker, right?"

"Mm," he equivocated. "You ask for information. You should seek illumination." He stepped into the shadows, leaving in sight only a hand that waved ghostlike in the lamplight. "But to answer this question, they are bioluminescents. Microbes, tiny little bugs that shine together or not at all."

"What makes them glow?"

"Electricity, of course."

"Where do they get it?"

"Can you guess?"

Cassie peered into the light near her head. She discerned a kaleidoscope of blinking squiggles rather than a solid beam. She thought for a moment. "A methane digester. You feed them waste." She hadn't seen any farm animals. "I'm guessing human."

The hand shot into the darkness. She heard him slink across the room. "Very good. You're familiar with the process?"

"I maintain one at home. For other stuff. I've never seen these before."

"They're my contrivance—with Tesla's help, you've not met Tesla yet—though similar kinds exist with various other practical uses. Tell me more about your home and the things you take care of there."

Maybe it was the atmosphere, but after the whipsaw of the past couple of days, it was a relief to unburden. The secret-keeper invited her to sit on the floor. Cassie reclined and stared into the simulation of infinite space. As she answered his questions, she settled into the obscurity it afforded. She told him about Inma, her desperation to leave the small world of her childhood, how the prospect of her apprenticeship was therefore exhilarating despite being for a Judge, and the abysmal realization that she had effectively lost it in the blink of an eye. He probed her tale gently and she was surprised to hear herself speak aloud of other things: her unknown parents, how May had scouted her on the playground and recruited her to be a water thief, the fantasies she had shared only with Mariah, the surprising force of her recently discovered desire for Teddy—and to help him.

Narrating that part brought acid to her throat along with visceral fear from her flight and inchoate fear of the future. But she felt pride, too, encasing the fear. What other water thief could have escaped as she did? The secret-keeper seemed impressed. He asked her to repeat the number of triumphs and went off on his own tangent, explaining the beauty of a number like sixty-four and all the ways it divided into symmetrical factors of eight by eight and four by four by two by two and so on. She kept thinking of sixty-five and its factor, thirteen, instead.

The only thing Cassie held back was the ring hidden in her pocket. While she spoke, her finger traced its silver sides and the thin, smooth strip of gemstone. In the moment, it somehow seemed more important to safeguard that object than her biography or feelings.

Even so, a raw vulnerability stole over her when her words ran out. Rising and reeling from head rush, she queried her interviewer, "You'll really keep it all secret?"

He brought his mangled face flush to a spotlight and triggered another on her face, inches apart so that they saw each other's eyes. This time she wished he didn't wear the patch. "I swear it, Cassandra, from your name on. I opine only as to whether or not I believe you to be sincere in intent and therefore safe to release or hardy enough to seek. If that is what you wish."

"And am I safe?" she asked, then added merely out of curiosity, "Or strong enough?"

"Hm," he non-answered. "You still keep secrets. Some you may not even know."

~~~

Instead of Dahlia, Viper and Cake waited for her outside.

"So what now?" Cassie asked them. The hour, at least, she spent confessing had rejuvenated her self-confidence. Her mind felt clearer.

"Breakfast," was Cake's happy reply.

They led her to a chow line. Each pried a cone of coarse eucalyptus paper from a stack, along with a narrow spatula with a tapered edge.

"Not what you're used to?" Cake watched Cassie examine the eatware.

"We had a dishwasher." Realizing she sounded snobby, and recalling the dishwasher's frequent strikes, she amended. "Inm—my guardian didn't like us to use paper in case it leached."

"No parents?" Viper picked up on Cassie's terminology.

"Gone. Dead, I guess."

"Yeah." Viper nodded. It was common enough in their generation.

"She never adopted me officially. What about you?" They had mentioned a father but not a mother, which could mean any number of things.

"Same. Mom's...gone."

"Definitely dead, though," Cake chimed in solemnly.

"We were too young to know, or know her. Dad's cool, though. And this place is kind of communal anyway. A lot of them helped raise us."

"Too many." Cake mimed asphyxiation.

"Yeah." Cassie knew the feeling, despite her very different upbringing.

They arrived at the front of the line. A lean woman with stringy hair streaked with grey and wearing pants and a smock manned an appliance that rested on a folding easel. It looked like the cylindrical satellites with flared solar panels pictured in Cassie's textbooks. The woman—Viper said her name was Lake—pulled a tube like a drawer from the cylinder and plucked the spatula from Cassie's hand.

"Not used to a solar cooker, either?" Cake ventured.

Cassie shook her head. "Biogas oven."

"These are easier to move around." Viper nudged her forward. The woman had dumped a few spoonfuls of baked black-eyed peas into Cassie's cone and handed back the spatula. The food was familiar, if that was any comfort.

There was only one other station. A short, grandfatherly man in a dishdasha punctiliously added three modest wedges to her cone. Potato went in the middle on top of the beans. He placed tomato and preserved lemon, peels up, near the edges.

"C'mon, let's sit in the shade." Viper sat on a curb of crumbling concrete beneath one of the ruined buildings and pinned his cone expertly between his knees. "I think this was a restaurant." The three of them stared at one another, then burst into laughter. Picnicking beside its hull was the closest any of them had ever come to eating in one.

Viper used his spatula to submerge the vegetables. "Tomato. Not bad."

"They're drip-fed in the greenhouse," Cake explained.

Cassie picked up the lemon wedge.

"Had a minor scurvy epidemic last winter." Cake curled his lips over his teeth to illustrate. "So they're taking precautions early this year." Without unfurling his lips, he ducked toward the cone and gobbled the wedge, peel and all.

Viper squeezed his onto the beans and tossed the peel to Cake. "Better eat before it sogs the paper," he said.

Cassie handled her garnishes like Viper and dug in. It was actually pretty tasty. A coating of olive oil kept it moist and palatable. "You grow the beans in the greenhouse, too?"

"Sometimes. I think we traded for these fresh. Or maybe flash-dried and rehydrated."

Cassie glanced from brother to brother. "Identical twins. What's that like?"

"Normal, for us," Cake shot back.

She hadn't thought of it that way. "Yeah, I guess so." She scanned the camped tribe. "I don't even have a sister. Well, Mar- my best friend basically is. But really there's just me."

It didn't take long to finish the food. Cassie followed the boys' example in unfolding the cone and using the tapered edge of the spatula to collect the last of the mash. A kid of maybe twelve or thirteen came around to collect the paper. Viper explained that the troop was coming from an area where paper was relatively abundant and would trade it to a recycling facility farther inland. Then he told Cassie to close her eyes and spin around three times. "Okay, open."

The twins stood side by side. They had removed their shirts and mussed their hair.

"Can you tell who's who?"

She couldn't from the voice. It was flatter, stripped of Viper's intensity or Cake's range. With them standing still, she couldn't distinguish Viper's even movements from Cake's goofiness. She blushed and hoped it went unnoticed in the daylight. Two half-naked guys were inviting her to scrutinize them. The differences in their faint, erratic tan lines were subtle. So were the tiny variations in the shape of their eyes and negligible bowing of one brother's elbows and knees. But their torsos reminded her. "You're Viper." She pointed to the one to her left.

"How do you know?"

"You're fatter." Not much, but the other was skinny for sure.

He laughed goodnaturedly. "Not always." He slapped his brother's puny gut. Cake cracked a sheepish smile. "I eat less when I use." Viper gave Cassie an exasperated look. She had a guess at the pseudonym now. There would have been more places to score in the city they had just left than on the open road. How Cake afforded it was a good question.

Viper pulled on his shirt. "In a few weeks, we'll be clones again."

"There must be a mole or scar or birthmark or something?"

"Wanna check?" Cake leered.

Before Cassie could retort, the server kid circled round again, this time bearing a bamboo platter and accompanied by an even younger kid. On it was a low mound of cooked carrot hash and sugar beets. The boys fluidly hived off a mouthful of the dessert with their spatulas. Doing likewise, Cassie couldn't help thinking of the chocolate birthday cake Inma had given her yesterday. Was it really only a day ago?

The little one painstakingly held out a capped glass breeq with both hands. Cake took the jug, tilted his head back, and tipped a stream of water into his mouth, letting it flow uninterrupted for five seconds. He deftly righted the pitcher without losing a drop. Viper did the same. He passed it to Cassie. She wasn't as smooth. Water trickled from the spout and spattered the dusty ground before reaching her lips. Out of the corner of her eye she saw the child's expression swell with alarm. The clean, cool liquid thrummed something primordial in her brain. She wouldn't stop drinking, even though she started choking on the pour, sputtering wastefully. Viper grabbed the breeq from her, sliding a digit beneath the opening to catch the last drops and sucking them from his finger. He returned it to the stricken child with a warning look and avoided Cassie's gaze. Cake scrunched his cheek as if to say: *I get it, but not cool.*

Out loud, he changed the subject by suggesting they check out the ruined castle across the main road. They handed their spatulas to the older server for reuse and went to kill time. It wasn't a real castle, of course, but up close it looked even less like one and more like a supersized playhouse attached to a giant apartment building. Cake poked around for a couple of minutes but digestion soon led them to hang sluggishly on the low hill next to the structure. From there, Cassie thought she identified the triumvirate who had more or less welcomed her earlier that morning, seated amid a larger group of adults. The cook, Lake, was there. They must be deliberating her fate.

Which was their right why, exactly? And what was she doing relaxing while they did? She'd been lulled into a false sense of security by Dahlia's kindness, the secret-keeper's tricks, and these two escorting her around like they were new besties. Guarding her was more like it. She saw Viper watching her. "What?" It came out a little more aggressively than she meant.

Cake answered instead. "He's thinking that if you go, he'll never learn your real name."

Viper leapt on him. "Shut up, hyena butter."

Compromised in a headlock, Cake play-acted the fainting romantic. "But he'll find you somehow, some way, someday."

Viper addressed Cassie. "What I was thinking was we get

strangers lots of times but it's the first time *we*—" he noogied Cake's scalp "—rescued anyone." He cut off Cassie's objection. "I knew you'd hate that word. You're kinda prickly."

"I'm gonna take a walk." Cassie stood and wiped the dirt off her pants. Prickly didn't bother her. She herself kind of liked Viper's directness, among other things about him. But he was right about "rescue." She was done waiting around worrying what either these people or those back home would do. Something this morning had given her an idea.

The boys broke apart. Viper seemed embarrassed but Cake said, "We'll come with you."

"No. I- I'm not used to being around so many people all the time," she half-lied. "I need a few minutes by myself."

♒

Cassie reconnoitered the vehicle from a spot between two others that seemed safely devoid of foot traffic. It looked sort of like a giant Conestoga wagon. Instead of canvas, it was hooped over with mesh. Inside, it was filled with plants. She hadn't been able to tell from afar if she recognized any or even would. But she had watched the man who served the tomatoes go get more from it. It must be the (mobile, naturally) greenhouse Cake had mentioned, although heat not being scarce, it was more of a semi-open-air garden.

From her scouting position, Cassie tried to peer between the mesh and greenery to see if there were people inside. She didn't see anyone. She waited long enough to feel relatively certain—it had to be too cramped and stifling to be a comfortable place for a postprandial nap. When the coast was clear, she darted to the wagon and inside the door.

A wave of scent struck her, akin to the bioswale's last

night but much stronger. And that had been in darkness. This—Cassie had never seen so much verdancy in her life. She thought about plucking some of the vegetables but they would be bulky to carry. Staying low so no one would spy her from the outside, she walked between the plants, running her hands through the soil.

She had done the math. Given the pace to which she had awakened, they couldn't have traveled more than a couple hundred miles. But she didn't know her coordinates or what lay on the way. The desert was madness but to follow the highway was risky, too. Even a proffered ride could be unsafe for a number of reasons. Yet it was too far to walk in three days and that was as much provision as Harv had offered. She'd need more. These people weren't wasteful; the bioluminescence in the secret-keeper's hut showed her that. With this many of them on the road, they must have their own water recycling system, too. Taking what she needed from whatever passed for a bathroom, even if she found it there, might get her caught quickly. But Cake had also said the crops were drip-fed. She'd be gone before anyone noticed a difference.

Cassie's hand found a narrow irrigation lateral lying beneath the soil surface. She traced along it until it met the wider submain at a right angle. So far, so good. She ran her fingers underneath the larger pipe until it, too, intersected with an even thicker one. It had to be the main line, running the length of the vehicle. Somewhere along it should be what she was looking for.

Crawling now, she followed the main to a spot where it suddenly stopped and ran perpendicularly downwards. Scraping away the soil, Cassie felt around the wooden floorboards underneath. She was looking for a seam and…a latch. A trap door. Trying not to uproot all the plants in the vicinity, she pulled it open and rummaged inside the cavity it exposed. Somewhere inside ought to be a urine filtration device. Its aquaporin protein membrane would allow only pure water through to slake the crops. If it was small enough, she would remove and carry it with her. Otherwise, she could find something to cut it. Then if she could steal a bag, bottle, anything, she could rig it for travel. She would thieve some water from the meal breeq (along with a little food) and reuse whatever she peed. With luck, it would last long enough to reach home.

After a moment, she hit upon the filter. It seemed manageable. She moved to get a better grip and started fiddling with it.

There was a noise at the door. Someone was coming inside. If these Transcendents punished thieves anything like the Dowsers did, Cassie could not afford to be caught. She couldn't hide the mess she had made but maybe she could disappear. Frantic, she swept her hands in the empty compartment beneath her. It was large—large enough to hold her. She took a deep breath and plunked into it, hoping not to land in the urine chamber.

She did. It stank. But it was mercifully empty. She quickly found the latch that let the gardener fill the container from outside. Just as someone entered above, she pulled it and dropped to the ground, clutching the filter membrane. Time to accelerate her escape plan. She crawled out from beneath the wagon.

"What are you doing." It wasn't a question. Cassie looked up, past the tattoos, into the unsmiling eyes of David, the scarily placid Transcendent leader. She stared back. They both knew what: she was thieving their water.

CHAPTER 10
CLEMENTINE & SHADOW

CLEMENTINE LAY FEVERISH on the flaking floorboards of someone's living room.

"She's awake." The unknown voice jarred her to panicked lucidity. She jerked but firm hands held her down.

"Almost done, My Darling." Truck's soothing bass preceded a sliver of pain through her backside into her spine.

"Who is that?" She pointed her head to where the other voice had come from. It took effort to keep her eyes rolling in sync with her cranium.

Shadow's face hovered into view over hers. "A friend."

Another face loomed and matched itself to the voice. "Actually, Gypsum's cousin, one way or another. Name's Lee Toby."

"You don't look Norwegian." *That wasn't right.* Gauze draped her thoughts.

"Nooo," Lee's elongated vowels stretched further as he laughed.

"She's trying to think of Naabeehó." Gypsum's perpetually

even tone contrasted with her cousin's. She sounded winded, though. "I took a look from the roof. Nothing."

"Good." Shadow turned away from Clementine to nod at Gypsum.

Truck stood and laid down his instrument of torture. He gestured with bloodied hands. "I removed most of the bullets and cleaned it out best I could." He nodded to Lee. "Thanks."

"Still, better to keep moving," Gypsum advised. Her voice grew even softer. "If we can."

"Where are we?" Clementine tried to raise herself on her elbows. Pain bolted through her lower body.

"Don't move. Or talk," Shadow instructed her. "Just rest for a while. We gave you a pill from Lee's emergency kit so Truck could work." Clementine sank back into the enveloping fog.

Shadow watched Clementine drift off and motioned for the others to follow him to the back porch of the ranch house. Tufts of shadscale and greasewood peppered the yard up to a wizened clump of sycamores that demarcated the property line. In the distance rose red cliffs like those through which they had recently passed. Shadow squinted into the blinding sun. Somewhere to the northeast were caves where exiled Aztec priests had supposedly secreted a golden hoard after the fall of Tenochtitlan. Maybe they had descendants. He looked from Gypsum to Lee. They didn't share many features. Lee's long isosceles nose and dark eyes set broadly in his cheeks conformed to Shadow's stereotype of the Navajo, whereas a wave rippled Gypsum's fading hair and her eyes were the milky gray of dried sage. It was a miracle she had found him in time to save Clementine. Or maybe not miraculous so much as another allegiance crisscrossed with the one she gave the Transcendents. Whichever it was, he was grateful.

He turned to Lee. "We used too many of your supplies. We owe you one."

"I owe her many," Lee replied graciously. He took Gypsum's hand between his own weatherbeaten ones. "She swore never to set foot here again. But when things got really bad, she did anyway, and brought the cavalry—hah—with her."

Gypsum pulled away shyly. She plucked an unseasonal panicle from a saltbush huddled against the planked steps and powdered its dried-up buds between her thumb and forefinger. "Better to keep moving," she repeated. "Back to the caravan."

"We can't leave her," Shadow objected.

"She can't stay behind anyway," Truck obliged. "She needs a surgeon and antibiotics."

"You won't find either here," Lee said. "Maybe in Dixieland."

"It's the right direction, at least." Gypsum had spoken openly in front of her cousin, so Shadow would trust him, too. "Harv and the others are that way."

"The main roads west will be watched," Truck worried.

A moan wafted their way from inside the house.

"I don't reckon you can spare the time to avoid it," said Lee. "I'll take you."

They lost little of that time tucking Clementine and then themselves into the fueled-up pickup Lee commanded as a tribal outposter. Clementine wedged lying down between Shadow and Truck in the bed. A make-do splint cushioned her bad leg. Lee covered them with a burlap tarp. The drive wouldn't take long, assuming no hiccups.

Shadow had Gypsum ride in the cab with Lee. If there were bulletins out, no witness from the raid would have seen and identified her. She also could claim relation to Lee. Meanwhile, she would be a second set of eyes and ears to scan for trouble. They headed out.

Suffocating beneath the tarp, Shadow pulled it beneath his nose. He ventured a peek above the bedrail. A stretch of shriveled farmland rushed by. He caught a few letters on a tattered sign staked into the ground as it whipped past. They implored water conservation.

The rear window was open. "It's nice to meet your family," he heard Lee say deadpan.

Gypsum didn't take the bait. "I've been through a lot with them."

"It's not like it was for you here anymore."

"More Cro—" whizzed by. Shadow mentally filled in the end of the old aid agency slogan: "—p per Drop."

Gypsum was crisply replying, "Nothing is like it was for anyone."

"That's my point." Silence again. Then Lee continued. "My kids, they weren't even born. They wouldn't have been if you didn't come back. I don't want them to go through what we did—hell, I don't want to go through it again."

Shadow could sense Gypsum shrugging the way she did to offset what counted as argumentative coming from her. "Not sure it can be stopped. The Dowsers have tapped into something. Pardon the pun."

"They're striking a match to tinder. Pardon the pun."

"You prefer the Judges' methods?"

"They show authority. You know how things stand. We can sort out what comes next after reunity's on solid footing.

Put back some checks and balances. Now the Dowsers, they pretend they're humanitarians, like that one from out in California, McClarrick. He's real slick. But if the rumors I hear are true, him and his pals are angling to take over and then they'll control everything lock, stock, and barrel." He spat out the window. "Pardon the pun."

Another ruined banner billowed beseechingly from the roadside: "Tell Cong—." *That would be an even older one,* Shadow thought. *No to this or Yes to that,* though the rest had long since blown away on the wind. All too little, too late.

"Come back, Joanna," Lee urged Gypsum with the name he knew her by. "Come back and help us Diné survive again."

Shadow heard a motorcyle. "Here comes your authority now," Gypsum said to Lee. "Can you outrun him?"

"Refurb LS battery. Perq of the job. She's old but she boosts better than the newer nanopods." He shouted to Shadow through the window. "Marshal on us. But I've seen those fancy bikes skid out at high speed. Regen wiring can't handle it. Retrograde ejac into the brakes, hah. Hang on!" He slammed the pedal and the truck instantly lurched forward.

In the back, Clementine's feet banged against the gate and she cried out. Shadow cradled her head and felt her hot breath against his cheek. He pinched the tarp tight over them.

The pickup reached an improbable speed for such an old lug of metal. It bowled into a shallow pothole. Shadow heard Lee holler with maniacal delight as they rocketed down a flat run of asphalt.

He also heard the siren as the marshal closed in.

"He knows," Truck whispered to Shadow.

"He just saw some bait." If that was true, Lee might talk or bribe his way out.

"They're looking for us," Truck insisted.

The truck got air bouncing out of a dip in the highway. Lee actually shrieked, "Yee-ha!"

A round pinged off the door frame. Marshals were well funded. This one's bike probably had a self-aiming, voice-commanded rifle. And now the truck was in its range. Shadow looked at Truck, who sighed unhappily but handed over his pistol. Shadow peeled back the tarp and sat up enough to see over the gate and take aim. His first shot decapitated a weed that had only just escaped a trampling by tire.

A heart-stopping crack obliterated their taillight.

An ear-boxing shockwave postscripted the reply from Gypsum's rifle. She had taken out the bike's side cam. Its rider hunched lower. He veered to the flank.

Shadow got off a second shot but one of their tires sucked in the next incoming bullet. The truck slued. Shadow felt the sensation of ice skating. It was amazing what the body remembered even after so many years. The next sensation was a sickening crunch.

Clementine came to and, for the second time that day, heard an unfamiliar voice through a haze. "I know this man," it said. It was male, elderly. "He's a Navajo officer." He was talking about Gypsum's cousin, Lee. So: *friendly, perhaps.*

"Be as may, he's way off the rez." This voice, too, was unfamiliar, also male but younger. Gruff. Not local. *From over the Fence*, Clementine thought vaguely. *Twang, that was the word, right?* He sounded like a marshal.

"Take these people to Dr. Beecham," the first voice said, though to whom Clementine couldn't tell. "Her, especially." *Her? To a doctor...right: me.*

"They were shooting at a federal marshal. And they fit the description of a group that waylaid a convoy in 'zona two days ago. They're coming with me." Yes, this second man definitely was a marshal.

Clementine worked on moving very slowly to get a view without drawing attention. She was in no shape to move fast at any rate.

"A federal marshal concerned for smugglers? Isn't that the Dowsers' job?"

"Concerned with criminals. Which these are."

"They need medical attention." The older man was persistent.

The marshal shouted. "Hey, you! Load them into that wagon and follow me." Presumably, he addressed the same onlookers she hadn't yet spied.

"I'm afraid I can't allow that." The older man muscled authority into his voice now.

"Look, chief—"

"—Judge. Peterson." *The man trying to get them to a doctor was a Judge?*

"Not a Judge judge, am I right?"

"Retired magistrate." *Oh.* This Peterson was merely a local authority.

"Then you'll understand that I have a plenary warrant." Clementine could see the marshal now, albeit upside down over her forehead. He was pointing to his dash. "Let's go!" the marshal commanded. Clementine saw a youth look anxiously from the marshal to a man in a creamy polyester suit and matching wide-brimmed hat. His almost equally wide necktie might have been repurposed from something else but its bright orange ends radiated like the sun from the impeccable

Eldredge knot—her grandfather used to tie his that way. Only his shoes betrayed the slow creep of shabbiness. He must be the first, older man: the magistrate, Peterson.

"Kanab is a closed town," Peterson said. "We have the governor's writ of immunity."

The marshal snorted. "My warrant applies everywhere, grandpa. I'm taking the prisoners and I'm commandeering that vehicle and driver to do it."

"This woman will die."

"Dead or alive, she and the rest are going before a real Judge."

"Or handed to your smuggling friends on the way." It was bold to accuse a marshal of corruption, especially that kind, but the ex-magistrate stared unflinchingly as he said it.

The marshal looked around. Five others stood there, plus the boy, three of them decently armed. He threw up a gloved hand. "Have it your way. 'Til I'm back with company." He swung a leg over the saddle and flipped the kill.

"Now," Peterson commanded his compatriots as soon as the marshal rode off. As delicately as possible, they retrieved Clementine. From her new vantage point in the wagon, she saw them help Shadow and Truck, too. They seemed okay. Like her they had landed in the soft shoulder of the roadway.

The truck had done a complete flip and landed upright—and not on top of anyone. Clementine saw Lee's face smushed into the deflated airbag like a half-popped kernel. *Dead.* His left eye winked open. *No, playing possum.* "So he's gone?"

"For now," Peterson said drily. His tone was more informal now.

"Thanks. For the record, I wasn't planning on ramming into your roadblock." Lee seemed to know Peterson.

"Or bringing a marshal on my town?"

"'Off the rez.' Jackass."

Peterson scratched his cheek with a knuckle. "You are, though. Technically."

"You know what he really meant. But sure, let's compare track records on *technical* treaty compliance." Lee grinned but his voice had an edge.

Peterson seemed to concede the point. But he pursed his lips. "Still, seemed to think you shot purposeful at him—a marshal an' all."

"How should I to know? As you said yourself, I am an officer myself. I don't feel obliged to surrender to every bandit costumed as a lawman." Lee got out of the pickup daintily.

Clementine saw Gypsum pop up on its other side. She stumbled woozily. Peterson moved lithely for his age to lend her his arm. He touched his hat but tucked a warning note into his effortless politesse. "I didn't know you kept company with raiders."

"She's my cousin. Just helping her out of a jam." Lee rubbed his bruised jaw and winced.

"Well. If you two can get in that wagon, we can head over to the doctor's. Sooner you're patched up, sooner you're on your way."

"No room at the inn, then?"

"The church gives us cover, but I don't care to test that shield against the full tactical might of the U.S. government."

Lee and Gypsum joined Clementine and the others in the wagon. The electric mule whirred to life and trundled toward the town center.

≋

Shadow sat with Truck in the wing of the hospital that was still in use. They nursed cuts and contusions with used bandages and thin strips of iodine paste from the cabinets. Gypsum, a black eye budding, stood looking around the room. "It's brighter than outdoors. Or crisper, at least," she mused aloud.

"Uh huh," Shadow was working quickly on his own injuries so he could be with Clementine.

"They knocked out a wall and set these up to trap the light coming in," Gypsum continued with fascination. Shadow looked up. An intricate set of mirrors chased the light out of corners where it might fade. Gypsum was enthralled. "Those convexes focus it on the table like a spotlight would." Shadow followed her gaze. The "table" was a bare gurney. Clementine lay on it, out cold and strapped down at the thigh and ankle. The binds framed her gruesome leg wound.

"It's a very old trick." Dr. Beecham looked up and smiled at Gypsum. Shadow thought he looked cross-eyed. But it was only on account of the simscim hooked around his ear to sync him optically with his tools. The doctor bent back over Clementine and picked at a flap of flesh with a surgical retractor. "Attributed to Edison, ironically enough. Hepha: hemostat...pin." His eyes guided the robotic arm holographically. It placed the clamp. "Quite the excitement you've brought us today, Terrence."

The old magistrate, Peterson, nodded carefully. "Feds chased them to our doorstep."

"Whoever took first shot at this did a pretty good job but there are fragments still inside. Hepha: zoom. Smugglers, then?"

"No," Lee answered as he daubed iodine on Gypsum's nose.

Shadow came over to watch the doctor. He changed the subject. "Your robot's name is Heifer?"

"Hepha. Short for Hephaestus, god of mechanical ingenuity. Hepha: forceps."

"Doctor: specify."

"Number four fine." The machine selected tweezers from a round magazine that rotated around one of its arms. It followed the surgeon's optical directions and automatically identified the shrapnel as foreign to the surrounding tissue. "Gotcha! Hepha: lavage. Then why was a marshal in pursuit?"

Beecham's casual tone was getting under Shadow's skin. He should concentrate on saving Clementine, not accusing them. "Marshals help the smugglers half the time," he said.

"Hm. This is not good. Hepha: biopsy...pull. Microbe sample. Why would the Judges' enforcers befriend water thieves?"

"What's not good!?" Shadow's frustration boiled over. "Pay attention to *her*!" He flung his hand toward Clementine's prostrate body. His elbow jostled the doctor. The man's gaze wavered and the robot veered infinitesimally off course.

"Unh. Hepha: hematic suction. You'd better step back, you made Hepha sever a vessel. Fortunately a small one."

Chastened, Shadow did as he was told. Clementine awoke, screaming. Beecham swore in his imperturbable way. Shadow rushed to cradle her head. "It's okay, it's okay." Clementine screamed and screamed.

Truck shouted, too. "Put her back under! Put her back under for God's sake!"

"I'd only sedated her to begin with. She was unconscious when she got here."

"Do it!" Shadow growled like a wolf sure of his threat.

"Hepha: midazolam." As the assistant calculated the dosage and punctured Clementine's skin to deliver the medication, the doctor added unhopefully, "And fentanyl. If you have any." To Shadow, he said, "I'm afraid sedation may be the best I can do. I have to ration painkillers around here."

"You give her whatever she needs."

Peterson intervened. "You are unexpected guests and this is Dr. Beecham's surgery. Why don't you let him do what he can to save your friend?"

"Here, give her this," offered the doctor conciliatorily. "Old school." He handed Shadow a strip of strap like the ones that bound Clementine and mimed biting down.

Shadow slipped it in between Clementine's teeth. "Bite." Between it and the drug kicking in, her screams turned to whimpers. He wiped the sweat from her forehead with a caressing thumb. She turned her head away to face the wall.

"To keep the Dowsers on their toes." Lee spoke into the relative silence that ensued.

"Who does?" Peterson asked.

"To answer the doctor's question. Why the Judges and marshals help the smugglers."

"Hm," Beecham demurred. "I assume you all weren't coming up the Honeymoon Trail to wed in temple."

"Who said we came up that way at all?" Shadow countered.

"No one," Beecham kept his bantering tone. "You have the look of wandering mystics is all. Transcendents, perhaps?"

Shadow stared at the pallid skin of Clementine's temple as it crinkled with each wince. Her eyebrows twitched as she rode the pain that surged and receded, surged and receded under the twilit enchantment of pharmacological dissociation. She shot a man and was shot in turn. But it was still

Shadow's fault she was there in the first place, mixed up with the Transcendents and their politics. She was a true wanderer and had begged him to wander again with her. Instead, this...

The doctor wouldn't shut up. "Well, us Saints were once wanderers, too, and no better loved." Beecham straightened his shoulders and picked bits of bone and flesh absentmindedly from his gloves. He cast his eyes across the assembled group. "So here's the situation. I got all but a couple of the shot fragments, and I don't think the rest will be a problem."

"That's good news." Gypsum reached a hand up to Shadow's shoulder.

"There's bad, too. She has a bug and it's not responsive to the antibiotics Hepha carries."

"How did that happen?"

"You're kidding. She's basically been rolling in dirt for what—two, three days?—and who knows what filth was on the original dressing—"

"Hey—" Truck interjected.

"I'm just saying it's not a surprise. Plus—" the doctor rolled a bit of shrapnel between his fingers "—some less savory characters lace their shot. Bounty hunter, if I had to guess."

Shadow felt Gypsum squeeze his shoulder. He took Clementine's clammy hand. "What are you getting at?"

"I have to take the leg from above the knee."

One of the mirrors overhead creaked in its casement. They seemed to stretch thirstily for the waning daylight. Darkness crept back from the corners to reclaim the room. No one breathed.

"NO!" Shadow thundered into the silence. "No No No no no no...."

"Where can we take her that will have the right meds?"

Gypsum didn't loosen her grip on Shadow as she fixed her sea-foam eyes on Beecham.

"You can't move this woman anymore. You've already done enough damage. Look at her leg, it's in shreds. Any more trauma and the rest of her will be no better off."

Shadow twisted and lunged across Clementine's body at the doctor, animal sounds coming from his throat. Gypsum bearhugged him, more concerned for her friend on the table than for the doctor, while Truck and Lee leapt to their feet to lock him back.

Truck spoke near Shadow's ear. "Shouldn't it be her choice?"

Clementine heard Truck's question as if from far away. She lay still, staring up at the indentations in the drop ceiling tiles as if they were stars of constellations.

"Miss?" It was the old man from the roadside. The first voice she had heard. She rolled her eyes down her side to find his. He had saved her life...for this. She betrayed nothing.

"You can regen, though, right?" asked Truck.

The surgeon shook his head and patted Hepha like a reliable horse. "Hepha doesn't have the capacity for epidermal blastema stimulation."

Truck looked worriedly down at Clementine. "Which means..."

"We can graft pixie dust."

"Great," Lee rolled his eyes.

"No, it's real. Basically pig bladder that might inspire her own tissue to regrow. A crude second-best to straight-up regen. They used to do it pretty often before the war."

"You raise pigs?" Lee asked skeptically.

"It's an expensive luxury, but comes in handy for a doctor,

so they indulge me. It's risky, though. I can't oversuppress her immune system with this infection present." He turned his attention to Clementine. "You understand?"

She nodded once. Then a second time, firmer. Beecham nodded back sympathetically, then uttered rapid fire instructions to Hepha. One of the robot's arms marked a line of ink into unbroken flesh above the wound. Another fit a hollow spherical scalpel around the thigh and pressed through the skin and muscle. A third revved a circular blade and sawed nauseatingly through the femur. Easy as pie, the bottom of Clementine's leg came clean off. It lay there on the gurney while Hepha screwed a titanium socket into the stump ("in case she needs a prosthesis later," Beecham explained) and implanted the misnamed pixie dust ("bacon strips," Clementine thought acridly). Sutures and a breathable cap completed the alarmingly efficient operation. Dr. Beecham scooped up the personless knee, shin, and foot for disposal.

All the while, angry tears streamed down Clementine's face as she clamped on her bit under insufficient anesthesia. She suffered each lash of pain as punishment for her sins of sentimental attachment. She had made herself unfree. *Martine, Martine*, she begged her absent sister voicelessly, *padoném, padoném*. Beside her, Shadow sobbed. His eyes also pleaded: *forgive me, forgive me*. But Clementine's gave him no quarter, reflecting only the vast universe she tried to will down from the ceiling to swallow her into its pitiless, painless eternity.

CHAPTER 11
CASSIE

*E*XECUTION. CASSIE WAS sure of it. All the ways she could imagine being put to death ran through her mind as she squirmed in David's unrelenting grip. After that one sentence—*what did you do*—he had said nothing else. He only grabbed her by the scruff and pushed her roughly toward Harv's camper. Cassie was equally sure David doubled as the executioner.

He shoved her to the ground in front of Harv. The other leaders were gathered, too.

"David," Dahlia scolded him. Cake had intimated that Dahlia was a pain but she had been kind to Cassie. Maybe that would come in handy here. Cassie let her lip tremble.

David held up the filter components. "She was stealing this. To go after our water."

"I wasn't—"

"She was in the garden piss pot." David seemed to have found fluency all of a sudden.

"Is this true?" Harv asked evenly.

"You were gonna, maybe, send me into that—" Cassie

gestured to the desert "—with enough water to make me a vulture snack." She hadn't been sure what tack to take but defiance won out. "So I figured you owe me the chance to survive." She'd go down swinging.

"A water thief. Told ya," said a mean-looking bear of a man.

"Griz is right." That was Lake, Cassie remembered. The cook. "Let's cut her loose." Cassie wasn't sure she heard right. Not "let's burn her alive" or "let's hang her 'til she's dead?"

"With the three days' worth," said another man. He was clean-shaven, smaller than Griz, shorter than David, but a little thicker, with black hair and something familiar about him.

"No, Meskit, with nothing, like the criminal she is," Griz retorted. Meskit—that was the twins' father. That's why he seemed familiar; they looked a little like him.

"She's a child," countered Dahlia. "We're not going to do that to a child." Cassie wanted to shout to stop calling her a child. But she was short on friends at the moment.

Everyone started squabbling all at once. Cassie tried to keep track. They weren't going to kill her and some opposed sending her away empty-handed. What, then?

Eventually, Harv raised a hand to quiet them. "We leave her in the next town. She can make her way from there." A few nodded assent to the compromise.

Not Meskit. "Castle's been listening. He can't tell exactly what the Dowsers know about her but they have something to go on because they're looking. We drop her off in a town, she starts asking strangers for help, one of them is a Dowser agent or happy to tip one off, and she's good as dead anyway."

"And so are we," Dahlia drove home.

For the first time, Harv displayed irritation. "What do you want me to do, then?"

"Let her test," offered someone with dark freckles who hadn't spoken yet. "The secret-keeper cleared her—"

"He was wrong, obviously," muttered Lake.

"He looks at insides, not actions," Freckles went on. "She has a skill and wasn't afraid to use it. She didn't take any food or water yet, only some plumbing. If she tests, she joins, and it won't have been stealing."

Griz wasn't having it. "That's the cockamamiest logic I've ever—"

"Tesla's right," Dahlia jumped in. Cassie renamed Freckles accordingly: the secret-keeper had mentioned this Tesla as well, who had helped rig the biolume. "She's a child—" Dahlia used that word again "—she panicked. Which of you hasn't? Who wouldn't, in her shoes? If Tesla thinks she could be useful..." Dahlia raised an eyebrow suggestively. Cassie had no idea what it suggested. But Meskit nodded vigorously. Harv seemed to consider it. Even Lake wagged her head wishy-washily. Only Griz and David seemed implacable.

"Do you wish to?" Harv finally asked. "Test?"

Cassie was startled to be included in the conversation. "What, like answer questions? I already did that."

"No. Our methods are practical. We would select one suitable for you. Something you must do."

Cassie looked from one to another. These people were exceedingly strange. But they governed themselves by some code. And they were clearly far more lenient than the Dowsers. Speaking of whom, the other options on offer didn't sound great. If she "tested" and joined these Transcendents, maybe she could persuade the softer ones to help her get home. "Okay."

♒

Cassie hardly felt self-assured as David escorted her to a long, low building at the perimeter of the complex. She had presumed it to be some kind of factory or fortification. She was about to find out.

After she had said she wanted to test, Harv conferred briefly with the others. Then they formed a semi-circle around him and stared at her forebodingly while he spoke in an even more lordly tone. "A seeker is never empty-handed in her quest because she knows how to call on the elements at all times. Enter that building. Bring us earth, wind, water, and fire. You have an hour." He cut off her incipient query. "No more questions from you."

David left her wordlessly at the smashed-in, multi-doored entrance to the ruin. The frame still held amid a heap of chipped, pinkish concrete and glittering ground shards. She crossed its tarnished threshold and looked back. David squatted a few paces away. He rocked his head sunward to indicate the ticking clock. He wanted her to fail. She faced forward and adjusted to the light lancing through the chalky air inside.

Debris defined the interior as well. The place was more wrecked than the water thief hangout. It was also cavernous. She decided to strategize while walking the lay of the land. The size seemed to confirm her initial suspicion, except for the copious glass slivers that suggested interior windows. It was segmented into spaces, some small and some huge enough to house large equipment. An open area appeared to have been a cafeteria.

She thought about Harv's riddle. Where to start? Earth was most obvious. She headed to one of the larger accumulations of rubble. There wasn't any dirt, really; it was all crumbled concrete and metal, while his request seemed elementally literal. She sensed the seconds tick by.

Fire and wind couldn't be literal requests, could they? Maybe they had hidden objects that represented those elements, like a satchel of earth or a flint rock. She dug with her hands and a fragment of metal for a few minutes. All she turned up was a cheap plastic bracelet and a scorpion that stung her hand and raised a welt. She threw away the first and leaped back with a yelp on account of the second.

Nursing her wound, she looked around the enormous space and began to realize what it was. A mall. She knew a mall in the city, only it was outdoors and far smaller. This one had been ransacked of whatever it once held, including much of its infrastructure. A few knocked-over racks or bits of wood shelving lay here and there, as well as some fixtures stripped of their most useful or salable components. It didn't even look like decayed glamour; it bore no trace of glamour to speak of.

The interior colonnade was sheltered from the sun but Cassie still sweated in the stifling, dusty air. Despite the building's vaulting height, the familiar claustrophobic feeling of a tunnel job prickled her skin. For the millionth time in a week, she fought it off with May's breathing lesson and pondered. There was no way they could bury four objects in this monument and expect her to find them in sixty minutes. Harv might be cryptic but he didn't seem blatantly dishonest.

Then again, he probably didn't care either way. They were toying with her, an amusement to while away a few hours in their boring, crappy, criminal lives. She stamped and swore, softly at first then yelling to see if her voice would echo. It didn't.

The stomping around did make her have to pee, finally. Decorum led her to the bathroom off a hallway behind the cafeteria. It was in no shape to use normally. She picked what she hoped was a snake-free zone. She added the incommodity to her list of present complaints. Would urine count as water? She imagined them making her drink whatever liquid she came up with. If only she still had that filter.

How long had she been in the mall? Too long. Forget this test. There must be some other way. She stood back up and, as she stepped clear of her mark on the ground, a thought struck her. The cafeteria. There was a way she might find water, after all, and maybe that would be the only element she truly needed. She had to hurry.

The mall seemed of the right vintage so that the food vendors might still have had functioning sinks while it was operational. The first one she checked had a clear drain so she didn't waste any time looking underneath. The second was more promising. Inorganic culinary flotsam covered the drain. Cassie swiftly opened the cabinet beneath. But a scavenger had already pried apart the u-shaped p-trap plumbing.

She scooted to a third stall. On the way, she spied a stray square of thin, translucent plastic sticking out of a cupboard like a surrendering handkerchief. It was about a square foot. If she did find any water, she would need to carry the proof back to the Transcendents. She snagged the plastic and tucked it at her waist.

The sink in the third mini-restaurant was clear of objects but a thick coating of sticky cooking grease was a hopeful sign. With luck, it had clogged the drain and prevented the horseshoe of water that sat in the trap from evaporating all this time. She exhaled and opened the cupboard. The plumbing was intact. Quickly, Cassie flipped onto her back and worked the screw nuts that connected the trap segment to the tailpiece above and to the wall tubing off to the side.

She popped out the trap, sat upright, and carefully tipped it over her hand with bated breath. Nothing. Empty. Dry as an ancient bone. Maybe the water had evaporated through an open vent pipe behind the wall. She should have known better. Water didn't last. It certainly didn't wait for you indefinitely.

A paralyzing blend of rage and panic combusted in her chest. Cassie fought it off. Whatever awaited her if she failed this cruel test was secondary now. Her professional pride was at stake. She closed her eyes and thought like a water thief.

Her mind clicked over. The sinks were both too obvious and too unlikely. There was somewhere else, though. All of these eating establishments gathered in one place had to feed a central biogas processor. Cassie sprang to her feet. There was still time.

Some of it was spent trying to locate the unit. The building was much older than its retrofitted technology. It wasn't immediately apparent where a central system might be other than below ground level. Although the floor was cracked in many places, there were no holes clear to the basement for her to jump down.

Then she remembered the small hallway that led to the bathrooms. They, too, would feed the processor so maybe the way down was between the human intake and output areas, so to speak. Cassie ran to it as fast as she could through the obstacle course of wreckage. Sure enough, the corridor contained a utility door. It took several hard yanks to open it but the reward was a janitor's closet and a vertical staircase inside that plunged to the lower level. Cassie grabbed the only tool left, a splintery hammer, and shimmied down the ladder.

Her excitement warded off the legion of fears that tentacled out of the total darkness. She used her hands and years of experience to follow a tangle of sewer pipes along the wall until they converged on a tank. That must be the digester. She felt her way around it until she found the outlet pipes that carried off usable gas and by-products. The latter was her target. In the right kind of system, it would have...

...that. A large canister hung off the pipe like a beehive from a tree branch. Cassie's heart skipped a beat. It was a condensation reservoir to collect water and separate it from the gas, much like an alcohol still. Normally, when the liquid accumulated past a certain point, a floater would strike a lever would trigger a valve would drain the water. But never fully. At some point, this device had discharged its last gulp and some was left behind with nowhere to go. It might still be there.

There was only one way to test her hope. She drew back the hammer and smashed it against the joint where the canister attached to the pipe. It clanged and nearly broke her wrist. She adjusted her grip and swung again. And again.

Finally, the tubing on one side gave way. The canister dangled and tipped—and its bottom edge hit the ground. It was too big. She had to dislodge the other side and tip the whole thing over. How many minutes were left? Would they look for her if she didn't emerge? Would they find her down here? Could she find her way back out? Cassie beat each question back with a hammer blow.

At last, the reservoir thudded to the ground, almost smashing her foot. This was the moment of truth. There was little room to maneuver in the passageway but she managed to plant her legs, hug the cylinder, and tip it over. She scrambled to the spout she had created by breaking the connection to the pipe, pulled out the plastic wrap, and held its corners to make a little basket.

She waited. Nothing. She nudged the overturned canister to roll it an inch or two, then resumed her position with the plastic at the makeshift spigot. She waited.

She couldn't see them, but she felt the drops of water trickle onto the plastic, depressing it with a glorious weight. There was more than she expected—a fistful, maybe, before the drip subsided. With exceeding care, Cassie lifted the corners of the plastic and tied them to make a pouch like a vagrant's bindle. Before she pulled it tight, she dipped a finger and cautiously tasted her prize. Maybe not pure, but it was water. She finished the knot and twisted the plastic to create a sealed sphere. If nothing else, she knew probably none of the people about to judge her could have accomplished what she just did.

Outside once again, she didn't see David waiting silently like a camouflaged predator until she almost bumped into him. His eyes flicked over her impersonally. If he registered what she carried, he didn't show it. "Time," he said gruffly.

"After you." She matched his tone and followed him back to the reconvened circle.

"Time's elapsed." Harv stated the obvious. "We asked for the four basic elements. What have you brought?"

Cassie held up the orb of clear liquid. "Water." She thought her voice sounded commanding. She certainly felt triumphant.

The acclaim she expected didn't quite materialize. Meskit muttered "brava" and one or two others nodded. Cassie thought she saw the corner of Dahlia's mouth twitch. But all held expressions of anticipation. One element was not enough.

"And?" asked Harv.

A long silence passed. Griz snorted. Dahlia drew a corner of her wrap over her head to fend off the beating sun.

Something pricked Cassie's other hand. She realized that she still gripped the wooden hammer. It had slid and a splinter stuck in her skin. Inspiration flashed. She broke off an unsweaty strip of the chipped handle and aligned it with the sphere of water and the sun like an eclipse. *This could be embarrassing.* She—and her inquisitors—waited.

At last, a ray glinted, magnified through the slapdash lens. A wisp of genie smoke rose from the wood to grant her wish. Cassie kept her hands steady. A black spot appeared on the wood, then a red ember.

"Fire." She spoke it as a challenge to her onlookers.

Meskit actually applauded this time. Someone else chuckled. Cassie saw Harv look at Dahlia. Dahlia shrugged but Cassie felt the older woman's keen eyes bore into her.

"Two. And the rest?" Harv's tone instantly deflated Cassie's renewed pride. Dahlia was watching as if she was trying to telepath the answer to her. But Cassie couldn't read minds. She threw the stick to the ground with a groan and shoved her hand in her pocket sullenly.

The leaders audibly lost patience.

"Well, then," Harv began.

Dahlia finally intervened. "You said a seeker always has the elements at hand. She yet may."

Cassie looked at her defender. She was being given a clue. She looked down.

"Not sand," Griz said. He followed her gaze to the burnt wood. "Too late," he warned with an admonishing look at Dahlia.

Cassie already despised this man. She had indeed thought belatedly that fire burns only in air and ashes return to earth. What now? The fingers in her pocket curled angrily. One caught on the ring she had hidden there. *At hand.*

"I have earth." Cassie slipped the ring on a finger and curled all five into a fist. She stretched it defiantly up to tall Harv's face. The sliver of red jewel glinted. Cassie willed it to dazzle them. She saw Dahlia mask a covetous twitch as an adjustment of her shawl.

"Glass?" Lake scoffed.

Harv quickly grasped Cassie's fist like a mantis and pulled her onto her tiptoes. Her heart jumped. He lowered his eye within a hair's breadth of the ring. "Or gem."

Cassie put steel into her voice. "Ruby. Pure earth."

Harv seemed convinced. He released her and she stumbled back. "Hm. Anything else?" Cassie detected less condescension in his voice.

Air was all around her but she couldn't think of a way to capture it. Still, she was winning and not about to surrender. The scorpion bite on her hand oozed a little. She scowled at it, then laughed spontaneously. One of May's lessons had been that, if caught in an ambiguous situation during a job—neither certainly culpable nor plausibly innocent—the best play was to make your captors think you were doing them a favor.

Cassie raised the satchel of water as high as she could. "The wind is these words: I *am* a water thief and you *will* need me. Everyone does someday."

The real wind made the only sound for a moment. Then Meskit burst into friendly laughter. Griz muttered discontentedly. The semi-circle broke into huddled groups.

Cassie stood confused by the sudden informality. Before she could ask what was happening, Lake seized her wrist.

"What happened?"

"A scorpion bit me in there."

Lake frowned. "Why didn't you bring it back for me?"

"Leave her be, Lake," Dahlia intervened. She put a protective arm around Cassie's shoulder. "It's a good sign if she's already putting you to kitchen work."

"I don't understand."

"They all need time to consider whether or not you passed."

"How long?"

"Oh, only a minute more, I think."

"Then what?"

"Then we vote." Dahlia registered Cassie's unease. "Your answer to the test was..." Dahlia searched for the right word, "unanticipated. Not everyone will find it as charming as Meskit. Plus, you confirmed a rather unsavory thing about your past outside the secret-keeper's confidence. The smugglers and water merchants are mostly considered enemies here, at least by tradition." She patted Cassie's arm like an auntie might. "We'd vote on your admission anyway. This just makes it a close call."

Had she miscalculated? "What do I do now?"

"You stay standing right there. You'll see."

Sure enough, the side conversations diminished and the circle reformed, this time with Cassie in the center. The Transcendents held hands and closed their eyes. A low chant rose among them. Cassie couldn't guess at its words or if they were words at all. The chant divided into parts along the scale and grew fuller. Then, in gradual, uneven intervals, each person spoke a vote. Griz said no without malice in his voice. Meskit said yes without a trace of humor. Lake was a no. Tesla's quiet yes must have meant she seemed sufficiently useful. Utterly lacking in surprise was David's emotionless no.

After the longest pause yet, Dahlia spoke. The delay injured Cassie to an absurd degree given that she had known Dahlia for less than half a day. But Dahlia said yes.

Harv's rumbling voice came last. "No."

The music stopped abruptly. Meskit spat, cuffing and hauling Tesla away in heated conversation. The rest of the circle broke up.

Cassie looked from Harv to Dahlia, the only two left with her. "What now?" she asked.

Dahlia gave her a pained look. By way of response, her squint drifted uneasily to the broken road that snaked eastward until it was a pip on the desert horizon.

CHAPTER 12

INMA

AT FIRST, INMA had been angry that Cassie pulled the same disrespectful crap two nights in a row. Then, she was annoyed that Cassie did it even after all the presents she gave her. Then mad at herself for treating Cassie too much like a grownup and sad again because Cassie was grown up. Anger and hurt jumbled together in a sixteen-year trip down memory lane and then some.

Stewing in the empty apartment all night left her exhausted when dawn bore no sign of Cassie's return. Inma pinged in sick (they'd dock her rations for it), slipped on her shoes, and donned her mask to fend off ash from the mountain wildfires blowing in on an early northeaster.

The court clerk was expecting the new apprentice that morning but seemed indifferent. Inma didn't anticipate finding Cassie at her old school, and didn't. She made her way to Cassie's best friend's house. A groggy Mariah suggested a couple of other places, which proved equally fruitless. It occurred to Inma that she really had no idea where Cassie spent her time. Desperate, she went back to Mariah. Inma's haggardness must have alarmed the girl because she finally gave up that the Bergson boy was at a medical clinic called Madre de Dios and Cassie might be there sitting vigil.

Inside, an orderly pointed her in the right direction. Inma made her way through the dismal ward. As she passed, a shriveled patient convulsed in a last-ditch effort to fend off the fever ignited from within. He would die in this place, sunken-eyed, tear ducts too dry to cry, heart and lungs fluttering for life, unrevivable by the sporadic ladle of water a nurse brought around. Such was the world now. And there was the boy.

"Theodore. Look at you." She kept her voice low given the lack of privacy but managed to convey scolding concern.

"Hi, Ms. Ruiz." He sounded like a sheepish little boy caught in a mischievous act.

Inma shimmied her hips into as much of a perch next to him as the narrow cot allowed. She peered at his face in the dim light. "I'm not sure I would have recognized you." She brushed a sweaty lock from his eyes. They stared at each other in silence for a few moments. "So you and Cassie stayed friends all these years?"

"Yeah. Kind of. I guess."

"Mariah thought she might be here. Visiting you. Has she been?"

"I...I don't know. Not since I've been awake."

Inma sighed and contemplated the spots that had started to discolor her hands these past few months. "What is all this about? What happened to you?"

He turned his head away.

"Does it have something to do with the...sculpture...I found in her room?"

He swiveled back to face her, though she left nothing to read in hers. "That was a birthday present."

"An odd gift, don't you think?"

"It's art."

"From a teenage boy to a teenage girl?"

Teddy shrugged. Inma pressed. "It must have cost quite a bit." She looked around the poor accommodations to emphasize the point.

His face reddened of its own accord. "She's worth it."

One evasion, one lie, and one truth so far. She changed tactics. "Where are your parents, Theodore?"

He sat up with alarm before the pain knocked him back again. "Don't—you can't."

"They don't know what's happened to you?" She repeated her unanswered question from before. "What did happen to you?"

"It's complicated."

"Which part?"

"Both."

"Teddy," she switched to endearment. "Can I help you?"

Her kindness cracked him. Whether from pain or fear or both, he spoke low and fast. "I couldn't just tell her what I was doing but I thought maybe she'd figure it out or guess or ask and think it was kind of cool and—I just wanted to stop doing the same thing over and over and nothing ever changes. And now—not just me but everyone who's doing it—they'll have to pay attention, and people will get it, it doesn't have to be like this." He paused for breath and sobbed, "Oh, God, I didn't know she would be up there, I never would have done it, I never would have hurt anyone. He didn't give me a chance to explain, he just came at me—" he gestured in bewilderment at his abdomen "—and it's all screwed up and—" he stopped abruptly. He opened his mouth again, then closed it and said only, "It isn't fair."

"Where!? Cassie? Hurt up where?"

"No, no." He looked like he was trying to straighten out his thoughts. "I wouldn't mix Cassie up in that part. But thieving's not enough." A fierce look broke through his daze. She knew it well: the bravery of the doomed. "We make a statement. Get people to rise against the Dowsers."

"'We'..." Inma trailed off. His disjointed screed began adding up in her mind. *Thieving.* Everyone knew that drink acquired in the black market, which even she did sometimes, was first pinched by nimble fingers in dark spaces. *Up there, a statement*—the water tower sabotage the Dowser candidate McClarrick spoke of in his stump speech. *Rise against.* This wounded boy who had played with Cassie as kids was a rebel. She felt a frisson of admiration. And something else. Envy. She suppressed it. What he did was reckless, wasteful, and indiscriminate, things that ran against everything she'd tried to build for herself and Cassie.

Cassie. That part. Thieving. The bombshell exploded. Cassie was a water thief. They were always young, which meant she had been one for quite some time. Shame assailed Inma. How could she not have known? Fear followed, of what might have happened all these years and yesterday to her daughter. Yes, her daughter, however much Inma had forbidden herself to claim motherhood. Out of love for the lost, she had insisted that Cassie keep the Killian name, though it was too dangerous to tell her everything it once meant to Inma— to many people. Or maybe the danger was in Inma's head, a hobbling habit that, it now seemed, had not prevented the wheel of history from turning after all.

She found herself standing, zombified. She turned to go. Teddy grabbed her hand. "The gift...." Inma looked at their clasped hands. Had the spots on hers multiplied since five minutes ago? His was bigger and she couldn't figure out why, when he was just a boy playing cops and robbers. "I don't know where Cassie is." His voice cracked when he said her name.

"Does she feel the same about you?" Was that pertinent? It had popped out.

Even his freckles blushed. "Maybe the gift—it was my idea, but Willie designed it."

"Willie?"

"Mariah's brother." Inma took that in. That cagey girl had withheld a lot of useful dots. Inma gave Teddy a last curious once-over, patted his hand comfortingly, and let her feet guide her back through the moaning maze. The collective misery clawed at her throat.

෴

The warehouse was close to downtown, an area that had actually grown as the city shrank back to its original center and its western reaches succumbed to flooding and depopulation. The building was old—more than a century old, Inma reckoned. Its brick was battered and corroding metal sheets covered the glassless holes of half the windows. The faded letters painted up top were a palimpsest of so many names over the years that they might as well have been Cyrillic.

The manufactory was well guarded. That didn't matter too much. If Inma had cultivated any skill in the most recent phase of her life, it was how to appear unthreatening and forgettable. She smiled disarmingly at the young man at the door and allowed him to slide open the heavy door for her.

Inside, the factory floor was dominated by two things. One was a bunch of computer-guided machine tools. The other was a jumble of salvage, which explained how a factory managed to operate in this part of the country. Nothing too energy-intensive or value-added. Mostly basic repair or recycling work. A state-sponsored chop shop.

Inma was only half-faking consternation when the foreman approached her. A few beseeching words got him to point out Guillermo so his "aunt" could share urgent family news. Guillermo was the boy—man—Teddy had called Willie. Cassie had even mentioned Guillermo's job here when she and Inma first discussed apprenticeships a year ago. She probably could have identified him from the same slightly round, healthy-looking face and body as Mariah. He was standing at an electro-lathe near the back corner. One hand was gesturing in the air like he was casting a complicated spell, while a 3D projection of a broken appliance responded to each move. The other held a piece of scrap and every once in a while he raised it to compare against the holographic model and tweak something. She approached as if she knew him well.

"Pretend I'm saying something tragic. Or wonderful. You pick," she told him. His surprised glance fit her cover story well enough.

"Who are you?" Guillermo said it with a smile. He was blessedly quick on the uptake.

"Inma Ruiz. Cassie Killian's guardian. And your aunt, for the moment."

"Oh, Cassie, yeah. Uh, okay, tía, what can I do for you?"

"What did you get her mixed up in?"

"Cassie? Nothing. Why, what's up?"

"I'm not playing a game, Guillermo—"

"'Memo,'" he laughed, and not just to keep up appearances for the boss. "That's what my aunties call me."

"No discuta conmigo," Inma hissed. "You gave her something."

He shook his head soberly. "I haven't seen your girl in a long time."

"You gave Theodore something to give to her."

"Aw, he came in here desperate for something unique. Special. I just spun it out on the CNC here." He said it like "cinci" as he patted the control panel of the machine.

"Why that…image?" The sculpted fist grasping water was burned in her brain.

"It's just a design. Because…" he trailed off.

"I know what she- what she did after school," Inma choked on speaking aloud of Cassie's criminal secret life. "You don't have to protect her from me. But that's not what that design means. I'm a lot older than you. I know what it stands for."

The worker at the next machine moved closer, maybe adjusting something, maybe listening. Guillermo measured Inma for a second. "Give me a hug." Inma complied. As they embraced, Guillermo whispered, "Everything's changing. Everyone's got a part. Cassie's something special. I figured it was a good way to break the ice, so to speak, so she'd be ready to talk about her part when the time came. Symbols are good for that."

Inma broke away. She would have smacked him if it wouldn't look weird. "What this one's good for is getting people killed."

The boss looked over at them. She'd stayed too long for a simple delivery of news. "I'm wasting my time here."

"You'll have to pick a side soon, Señora Ruiz. Are you going to choose the Dowsers?" His whisper sounded like a threat.

"The Judges are in charge." She whispered without conviction, "They offer reunity."

"They're worse."

"You have no idea what worse is." She straightened to her full height. "You're telling me Cassie didn't—yet—get wrapped up in this business. If you have nothing else to say that can help me find her, we're done."

Guillermo moved his body between the machine and any prying eyes. "Mire, tía Inma." She thought it was an apology but he was gesturing imperceptibly with his head at the electro-lathe. The design he'd been working on was gone. The projection was now a pale green polygon of twelve pentagonal sides and twenty vertices where the edges came together, like a stunted version of the soccer balls of her youth. It rotated slowly.

While she watched with dread, his fingers wriggled over the controls. A second shape grew inside the first. Light blue, this one was like Cassie's trophy: twenty triangular sides and twelve corners. It grew until its points pierced the other's planes and vice versa. Twelve and twenty, twenty and twelve— they were reciprocals. Geometric duals. Partners. Interlocked and spinning faster and faster, they gave the impression of the business end of a medieval flail. Inma grew dizzy. She choked on her words again and managed only, "Stop."

Guillermo let the pattern explode in a starburst and dissolve away. He patted her hand as if to comfort her. Maybe he meant to. "I thought so," is all he said, quietly.

Inma pulled her hand away and rushed as fast as she could out of the factory, tossing the boss a look of thankful apology that she hoped fully explained whatever complicated family business she'd been pretending to conduct.

She didn't dare breathe until she rounded the corner of the building. What the boy—man—had done, it was more than a symbol. It was a signal. The second shape was an icosahedron, the geometric representation of water according to Plato. The shape of a precious, perfect droplet. The first was a dodecahedron, the shape, the philosopher had believed, of the universe itself. United, they were a call to solidarity to reclaim the life force of a dying land. That's what it meant more than fifteen years ago. And given the brazen pyrotechnic display she had just witnessed, she had no doubt that it could mean only the same thing now: revolution.

Once she caught her breath, she spent the rest of the day looking wherever else she could think of, although without real hope. Someone was putting the girl in danger, Inma was sure of it. But filing a missing person report with the Dowsers or marshals was out of the question now.

She hated herself for it, but she almost felt excited. Ever since she had heard McClarrick's campaign speech, she'd been feeling antsy. When Teddy told her Cassie was a water thief, besides shame and fear she had felt unexpected pride. Her otherwise infuriating chat with Guillermo had not helped. Now that her eyes were open, she began to see the hand grasping a stream of water graffitied over and over on walls and sidewalks. It spoke to a part of her she had long ago buried under middle-class (ish), middle-aged (ish) respectability.

It was also terrifying. Everything seemed to be happening again. Which meant whoever was behind it this time hadn't learned a thing.

CHAPTER 13
CASSIE

THE ONLY THING more humiliating than failing the test was being forced to hang around for so long afterwards. Harv's original compromise was settled on: the Transcendents would leave Cassie at the next town on their route. That meant the rest of the camping day and traveling night to feel like that tube star who'd told a talk show host how she threw up on her date five minutes into a two-hour sub-orb. Awkward.

The nomadic community made no exceptions for transients among them, which was a relief because it gave Cassie something to do in the meantime. When she displayed some familiarity with a few of the tools, she was put to work for the day as assistant mechanic to a raven-haired woman of thirty whose face bore shades of tiger. Cassie had seen vitetics a few times before, but usually on actors in the sizzles and rarely in person. The commentators always went on about the upkeep required. It wasn't ink, like May's, but a deeper subdermal injection that sent color back up to the surface and shifted as its bearer changed expression. Despite their subtlety to begin with, tiger woman's—her name was Sierra—feline features were visibly dulling. They must have been done a while ago and it was no surprise she had little chance to maintain them on the road.

Sierra lent Cassie a spare polyester jumpsuit blotched by Rorschach grease stains. Cassie went along to troubleshoot a finicky body panel battery system on a motor home, trying to translate her limited knowledge repairing household appliances to fixing vehicles. The mechanic was brusque while she worked but also kind enough to chalk up Cassie's incompetence to the archaic nature of the fleet rather than near total incompetence concerning modes of distance transportation.

Despite the welcome distraction, it did suck doing someone else's literal dirty work again. The brilliant future she had suddenly lost seemed all the brighter by comparison. While she tried to match components and avoid errant electric shocks, she wracked her brain for a way to get back. Or to get a message to Inma. However much she had chafed under her guardian's thumb, the thought of Inma alone and worried made Cassie's heart ache. Then she thought of Teddy. Was he still comatose? Was he even still alive?

After work, they sloughed off the grime with the same cleansing gel as city dwellers, but more of it with less water even than in the stingy carafe back home. They scrubbed their suits and rags clean with dry soda ash and beat them with the flat of a hammer to send the residue drifting on the desert wind. The flecks floating away seemed like a metaphor for the air of temporariness around everything in the camp. If you set out a table or cooker or work station, you might have to pack it up again in a few hours. If you found a good spot to carry the collection bucket to and do your business, you'd have to find another the next day. Every task was conditioned and coordinated to maximize the efficiency of transport. When she had asked Sierra why they didn't travel by day and work at night, the mentor pointed to the cars. "Half of these will overheat if they're run that long under the sun. And we don't have the spare generation capacity to light a working camp at night." Sierra wiped her brow and looked toward Harv's camper. "Other reasons, too." She left these vague and resumed refitting the engine hood.

Viper came by while Cassie helped pack up Sierra's truck as the sun faded. "Hey—girl," he smiled, unable still to call her by any proper name.

"Hey, boy," she shot back. It was hugely embarrassing to see him in light of her epic failure. Still, it was nice that he came to check on her. "Can I ask you something?"

"Yeah." He picked up a tin of bolts and rifled through it idly.

"Are Viper and Cake your real names? I mean, your real fake names?"

"These aren't fake names, you know."

"I know, it's just—"

"No, I get it. If you'd—" he hesitated "—passed the test, you would get to choose right away because you're old enough. We weren't. So they called us something else but we got to keep it or not later. Or like my dad, Meskit, you know? They called him that to tease him 'cause he was a pest, but he liked it, like a badge of honor, so he kept it."

"What were your and Cake's names before?"

"Hah. If we had any, it doesn't matter. They're gone now."

"But not dangerous to know, like mine is."

"No."

She threatened him with a cable. "So what were they?"

He smiled and shook his head. "You'll need a sharper torture implement."

"Fine. Then why Viper?"

"You really do ask a lot of questions." He changed the subject. "Hey, look. No, look!"

She followed his pointing finger. High in the sky were lights that arced like stars falling in the wrong direction.

"They're launches from Space City."

She knew the name. A "jewel of national industry," a holograph in physics class called it. Set deep in the desert, defended more vigorously than the population centers, and so valuable it had been rebuilt despite its remoteness from civilization. The parents of some of her classmates worked stints there. For a whole year when she was younger, she believed fervently that her own were on assignment to that place and would return home. The home she might not return to now.

Sierra appeared at the inside edge of the truck's hold. "Time to go."

Cassie looked back down to find Viper watching her. For the first time, his careful demeanor cracked. He gave her a wild grin that made him look exactly like his brother, as if he might grab her suddenly. Instead, he clicked his tongue and casually saluted before vanishing between the wagons.

Dahlia had insisted that Cassie not ride with Meskit and his sons so Sierra made room for another bedroll amid a jumble of spare parts in her box truck. She helped Cassie into the hold and closed the doors. A hunched old woman named Cray took the wheel of the truck—these people apparently mistrusted autopilots. Sierra went under almost immediately. Cassie lay awake for a while, trying to adjust to the lumbering pitch that took her farther from home and farther into the world—this part of it anyway—than she had ever imagined, hoped, or desired.

She must have drifted off because she awoke disoriented to Sierra saying something about increased security and checking identities. Her tone seemed slightly accusatory, as if one fugitive water thief could singlehandedly ratchet up impingements on free movement. The caravan slowed to a crawl at the outskirts of the town, so Cassie jogged from Sierra's truck to Castle's. Someone else was driving him tonight and he was waiting at the back door. He hoisted her up among the silkworms.

Still drowsy, she thought they murmured to her in an alien tongue. Her ears tuned and she understood it was a chorus of disembodied voices coming through Castle's array of listening devices. Some sounded like friends, using slang and call signs. Others were more official; she caught the familiar monotone of newscasts aka government propaganda.

"Castle?"

"Yeah."

"You *can* hack them, can't you?" The first time she had asked him that question—ages ago that morning—he sidestepped it. She hoped her vulnerable position might move him now.

"Come on, we've got to hide you before we're searched."

"Please, there's someone I need you to send a message to. So she knows I'm okay. Maybe she can help me get home."

He looked upset but didn't cave. "I'd give up on 'home'— at least that one—if I were you."

The thought had been torturing Cassie all day but to hear someone else say it out loud caused tears to well in her eyes. "Then what am I supposed to do?"

He avoided her gaze. "I wish I could, I do. But I'm not supposed to know anything about you, and that includes whoever you'd want to contact. It's way too risky anyway. If they trace the hack, they'll either find you here or it'll ruin any head start we give you in town."

"Head start? Like I'm a- a rabbit you're throwing to the coywolves?" The tears flowed in anger now. "I guess you would, 'cause all you do is run away. You all talk noble about your secret society but you're cowards. Hey, here's an idea. It'd be a lot easier to hand me over to the Dowsers right now, skip the fun and games." She swiped her hand across her nose.

"We're not like that. I don't like it. Neither do the boys. Or their dad. Others, too. But it is our society and we have to have rules. Come on, don't give up." He looked at her, his own eyes filling. "Look, I'll try, okay? Once you're safely out of our hands. Now sleep. You'll need the rest."

Cassie nodded gratefully. Leaving Inma's name out of it, she gave him the IP tag where Inma worked and Inma's ID. Calmer, she let him nestle her in the back amid the machines against the far interior wall. He replaced the silk curtain to conceal both stowaway and contraband.

≋

Carrying her bag with her sweater and half a day's ration (thanks to Dahlia), Cassie followed Sierra through the town's strip of bustling activity. It had the atmosphere of a carnival the day after. Around her rose hulking buildings of extraordinarily diverse and imposing style unlike anything she had seen at home. Half were cratered beyond occupancy. Others were pocked with bullet holes but still serviceable. Those, Sierra explained, were hotels that catered to a niche in archaeological wonder-slash-adventure trip. The city was built for partying and Eastern tourists still came for that purpose.

Only now it was to party among the ruins. Barkers titillated them with invitations. *Come thrill to the debris of a glittering age that choked on its own hubris. Take our aerial tour of Caprian follies that stud the whittled hills; far beneath lies proletarian sprawl conjured from a dream. Camp among ghosts of a world that sputtered, then burned. Sift through its ashes for a souvenir of opulent ignorance. Sate your schadenfreude with the wages of a city of sin.*

This was where the Transcendents were going to abandon her. Some had stayed further afield to make camp, while those with business or needing a distraction went into the center of this bizarre town. They fit right in. Cassie figured Sierra would simply drop her at some inconspicuous corner. Instead, she stopped in front of a tattoo parlor.

"Wait here. When I'm done, we have an appointment with a biometric forger."

"I thought I was on my own."

"You are. But Meskit asked me to do this, so I'm doing it." Sierra seemed reluctant but she continued, "The forger owes me. Can't give you any money, but this should get you some low-budg papers. Good enough for hitching. Maybe even a bus'll take 'em."

Compared to zilch, it was more than good enough. "Thank you."

"Thank Meskit." Sierra added less brusquely, "I will for you. He'll pay me back one way or another. Stay out of sight." She entered the parlor. Cassie watched her haggle with the artist through the window, then disappear behind a curtain.

She shifted her attention to the street. The tattooist's place was in a colonnade along a thoroughfare crowded with tented stalls. Locals and travelers like Sierra rubbed elbows with intrepid Easterners who took a break from copter tours and choreographed spectacles to visit the trinket sellers who displayed recovered kitsch of the city's improbable past. It was too tempting not to explore.

A stall selling multicolored glass caught her eye. Perched on a small rug was an object that waved delicate tentacles like a sea creature, one of them chipped as if chomped by a predator. It made her sad. And lonely. She reached for it. The vendor smacked away her hand. Cassie faked a swipe at the trinkets on the table merely to spook the vendor. She walked out and further into the warren. A thin boy crouched by a thin flame chased her out of the next one she entered, banging his spoon on a pot to rouse his sleeping father. She backed out without protest. Some of these shelters were homes.

A body whammed into her back and sent her spinning into a table laden with scraps of brocade. Her first instinct was "pickpocket" (*joke's on them*, she thought, before reaching to the pocket with the ring and the private chip Castle had returned to her). But when she turned to give whoever it was a piece of her mind, she instantly recognized the back view of limbs pumping in extreme haste. Viper. Or else Cake. Yes—Cake. She barely had time to adjust the expletive she hurled after him before two men came barreling through the narrow alley, overturning whatever impeded their pursuit.

Cake must have stolen something. A water thief's fealty kicked in along with a dose of sheer curiosity. Cassie rolled the kink out of her shoulder and chased after them. Cake was making good use of the maze but hadn't shaken the men. The trail of upturned wares left clues. She caught a glimpse of his flailing arms as he kicked around another turn and doubled back one corridor over. She cut a corner and headed to the far sidewalk, anticipating that Cake would sprint to the edges for an escape.

Her detour gave her a few seconds if he didn't turn again at the last minute. There was an alley to her left. She scanned it quickly. Her expert eye immediately spotted the cover for a maintenance drain. It was missing screws. She pulled on the grate and up it came. Disused. She wheeled around as Cake came blurring by. She grabbed his arm and pivoted into the alley. Their faces almost crashed into each other. His eyes were wild. Without a word, she shoved him into the hole and replaced the grate, making herself as unobtrusive as possible when the pursuers raced past.

The grate rattled. "Stay in there," she growled between heaving breaths.

"But—"

"I said stay down!" Until she could make sure the danger was over. "Alright, hold on." She pulled away the cover again and gave him a hand up.

"Thanks!" Cake smiled as he heaved himself onto the asphalt. He didn't seem to register what she had risked for him.

"Hey!" Another surge of adrenaline whirled Cassie around, ready to fight this time. But it was Viper. He was out of breath, too. "What the hell, man!?" He dragged Cake the rest of the way out of the sewer and threw him against a brick wall.

"What?"

Viper looked anxiously from one of his brother's eyes to the other. He let go of his shirt and looked away. "I hope it was worth it. You know what happens if the dealers catch you."

Cake winked at Cassie. "Under control. They didn't."

Viper cast her a casual glance and a "Yeah, thanks," before turning back to Cake. "One of these days they will and you'll never see me or Dad or anyone else you know ever again. If you're lucky."

"Lay off." Cake knocked into his brother's shoulder and started to walk back toward the main street.

"Not that way." Viper tugged him back.

"Here, follow me." Cassie walked them down the alley and up another way, winding around until she found the tattoo parlor again.

Before they reached it, someone grabbed her arm and yanked her around the corner into a side street. "What the hell's wrong with you?" Vitetics were supposed to capture humanity's animal nature and Sierra, entigered once more, looked like she might bite Cassie's head off. "Come on. We've gotta get out of here."

"What about getting my pap—"

"They're looking for a thief. I'm guessing that's you."

Viper started to object. "It wasn't—" Cake punched him and they were at it again.

"I'd leave you but I don't feel like explaining it to Meskit. He can deal now." She glared at the twins. "I'm taking your girlfriend back to camp. You two do what you want but I wouldn't stick around unless you wanna haul ass to catch up. After whatever just happened I'm guessing we're gone and not stopping 'til St. George soonest."

"That's a four-day trek," Cake said as if it were seriously on the table.

"Come on," Viper shook his head.

They fell in line and followed Sierra away from the market quarter. Cassie scowled at her back. She didn't mind taking the heat for Cake but that was the second time this week she'd been dismissed as just somebody's girlfriend.

CHAPTER 14
TEDDY

YESTERDAY, TEDDY HAD come out of a coma with a pasty mouth and an empty saline pack strapped to his arm. His thief's eyes hunted for a squeezable drop but the osmotic double membrane and micropump had pushed every last one into his body. There was no sign of anyone replacing it soon. He inhaled through a starched nose and weakly called out to the orderly doing rounds with a bucket and a spoon.

Using his voice hurt his diaphragm. He examined his belly. Waldo's knife had sliced a wry sneer into it. The medics had cleaned up the skin and sutured it roughly—no scarless reprints in a place like this. It itched but then again all his skin always itched in this oven.

A streak of white-hot agony ripped through him. He dropped his head back to ride it out. His grasp of time slipped amid the checkered tiles and colorless lighting. So much time. Time to think. He thought of how Waldo had accused him of the worst crime: murderous treason.

It was true. He had sabotaged the tower. He remembered in exquisite detail. He and Bridget had gone to thieve its water. The ladder was inside. He climbed first, up to a catwalk landing, carrying a coiled hose and trying not to think of falling from the dizzying height. While he waited for Bridget to scurry up behind him, he made a side trip up a shorter ladder that rose inside a tube through the heart of the tank. It put him on the roof, where he had a falcon's view of the husk of a city below. He recalled his grandfather telling him that its lights once filled the valley like poppies in bloom. Teddy had only ever seen a field of flowers ontube.

Back at the landing, he found Bridget drilling into the tank at a point above the existing water line to avoid a pressure blowout. One end of the hose went through the hole, coated in an adhesive to bond it to the tank's interior wall. Next time the pumps ran to partially fill it, the hose would drain the new stuff, at least until it was discovered. Teddy ran the other end back down to screw it into a pipe sticking out of the ground. An advance crew had prepared it to carry off the water. That was all he was supposed to do.

He had done more, however. Up on the roof, before he closed the hatch, he dropped in something one of the bosses' lieutenants had given him along with some extra cash and reassuring words. Down on the ground, he felt the boom before he heard it. Debris rained down, the tower swayed, and then actual water from the tank rained onto him.

He should have waited for Bridget. He had assumed she was right behind. The job was done. You always scrammed before anything could go wrong. She should have been out when the bomb timer went off.

He was sorry—crushingly sorry—that Bridget died. But he was still proud of what he did. He needed to explain that to Cassie when she visited. If she visited; the nurse said no one had while he was unconscious. The last thing he remembered before waking up was telling Cassie that he didn't sabotage the water tower. He could absolve himself of everything else, even Bridget's sacrifice, but not lying to Cassie. It was a coward's deathbed confession after Waldo stabbed him. But now he had the chance to be brave. To explain himself to the only person who mattered. The person he had gone to the party to see, to give a present to, to make crack a smile, to fall harder for as she spoke dreamily about water thieving, to feel loved by (maybe not love, but something real) when she teased him too harshly.

He had tried to tell Cassie's godmother so when she visited him. But the nurse had given him some street-cut pill and he worried that his words had been muddled, collateral damage in the molecular war between pain and its killers. And then Ms. Ruiz said she was looking for Cassie. Something was wrong.

〜

That was yesterday. Today, Teddy was still trying to process the news when a second visitor arrived, a middle-aged man with salt-and-pepper hair, a five o'clock shadow, and an ample paunch he was using like a cowcatcher to clear a path through the ward. "Finally found you, my boy!" Boss Treviño made no effort to keep his voice down. As usual, he wore his shirt with the collar open, darker slacks of the same hemp linen, and his famous cheshire grin. That ivory accessory worried Teddy.

He watched the bulbous belly come perilously close to jostling him off his cot as the boss leaned in to pat his shoulder roughly. There was no way to run and nowhere to hide so Teddy put on his game face. "It's a jungle out there."

"It is, it is, and more so every day." Treviño laughed heartily. "I guess you found that out the hard way." He pointed a finger dangerously close to Teddy's wound. "I'm also guessing someone will finish the job now the truth is out."

Teddy's blood froze.

Treviño laughed again, too loudly for the space or circumstances. "Not to worry, my boy, if I wanted it so, it would be done. By someone competent." He leaned in with a twisted grin and wagged a scolding finger almost playfully in Teddy's face. "You've cost us quite a penny. And bad PR besides. Whose idea was it?"

The jig was up. But Teddy still had pride, loyalty, and conviction. "Mine."

"No, I think not." The grin turned cruel. "Tell me or I throw you to the wolves."

Teddy pursed his lips and, futile as it was, balled his fists.

Treviño's echoing voice was replaced by a hiss through lupine teeth. "You're worth nothing, you water thieves. You're urchins we scoop from the piss pit and make into something. You bring us money, you get a little yourself. When your time is up, you are as useless to us as a raincoat and worth less as scrap. I'll ask again: who is behind the sabotage?"

Teddy tensed, his limbs splayed like a stick figure's, and stared at the ceiling resolutely.

Treviño smacked his shoulder again, hard enough to make him buckle in pain. "Good, good! I knew you were made of tougher stuff."

Teddy ventured a wary sideways glance. "What the—"

"A test of mettle, my boy. Passed with flying colors. Now, how would you like to get out of this place?" Treviño gestured disgustedly at the pink and bloody patches on Teddy's abdomen. "I can take you somewhere they can fix all this, print you some new skin, new gut if you need it, too." He looked around and added almost to himself, "Such a pitiful backwards time to live in."

"But I- you—man, you're sicker than these people if you think I'm going anywhere with you after what you just said."

The boss stood up. "I have a proposal for you. If you want to hear it, tell the staff. They'll know how to reach me." He wheezed and patted Teddy's shoulder for the third time. "Think about it." He poked near the wound again. "But not too long. I wouldn't trust them to save your dishwater here, let alone your life."

≈

An hour after Treviño left, Teddy made the call. Treviño had threatened him, only to laugh it off as a test—or trick. But what did the man have to gain by toying with him? And Teddy hadn't before considered that he still might die in Ma'dio. What finally made up his mind was a growing fear of the sort of trouble Cassie might be in. Only if he healed could he be of any help to her.

He found the orderly. Soon a private car pulled up. The driver bundled him into it. Teddy had never been in a car before. His perspective did an immediate one-eighty. For the first time in his life, he was on the inside, where it was cool and smelled faintly of washing gel.

The car drove to one of the more or less fortified hills where the city's elite barricaded themselves. It wound up the road past a guardhouse but not too far. Even the rich were too scared to occupy the denuded hilltops anymore. Infernos could sweep through suddenly, though there was little left to burn—which meant landslides. So they huddled on high enough ground. Hired guns protected them from the hoi polloi below while massive retaining walls held their backs.

Treviño's house was another revelation. It seemed as big as an apartment building. A servant opened the door without anyone ringing the bell. The driver pushed Teddy in a wheelchair through hallways wide enough for one. Through an open door, he caught a glimpse of art and furniture packed in a room like it was a storage locker. At a staircase, the driver cradled Teddy in his arms and carried him up. He laid him in a proper hospital bed in a room with a window looking south onto a blanket of haze.

A doctor came, examined him silently, and hooked him up to an IV with two bags. One must have been real pain medicine because his head bobbed and he went out like a light. The other must have been equally real antibiotics because by the time the servant prodded him awake to eat he already felt better. The doctor came again and said his internal organs would heal. She offered to strip the skin where the stitches held it together and print a scar-free replacement from an epidermal swab of his tissue, but he declined. For now. He kind of liked it.

After the meal, he met with Treviño in the boss's office downstairs. It had French doors that opened onto a patio decked with potted fruit trees. Flowers grew in the yard.

"You see what I can offer," the older man said when Teddy's jaw dropped. "These are things that even money can't buy. Only water—and power over it."

"Don't, like, the Dowsers know? I mean, why aren't you executed yet?"

Treviño laughed. "There are understandings. One of

which is that I don't flaunt it. But my friends can enjoy it with me."

"Uh huh." Teddy faltered. "Um, thank you. For, you know, saving my life."

Treviño picked a fig from one of the trees. He picked another and handed it to Teddy. Treviño peeled the sticky fruit and popped a perfect teardrop of pink flesh into his mouth. Teddy devoured his whole, petal-like skin and all.

"My pleasure. Now, as my friend, you can do something for me. What you did to that water tower was already useful, if clumsily executed."

"I've been thinking about that and I still don't get it. I ruined a thieving job. The Dowsers will crack down. Why are you so happy about it? Wait—did you order it?"

Treviño eased into a chair in the shade. He put a handful of figs in a bowl next to it. "No. If I had, there wouldn't be a dead body to call attention to our business." Teddy flinched but the boss continued without noticing. "We—you and I— thrive in the shadows. But shadows are short at high noon."

Teddy returned Treviño's knowing look with a blank stare. "Sorry, the uh, pain, medication—I don't follow."

The boss tried again. "You know the game, cops and robbers? It's like that. It's no fun for anyone if the Dowsers round up all us thieves and smugglers. There's a balance. Or there was one. The Judges used to tolerate it while they cleaned up the bigger mess left by the war. But now they want to illuminate everything under a spotlight and drive away all the shadows." Treviño mimed it with a swipe of his hand. "Drive us out of business."

"But I mean, despite your 'understandings,' don't the Dowsers want that, too? They work for the Judges."

"Because they don't have a choice. But elements among them—Mr. McClarrick, for example, if he wins—wish to transform the water council into an institution of legitimate democracy in place of those castrated mandarins like the governor. A real check against the usurping power of unelected arbiters."

Teddy was lost again. "Pain. Meds."

"What do you fear if you get caught thieving? The Dowser cops, yes, but the real terror is the Judge who will have you executed in the blink of an eye. Lord knows I've used that threat more than once to scare you kids into doing the job right. The Judges are the law because they provide order. Take away order—say, through sabotage—and why should they rule?"

"You're saying the Dowsers *want* the Judges to crack down?"

"Some do, if it impels the populace to cast off the yoke of occupation. Then the Dowsers can step in with their democracy. They don't like us and we don't like them, but we have a common enemy, so it makes sense to be friends. For now."

Teddy took another fig from the bowl. Treviño didn't object. As he chewed, Teddy said, "A Dowser cop broke my mom's skull when she went to beg for an extra ration 'cause my sister had scarlet fever. Last month, they cut us down to two gallons a day for six of us. They let people die of thirst and then go around telling everyone how stealing this much—" he cupped his palm "—makes us public enemy number one. No. They're the enemy. I know that much."

"There's a price to pay for getting in bed with them, I admit," Treviño persisted. "As you say, they'll always demonize me publicly. Maybe still string up a few water thieves. But that's the cost of doing business. Think about the upside.

Elections, local control." He seemed almost entranced. "A little bribe here, a blind eye there, cops and robbers and everyone's happy again."

Teddy's face flushed. "I don't want corruption. I want freedom."

Treviño sighed. "So do I, my boy. I picture it a little differently is all. Maybe you'll get your way and it all comes tumbling down like Niagara Falls. Daily baths and iced lemonade all around. But if not, halfway there's better than the spot we're in, right? In the meantime, you get to do more sabotage and I get to make sure it's done right, by someone I can trust."

There was a long silence. Evening was falling—*longer shadows*, Teddy thought. He watched two insects jumping on a leaf. Fighting. Or mating. "There was this other job I was supposed to do for you before—" he pointed at his belly "—this happened. I think my friend covered for me. A girl."

Treviño frowned in thought for a moment. "Yes, right. She wanted the job. It was a new sort of thing in the eastern district. Out of her usual range. I thought she was finished with us. But she was adamant so I gave it to her. She had been one of our best. I guess I pushed our luck."

Alarm buzzed through Teddy. "What do you mean?"

"The job didn't get done—was a total disaster, in fact—and one of my subordinates, a very promising young man, was arrested."

Blood beat in Teddy's ears. "What about Cassie?"

Treviño shrugged. "Who knows?" He plucked another fig. "Anyway, she's through. But do this and your debt is absolved. So? Are we agreed? I have other business to attend to."

Teddy watched him suck the fruit into his mouth. The

rational part of him knew the boss didn't care about the water thieves. But rage filled him nonetheless at Treviño's cavalier unconcern for Cassie. Teddy had been trying to convince himself that he was doing this for her. But she would never make this deal. He took a deep breath. "No."

"No?"

How did you say no to a boss? "I- I'm no good to you like this."

"My doctor didn't do a good job?"

"No- I- she did. But I- don't feel up to it. Maybe later. When I'm healed more."

Treviño worked the fig inside his mouth. A piece of it stuck to his lip. Teddy watched it bob up and down while he chewed. "Very well," the boss said.

"That's it?"

"I made an offer. You refused. I trust you'll be discreet." His sentences were staccato now. He grabbed a few of the figs and tossed them to Teddy. "No hard feelings." He pointed across the patio. "The gate's through the garden there."

Expelled from Eden, just like that. Teddy pocketed the fruit and walked through the flowerbed, wondering if he had made a gigantic mistake. He turned down a chance to do even greater work for the revolutionary cause. If he had said yes, maybe Treviño would have used his considerable resources to find Cassie. He stepped through the gate. It led to a narrow, crumbling staircase built into the hillside. Things were even worse than he had feared. Cassie was either caught by the Dowser cops or on the run or….

He was still trying to keep the word "dead" out of his head when the shovel came flying at it. He dodged barely in time to evade decapitation. The thug had swung so hard the follow-through knocked him off balance. Teddy pushed him down the stairs—it felt like being stabbed all over again—and ran up them. He cursed himself for being so stupid. Of course Treviño wouldn't let him go. He only wanted Teddy out of sight and off his property before his goon splattered brains everywhere.

The stairs came out onto a slanted road. Teddy broke for downhill. He didn't see the assassin behind him. But even if he escaped his tail, how was he going to get past the guards at the bottom, who surely were in Treviño's pocket?

He rounded a bend and stopped in his tracks. The thug was coming up the other way, walking, grinning. Teddy heaved and coughed up acrid spit. His injury was too much. He was done running and they both knew it.

He heard a car approach behind him. Treviño must have sent the driver to make sure. He turned. The lights blinded him. Someone got out. "Hey!" It was a woman. Not Treviño's driver. She was in a uniform, albeit a shabby one. "Hey!" she shouted again and pointed her weapon. A Dowser cop.

Until that moment, Teddy would have bet his life that he would never, ever voluntarily approach the mortal enemy. But now he had to gamble the other way. He glanced behind him. The thug was hesitating a few yards away, unsure how to handle the development. Teddy put his hands up and turned back to the cop. "Help!"

She looked him over. Treviño had put him in decent clothes but he wasn't wearing them well, especially after the chase. "You live up here? Or got a permit?"

"I- uh—" He patted his pants out of habit.

"What's in your pockets?"

The figs.

"He stole fruit, Officer," the thug called out.

"Who are you?"

"Gardener." The thug hefted the shovel as proof.

Teddy saw the cop waver. "No, listen—"

"We let people deal with ordinary thieves themselves up here." To the waiting killer she said, "He's all yours." The man nodded graciously and stepped forward.

Teddy had only one card to play if he wanted to survive the day. "What if the thief in question is wanted for sabotage?"

CHAPTER 15
CASSIE

THE TRANSCENDENTS WERE anxious not to get caught up in a dragnet or any sort of official business whatsoever. They left their encampment on the eastern outskirts of Vegas hastily. In the commotion, no one commanded Cassie to depart.

On the contrary, Meskit hid her in his truck until the next stop. Cassie didn't rat but Viper told his father how she saved Cake. He said he needed help keeping his brother clean, although while he spoke, he kept looking at Cassie as if he was as worried about her. The whole way there, Cake alternated between whaling on his brother, who let him out of resignation, and pacing a corner, expertly keeping his balance with every bump and swerve.

When they arrived, Meskit brought her to the—whatever the seven leaders called themselves—yet again, his hand heavy and comforting on her shoulder. This time, Cassie stared them all down as they appraised her. Besides Meskit: Harv, the apparent honcho, who cast the deciding vote to kick her out before; Dahlia, who had been nice to her and smiled apologetically now; Lake, the crabby cook, who seemed the most surprised to see her again; David, the monosyllabic grump; Griz, the unfriendly man who, Viper explained on the way from Vegas, was only standing in for a woman still "out in the field," whatever that meant; and Tesla, the young, freckled nerd Viper also told her about, so named for their engineering nous.

"You bring us a dilemma, Meskit," Harv said in his gentle voice.

"She saved my son back there. It was his doing, not hers," Meskit replied. "I'll deal with him. But I wasn't going to leave her behind after that."

"You weren't going to, anyway," said Griz. "This is all a ruse. I know you've got a soft spot for orphans and all—"

"Don't," chided Dahlia. "That's not fair."

Griz wheeled on her. "So do you, apparently." Dahlia backed off.

"Wasting time," David grumbled.

"He's right," Lake added. "We have bigger things to worry about."

"This girl saved my boy, which would have cost you more than time." Meskit practically growled at them.

"That only proves our point," Griz insisted. "We can't afford delays, let alone being stopped for good. The other caravans are depending on us."

"The plan was to leave her in a town she could get home from. We're two states away by now." Tesla's brow puckered from unspoken calculations.

"Yes, and the towns around here are all closed."

"The Saints'll take her in."

"Not if she's a thief."

"Or a Dowser spy."

"Or if they think she's a spy for us."

"Does anyone seriously still think she's a spy? We should vote again." Dahlia seemed atypically agitated to Cassie. Then again, they all seemed more restless than yesterday, which was her only point of reference.

"I agree," their leader said. "Do you?" he asked Cassie.

Did she want to be one of these people? Not especially, after what they had put her through. But the options had narrowed like those hated tunnels until most were obscure to her. She was even farther from home, even less likely to survive a solo journey, and perhaps even more wanted than before, if any surveillance or witnesses tagged her back in town. Maybe the road back lay ahead. Maybe she could join this traveling flea market and find a way to use them from the inside. Some of them were clearly pliable when it came to her. Dahlia had taken a shine. Sierra, despite her crusty demeanor, had brought her back rather than abandon her. Meskit and Castle had bent rules for her already. She tried to sound convincing. "Yes."

Harv nodded and the seven began to form the circle around Cassie. Suddenly, a wave of audible emotion fluttered through the camp. A pickup, much the worse for wear, sped to its edge and kicked up dust clouds as it braked hard. Cassie saw people tumble out like it was a clown car. She counted five, plus the driver, who kept a respectful distance while the others leaped into action. Three of them lifted a sixth passenger, a woman, out of the bed. Wounded, it looked like. Another woman, who had been sitting in the passenger seat, made a beeline for the circle.

"Gypsum!" Harv cried as Meskit bear-hugged her. "What happened?"

"Clementine. An ambush." Gypsum turned to Dahlia and swallowed hard. "We got her to a doctor but he had to take most of her leg. Buckshot infection."

"Oh my god." Dahlia glanced at Harv, then broke into an uncharacteristic run for a parked bus. Gypsum looked around the circle, settled on Cassie for a moment, then followed.

The rest split, too, some following Dahlia, others rushing to help carry Clementine to the hospital bus, and still others scrambling for whatever they could do to help. Lake headed to her pantry. David and Tesla went to confer with the pick-up's driver, gesturing variously at its damage and the direction it came from.

Cassie was left on her own. She wandered around until she found the secret-keeper, who was carefully tying stems he had plucked into bundles. He answered the question in her eyebrows before she asked it. "The best thing I can do is stay out of their way. Dahlia's our doctor, she'll take care of it. If there's a story to tell, someone will come by to tell me later. Here," he said in his thin voice, seeing that Cassie looked like she didn't know where to put herself, "help me with these." He handed her strings made of fibers stripped from some plant and dried, and pointed at the stems. "Mormon tea. Good for my bronchitis. The wait is pretty hard, isn't it?"

"I'm not used to other people deciding for me," she answered. That wasn't true, actually. Inma decided plenty of things, so had her teachers and the smuggler bosses, and so would have the Judge. Still, this felt weightier or something. Also, "It's annoying."

The one-eyed ex-lawyer smiled like a jack-'o-lantern. "Do you believe in fate?"

"Not really. I mean, there are things you can't control. But that doesn't mean they're predestined or anything."

"Some would say there's no difference."

"You're saying I'm here for a reason? Like, a cosmic reason?" She thought about Waldo stabbing Teddy, her going on the job with Gray, the job going wrong. It was all accidents. A cascade of bad luck. And she had chosen to get involved because of Teddy. Was that fate? How she sort of felt about him, which she wasn't even sure she could pinpoint.

The secret-keeper stopped working. He sat on the ground in the shade of his truck and motioned for her to do the same. She thought he looked around and lowered his voice a little before he answered. "You know what we're called, this caravan and others like us?"

"Yeah, Transcendents."

"Do you know what that means?"

"Not really. Something religious."

"Not quite. But spiritual, yes. There are those among us who believe there are forces at work in nature that command reverence."

"Like witches?"

"More like—" he searched for the right example "—more like the scientists like Newton, who theorized gravity, and even Einstein. And philosophers going back all the way to the ancients. We call ourselves Alchemists."

Cassie didn't respond. She grabbed a rock and turned it over between her fingers, waiting for him to continue. He was going to tell the story whether she encouraged it or not.

"You know that number you told me—sixty-four?"

"Yeah." Her thieving record, until the last job got fouled up.

"It means something."

"Yeah?" *Here we go.* There were kids at school who obsessed over signs and portents of this or that epochal event. She got into it with one of them once, trying to convince him that there was no point looking any farther than what you had to get done that day. The next thing she knew, she had detention for skipping three classes in a row. After that, she never argued with one of them again. It gave her a headache.

"What's the most important thing to us, all of us out here in the desert lands? The thing we spend all our time worrying about?"

"Water." Obviously.

"To the ancients, water had a form, a shape."

"Yeah, chemistry, I know. H two O."

"No, I mean a symbolic shape of geometric perfection. Earth has one, fire another, air its own as well. And water."

"Okay."

"The shape for water—an icosahedron—has twenty sides and twelve vertices, corners where the sides all come together. Remind you of something?"

The present Teddy gave her. Cassie had told the secret-keeper about it. He was using it now to get in her head for some reason. Instead of answering, she tossed the rock as far as she could. It was getting dark and she only saw where it landed by the scuff it kicked up on the ground. She picked up another.

He was undeterred. "There is another shape, one that represents the whole universe rather than one element. This shape reciprocates not fire, or earth, or air, but only water.

It has twelve sides and twenty vertices. Inverse." The secret-keeper drew numbers on the sand with his finger, twelve and twenty and twenty and twelve, and drew a line under the column. "Add them up."

"Sixty-four."

"You see?"

She didn't.

"You think I'm delusional."

She didn't understand, let alone buy, his numerology. To her, sixty-four signified concrete events in her real life and tied her to everything and everyone real she'd left behind: Inma, Mariah, Teddy, even the screaming Sendhal baby. Whether or not she had any chance at resuming that life was—in the immediate future, at any rate—in her hands and those of the seven leaders. She aimed for diplomacy. "I think you're looking for something that's maybe not there. Some reason why the world is like it is and you and me of all people ended up sitting here together on the edge of it. That is, other than bad luck and stupid choices." It sounded cold even to herself but it was liberating to feel clear-eyed about the situation. It made it easier to face whatever came next.

Footsteps sounded around the corner of the truck. The secret-keeper hastily scratched out the numbers.

"We're ready for her," Lake said as she found them.

Cassie scrambled to her feet and gave the secret-keeper what she hoped wasn't a totally dismissive smile. His eye seemed to pierce her for an instant. She followed Lake back to the gathering place for the circle. The others were there, except for Griz. In his place was the woman from the truck. Not the wounded one. The passenger. Meskit had called her Gypsum. She was lithe, older than Inma but younger than

Dahlia, Cassie thought, with dark chestnut hair fading to white and grey eyes that seemed to absorb everything and let little out. Cassie had the feeling she'd been watching her for some time. She must be the one Viper told her about, whom Griz had merely been proxy for.

No one said anything. Like before, they held hands in a circle around her and began a low chant that moved along the scale and switched keys seemingly at random. Then, one at a time, each spoke his or her vote. This time, Lake began: "no" again. One by one, each cast the same verdict as the first time around. David and Harv against—so much for the favor she did them in Las Vegas. Dahlia, Meskit, and Tesla for, like last time.

The vote was even, however, because Griz was no longer among them. The new woman—Gypsum—took her time. She voted last. Cassie could have sworn she broke from the chorus into a trilling whistle, although watching her face she wore nothing but a peaceful expression that hummed along with the rest. Perhaps the secret-keeper's magical thinking had infected Cassie, after all.

Finally, Gypsum spoke. Her voice was almost too soft to hear above the chant. It took Cassie a moment to register the word: *"Yes."*

Immediately, the chant ended and was replaced by congratulatory shouts. The seven pressed in to give Cassie a giant bear hug. They were all smiles, including the ones who voted no. Harv saw her bewilderment and explained that holding a public vote cemented the bond. The doubters could harbor no secret grudge while the supporters could insinuate no secret obligation. The air was cleared and all were Cassie's sworn friends and family.

Harv's voice carried through the crush of sweat and body heat. "Now, seeker, you are one of us. Once in, never out." A whoop went up from the others and was returned in solitary shouts as it resounded through the encampment. Transcendents young and old who were nearby rushed to pile on. Cassie felt panic build from the airless squeeze but the part of her that had no name yet among these people rejoiced to be joined to this unity. Gasping for breath between the armpits and hips that pressed around her, she saw Viper and Cake peek their heads into the mosh. Cake stuck out his tongue playfully. Viper winked at her.

Harv was the first to pull apart the knot. "There is one final thing." Cassie groaned in exhaustion and he laughed. "No, no. A good thing. You need a name." He raised his voice to reach everyone assembled. "A new name for a new life." A few voices amened assent. He continued. "When conflict stained old names, we chose new." More amens. "We choose still, so that in our names, we might transcend." The last words thundered because many spoke in unison with him.

Harv looked down at Cassie and instructed, "You will choose it." He led the circle to re-form around her, more populated and layered than the voting one. The stars were out above them by now. They began chanting again, this time a mélange of syllables, filling the air with sounds that might coalesce in her ear.

Cassie closed her eyes. At first, she tried to choose which ones to put together into something that matched the vibe of the Transcendents' unusual pseudonyms. Uninspired, she finally let go into a trance and let the phonemes rise and fall around her, some striking a chord that lingered, others fading quickly. A thousand words formed in her mind and painted memories of all the times and places of her life. It was a small moment that lodged most vividly. A moment when Inma broke her usual silence and told Cassie something about her parents when she thought the girl was still too young to remember. She was, but not to remember the pride in Inma's voice. That feeling had imprinted upon Cassie and never left her. She came back into the susurrus around her. She wouldn't choose a name. She already had one.

"Cassandra." It was a real name but also mythological, even more so than David.

The others' tones bled together into a whoosh of white noise and ceased. Harv smiled, all trace of haughty skepticism gone from his look. "A bold name. For a bold girl." David caught her eye and nodded companionably, as if seeing a person there for the first time. Everything else changed immediately, too. Cassie's new family kicked into gear to settle her in. Dahlia hugged Cassie warmly. She seemed as happily nonplussed as Cassie was.

The best part of the day came with dinner. Although she had to wolf down her meal, it was so that she would accompany the breeq bearer on his rounds. At each group, Cassie would formally introduce herself and be introduced, even to those she had met already. She shared a drink in each round of the pitcher, only a ceremonial sip every time it came to her, but there were enough stops that by the end her tissues bloomed head to toe and her belly sloshed with a wonderfully uncomfortable fullness.

She even learned to tip the jug back and forth without spilling, to Viper's relief. They laughed together as she used to with Mariah. Then a voice in the back of her head warned that she oughtn't get lost in the moment. Harv had said "never out," but Cassie was already planning her exit.

She raised the pitcher to her lips and drowned the voice with a joyous gulp.

☲   ☲

"Just tell me." Dahlia loomed over the secret-keeper.

He crouched outside his yurt-truck gathering up bundles of herbs in the eerie light of one of his worm lamps. It was time to be on the road after the delay for the ceremony. "You know I won't."

"Your eye is oozing again." She pointed at the liquid dripping beneath the patch over the scarred hollow. "I can help you with that."

"You can't reprint an eye."

"No, but I can fix the skin around it. It won't bother you as much."

He matted a ragged square of cloth around his eye socket. "Doesn't bother me much now."

Dahlia frowned. She didn't buy into the mystic mumbo-jumbo of Alchemists like the secret-keeper but it was starting to feel like fate had brought the girl to her. It certainly seemed as if Gray had. The beacon that alerted Castle, who told Dahlia, who sent Meskit and his boys to check it out—that beacon likely belonged to Gray. Yet instead of Gray they picked up a girl. Some years ago, an intermediary for an anonymous individual had put out furtive word offering a reward—a rather nice one—to find a young girl. There had been little to go on, no picture, not much else. But of all the contacts in Dahlia's own far-flung network, Gray had delivered. He brought her a name and location. By the time Dahlia approached the intermediary, however, she'd been beaten to the punch. The reward went to someone else, if it went to anyone. She never got confirmation that Gray's lead was correct but she convinced herself she'd been robbed. She had deposited her resentment with similar treasures in the back of her mind and forgotten. Until now. Could it be a fluke that Gray (if Gray was behind it) had delivered her another girl—older, to be sure, but that made perfect sense—from the same city?

Neither pleading nor bargaining had worked so far. "I want her name," she said sternly. Her real name. When the girl had uttered the one she chose, Dahlia thought it chimed with the one Gray had told her way back when. But her memory was cloudy. It could be wishful thinking, confirmation bias. Besides, this girl was a water thief, a punk unworthy of a search, let alone a reward. The coincidences and circularities irritated her mind. Madness, whereas Dahlia preferred method.

"And I told you, you can't have it."

"I'm trying to protect us all," she lied.

"Then you should have voted to send her away."

In fact, the first time, Dahlia had hung back, almost wishing the vote would swing one way or the other before her turn. It was the safer option. The cons were solid. A yes was risky because Meskit had already indicated her role in the rescue and the others were annoyed that Dahlia nudged the girl along with respect to the test. Generally speaking, Dahlia preferred to watch how the chips fell. She had felt fairly certain that Harv would vote yes anyhow. But he waited for her so she did what she had to in order to keep open the possibility of more information. Besides, the girl's resourcefulness reminded Dahlia of herself in a small, sentimental way.

The second time she simply repeated her vote, which the others did as well. Only Gypsum's fortuitous arrival and substitution for Griz made the outcome uncertain. Dahlia would never in a desert's drought dream of overtly trying to influence Gypsum. But while she tended to Clementine's immediate needs she answered Gypsum's questions about the girl in a way that might impress her favorably. Whether or not it worked, Gypsum had cast the deciding vote to welcome the girl—Cassandra—to their community. It still didn't answer Dahlia's questions, though.

None of that was for the secret-keeper to know. Instead, she sneered, "That's not very spiritual of you."

"And this demeanor isn't very rational of you," he retorted.

"At least tell me something more of where she came from." Maybe she could piece it together with the data points she already had.

"Dahlia, every time there's a newcomer, you ask me to break my vow. Every time, I tell you no."

"This one might be important."

"Why?"

"Because everything's important these days," she bluffed. "We can't afford to miss any signs—" that was to appeal to his mystical side "—or make any mistakes—" that one was for herself.

"I suppose it's a risk you'll have to take." He straightened and looked over to where the first trucks were already pulling onto the road. "Time to go."

"I won't forget your pigheadedness."

Standing up, he loomed over her. "You know better than to threaten me, Dahlia. You forget I keep everyone's secrets."

"Maybe you'll take them to the grave sooner than you

think." She huffed away before he could laugh at the ridiculous threat. She might be a lot of things but a murderer was not one of them.

His intransigence was infuriating but her sour mood sweetened as she settled on her tabletop. Momentum was the thing. She knew more today than she had yesterday, and yesterday had delivered potential that had not existed the day before. She had been too patient for too long to let a stubborn man ruin her rest.

That night, as the caravan rumbled eastward yet again, Dahlia slept serenely. For the first time in ages, the earth didn't shake in her dreams.

INTERLUDE: ORTZIKARA
The Judge & The Dowser

Judge Reynard Meiklejohn spun in someone else's chair in a borrowed office. Los Angeles always brought back bitter memories. It didn't help that this session had already been grim and he had several more criminals left on the docket. One of them was still a boy.

He needed a drink to stiffen his spine. He unbuckled the straps on his monogrammed bottle suitcase and lifted the lid. Inside were the most heavily secured of the few belongings he lugged from one depressing place to another. Drawn from the Great Lakes and purified through electrodialysis. He poured a glass and contemplated its contents. He peered closer. There was something floating in the water. He dipped a well-manicured finger to scoop out the offending particle. Dust or else a tiny, desperate insect, both of which hopelessly contaminated the godawful atmosphere out here. He flicked it away. He didn't consider himself especially persnickety. It was more the principle of the thing.

Order was built atom-up. That was what he tried to teach the new apprentices.

Speaking of which, he wondered what happened to the latest one. She never showed. It was no skin off his back but it was untidy, and he had made a promise to mentor the girl as one orphan of the city and another. He took a long sip.

"Your Honor." Owen McClarrick stood in the doorway.

"Councilor. Congratulations." The Judge had never met McClarrick in person, but he was well aware of the newly minted Dowser, as the locals called them. The Judge had mixed feelings about the Dowsers. Founded more than a hundred years ago to mediate interstate water relations out West, their council had shouldered increasing responsibility. The dam burst under the pressure of an impossible task. The council washed away along with the states it served. The latter remained moribund, little more than chalk outlines smudged on the map where they fell in a fratricidal heap. When the Judges sent in their army of marshals to reimpose control, they kept it that way, sidelining the traditional politicians. It wasn't so very different on the other side of the Fence. Over here, however, the Judges revived the council to oversee the most crucial resource. A necessary evil, in Meiklejohn's view. What troubled him was McClarrick specifically. There was something chaotic in the man's eyes.

"I don't mean to interrupt your meditations," McClarrick was studiously obsequious. He brushed a hand through his wonderful hair and grimaced politically. "However—"

"It's fine. Have a seat. I know why you're here. The graffiti." The symbol was sprouting up everywhere, even in heavily guarded areas downtown.

"You know what comes next."

"We smashed the networks years ago. I doubt anyone has the

capability to build bombs, let alone plant them. Or wants to, really. Terrorism's only romantic in the abstract." The Judge took another sip. He didn't offer McClarrick any. "It was bound to happen as a new generation felt their oats. This is children playing at stories their parents told them."

"The one you're about to sentence managed some pretty concrete terrorism."

"Try."

"Yes, of course. Try, then sentence. He brought down a water tower. It's not an isolated incident. People are nervous. You have the marshals but are there enough of them? Things are still precarious. We can't risk backsliding."

Judge Meiklejohn frowned. McClarrick was sitting with an ankle across the other knee. It was too familiar. "Remember your place, Councilor."

"Oh, I do," McClarrick brushed it off. "It depends on yours. I'm only offering input from closer to the ground. Worm's eye view." He smiled broadly.

Too broadly, thought the Judge, mistrusting those dancing eyes. "Which is what?"

"Make it a public example. Your own policy is zero tolerance for sabotage and theft."

"Public? We're trying to work with the citizens, Mr. McClarrick, not drive them deeper into the smugglers' arms."

"My constituents want it, Judge. They crave order."

"He's a child."

"He's—he was—about to be apprenticed. Old enough to work and old enough to topple a town's worth of the only thing between us and an abyss no one wants to see again in our lifetimes." McClarrick stood and smoothed his pants to the extent

permitted by the wrinkly hemp. "Thank you for your time, Your Honor."

Judge Meiklejohn sucked his teeth in thought as he watched the Dowser leave. "Crave order." *Was McClarrick right or was he playing to the Judge's sensibility for a devious purpose?*

Outside the room, McClarrick allowed himself a genuine smile. He had softened up the Judge. Now to bring it home with the star witness. Treviño had come through nicely on that front. McClarrick had been honest about that in there: it was the perfect case to, well, make the case to the public. The world was ripe for change and McClarrick intended to be its agent.

Softly whistling some trivial tune, he wound his way down the old emergency stairwell to the ground floor and back up the main steps to the courtroom so he wouldn't be seen coming from chambers.

PART 3

—As beyond transition its crystal blossoms,
beyond seeking we transcend.

—Catechism of Transcendence,
Affirmation

CHAPTER 16
CASSIE & CLEMENTINE

"I'M SORRY, CHAMP."

Cassie stared blankly at Castle's outstretched palm and wrinkled her nose. They were in his truck. By now, the silkworm stench hardly tweaked her nostrils. What made her recoil was his request—his demand.

In what seemed only a few days, the thrill of her initiation had faded. Life took its course, quickly and impersonally filled with workaday concerns. She was an apprentice, only to a vagabond mechanic instead of a princely Judge. *Traveling after all*, she thought grimly more than once. She had used the unending repairs Sierra increasingly trusted her with to avoid this meeting with Castle for as long as possible.

"Everyone has to do it," Castle continued. "Wiping traces of your old existence is part of becoming a Transcendent."

"What does it matter? My records, my identity, that's all somewhere else. I'm here. It's not like I'm gonna forget just because you delete a government file."

"Disremembering is also part of becoming a Transcendent,"

Castle persisted, though Cassie detected less conviction this time.

"I know you're good but won't the Dowsers notice that something's gone? You can't make it like I never existed at all. I have fami—"

"Once in, never out." Castle's voice was firm again. It was the Transcendent motto Harv had spoken when she was accepted among them.

"Did you try to reach my relative?" Aeons ago, when they were about to abandon her, he had promised to contact Inma, though he refused to let Cassie tell him her name or even her gender.

"I did. Try." He paused. "Honestly, I don't know if it succeeded. I pinged their work ID with a gossipak buried in some audio spam. If they authenticated instead of an admin and if they let the spam play long enough to load the packet, then it should have decrypted. It's supposed to ping me back as part of the self-destruct, if it hadn't done that already 'cause it expired unread." He paused again. "It didn't. Ping me back, I mean." Seeing her crestfallen, he gestured toward the hidden electronics. "But these things are dicey given my setup." He looked at her apologetically and licked his lips. "That's a lot of ifs, I know."

In a small voice, Cassie asked, "Can you try again? Maybe Tesla knows a way."

He rocked uncomfortably. It obviously hurt him to be such a stickler. "I'm sorry, no. And you know I can't ask." Before her protest was out, he continued, "Haven't you been listening to me?" He added more gently, "You're in a different situation now. Speaking of which, Cassandra, I need your chip back."

It had felt strange when she first arrived that none of them could call her by a name but now it felt strange and, worse, violating, to be called by her real one. They had made her drain her heart to the secret-keeper. Why should he hold onto it while she was supposed to forget? Everything here was shared, every moment communal. Couldn't she keep one private anchor? Especially what was on her private chip.

"What—you got a fortune on there?" Castle tried a joke to shake the tree. "No, don't tell me. But seriously, if that's it, you really should tell me."

"If I did I'd be…I don't know but not here right now."

"Then…" he motioned to hand it over.

She looked down. "I'm not ready."

Castle fut-futted air between his lips. "Okay. I got other things to do. I'm supposed to send you to Dahlia for your physical after this. I guess you've been putting that off, too. Go do that then we'll talk." As she jumped out of the truck before he could change his mind, he called after her, "And by talk I mean you're giving me that chip by the end of the day or I'm feeding you to my worms."

᪲

"I'm sorry, dear."

Clementine stared blankly as far into the distance as she could inside the ambulance bus that served as a mobile hospital. It was mostly empty. One or two of the usual patients suffering from dehydration or a sprained ankle slept strapped into the gurneys fastened to the sides of the bus. She sat on a lower bunk. It could be worse. Meskit's kid wasn't in here wailing through withdrawal like a year or so ago when Clementine spent a couple of days with acute bronchitis.

"It's the location," Dahlia explained. "I don't have the materials to cover that much ground. If you had knocked out a tooth, burned a patch of skin, even severed a finger...but a limb? Below the knee, maybe, but even then, the risks of reopening the wound—"

"Reopen it. You said you would."

"I said I'd try once you were stabilized. I'm sorry, Clementine," Dahlia repeated. "My printer can't handle it. In the old days..." she trailed off, uncharacteristically at a loss.

"You told me you did a heart valve that time in Sacramento," Shadow interjected. He stood beside Clementine like a sentinel.

"Yes, and I also found the inputs for some delicate blood vessel work. But I had contacts there willing to cut me a deal and a surgeon to assist me without asking too many questions. Out here, these days—there's no way."

"Okay, then." Clementine steeled herself to stand on the prosthetic Dahlia had been able to print. Shadow lurched to steady her. She batted his help away. She was still getting used to it but the synthetic material was responsive to intuition. The knee and ankle joints and even the knuckles flexed naturally. Her hip and what remained of her thigh were already habituating to the movement. Even her eyes and hands were sometimes tricked by the naturalistic skin. All of which her brain had resisted while she held out hope.

"Wait," Dahlia pleaded. "I do want to perform chelation. They should have done it before—" she caught herself "—but of course there was no time."

"Chelation?" Clementine spun on the artificial foot.

"To leach out any lead from the bullets."

Clementine snorted. "The bullets were in my leg."

"She doesn't have symptoms," Shadow added.

"She's looking peaked." To Clementine she added, "You told me you vomited this morning and you're stopped up."

Just then, the new girl stepped onto the bus. She stared at Clementine, who stared back harder. Freshly initiated. The pòv pitit didn't know she had fallen into a fly trap. "Sorry," she said, looking quickly from Clementine to Shadow to Dahlia. "I'm supposed to have my physical."

"Yes, okay," Dahlia nodded. "Let me finish with Clementine. You can wait right there, Cassandra."

Cassandra, that was her name. A runaway Meskit had found. Clementine watched her shrink into a corner amid the bolted-down shelves lined with drawers full of medications, syringes, tubes, and whatever else Dahlia could scrounge to stock it. "Everyone is," Clementine laughed acidly, picking up where they left off. "'Stopped up.'"

"She had an infection," said Shadow. "That's why she threw up."

"Nonetheless. Lead poisoning can occur quickly and we don't know if all the fragments are out. You've been obsessing over that one—" Dahlia pointed at the prosthetic "—but there's a wound there, too." She indicated the bandage around Clementine's other leg near the knee. The amputated leg had borne the brunt of the bounty hunter's gunshot but it was true that she took a hit in both. It was only a nick, comparatively. Dahlia continued, "If there's something in your popliteus, or in the joint, it could leak into the synovial fluid. The surgeon who treated you was right not to go fishing for pellets given your more pressing problem. But I want to take the precaution now." When Clementine didn't answer, Dahlia confessed, "It's a chance to hydrate you a touch more intravenously. You've been through a field amputation, a near-fatal infection, and a flight from justice. You need the juice. The rest is probably unnecessary but where's the harm?" Dahlia puckered her cheeks hopefully, motherly.

Clementine sat back down with a shrug. "Jan ou tanpri. It's not like I'm going anywhere anytime soon."

From her corner, Cassie ventured a word of encouragement. "The prosthetic is beautiful. I mean, you're beautiful, and I've only met you this way."

Clementine's look was withering. "No one asked you." To Dahlia, she said, "I thought no more stragglers."

Dahlia gently pushed Clementine to a reclined position. "Long story with this one. Shadow, can you bring me an IV needle from the third drawer there near the gauze? Cassandra, there's alcohol in the bottom." While they found the supplies, Dahlia prepared a bag of solution. "I've been husbanding this EDTA just in case."

Clementine watched dispassionately as Dahlia inserted the needle into her arm. Shadow hovered and bobbed like a hummingbird. Clementine could feel the anger and guilt competing to consume him. It was only a needle—*honestly, compared to everything else recently?* "It's a needle," she said aloud.

She noticed that the urchin watched her interaction with Shadow. It was none of her business. But there were always eyes on you in the Transcendent camp.

"Shadow, slide this up high for me, will you?" Dahlia had placed the medicine bag on a hook bracketed around a bus pole.

He unlocked the latch and started twisting the ring. It was stuck. As he stepped to get a better grip for loosening it, he tripped over Cassie. "Move," he grunted irritably. She scuttled aside.

Clementine's pleasure to see it was fleeting. She and Shadow must be the most intimidating Transcendents this child had met yet, leaving aside David. "He's nothing to be scared of."

"I'm not scared," Cassie boomeranged.

"Oh. Good." Clementine gave Shadow a nudging look.

"Sorry," he said to Cassie.

"You didn't do anything," Cassie insisted. She sounded irritated, like they were making a big deal out of nothing. In spite of herself, Clementine grinned. She was warming up to this one.

"She'll be fine," Dahlia cooed absently as she checked the flow in the tube.

Clementine turned to face the bottom of the gurney bunk above her. Someone had keyed a smiley face into its hard orange plastic. "Don't make promises you can't keep, Doctor."

Dahlia was satisfied all was in order. "This will take an hour and a half. Don't move. Let's go take a look at you," she told Cassie.

Clementine could tell this newcomer was fit. They would have her raiding in a year or so—assuming any Transcendents were left. The girl had naively scrawled her name to a compact Clementine wanted to shred. "Hey," she called out as Cassie followed Dahlia toward the front of the bus. Cassie looked back over her shoulder at her. Clementine indicated her own banged-up body. "This is what you signed up for," she said, utterly without malice. "So you know."

The girl didn't blink but Dahlia glared beratingly over the back of her head. "Come on," she said, pulling the girl away.

When they were more or less alone, Shadow reached for Clementine's hand. She didn't swat it away this time. But she didn't grip it, either, or say anything, or look in his direction.

Instead, she closed her eyes and drifted elsewhere...

Back to the garden behind the enormous cinderblock home where little Elita and Martine chased each other through rows of cassava plants. She could still feel their languid leaves brush her shins as she raced after her sister. One played a hero of the revolution driving the other, a slaveholder, from the island. She no longer remembered who was which that day. From points on the hillside where their grandfather's farm was among the last holdouts against erosion, they could glimpse the colonial architecture of the port and imagine the American ships to be the French navy sending reinforcements, for Napoleon might tolerate emancipation but not independence. Soon, one of those ships would take Elita to the mainland to live with a relative. A few years later, she would go West to college where scholarships were plentiful. Then the American war began. No more ships sailed to Haiti. No planes, no news, no contact. Elita took the nom de guerre of Clementine to remind her of the scent of citrus, the tickle of the cassava leaves, and the voice of her sister laughing merrily in the Caribbean breeze.

"Well, she's a poopsock," Cassie whispered to Dahlia.

"Shh," Dahlia admonished. A few yards away in the back, Shadow sat on the floor with his head on Clementine's belly and his eyes closed. Clementine, too, seemed asleep. Dahlia drew a curtain to compartmentalize them. She began retrieving implements to conduct the physical. "Clementine has been through more than you can imagine."

Cassie doubted it. When Shadow barked at her, she

pictured herself in his shoes, tending to Teddy while he lay unconscious in Ma'dio with a hole in him *(was he still there? was he alive?)*. That was why she didn't blame Shadow for being curt; he was only trying to care for Clementine, the apparent queen of curt.

Dahlia must have read her face. "You have a story," she conceded, "but so does everyone here." A bitter note crept into her voice. "None of them very happy."

It hit home to Cassie that all of these people were social orphans like her. "How long have you all been doing this... on the road thing?"

Dahlia rubbed a mole on her hand as if it might come out. "The caravans began before the war, I suppose. But the tribe—the Transcendents—that coalesced sometime after."

Cassie was almost shocked. Dahlia said "the war" like she was talking about "the tubecast" or "the potatoes." Back home, no one ever openly discussed it except for a quick unit in history class. It ended with a moral about the Judges' beneficence in restoring law and order and the Dowsers' judiciousness in managing water. The only other thing she knew was that sporadic violence erupted into full-scale conflict the year she was born. "I don't really get what happened in the... war," Cassie confessed. It felt illicit to say the word out loud.

Dahlia motioned for her to open her mouth wide. "Ahhh," she modeled with her tongue out. "You must know why, though."

"Ahhh. Water."

"We used to read about it when I was younger. In other parts of the world. It sort of bubbled up to the surface. Conflicts thought to be about oil or religion or national pride. So many of them were really about water when it came down to it. My parents told me some even took a stand in this country, before I was born. Nothing like the war, but still. The Transcendents are right about all that, in a way."

"Right about what?"

"That water is the sacred element, the twin to universal essence."

Cassie remembered what the secret-keeper had rambled on about. "Yeah, the secret-keeper was trying to tell me something about that."

Dahlia put in the earbuds of a stethoscope that looked like it was two hundred years old. "Don't worry, you'll get an earful from that sort in due time. Deep breath."

Cassie breathed. "You talk like you're not one of them. Of us."

Dahlia laughed an almost girlish, innocent peal. "Oh, I very much am, by circumstance and force of habit. Deep breaths. But I'm a scientist. Not that I blame them. If ever there were a time for revivalism to grip the imagination, it's now. Anyhow, we were not spared the water wars. There was no plan for when it ran out here. Tempers boiled and what started as civil disobedience or insurrection or self-determination or whatever you want to call it dragged in the governments. You think there's a system in place, that your country operates according to certain rules and principles. But the truth is that it's all hodge-podge layers of historical accident papered over by a confidence game. Like the stock market."

"What's that?"

Dahlia placed the stethoscope on Cassie's chest and listened for a moment. "Never mind. What I mean is, stability exists because people think it does. But there are a million fault lines beneath the surface. If lots of them snap at once it's- like the Cascadia Event."

Cassie knew that one from science class. "The Northwest."

"Cup your hands beneath your leg and let it dangle. Yes, like that." Cassie's knee jerked as Dahlia tapped it hard with two fingers. "Exactly. You have no idea what those cities were like. Now it's a feral marsh. In a hundred years some anthropologist will find survivors and call them the last uncontacted tribe on Earth."

Dahlia started prodding beneath Cassie's jawbone, clavicle, arms. "The point is, so many things finally snapped—the drought and Exod in the West, seabord evacuations in the East—that, well, it's no wonder they don't teach you much about it. The past is past—that's the philosophy around here, too."

Cassie thought of Castle's word for coping with her identity loss. "Disremembering."

"Precisely." Dahlia pulled Cassie's earlobe and peered inside with a magnifying glass.

"I don't get how that helps anyone."

Dahlia didn't answer. "I'm going to do just an external pelvic if you'll lie back and scootch down your pants." Cassie complied. Dahlia was quick. "Okay, sit up. I assume you menstruate?" When Cassie nodded, Dahlia handed her a small plastic cup that looked like a miniature plunger. "Hard to come by. Don't lose it. And—" she looked gravely into Cassie's eyes "—you can come to me about anything, okay?"

"Okay."

"Last thing…." Dahlia pricked Cassie's finger with a pin. Cassie flinched involuntarily. Dahlia grimaced. "Barbaric way to do bloodwork, sorry. You know by now that we're forced to be quite old-fashioned. I suppose that's true for most, west of the Fence."

"Are we near it? We've been going east."

"The Fence? No. Not near. But you'll see it soon enough, I suspect." Dahlia began putting away her instruments. "It's not what you'd expect."

Cassie grabbed a pole to help herself up. She stopped short. Dahlia was humming. "What is that?"

"I didn't mean anything by it, dear."

"No, that song. What is it?"

Dahlia seemed genuinely surprised. "I don't know. From a dream, maybe. I think my mother used to hum it. Talking about the past must have dredged it up." She turned her sharp eyes on Cassie. "Why? Do you recognize it?"

Cassie wasn't sure. It triggered a memory in her, too. Something vague. It would slip away if she tried to sing it herself. But deep in her inner ear it was complete. "I don't know."

"It's probably a lullaby. Maybe your mother sang it to you as a baby. Music is supposed to leave deep traces." Dahlia put a hand on the curtain. "You can leave whenever you're ready." She went back to where Clementine lay.

Cassie pictured Inma rocking her to sleep when she was young. Was that it? With the memory of her real family, the feeling of estrangement from these people came back. They were going east but she ought to be going in the other direction. Her hand moved to the ochre strand of silk around her neck, the one Castle gave her on her first day with the caravan. She had tied to it the ring from Inma. For the umpteenth time, she counted its several metal sides and single ruby one. She read the inscription: *e pluribus unum*.

"That's a pretty piece."

Cassie jumped in her seat. Dahlia was back, standing over her shoulder.

"Uh, thanks."

"I remember you passed it off as earth at your test. May I see it?"

With a reluctance that surprised herself—as if doing so betrayed Inma somehow—Cassie placed it in Dahlia's palm. The older woman examined it. She didn't say anything but handed it back to Cassie with a smile.

"It's junk," Cassie said apologetically. She immediately felt guilty. Disparaging the gift to Dahlia also felt like betraying Inma.

"Not if it means something to you," Dahlia reassured her. She took Cassie's hand in hers. "There are many reasons we don't talk about the past. For some it's too painful. With others, the group is better off not knowing who they were and what they did before. But a lot of us find it liberating. Or simply normal. It's been so long for me but I imagine it must be hard to suddenly be away from family and friends. It's good to have something concrete to remind you when they wipe everything else."

Cassie felt her cheeks flush. She was primed for tears and Dahlia's kindness wasn't helping. Castle was going to erase her chip soon and there was something she needed to do first. "Is there- do you have anything I can use as a screen?"

"Here," Dahlia pulled down a metal shield that covered a small screen. "I use this to look things up in my sadly meager library. I'll give you some privacy." She left out the front door of the bus.

Cassie thumbprinted the chip to unlock it and passed it in front of the screen. An image appeared. She felt the ache of nostalgia. Not good-old-days memories but yearning for a past she never could have remembered because she wasn't there in the first place. The pic showed a young woman somewhere in a desert. Strong, lithe, with blond hair. She wore clothes that struck Cassie not so much as vintage but alien, though probably quite fashionable—and available—at the time. She stared at something or someone off to the side with a fierce but playful look. Cassie couldn't stop her lips from trembling or the rise of salty phlegm in her throat.

She heard a gasp. She killed the image and whipped around. It was only Dahlia, fanning her face in the doorway. "Didn't mean to startle you, dear. I get out of breath," she said. Her brow furrowed sympathetically. "Castle's looking for you. It's time to become a ghost."

CHAPTER 17
INMA & TEDDY

TEDDY LANGUISHED IN jail. He wasn't exactly sure how to languish. Like was he supposed to lie back on the mattressless cot with his feet up on the wall and count imaginary slashes in the wall that marked the days? Or maybe grip the bars on an imaginary window and gaze at the moon and think of a lost love. Probably, he hadn't been here long enough to languish. Languishing sounded like a stranded-on-a-desert-isle sort of activity.

It had only been a few days since his split-second decision to throw himself on the mercy of the Dowser cop instead of receive a skull-bashing from Treviño's henchman. Confessing to sabotage had gotten her attention. Later, Teddy tried to retract it and give them the boss based on what Treviño had frankly confided to him. He wasn't a rat but Treviño had earned it. The authorities were uninterested. He wasn't surprised. Treviño had bragged about his connections and his bribery.

So he did spend most of his time lying back, wondering where Cassie was and how he might get out of this new predicament. The cell itself wasn't great but it wasn't that terrible, either. For one thing, he had it to himself, a perq of depopulation, which was good because no one was rushing to empty the crap bucket. The food sucked but most of the food he normally ate did, too. The Dowser guards showed no love for a thief and saboteur but his age and precarious physical condition seemed to take the fun out of anything more than verbal taunts, which, again, had been a feature of much of his life.

"Bergson: time. Let's go." An officer flashed a chip against the wall to open the cell.

The holding pen the officer led him to was crowded. The stink of a dozen unfamiliar unwashed bodies hit even before he shoved Teddy in. The men who watched him enter with unfriendly glares were much the worse for wear. Teddy realized his own appearance must be equally sorry. The only spot to sit was darkly stained and—yep, damp. He stood instead. A moment later, everyone shifted with ruffled feathers as the guards pushed yet another man inside. Teddy closed his eyes.

"Hey."

Teddy didn't respond.

"You're a kid. The Judge might go easy on you." This person was trying to be nice. Or pretending to.

"I'm not a kid."

"Sorry, man. No offense. Just trying to cheer you up."

Teddy opened his eyes. His interlocutor was the new entrant. Taller, leaner, and a few years older. He didn't seem predatory. On the contrary, he looked like he'd taken a bad beating, though it didn't dispel a beatific aura about him.

"I'm Gray." The man jerked a thumb toward the door.

"Execution pending. Waiting on when but it'll be probably, you know, prime time tubing."

Teddy had watched public hangings of adults. Cheap and relatively effective. Even a botched one that decapitated the subject got the job done. Strangulation was possible but a sharpshooter was on call in case. Hanging was a terrible way to go but terror was rather the point. This man was too cheerful for a convict facing that imminent prospect.

"Why?"

"Maximum eyeballs."

"I mean, why are they..."

"Killing me?"

"Yeah."

"'Cause the world is f'ed up. But you want to know what I did. If I did anything." Gray looked Teddy up and down. "I'm guessing the same thing you did, thief."

Teddy balked. Maybe this guy was a plant trying to get him to incriminate himself further. "Forget I asked." He turned to stare at a spot on the wall. He'd gotten good at that.

"Sorry. I didn't mean to scare you. Like I said, maybe you get off easy."

Teddy's pride was pricked. "Maybe I don't want to." He didn't look at Gray.

"Okay. I respect that. Front line honor. You're a foot soldier like me."

"You're too old to be a thief."

"I was a lieutenant."

Teddy froze. Did Treviño send another assassin? There was nowhere to run. None of these other men would care. Could he fight this Gray to the finish in his condition?

The man moved closer. "The truth is, I'm a double agent," he said conspiratorially.

Oh. Teddy inwardly rolled his eyes. "Wow, cool," he half-heartedly humored him, hoping to be left alone.

"I'm serious," Gray insisted. "I started as a kid and worked my way up. But someone else found me, too. Someone with principles." His voice grew even softer. "A Transcendent."

Teddy was trying hard not to pay attention. "You mean, like, you meditate?"

"Yeah, but—no, I mean a person. People. People who looked around and believed there's a better way to be and began searching for it—seeking it."

"God."

"Uh. Can be. For me, more like Thoreau. Emerson."

"That's who found you?"

"What? No. The Transcendents did. The caravans?"

"Oh. Travelers. I thought you said you were caught thieving."

"I was. I told you, that was my cover."

Teddy turned back to Gray. "Why are you telling me this?"

Gray sighed but it wasn't melancholy, more like…expectant. "I don't know, you seem like the kind of guy I would have recruited if the Dowsers hadn't gotten both of us first."

That and every other foreclosed possibility filled the air for a minute.

"How'd they get you?" Teddy finally asked, merely to end the yawning silence.

"I let them." Gray saw Teddy's skepticism and elaborated. "There was this water thief like you. Treviño had me on a job on the east side. I thought a dude was coming but this girl shows up instead."

Teddy swallowed. His fingers squeezed the bars of the cell.

"You with me, uh—what's your name, again?"

"Teddy," he managed to croak. "Yeah."

"So she shows up. I'd never met her but there was something familiar about her and then I remember it's from this thing I did for the Transcendents once."

"Uh huh." Teddy sucked in the stagnant air reluctantly. He needed oxygen.

"So I decide to carry on and maybe afterwards I could feel her out, see if it made sense to say something. But I didn't get the chance. Something went wrong. The guards got onto us, called the Dowsers in."

"Hhhhh." Teddy slumped to the filthy floor. "So they have Cassie, too?"

"You knew her?" It was Gray's turn to be surprised.

"The Dowsers have her?" Teddy repeated.

"I don't know. There's a chance not. Right before I was nabbed, I slipped a transponder into her bag. She took it when I told her to run. I used it to set meetups with this Transcendent high-up when she's in town. So maybe they found her."

"Or maybe the Dowsers tracked the signal."

"They might've. We try not to use their frequencies. Hey, Ted?" Gray looked at Teddy with concern in his eyes.

"Yeah?"

"Get a grip. You go to court like that and they'll spike you with an upper and you'll end up confessing to a hundred crimes you didn't commit."

"Bergson." The officer was back.

Gray smiled. "Good luck in there. We should hang again." Teddy's escort walked him down the hall to the sound of Gray laughing at his own gallows humor.

⌁

The courtroom, like the building that housed it, was a relic of a more confident era. Its ceiling was high, its walls lined with chipped green marble down to cherry wood wainscoting. Pews of the same winy color lined the back of the room like in church. Most of them were missing, though, as were the posts of the bar that separated them from the action. Looted long ago, most probably. It facilitated the standing-room-only crowd. Even the Dowser leader, McClarrick, was there. Teddy recognized him from the posters. He was surprised by the attention. Most people steered clear of this complex whenever possible.

He sat at a table on the other side of the bar. A lawyer he had never met before sat next to him. She told him he could plead guilty or not guilty. Her tone made clear which she thought best. Juries didn't apply to crimes of insurrection so the success of a not guilty plea depended on persuading the Judge that he was telling the truth. That was going to be difficult in light of his initial confession—and the star witness. Waldo stood eagerly at the bar, dressed in a borrowed suit, his hair combed and his nails cleaned. He flashed Teddy a vengeful private smile before resuming a heartbroken countenance.

There was no prosecutor. The bailiff announced Judge Reynard Meiklejohn and everyone stood. The Judge took his seat and straightened the items in front of him. There was only one: the gavel. The Judge and Teddy's lawyer went through a bunch of things. Whenever the lawyer poked him, he answered politely with yes or no as she instructed. He half-listened; she seemed to be requesting leniency on account of his age. She didn't sound confident.

Something tugged at his sleeve. He realized that his lawyer had sat down and was trying to make him do the same. Waldo shuffled mournfully between them and the Judge's bench and took his place at the witness stand.

"Do you swear to speak the truth on pain of justice?" Meiklejohn asked him.

"I do, sir, Your Honor." Teddy had never heard Waldo sound so meek in his life.

"You are familiar with the defendant—Mr. Bergson?"

"I am, sir. From school."

"I'm told you are also familiar with the events in question concerning the sabotage of a city water tower of which Mr. Bergson is accused, is that so?"

"I was there if that's what you mean."

Teddy's knees spasmed involuntarily under the table.

"Go on."

"I mean, I was there with my friend, Bridget, the girl he killed." Waldo choked.

That part didn't seem like acting to Teddy. He would have felt sympathy. Except Waldo was lying.

"We were, you know, looking for some privacy. I wanted to impress her. I thought I could scale the fence or something or get past the guard and get inside to climb up it. I had no idea what kind of security they have around those things."

Teddy barely suppressed a snort. As if Waldo wasn't equally a thief. His lawyer gripped his arm to quiet him.

"But it worked out, actually," Waldo testified. "Bridget could sweet-talk anyone and she got the guard to open the door to the tower so we could check it out. I- I don't want to get him in trouble—"

"That's alright, our concern here is what happened next," the Judge reassured him.

Teddy couldn't believe he was eating up this crap. But intervening would probably backfire.

"We climbed up. We got to the roof, I don't know how many feet up, and we sat down and dangled our legs over the edge. I was terrified, actually, but I didn't want to show it. And we started to, you know....And then all of a sudden he—" he pointed at Teddy, who jumped in his seat "—came up out of the hatch in the tank and shot down the ladder like a- like a rat."

"Rat" was a nice touch. Teddy met Waldo's eyes and saw pure hatred.

"We didn't know what he was doing but, you know, someone runs like that and you run, too, just because. I made Bridget go down first. Then there was this boom, like you felt it first and then you heard it, and sh- stuff was falling all over the place and the whole thing swayed, I mean it was just coming apart. Something hit Bridget and she fell and by the time I got down there...." Waldo was full-on crying by now. "I know we never should have been there but she's dead because Teddy wanted to sabotage everything and it worked, I guess, because he killed an innocent person and that's what they want, isn't it, to hurt us?" He turned baleful eyes on the Judge.

Teddy's cheeks flushed with outrage. Waldo was signing his death warrant and relishing it. He felt eyes on him—the Judge's. He must look guilty as sin. The crowd behind Teddy certainly thought so. They had grown increasingly restless as

Waldo went on. A few started a chant. The rest now picked it up. They screamed one word: *"Rope!"*

Inma watched the politician, McClarrick, surreptitiously stir the courtroom mob to clamor for a public hanging. Of a child. It seemed unusually vicious, even for a Dowser, but she remembered his stump speech calling for change. Whatever his plans, public anger would fuel them. It sort of explained why someone of such high position would take an interest in a water thief's trial.

Inma herself was there after cloaked inquiries about water thief arrests led nowhere concerning Cassie. They did point to Teddy, however. She came to lend moral support but the crowd was so thick she could neither see nor be seen by him.

She hung around the justice complex until Teddy would be back in his cell. Then she pulled her auntie routine to gain access as a visitor. The guards were reluctant to deny a family visit on the eve of…of….

Teddy seemed in shock, naturally enough in light of the outcome. "Has your family come to see you?" she asked out of genuine auntish concern.

"Huh? Oh. No. Once. When I first ended up here. I guess the Dowsers notified them. They scrubbed their hands of me." He smiled apologetically. "They're law and order types. They thought my after-school job was trashpile sorting."

Inma swallowed. She felt responsibility landing on her shoulders. "I see. Theodore," she swallowed again, "you understand what is going to happen next."

He stared past her at the wall outside his cell. "Yeah. Gray told me."

"Gray?"

"Someone else headed to the gallows."

"I see," Inma said again. No sixteen-year-old should have to utter a sentence like that.

"Oh." Teddy seemed to remember something as if it was from a long time ago. "He knows Cassie. He knows what might've happened to her."

By the time he finished relaying what Gray had told him, Inma's brain was crackling. The tide she'd held back for years, the one building to a wave this week under the pressure of some deep rumbling of the earth, finally crested and smashed the dam of respectability. Everything else fell away as her priorities crystallized. She was a middle-aged ex-insurgent creaking towards inglory but her heart leapt like she was spinning into her superself. "Thank you," she cried. "And Theodore, don't lose hope. There's always hope until the end."

"Yes, ma'am." He spoke like an automaton.

She laid her hand over his on the cell bars. "I will be there. Look for me. Look *at* me."

"Okay." His voice was still colorless but he placed his other hand on top of hers and squeezed. After a moment, she pulled away, unable to bear it any longer.

CHAPTER 18
CASSIE

THE CARAVAN WAS parked on the near side of Utah Lake. It would stay there. Across the water lay an oasis of sorts afforded by an unpredictable but self-contained hydrologic cycle.

"Saints territory," Sierra told her while they scrutinized a telematics unit. It was actually a holographic model of one, using precious equipment Sierra cajoled out of Tesla for the day.

"Those are the people who helped Clementine, right?" Cassie, like everyone else, knew the story of the raiders' flight to a closed town where a surgeon cut off her leg.

"Yep."

"So why don't they let us in?" The city across the lake was off limits to all but one or two Transcendents like Castle, who went to trade his precious silk.

"'Cause helping her made trouble with the Dowsers and the marshals. We are unwelcome at the moment."

"How can they do that—keep us out?"

"Watch it! You almost warped the honeycomb." Sierra pulled Cassie back roughly. "I told you, it's interactive."

Cassie was sure she had gotten nowhere near the projection's motion sensor but she stayed silent. They were trying to fix a biomimicry function that had gone haywire, reading sandy terrain as two inches of flooding and shaping a vehicle's tire grooves accordingly. It was bad for handling and bad for efficiency. Transcendents hated inefficiency.

Especially Sierra, who consulted a manual projected on a screen from her chip. "These instructions are ancient," she complained. "It's like reading how to fix your fridge."

"We had one of those. Back home," Cassie volunteered.

"Did it work?"

"We never really needed it to."

"Uh huh. Any more helpful hints?"

Cassie shook her head. Sierra was cranky on a good day. It was not a good day. Sierra had been growing grumpier as the caravan's pace quickened because there was never enough time to charge the EVs and they had to spend a lot of time switching out batteries. As soon as a travel pause solved that problem, drivers came at the mechanics with irritants like these stubborn wheels.

"I have to troubleshoot this. Check the maglev," Sierra commanded. Cassie went to the spherical tire sitting nearby. Sierra made a motion corresponding to a tiny physical adjustment to the graphene processor. "Did the treads change?"

"No," Cassie replied.

"Are you sure?"

"I'm sure."

Sierra swore.

Cassie felt superfluous, which was why she was making conversation. The only people she knew of who could check your papers were Dowsers or the federal marshals. She didn't even know if there was a city council back in Los Angeles. "So," she repeated, "what gives them the right to keep us out?"

Sierra looked up, befuddled then annoyed. But she answered as she turned back to her work. "In the civil war-slash-rebellion-slash-insurgency, the Saints spearheaded the formation of the Wasatch Front, a militia. They had weapons. Good ones. They withdrew to that strip between the lakes and the mountains and negotiated a truce. They see to their own affairs in closed towns and the government doesn't get any trouble near the Bumblehive. What about now?"

Cassie watched the tire. "Nope. What's the Bumblehive?"

Sierra stood to stretch. She did even that with a feline yawn. "An info-suck. 'T's where the government keeps all the intel it gathers. And it's thirsty, uses a ton of water to cool and clean all those spy machines. Which is why the situation with the locals is delicate and we are personae non gratae. Have I answered all your questions?"

Cassie cast her gaze downward. "Yeah. Sorry."

"Look," Sierra sighed, "you've been half-bad 'til today. Probably just need a break. It takes a while to match our speed. Take the day, get your focus back."

In Cassie's opinion, she'd been superb. But it was true enough that she was distracted. That day in the ambulance had stayed with her. It was her last look at the pic she had carried forever before it poofed into oblivion. *This is what you signed up for*, Clementine had told her. There was something honest in the way she said it, although Cassie still thought Clementine was a jerk. So all she said in reply to Sierra was, "Okay."

"What's on top?" Cassie eyed Lake's latest lunch concoction, a piece of sorghum bread with a dark, dry spread.

"Grasshopper crumble," Cake sprayed the crumbs as he spoke and scrambled to scoop them back into his mouth.

She tried to flick it off discreetly, although she knew where the protein rations at school came from. It was more out of frustration—the small differences from her old life loomed largest in her homesickness.

"I wouldn't do that if I were you," Viper admonished.

"You won't get a protein pill here."

"No G-rations for outlaws."

"It's tastier this way anyhow," Cake concluded.

"Come on, we want to show you something." Viper stood and motioned for her to follow.

"Lemme guess, beetle brulée."

"No. I promise you'll like it." His wide smile was convincing.

The caravan's vehicles were arrayed in their special pattern all along a patch of dirt that clearly had been divided once upon a time into the lawns of a housing development. Some of the homes still stood. They were palatial next to anything Cassie had ever been in, though some of the richer folks' homes she thieved were comparable on the outside. The trio wandered into one—all the doors were missing or bashed in. She thought of the test the Transcendents put her through at the mall back at the Nevada border and kept an eye out for scorpions and snakes. There wasn't much to see. It felt both lived-in and unoccupied, like a model home in Pompeii. It was filthy and stank and she preferred to go back outside, where across the lake was a magnificent mountain with a hint of snow brushing its cheeks.

And there was the lake itself. It was only the second time she had seen such a body of water. The first was on a school trip to tour one of the mammoth plants that lurched into operation whenever there was sufficient energy, gulping seawater and regurgitating it plucked clean of salt. The hydro engineers were paid well but Cassie had found the idea of an oceanfront apprenticeship depressing. For one thing, it was thankless. The city's residents hated desal because the output rarely benefited them. Worse, the western rim was a sludgy wasteland that stank of stagnant eddies filled with rotting organic matter and molding manmade junk. A drowned carnival ride breached the water beside the long pier that stretched over the waves to reach the plant. The ocean wore an ugly, resentful shade. Though infinitely smaller, this lake called to her. Its flat shore was marsh. She could wade right in.

"I wouldn't do that if I were you," Cake exited the house behind her laughing and gesturing to suggest what kinds of horrible death awaited her if she dared to.

"It's gross. And electrified. We're not going that way anyhow. Come on." Viper grabbed Cassie's hand, to her surprise, and stalked off northwestward. It was a long hike under afternoon sun but he was bent on it, so the others followed, kicking up dust as they trod the broken rural roads. In this direction, the horizon was flat until it met with low iron-colored hills. Cassie couldn't imagine what was going to be so special out here.

Suddenly, Viper pulled up short and pulled Cassie down with him to a crouch in a stand of brush. He put his arm around her neck like they were pals. Which they were. She focused on where he was pointing instead of his shoulder curved around her.

"Holy sh—"

"Shut up and get down," Viper hissed at his brother. "You knew it was here!"

Cake obeyed under protest. "Relax, loverboy. I was trying to help you with the element of surprise."

"That's not what that means." Viper turned to Cassie. "And I wasn't trying to impress you. Not like that."

"Oh." She faked disappointment. "Didn't work." She stared back at him.

He blushed and turned back to the orchard. "Now to get us some of that."

It wasn't a large farm but Cassie had never seen so many trees in one place. It was like a Halloween forest. Slender branches crooked out from the trunks and waggled at the earth, ready to snatch up unsuspecting travelers. They were laden with bright orange fruit that looked like a cross between tomatoes and pumpkins. "Persimmons," Viper explained.

"Let's go." Cassie stood but he pulled her back down.

"Look." The trees were fenced in with barbed wire.

The rows and cross-hatching had huge gaps in between from a water thief's perspective. "Please. That guy Truck could walk through there without a scratch."

"There's also that." He pointed at a farmer working near a tree in the middle of the orchard. A gun rested against it.

"So you run in and distract him, and me and Cake'll grab the fruit. I promise to get you some."

"Haha. It's a her anyhow."

"Great, you're good with the lad- oh—" Cassie feigned disappointment again "—I guess it is a long shot."

"You're cracking me up. Maybe you ought to go in with

your comedy routine and when she uses the shotgun to pierce her own eardrums us two will get the fruit."

"How 'bout we send Cake and see what happens," Cassie joked again.

"Hey," Cake protested reflexively. But he seemed game. "Okay."

"No, you dryhump," said his brother. "Hold on a minute and let me think."

"I thought you guys have done this before."

"We've been here before but we didn't actually get away with any of it," Viper confessed.

"Great, I'm dealing with amateurs. Alright." Cassie thought for a minute, too, and came up with a plan. Sometimes, in water thieving, if there was a guard you couldn't bribe, one thief played decoy while another got the goods. It worked as long as you trusted the person you were working with.

"Which one of you is faster?"

"I am," Cake spoke up. "I've got a lot of practice," he grinned, reminding her of their recent escapade.

"Okay. Cake, you're gonna go to that tree there." She pointed to one whose branches overhanged the fence. It was within the farmer's sight if she turned around. "Make some noise to get her attention and make like you're stealing the fruit."

"Can I?"

"Sure, if you can jump high enough and get it and land and run before she starts shooting."

"Yes, ma'am." He stretched out his neck and cracked his knuckles.

"Wait. Go when I say. I'm going to climb through the wire over there—" she indicated a spot at the other end "—and grab as many as I can."

"You—" she poked Viper in the chest "—are going to stand on this side and catch whatever I throw to you." She turned back to Cake. "Give me as much time as you can. Does anyone else live here?"

"No, only her."

"Good. Stay clear of her sights. Run around the other side of the building if you have to."

"Then what?"

"I'll call out when I've got as much as we can carry and then we run for it. We can regroup later. Is there somewhere you both know of that we can meet at?"

The boys thought for a second. "The desorp garden," Viper suggested. "Cake, you know, the things." He shaped something in the air.

"Yah. Okay."

"Okay," Cassie agreed. "I have no idea what you're talking about, so you—" she slapped Viper's pecs full palm this time, because why not, they were pals, right? "—wait for me. Ready?"

"Ready," they answered in stereo. Twins had weirdly synced timing.

"Go."

Cake loped in a wide arc toward his target, hamming it up as a secret agent for their benefit. Cassie rolled her eyes and sprinted to the barbed wire. She wanted to time her entry to when Cake drew the farmer's attention. Viper held back a minute since he would be the most exposed and didn't want to draw it instead.

Cassie reached the trees. Up close, they were even more otherworldly. They had few green leaves left but were covered with ripe, plump fruit that dangled like fairytale temptation.

She wasn't sure what they tasted like but it had to be good. Her mouth watered, drowning the aftertaste of grasshopper crumble on sorghum.

The farmer's shout brought her back to the task at hand. She scrambled to the main fork in the nearest trunk. Cake was out there with a persimmon in his mouth and another in his hand, flailing to get the farmer good and worked up. She came after him and—Cassie gave him credit—he had the sense to draw the angle between them so that she had to exit the barbed wire and move away from Cassie.

The fruits came off easily into her hands. She hurled them out to Viper waiting on the other side of the wire as fast as he could catch them. The shotgun blasted. She flinched, not out of fear but remorse. She hoped Cake could handle it. The brothers seemed tough, in some ways more world-wise than she was, but she didn't really know them. She, on the other hand, had years of experience with tight spaces and close calls that could result at any moment in capture or death. She looked up but couldn't see Cake or the farmer. Probably, they were behind the farmhouse. She panned over to Viper. The pile by his feet was about as much as the two of them could carry and run with. She ought to jump down.

A growl stopped her. No other person might live here but a canine with an unhappy look on its face apparently did. The mutt was the same size as those that guarded her thieving targets. She tossed a persimmon a few yards away. The dog didn't bite. It barked.

So did Viper. Cassie nearly fell out of the tree laughing to see him trying to distract the beast's attention with what was either a combat challenge or a mating dance. Whatever, it worked. The dog rushed the fence. Cassie slipped down the tree trunk and pelted toward a section of it a respectful distance away. Viper scooped up as many persimmons as he could while the dog lunged at him. But it stopped at the fence. Too high to jump, too sharp to risk, or else the dog was too well trained to breach the perimeter. Instead, it raced after the intruder still within its domain and snapped its jaw shut within a millimeter of Cassie's foot as she tumbled to the ground on the other side. She heard the farmer shout and picked herself up to chase after Viper, who was desperately motioning for her to hurry up. She caught up to him, took a share of the booty to carry, and they booked it barely fast enough to escape a blast that blew a hapless pink pixie Apache plume to kingdom come instead.

Cassie was still laughing when they collapsed together behind an old industrial shed a couple of miles away. Her sides hurt in the best way. It felt like forever since she'd had this much fun. She looked over at Viper, who was heaving for breath with his eyes closed. He opened one eye and winked. "I'm glad that cheered you up."

"What do you mean?"

"At lunch you were Miss Mopety-Mope. I know it wasn't only because of grasshoppers."

His calling it out brought Cassie down a little. The last person she did have this much fun with was her best friend Mariah. What was she doing right now? Was she worried? (Of course she was, Mariah was always worried.) Was she looking for Cassie while Cassie was juvieing around with these two?

"No! I didn't mean to bring her back," Viper entreated. He rubbed one of the persimmons on his shirt, which probably made it dirtier, and pulled out a pocketknife. Its skin gave way easily. He cut out two slices and handed one to Cassie. "Here."

They each took a bite and giggled like kids at each other. The fruit was firm and sweet. When they were done, Viper took off two more slices and repeated until they finished it.

Cassie let out a contented groan.

"Right?"

"So worth it. Now I'm thirsty, though."

"Ah, therein the genius of my rendezvous plan." Viper tapped his temple and winked again. "Come on."

They stood and gathered the remaining fruit. Viper led her around the corner of the shed. Another candyland orchard was laid out before them. This one was artificial. Titanium teardrops twenty feet high staggered along the landscape. Each was a scaffold, and through that outer shell Cassie saw huge clay-colored urns suspended within. They reminded her of the bonbons Inma brought home from work once, impossibly sweet sugar candies wrapped in cellophane.

"What are they?"

"Suckers. Aka a 'desorption array.' They draw water from the air."

"How?"

"Come on, I'll show you."

She looked around nervously. Life-threatening adventure was great but a single daily dose was sufficient.

"It's obsolete. Didn't work. Or not on the scale they needed. But it's good enough for us." Viper walked over to one of the towers. Cassie followed. It dwarfed them like a temple statue. She saw now that the urns were made of some kind of plastic. "Mesh," Viper anticipated her question. "The air goes through but water droplets don't. When it's cool at night, the dew condenses and drips down into a bucket." He rapped on the outer shell and it echoed a little across the flat land. "It's supposed to catch rain and fog, too, but there wasn't enough. That's why it failed. But look." He stooped over a foot-high gate at the base of the tower. The latch was padlocked but Viper pulled a couple of thin, oddly shaped wires from his pocket and got to work picking it.

"Won't it ping a security station?" Cassie asked. It would, in her experience.

"'T's not electronic," he answered through teeth gritted with concentration. "Too remote for rapid response once they gave up on the place. So people pick 'em and some poor Dowser who screwed up a real job comes 'round and replaces 'em and people pick 'em again. There," he said as the shackle clicked open. He opened the latch. Inside was a pipe leading from a cauldron-like bucket to a spout. "Hold out your hands." Cassie squatted next to him and cupped her palms together beneath the spout. Viper turned a valve. Crystal clear water trickled out. Cassie scooped it to her mouth and drank. It was glorious.

"My turn." Viper nudged her aside and leaned his shoulder against the ground so he could stick his head inside the gate, tilting it close enough to the spout to get the water into his mouth.

"I could kiss you." She said it without thinking.

"Yeah?" His head popped back up.

"Nice! Real nice, roachturds." An irritated voice broke the spell. Cake. Cassie had completely forgotten about Cake. "Yeah, while you're lapping it up like- hamsters or whatever, good ol' Cake nearly got his ass blown off by Old MacDonald."

"Smells like you've still got it, though," Viper jibed, wiping his mouth with his sleeve.

"Move over and let me drink." They got out of his way.

"Thank you," Cassie said, and meant it. "Here, have a persimmon."

Cake glared at her but took and bit into it, spitting out bits of peel as he chewed furiously.

"You should savor it," Viper scolded with a smirk.

Cake pointed the half-eaten fruit like a weapon. "You two owe me big time," he sputtered through a full mouth.

"Tomorrow," Cassie conceded, laughing.

"We can't go back there. She'll be ready this time," Viper countered.

"Yeah, but one of the other ones," said Cake.

"Other farms?" Cassie asked.

"There's a few," Cake confirmed. "They co-op. Kind of like us, without the wheels."

"We'll see. Let's go. Spinney and Laurel can give us a ride back." Viper pointed at a pickup parked at the other end of the field. It was loaded with plastic barrels. Two Transcendents were tapping the suckers. Cassie recognized them from the night Clementine was brought in wounded.

"You owe me," Cake repeated solemnly as he backpedaled, then turned and jogged to the truck.

"You good?" Viper asked as he and Cassie strolled to the truck. She had grown pensive again.

"Yeah." She was good. Well—better. The day's diversion had given her a new idea.

CHAPTER 19
INMA & TEDDY

INMA MOVED DEFTLY through the apartment gathering supplies. She chose things that were obvious, like food, and others that served one purpose domestically but another on the run, like the tarp that patched a hole in her bedroom wall. As she moved, her limbs and joints began to recover their muscle memory of a more virile period in her life, albeit under enough protest that she had to stop and catch her breath now and again.

Finally satisfied with the bag she packed, she remembered where she had a bit more money stashed on separate chips in secret hiding places. Plus the one she had found in Cassie's chest along with the sculpture. She decided against taking her favorite fork, after all, and made a final pass over the place.

Days spent turning the city upside down had produced no sign of Cassie. The last time Inma had actually gone to work on the off chance there was a message from her, the supervisor fired her at the door for absenteeism (after what, fifteen years without missing a day). Then came Teddy's news that Cassie might well have been spirited away by travelers.

The only reason Inma had not left town sooner was the vow she made to be there when he was executed. A sense of foreboding crept over her but she packed it away, too.

She power-napped and woke more refreshed than she'd felt in ages. She dressed, drank a ration, closed the door, turned the key, and walked out on her old self. When she returned—if she returned—she would no longer be this Ms. Inmaculada Ruiz, office drone and erstwhile guardian of a teenage girl.

⚏

Teddy had nowhere productive to spend his wired energy. Suddenly, it seemed like there were a million things he ought to do before the big sleep shut it all down. But there were only the cot and bars and crap bucket and that thing on the floor that hadn't moved in a while and may or may not be or have been alive and therefore also possibly dead and/or biding its time. Teddy thought people in his situation reviewed their lives so he tried to make a list of his good and bad deeds, prides and regrets. Thinking about his family took up most of that. They had abandoned him, which made him sad and angry, and they were ungrateful for the money he brought in, although he felt petty for bringing that up even to himself at this point. And he loved his younger siblings and would miss seeing them grow up. He was a pretty good big brother, which wasn't an example he learned from his own older brother.

He fended off his sole regret as long as he could but it wouldn't be denied. He loved Cassie and the last thing he said to her was a lie to make himself look good. A half-lie, maybe—he had sabotaged the tower but he never meant to hurt Bridget—but a lie nonetheless. Now he would never have a chance to correct it.

Fatigue had finally knocked him out when the Dowser guards rousted him. He was led out of his cell, cuffed, and lined up behind the other condemned from various cell blocks, both women and men. He saw Gray among them. They exchanged a somber nod. Teddy wondered if he looked as calm as Gray did because on the inside, Teddy's guts churned.

The corridor seemed much longer than it did on the way to trial the other day. The guards led the chain of prisoners through a few turns until they reached a side exit. Before leaving the building, all were hooded. Teddy thought he saw Gray wink at him before the burlap blocked his vision.

The hood was the worst thing so far. Binding his hands was inconvenient but blinding his head from sight, sound, smell, taste, direction—it wasn't even like the confined spaces he knew as a water thief. At least then he was free to move while his surroundings were dimmed. Now, the world buzzed with threats he couldn't anticipate or respond to: the guard who yelled near his ear, the prisoner who stepped on his ankle and punched him in the back for good measure, the bystander who pelted him with rotten food. All the while, the hot November air doubly suffocated him.

With no sense of bearings, Teddy tried to recall watching executions ontube in civics class or at dinnertime at home. They probably were headed to the Hall of Justice, where a scaffold would have been erected and a crowd gathered to watch it live. It was one building no one successfully bombed during the war, although it bore snipers' pockmarks and a few streaks of char where a firebomb had blown up a Judge early on.

The guards stopped the line. They prodded the prisoners into shorter queues. Some jittered, one ran; Teddy heard the patter, then the thud of a baton and a body dropping to the ground. The fidgeting stopped. Teddy sensed the person in front of him shuffle forward. Then it was Teddy's turn. A guard grabbed his elbow and yanked him up a few steps before pushing him into a van.

Second car ride in my life, all in the last week, Teddy thought, wryly turning over the word "last." The van took a lot of turns. Like the corridor, this road seemed awfully long. It was strangely quiet inside, even taking into account the hood. He had expected to hear a crowd as they approached the hanging square. None of his fellow prisoners wailed, pleaded, anything. Then again, neither did Teddy. They all were in their own head-spaces. If he concentrated, he could hear the erratic breath of whoever sat beside him. She or he seemed equally nervous.

"Okay, you can take it off now." A man's muffled voice.

Someone pulled the hood from Teddy's head and his heart almost did the executioner's job. He was face-to-face with Ms. Ruiz. She was the one sitting next to him breathing the whole time.

"What the—"

"You're good at making friends, Theodore," Inma drily cut him off.

"Uh, not really." He was still in shock.

"Well, you made one, anyway, back there. Gray? And me, that's two. And Guillermo—" he waved from the driver's seat "—who took a big risk borrowing this van from work, that's three."

"What…" was all Teddy could repeat.

"Gray had a ticket out," Inma cut him off again. "He gave it to you."

"Ticket?"

"He has a lot of friends, too, it seems. Or the right ones. They found a guard willing to help him slip the noose in exchange for…whatever. Gray gave it up for you."

"You know Gray?"

"After you told me about him, I visited him, too."

"She's more than meets the eye, man," Guillermo offered from the front.

Inma frowned with worry. "He could tell me only a little more about where Cassie might be." She brightened a little. "But he set this rescue mission in motion."

"Where are you taking me?"

"Have you ever left California?"

Teddy looked at her like she had lost it. "Of course not."

Inma didn't answer for a moment. She seemed absorbed in thought. "You know, it was its own whole country for a second. I mean, in the 1800s. Way before the Judges. Or- there were judges, but they weren't so important. Not even when I was your age. But then…well, the war, and by then back East only the Judges could do anything, which was to send in the marshals, who'd been beefed up over the years without anyone quite noticing, and…well, here we are." She shook something off and smiled at Teddy. "Leaving California."

"You look different, Ms. Ruiz."

"I feel different, Theodore. Now, put your head down for a while because we're not out of the woods yet. Or rather, into them." Exhausted, he was only too happy to oblige.

Inma watched Teddy slump and close his eyes. He would need the rest. She had instructed Guillermo to steer northeast. It wouldn't be long before the authorities realized that someone on the inside had helped a prized prisoner escape.

They would be on the hunt. Guillermo had concocted a legit story about a machine delivery, which would buy some time and keep anyone from looking specifically for their van, but soon road blocks would be raised and drones deployed. They had to be out of the city before then.

And they were. Guillermo drove up past the abandoned foothills, where the highway had narrowed to one crumbling lane because of landslides and disuse. When he pulled over, Inma had another surprise for Teddy as he got out of the van: Mariah. "Another friend," Inma smiled.

Mariah held up a pack like the one Inma had made herself. "I found everything you asked for." She gave it to Teddy and hugged him. "Find her," she whispered fiercely to him.

"I will," Teddy promised, still clearly bewildered by it all.

Inma and Teddy waved goodbye as the siblings turned the van back toward the city. Then Inma pointed north to wildfire country. It was a perpetual tinderbox where the slightest change in wind ignited new conflagrations in a neverending season of hell. Only the depletion of kindling ever kept it in check. No one lived here anymore. No one in her right mind would even pass through it. Which is why Inma chose this route to steal away a fugitive wanted dead or alive. They donned masks against the smoke and she led the boy into the inferno.

〜　　〜

In the city square, Gray stepped to the noose willingly, rapture upon his face. He looked at the doomed men and women to his left and to his right. They did not return his smile. The rope slipped around his neck. A call went out. The floor dropped. His body fell and his neck snapped. The last electric pulse through his brain released chemical elation, for Gray died knowing absolutely that in giving his life for Teddy's he had finally, truly transcended. Dahlia, he hoped, would have been proud.

CHAPTER 20
CASSIE

"**D**ON'T SHOOT!"
"Why not?"

Cassie didn't anticipate such a practical question. "Uh-I'm unarmed?" The persimmon farmer had called halt when Cassie was ten yards from the farmhouse door. She couldn't quite make out the gun in the moonlight but she knew it was there. Also the dog, which was rumbling a low growl.

"So were the runts who robbed my trees. Was that you?"

This woman was direct. Cassie decided honesty was a better policy than spooking her further. "Yes," she ventured slowly.

"Starlight, kill!" the farmer commanded.

Three thoughts zipped through Cassie's mind: *kill seems a little extreme, this thing's name is Starlight?* and *oh yeah—* "Wait!" she shouted. "I brought a gift."

The farmer repeated the dog's name and a word Cassie didn't catch because she was too busy standing her ground against a muzzle of slobbery teeth. A whiff of beast breath hit her as Starlight put on the brakes pretty gracefully with inches to spare, rounding her and staying close in case the farmer changed her mind again.

"To make amends," Cassie added as Starlight's tail swept into her as a not-so-gentle reminder.

"Let's see it."

Cassie stepped forward cautiously until she closed half the distance between them. "Your wire has too many gaps."

"Scrap's hard to come by. Anything left's rusted to useless."

Cassie reached into her pocket and held out what she had brought. It glinted off the moonlight for a second.

"Doesn't look like much," the farmer said from a few paces away, her weapon still trained on Cassie.

"It's spider silk."

The farmer snorted. "Cobwebs won't mend a fence."

"It's from silkworms. Spliced with spider genes. And fed something to make it even stronger." Despite distractions like the other day at this farm with Viper and Cake, Cassie had not neglected her personal mission. Keeping alert for anything in the Transcendent camp that might be useful, she had stumbled upon Castle and Tesla discussing this supersilk. It hadn't been hard to steal a few strands as a sample for the farmer. She'd steal more if she had to—the worms themselves if necessary to make this plan work. "There's more where it came from."

"Good, 'cause this i'n't much," the woman sniffed, before adding, "How d'I know it's like you say?"

Cassie heard the curiosity in her voice outweigh the doubt. "It would be a lot easier to show you inside," she pressed.

The farmer eyed her, then stepped aside and motioned with the gun barrel. "Go on."

The farmhouse interior was snug. A crusty pair of boots

and a few caked tools cluttered the entryway, which led straight into a room with a stove and cabinets, an ancient wood table and two chairs that all seemed to be handcarved, and a metal bed piled with much-mended blankets. Another on the floor had telltale signs of Starlight's ministrations. Cassie didn't notice any of the appliances she and Inma had in the apartment back home. But that wouldn't be a huge deal, maybe. It wasn't like they could afford to run the operational ones half the time. The bathroom was probably through a small door she saw at the far end. The farmer likely converted her own biofuel. Cassie grimaced. She could do that. The place seemed smaller on the inside than out but there might also be a storage room she didn't know about. The thought struck her: maybe even livestock. Would that be possible in these conditions?

"Sit 't the table. Both hands on 't if you want to keep 'em," the farmer said as she patted Starlight. She sat in the other chair across from Cassie. "You can leave the wire there, too."

Cassie did as she was told. It was her first good look at the woman. She was tall, with broad shoulders cloaked against the evening nip and muscled legs she planted wide as she sat. Her gray hair was tied loosely at her neck. On the same arm as her trigger hand, a scar ran from her wrist to above the elbow.

"Thanks, Ms. uh—"

"Chief. That was my rank in the fire brigades—battalion chief." The Chief inspected the silkwire, pulling at it and coiling it around her hand. "Could see this catch a thief or slow her down at least," she said appreciatively with side-eye at Cassie. "Where'd you get it—what's your name?"

Cassie had planned to give her name but seeing as the Chief had declined to mention even her own last name, it seemed risky now, asymmetrical. "I'm um, Mariah. I grow it."

The Chief put down the silk and sat back. "I see. Well, Mariah, if what you want for the wire is more fruit you're out of luck. You took more than that's worth. Besides, what I had was promised. I'm in deficit 'cause of you."

"Promised—to the cohop?"

"Figured you weren't a farmer," the Chief scoffed. "I know everyone around here who is. Yes, promised to the co-op." She peered suspiciously at Cassie. "Nothing wrong with that, if you're government."

"I'm not." Cassie fluttered her hands, causing Starlight to perk up. She planted them firmly back on the table. "And I don't want more persimmons, although—thank you? And sorry again. What I want is to know about the co-op."

"How's 'at?"

"I think it might be good for us." The Chief twitched and glanced at the door, so Cassie hastened to add, "My uh, mom and me, but just me right now. My mom is—it's a long story."

"They all are," the Chief sighed, almost friendly. "There's not much to know. You've seen what I grow. I'm good at it. But I can't live on that all day all year. So I share with those'o grow other things. One or two don't grow but know how to fix." She nearly smiled. "Say, a fence."

"How? The lake?"

"That pond's off limits now. But we're on the edge of a microclimate. There used to be more but the Dowsers keep shooting out straws to feed 'at Bumblehive. Thing's unquench-able. Nearest fellow had to give up anything but tepary beans, and those barely."

"But what you find, you keep? It's not rationed by the Dowsers?"

The Chief pursed her lips up to her nose. "Where you from?"

Cassie wasn't sure how much to say. She tried to match the Chief's terseness. "City."

"Ah. Kind of the opposite here. Not a lot of us. Honest, the Dowsers don't pay us attention. We're an afterthought 'til they reach our sources. And then, like I said, they take what they want." The Chief sucked in her cheek like she had bit a lemon. "Look, Mariah, I can tell you've been through a thing or two, and you got the better o' me the other day, which shows something. But farming—this kind, anyway, not those giant agros over the Fence—it's a hard life, harder maybe than in human history. I don't know what you and your mom are used to but this i'n't it."

Cassie was certain it was. A fixed place, ignored by the government, where people took care of themselves. She could escape detection, which ought to be enough to convince Inma to join her. She wasn't sure what Inma could do—maybe this co-op needed an accountant or something—but Cassie wasn't afraid of hard work. She would take care of them. She owed it to Inma now. And she could bring her friends. They would help. She reimagined the farmhouse as a bigger, cheerier one with a fire in the stove and Inma, Teddy, and Mariah laughing with her as they feasted on a tableful of fresh food. She only had to set it all up, maybe even find a way to holo it, so they would believe her and come.

The farmer stood. "Okay, time to go." She waggled the gun at Cassie.

"Hold on—you're wrong. I need to know how to start my own farm here."

"You won't be doing that. No one we don't know."

"You know me!"

"I know a city girl who's a thief. Who still owes me." The Chief was at the door now, holding it open, while Starlight shepherded Cassie toward it. "We made conversation. Now we're done. Don't come back unless it's to repay."

"Please," Cassie pleaded as the Chief pushed her outside. "There's gotta be something. Name your price."

The Chief laughed mirthlessly. "Not if you could squeeze a drop from a Dowser. Good-bye." She started to close the door.

"Wait." Cassie put her hand out to stop it. "What if I can?"

꙳

The nictitating membrane slid over the lizard's eye and back again. From her vantage point lying on her belly, Cassie had watched it do that three times, as creepy the third as the first. Then again, a nocturnal lizard perched on a rock was one thing. The snakes that she belatedly realized were probably out hunting were another. *And scorpions,* she thought, remembering the one that stung her during her failed initiation test. The sooner she learned something, the sooner she could leave. She forfeited the staring contest with the gecko and looked out at what lay beneath the ridge she had crawled up.

In the moment the Chief had almost slammed the door on her, desperation had cooked Cassie's half-baked dream into a plan. She didn't belong with the Transcendents, however much some were becoming her friends. She wanted her real friends, her real family. Settling down here felt like the last chance she would ever have. They hadn't traveled so far that it was inconceivable to contact home. The life was one she had never imagined before but it was in front of her eyes so she could now. And to live in this bubble, filled with fruit and relatively free of Dowsers—that was worth almost anything. So she had stuck her hand in the doorway and made an offer.

The Chief had mentioned the Dowsers extending "straws" out from the Bumblehive—which Cassie could still picture only vaguely as a tiered complex teeming with drones—to draw ever more water from the surrounding landscape. It made Cassie think of the capillaries Gray described as they went on that fateful water thieving job that ended in her flight. Trying to sound like him, she began spouting off about lapidarious strata and fiberoptic beacons. The Chief bit her top lip, then her bottom lip, then agreed that if Cassie could deliver a viable mechanism to re-thieve that water in dribs the Dowsers would never follow up on, she might earn a place in the co-op community.

It felt so good to have a familiar, concrete task that Cassie wanted to start scouting immediately. She had to be sure it could be done before she risked trying to obtain any of the necessary materials—more stealing from Castle, probably, she thought with a slight twinge of guilt. So she continued from the farm in a direction the Chief pointed, sticking to an old road to avoid getting lost in the dark as she approached the outskirts of the Bumblehive's restricted zone.

It had brought her past another abandoned subdivision to the embankment she lay on now, eyes peeled as open as the reptile's beside her. It was difficult to make things below out clearly without much light. But her tunneler's vision discerned a meandering line of disturbed earth running at changing angles to her position. The far end stretched toward where the Bumblehive would be, disappearing through a clump of greasewood. Nearer to Cassie, it simply ended. The authorities were digging trenches to lay pipes, like the Chief had said. No one was working at this hour but a couple of Dowser cops patrolled lazily, kicking at unseen pebbles or nightlife as they shuffled along.

The brushland in this area was dry and Cassie couldn't understand why the Dowsers bothered extending a finger this way. Then a cloud shifted and the topography became clearer. The trench intersected a tiny streambed and one or more further east. When they ran, the streams probably flowed to the lake—and to the downstream farms. The Dowsers were trying to collect the water while it was cleaner and closer to their data fortress. Interfering with their lines would be noticed. But she thought her promise would work. Threading underground tubes upstream of one of the intersections would let the farmers extract small amounts of water before it reached the Dowser pipes. The placement of a guidance beacon like the one she had planted in the bioswale for Gray didn't even have to be as precise here. And it would be easy to cover up in the soft soil. Excited by her brilliance, Cassie memorized a few features of the landscape to mark a decent spot and started scooting backward down the hill.

A foot on her back stopped her cold. "Stay down," a voice commanded. Cassie felt something sharp against the back of her head as a man knelt beside her and grabbed her wrist. She squirmed but he repeated, "I'll kill you here if you make me. Give me your other wrist." She obeyed. He strapped her wrists together and nudged her stomach with his boot. "Roll over."

She did and found herself staring up at a Dowser cop. The ones back home were often dressed in faded uniforms but this man almost passed for a federal marshal. There was an insignia on his shoulder that she didn't recognize.

"You're trespassing on federal land," he said, shining a thin light in her face.

"I- I'm sorry, I didn't know, I was—"

"You were spying. Who for?"

"No, I'm lost, I—"

"Get up."

She did.

"Lost from where?"

That was a question she didn't know how to answer without betraying either the Transcendents or the Chief. She had no idea what a plausible answer in this region would be. Her hesitation was enough for the officer.

"Walk." He prodded her with his rifle.

"Where are you taking me?"

"Walk."

He fell in behind her. Cassie twisted her face in rage and screamed silently at herself for being so stupid. She didn't know the punishment for trespassing but she knew it for water thieving once they identified her, which would take two seconds at the Bumblehive with all its supposed technowizardry. She considered making a stand while it was still one-on-one. Given her straits, she might have risked it with a regular Dowser cop, but this one had a gun and the air of someone much better trained.

Snap. Swoosh. Rifff.... Cassie heard the Dowser let out an "unnngh" and drop to the ground. She whirled around, heart pounding.

Clementine stood in his place. She held a knife dripping with blood. Cassie looked down. The Dowser jerked a couple of times, his begging eyes fixed on her before darting wildly and extinguishing. His leg jolted once more in death.

Cassie flashed to Teddy lying on the ground at the hang-out after Waldo stabbed him. But Teddy had been viscerally alive, fighting for his life. This man was unsuspecting prey who twitched his last in front of her. Waldo's knife thrust had been impassioned. Clementine's was clinical.

As was her gaze when Cassie looked up again. "Where did you come from?" A whisper was all Cassie could muster.

Clementine regarded her for another long moment before she answered. "I was walking, practicing—" she pointed the glistening knife at her prosthetic leg "—and saw you leave camp. I followed."

"Why?"

"I don't know. I…took an interest. I saw you talk your way into a farmhouse. I was curious so I waited. Then you came this way so I followed some more."

"You killed him…to save me."

"Once in, never out." Clementine wiped the blade on the Dowser's clothes and started going through his pockets.

The all-too-familiar phrase cracked the spell. "What does that even mean?" Cassie cried, blood finally flowing to her limbs. She suddenly had to pee very badly.

"Shh." Clementine stood and began striding quickly south. Cassie hurried to keep up. "It's a promise," Clementine whispered. She glanced at Cassie. "And a warning."

Cassie's blood re-froze. *Had Clementine heard her conversation with the farmer? Seen what Cassie brought as a gift? Guessed at her intentions?*

Clementine continued, "My first month with the Transcendents, I saw them bring a distraught man in front of the elders. They judged him, then one of them—a person like David, at that time—marched this man a few hundred meters from the road. He was crying. He carried nothing, no ration, no drop. He walked into the dunes. There was nothing for miles. Probably he died. I asked what he had done. They told me he was a deserter."

Clementine finished her story. They walked in silence for a while.

"What about the dead Dowser?" Cassie finally asked.

"That's my problem," Clementine said. "I killed him."

"Will you tell the elders what I was doing?"

Clementine broke her stride and faced Cassie. She was the most intimidating person Cassie had ever met. More than any of the smuggler bosses, more than David. Cassie half-expected that knife at her own neck. Instead, Clementine simply said, "You're not ready to desert."

Cassie fumbled for a response, torn between deceit and defiance. "I—"

Clementine cut her off with brutal honesty. "It's not an insult. Only the truth."

CHAPTER 21
CLEMENTINE & SHADOW

NORMAL PROTOCOL WOULD have been to confess to the secret-keeper first but Clementine understood the stakes. She bypassed his ghoulish glowworm emporium and went straight to Dahlia. Once the elders were gathered—plus Shadow, whom Clementine did not tell but Meskit brought anyway—Clementine announced that she had killed the Dowser soldier. Harv dispatched David and Shadow to handle the body. The rest waited silently for them to return with a report. Clementine scrutinized each of their faces for a long while: meditative Harv, calculating Dahlia, kind Meskit, impatient Lake, stalwart Gypsum, and Tesla, fingers typing down the other palm as if they were working out a cascading code.

She looked up when David reappeared. Shadow trailed him. He shot Clementine an uneasy look and went to one knee outside the semi-circle around her to watch and wait. She cracked and smiled reassuringly at him before resuming a stony demeanor.

"No alarm," David said flatly. "We should be good for the day."

"But?" asked Harv, sensing the incomplete thought.

"Move up the raid. Do it tonight before they notice," David answered.

Doubt rustled through the circle. "Are we ready?" Lake spoke for them all.

Tesla computed mentally. "It's not ideal. But if we have to…we can be."

Lake turned to Clementine. "What were you even doing near the Bumblehive by yourself?"

Clementine felt the heat of their stares. The simplest answer was the truth. She had followed Cassandra out of camp to a farm then to the data center's perimeter. She had killed the soldier to save the girl. Something stopped her from telling them, though. She had spoken honestly when she said Cassandra couldn't survive expulsion but she didn't feel moved by mercy. Nor did she see her young self in the ingénue—the thought repulsed her. What it boiled down to was that Clementine was sick and tired of justifying herself.

"Were you test-running the prosthetic, making sure you had things in hand before the raid?" Dahlia asked. Clementine looked at her. Dahlia was trying to be helpful. But that way lay pity. Clementine said nothing.

"Well, that's understandable, in a way," Harv offered, grateful for the out. "Our proscription is on needless killing, but need was upon us soon at any rate. If this soldier threatened your life, necessary self-defense is not wholly reproachable. You're a valuable Warrior and we can't fault you entirely for doing yourself today what we would ask of you tomorrow."

"Was that it?" Meskit asked hopefully.

"If you're asking if I had to kill him, the answer is yes,"

was all Clementine would concede. Out of the corner of her eye, she noticed Gypsum part her lips as if to speak, but no words followed. Gypsum wouldn't question her here. Many field missions together bonded them in a way even this council couldn't touch.

But Dahlia saw it, too. "There's something you're not telling us." A reflex from Shadow stoked Dahlia's suspicion. "Did something else happen on your last raid? When you were shot?"

Now the others were onto it, too. Clementine said nothing. Neither did Gypsum. "Shadow?" Harv called to him. Shadow seemed supremely uncomfortable. He didn't budge from outside the elders' circle. "We have all taken oaths," Harv reminded.

Shadow rose heavily to his feet. Clementine watched him fidget. She knew his movements like a beebot knew its hive dance. He would agonize—and he would tell them. "The convoy driver. Clementine took his life, too." He hastily added, "Out of necessity." A loyal liar. Clementine didn't hate him for it. It wouldn't be fair.

Tension rippled through the circle again. "Was it?" Harv asked Clementine.

"From what I saw from above," Gypsum spoke for her.

But Clementine had made her peace with anything but diminishing herself. "No."

"Then why?"

"Because I was angry." It was the answer she had not given Shadow way back on the plateau, right before the bounty hunter shot her. She glared around at them. "Aren't we all angry? Aren't we prepared to kill because of it? You just said so, Harv."

"I said the armed enemy, in self-defense."

"We can't be reckless," Tesla, too, objected.

"This will make it harder to keep the smugglers neutral," Dahlia mused almost to herself.

Lake knitted her brow. "A driver." The word carried weight with the Transcendents. It was a vocation they esteemed, given their lifestyle. "It's wrong."

Even David chimed in. "Coulda gotten your team killed."

"This changes things," Harv said grimly. "You admit to willfully breaking a cardinal rule. Perhaps twice. I think we have to consider your situation in a different light now."

Clementine had opened herself up to an expulsion proceeding. It was repellant that these people—whom she had literally given a limb for—should debate whether or not to ostracize her. It wasn't going to happen. Since the moment before she slit the convoy driver's throat, Clementine had decided to take responsibility. Her "situation" was her fault, her mistake made years ago when she followed Shadow into their orbit. Everything from now on would be on her terms. "Don't bother," she said. "I'm finished." She rose and stalked off between Tesla and Lake without looking at anyone, including Shadow.

〰

"I had to tell them."

Clementine didn't turn around. "I know."

Shadow came closer behind her. "Clementine, please." When she didn't stop packing her bag, he put a hand on her arm. Then she stopped. "I'm sorry," he said.

"I don't blame you." She faced him. "Really, I don't. You made it easier to do what I had to."

He eyed her pack. "Come with me a minute."

"I want to go, Shadow." Every passing second made it harder to keep her nerve.

"I have something to show you."

She let him take her hand and lead her away from the caravan toward the nearby abandoned mansions. "You can't change my mind."

"Okay."

"I hate them. The Dowsers, the Judges, marshals. But I hate the Transcendents, too."

"Because they fight by rules you don't agree with?"

"Because they believe fights like this *have* rules. Because they think they make them. But most of all because they convinced you, took you from me to fight their fight." He started to speak but Clementine continued, "You were all I had left. I lost everyone else."

"Me, too," Shadow said softly. He led her into the foyer of one of the houses and started climbing the staircase, still holding her hand.

"No." It came out harsher than she intended. "I'm sorry. I know you carry that pain but it's not the same. You lost them in war in your country. This wasn't my country. Isn't my country. It was like...being stranded on a desert island. Until I found you."

They reached the landing. "If we succeed, maybe you can find them again. Go to Haiti. Bring your sister here when we fix things." He squeezed her hand. "Don't give up hope. Don't give up on me."

Clementine searched for words to make him understand as he drew her over a threshold into a bedroom. He had already cleared it of debris and cleaned it of bugs and mildew and found sheets that had been wrapped in nylon to spread on the mattress. Had made them a tiny bubble against the entropy outside.

In spite of everything, Clementine felt her insides unwind. She leaned against him, then into him, their foreheads pressed together, fingers intertwined. She stepped toward the bed. Neither spoke a word while they made love. Their hands and lips and tongues spoke what was needed, tender, rough, injured, forgiving, as they moved over each other's curves and heat and scarred places. Only when they lay spent and sweaty did she caress his cheek, kiss him for a long minute, and say, "We can stay here."

"A little longer, then—"

"I mean stay. Let the caravan go on." She giggled. "We can live here." She propped herself up on her elbow, serious again. She stroked his cheek. "Or come with me now. You and I, like it was once. This cult, their suicide mission, it isn't you."

Shadow stared at the ceiling. "It's more the old me than you know. I can't take the way things are anymore. Maybe it is suicide. But something has to break even if it's me."

"The old you...." He rarely spoke of the time before they met. "I don't understand," she heard herself complain. She needed to understand.

Shadow was quiet for a minute. He seemed to be weighing something. Then he reached for his pants and pulled something from the pocket. He turned to her and opened his palm. On it lay a tarnished silver ring, not round on the outside but angled. One of the resulting facets was green. An emerald, or else a good imitation of one. He held it out to her until she took it, raising it above their heads so the sunlight through the window caught the jewel. She looked back at him. His dark eyes plumbed hers.

Clementine was flummoxed. They had been partners for a long time. No one ever spoke of marriage. It was irrelevant to their lives, an anachronism. Was this a proposal of love? Or an attempt to control her actions? "You- you're—"

"Look." He pointed at the inscription inside the ring.

"E pluribus unum."

"It used to be on our physical money."

"I know." It was stamped on the coins fashioned into the weapon she used on the convoy driver. "It sounds like Transcendent b.s."

He shook his head. "It's not. I don't know, maybe, a lot of things morphed into their smorgasbord of religious kitsch. But to those of us who fought…back then, it meant something real. A broken promise that had to be restored. And a promise to each other."

She drew in a sharp breath as suspicion dawned. There were rumors about tokens that marked the revolutionary inner circle during the war. How many years and she never guessed? "What's your real name?" she whispered.

"It doesn't matter. That man is dead." His tone grew bitter. "We failed. I failed. I know you, and I, and Truck and Gypsum and the others give more to these people than we get. But they let us be part of something bigger, something that maybe has a chance at changing things." His voice became almost inaudible. "At fixing some of our mistakes."

Her face scrunched. "A failure is not always a mistake." When he didn't reply, lost in a thought she knew he wouldn't share, she continued, "You said a promise to each other. How many others with rings like this?"

He was silent for a moment. A fly buzzed in through the broken window. Entropy would resume its course in this room once the magic wore off. "Three."

"Where are they now?"

"I don't know." His voice was mechanical, like he had rehearsed distancing himself from the words. "Dead, most likely. One for sure, executed by the Judges' postwar tribunal. I lost track of the other two when the marshals were mopping up after they crushed us. I only survived because the caravans were forming and one of the leaders took me in and hid me."

"Harv."

He didn't answer but she finally understood it all, including his new name. "What are you asking of me?"

"Stay. Stay with me. I'm angry, too. Fight with me. I'm not trying to control you. This ring is my heart. If you take it, I know you'll stay."

"They won't let me."

"They're jumpy because of the mission. You're off it now anyway. We'll find a way to explain when things settle down afterwards."

Clementine felt resentment seep back into her blood. "To a philosopher and a- a tinkerer and a cook who spends her day plucking the wings from insects?"

Shadow kissed her and slid out of the bed to pull on his clothes. "I have to get ready." He kissed her again.

She held out the ring. "Here."

"I gave it to you."

"I—"

"Hold onto it until I'm back." He was at the doorway before she could protest further. "We'll figure everything out then." He disappeared.

Alone, Clementine slipped the ring onto her finger and held it to the light again. Their lovemaking still filled the room. Shadow had created a cocoon of normalcy in this place. It was an illusion. She loved him but love bowed to self-preservation. He wouldn't change and she wouldn't stay. To the hope he had left lingering in the dusty air, she responded softly: "Adyeu."

≈

Shadow looked around at the small team assembled to raid the data hive. Tesla and Castle would perform the technical operation with three Warrior escorts: Shadow leading, David deferring to his stealth experience, and Meskit substituting for Clementine. Meskit was a good friend, welcome and trusted, but no one could replace Clementine by Shadow's side. For a while, she had been drifting away. Recently, she was pulling away, ever harder, and pulling him apart. He had convinced her to stay for now, at the cost of dredging up and exposing regrets and what-ifs from that other life he once had. Tomorrow, he would have to find a way to heal the rift between her and the elders if he was going to remain devoted to both.

"Shadow? With us?"

He blinked. "Yeah. Sorry. Go ahead."

Tesla nodded. "Okay. As you all know, our target houses whateverbytes of data scooped up from drones, chips, and your standard electronics like holophones. And it's getting worse. Rumor is R&D is close to cracking a technique to apply targeted magnetic fields that could induce and measure state changes between ortho- and paramagnetic H_2O."

"Ortho what?" Meskit asked.

"The spooks could monitor every sip and slosh in a human body. Big Brother on a seriously subatomic level."

Shadow didn't quite follow the science, either, but he knew that this escalation in surveillance was why the Transcendents had a chance at winning over the smugglers. As for the enemy, he wondered if the Dowsers realized that such pinpointed technology could render them obsolete from the point of view of the Judges.

"The point is," Castle clarified, "too many eyes in the sky and who knows where else is a problem when we reach the Fence."

"Right," Tesla nodded again. "So the objective tonight is to install a sleeper rootkit that can evade scans or storage dump detection 'til then."

"So how do we get in?" Meskit asked. "Did we ever get someone on the inside?"

That had been the plan. The Transcendents' tentacular reach often let them compromise insiders. But, "No," Shadow replied. "We couldn't. The workforce is strictly Easterners. Vetted and flown in and out for six-month tours. They're sequestered the whole time."

"Which doesn't make them immune to temptation," Tesla chimed in. "The rootkit's dropper rides in on a Trojan horse."

Shadow cringed inwardly. With the cat out of the bag, he had told the elders that the marshals were after Clementine. The run-in with one back in Kanab was serious enough to be reported to Salt Lake for the Saints leaders to resolve directly with the feds. So, although those leaders forbade the Transcendents to enter, Castle had snuck in posing as an unaffiliated merchant. There, he had let drop a chip with Clementine's biostats where it would be quickly found and taken to the

Bumblehive. The data were fake but it still made Shadow uncomfortable to use her this way. The others insisted it was sweeter bait than their original plan, though.

Tesla was still speaking: "…and once some analyst plugs it in, the chip will ping. They should think it's trying to locate Clementine's medimplant—"

"Hopefully they won't realize we never use those," Castle added.

"By the time they even might, I'll have piggybacked a loader in reverse using a modded Blue Pill protoc—"

Shadow cut Tesla off. "We'll get control over their system from the outside. A shadow computer."

Tesla was too giddy to resist correcting him. "Actually, a virtual hypervisor. Think of it like a non-shadow cast by the sun at noon, in the tropics, on the solstice. Virtually unde-tectable. It sits there waiting until I execute a kill function on it that tricks the real computer into stroking out, too, long enough for me to knock out their tracking systems."

"Gives us th'element of surprise on D-Day," David summarized.

"Now we—" Shadow indicated himself, David, and Meskit "have to get them—" he pointed at Tesla and Castle "—inside the center's EM barrier and buy time to set this all up."

"Plus make a wormhole in the barrier so the kill switch works later," Tesla said.

"Plus I ain't lugging the gear myself and you make a good mule," Castle ribbed Meskit.

"Plus get these geeks back out 'cause if they die we're screwed on the B-side," Shadow teased with a genuine smile. He was relaxing into the familiar rhythm as game time approached and anticipation limbered up his mind and muscles. The others joined in his laughter, except for Meskit, who seemed preoccupied. Shadow put a reassuring hand on his friend's shoulder and looked him in the eye. "I know you didn't expect to be going in. You good?"

Meskit shook off his nerves and nodded. "All good."

"Good." Shadow thumped Meskit's shoulder and addressed the team. "Let's do it."

CHAPTER 22
CASSIE

CASSIE'S WAIT WAS less nerve-wracking than she expected. Sierra said the caravan might have to launch quickly so there was plenty of work to occupy her for a few hours. Afterwards, she wiped down and spread her bedroll on the ground beside her home-truck.

She didn't sleep, though. Her resettlement was so close she could taste it. She wanted to be ready to send a message home as soon as she joined the Chief's commune. Her tussle with Castle had convinced her that digital was out of the question so she was going analog. She had bartered her dinner to a taciturn Transcendent who gave her a sheet of imported straw paper in return, and begged a vial of sumac ink and nib pen from Dahlia.

She sat on the bedroll and carefully sketched lines from memory. Slowly, the sculpture Teddy gave her took shape on the page: the faceted sphere (shaded by diluting the ink with her saliva), the raised fist, the slash of water. The hard part was putting its dimensions into perspective. She reminded herself that it didn't have to be art. It was a code. She didn't dare write anything that might endanger her or Inma, who might be under surveillance. But if a messenger could take this image to Mariah or maybe Teddy, they would know it came from her and where to find her.

While she drew, a smile kept crowding her frown of concentration. Meskit would be back soon. He had promised her when she went to ask...

"Can I talk to you about something?"

"Cassandra. Of course. What do you need?" Meskit's troubled expression instantly morphed into a grin. He had been the one to rescue her from the Dowser drone but ever since she saved Cake in Vegas he had been even friendlier, if that were possible.

"Maybe somewhere more private." She had found him coming from the elders' circle.

"Sure. How about the truck? The boys should be out scavenging fuel."

"Did something bad happen?" she asked on the way there. She tried to keep the anxiety out of her voice but she was on tenterhooks waiting to hear what happened with Clementine. "Your face a second ago—"

Meskit exhaled loudly through his nose. "Clementine...did something. It needn't worry you."

It didn't sound like Cassie was in any trouble. "Is she in trouble?"

They had reached the truck. She hopped in expertly—a far cry from her first day with them. Meskit followed. "Don't worry about it. I don't have a lot of time," he added apologetically.

Cassie bit her lip. She was about to broach a subject that could land them both in the cooker. She had chosen Meskit because of his fondness for her, which she suspected stemmed not only from what she did for Cake but also her orphaned circumstances. Ever since the twins had told her a little about their mother, she had paid close attention to how Meskit treated them. He was tough when he had to be but everything he said or did seemed tinged with guilt.

"I don't know if Viper or Cake told you, but my mom's... gone. My dad, too," she began. "I never knew them."

"Cass—"

"I know, I'm not supposed to talk about it. But that makes it worse. I- I don't have anyone. I know you all are my 'family' now but it's not the same. It doesn't feel like it's supposed to." Her voice cracked. This gambit was meant to manipulate him but genuine tears threatened to overwhelm her.

Meskit's eyes wilted. "I can't imagine," he said quietly. "I couldn't ever replace them but if you need someone—"

"I know," she wiped her eyes and smiled at him. "I didn't mean to get started on that. I wanted to explain why I need your help to...to leave."

"Leave—the caravan?"

Cassie nodded. "I know it's a huge deal, even if I haven't been here that long. I'm not worried about me so much but what they'll do to you if you help me. I know this is your home." Her voice cracked again on the last word, sincerely. She was on emotional autopilot now. "But it isn't mine. I didn't understand when I joined. I thought it was the only choice I had, that I could find a way back home after. But then—wiping my identity, and Castle telling me to forget about that place forever.... I don't have parents, not like that, but I do have a godmother, and...others I love." She stopped and looked up at him. The air inside the canvas cover was stifling. Meskit puffed his cheeks. The spicy-sweet hint of some herbal stalk he had been chewing wafted toward her.

"Cassandra," he finally spoke. "No one wants you to stay against your will. That's not what it's about. But it's dangerous out there. The Dowsers are looking for you, you're a long way from where we found you, you're—"

"A kid?" she said wearily.

"Yes. I know that sounds condescending but I only mean you haven't been around as long as someone like me. Being around a while helps." He shook his head. "Where would you even go? Nowhere's safe."

"I have a plan." Her voice was clearer now. "I found somewhere that is. But I have to do something first so the people I met will trust me."

"What people?"

"Farmers. Here, nearby. They're like you in a lot of ways, they just don't move around so much and that means I can stay and figure out how to get my godmother here. It's a life I think she can handle." She gestured around the truck to indicate what Inma definitely could not handle.

"What do these people want you to do?" Meskit asked cautiously. Cassie couldn't tell yet whether he was on board or hunting for information to shut it all down. Either way, she had to keep going.

"That thing, the uh Bumblehive—they're taking more and more water the farmers need. I told them I knew a way to sneak some of it back without the Dowsers finding out." She saw skepticism shimmer in his eye and reminded him, "I was a water thief."

She could feel his resistance crumbling on that front. However, "You can't go up there," he said sharply.

She ignored the admonition and instead described the beacon Gray had given her at the bioswale. "I already stole one from Castle." Castle trusted her near the silkworms and she had taken *advantage of him to pocket it earlier, plus a mate to put on the siphon tubing. She had stolen the latter, too, from the garden supplies, and spirited it to a hiding place in one of the nearby crumbling houses. Being an official member of the clan made it easy compared to that first day among them. Besides, everyone seemed preoccupied these days, especially hawks like David.*

Meskit scowled but Cassie was going all in on honesty to make him see how serious she was. She barreled forward. "I need a- thingy, something to sync it to the uh—"

"Receiver. Remote control," he offered wanly, catching up to speed.

"Uh huh. Tesla must have one but all that really fancy stuff is locked away." It had been a huge pain even to borrow the projector for the maglev tires. "I can't ask and I don't even know where to look exactly. And if I get caught...." She twisted her fingers and avoided his gaze. "I know it's too much. I just- I'm so close. I'll find a way to repay you. I'll bring it back—or leave it for you somewhere. I'm sorry. After how much you helped me already...." She forced herself to look him in the eye. "Will you ask for it for me?" She stared at him pleadingly. It was all on the table now.

A range of emotions flitted across Meskit's face. He landed on a grimace. "I don't know how to ask for something like that without a good explanation, either."

He wasn't going to help. Cassie was crushed. She put her head in her hands and started convulsing with exhaustion. Everything she had confessed to him was true. She had done so much herself. She only needed him to help her with this one thing.

"But," Meskit continued. Cassie looked up. Meskit's eyes betrayed his agony. His chest rose and fell with a deliberating breath. "I might be able to borrow one tonight."

He emphasized "borrow" but Cassie knew the fight was won.

Her grin was so huge, so heartfelt, that Meskit couldn't help matching it and returning the embrace when she threw her arms around him...

All there was to do now was wait for his return. He had divulged that he was going on a raid of the Bumblehive that night. He would have access to Tesla's electronic gear. He also insisted on taking the beacon and knowing where to put it so she wouldn't go there herself. Her description was so precise that he guessed she had already been there—and put two and two together concerning Clementine. Her apprehension swelled again but Meskit said Clementine was in quicker sand of her own doing and any exculpating details could wait until Cassie was gone. Then he had hugged her goodbye because as soon as he got back the caravan would make a hasty departure. That would be her window to slip away.

Cassie put the finishing touches on the sketch. With nothing left to keep her busy, the adrenaline began wearing off. She drifted into a dreamstream of the court clerk prattling on about a hologram that turned into May giving her a tattooed finger and lifting the patch over her bad eye to reveal the scarred socket of the secret-keeper who was munching potato chips at the hangout while Teddy and Waldo were hippopotamus men crashing into each other next to a lake whose surface was made of Mariah's spreading curls and her friend lifted a humongous head from underneath the water and tried to tell her something but all that came out was a squadron of Dowser drones that tangled into the shape of her trophy with Inma trapped inside while Shadow chomped her legs and Dahlia and the woman in Cassie's chip pic tore her apart by the arms....

"Hey. Hey, you awake?"

She opened her eyes. It took a second to realize she wasn't in her bedroom back home and another to realize that she wasn't hanging upside down but rather someone was standing over her head.

"What's this?" Viper was holding the sketch.

She sat up. "Nothing. Give it back."

He didn't. "You should burn it."

"What? Why?" She scrambled to her feet.

Viper looked puzzled. "I'm not sure. But- I can't remember right now. It gives me a bad feeling."

"Well, that's a good reason." Cassie grabbed it from him and rolled it up. "What are you doing here?"

"I can never sleep when Dad's out on mission."

"Where's Cake?"

"He likes to wank away his anxiety. It makes for awkward conversation."

She was wide awake now, too. The least she could do was keep him company while his dad was out risking himself for her. "Let's go for a walk. I want to see the lake at night."

〰

"So, 'Cassandra,' how did you come up with that?" he asked as they reached a colony of cattails near the water's edge.

"I don't know, it felt right. Did you pick yours standing there with them all chanting around you like that?"

"Nah, kept what they gave me."

"So how did you become 'Viper?'" she countered. It was strange that she didn't know his "real" name. Hers had always been so important to her.

He jabbed at the air and danced around her. "Boxing. Float like a...something."

"Rock?"

"Oh, well, if you don't want me to tell you."

She pushed him toward the water. "I do!"

"Okay, but seriously, let's move over there. I have no idea what lives in these reeds."

"Vipers?"

He bumped her this time, then leaped back and ran to a clear plot of dirt near the shore. She caught up.

"So tell me for real."

"It's not that interesting." He bent down and picked up a pebble. "Cake was stronger than me when we were little. So I used to bite him." He wound up and flicked his forearm. The rock skipped across the water.

"How'd you do that?"

"Pick one up. A flat one."

She did.

"Here." He stood behind her and put his hand over hers. He drew her arm back in a scything arc and then pushed it forward again. "Flick your wrist like this at the end. Keep it sideways, like you're aiming at a scorpion."

"Uh." But she got it. He moved away and she snapped the pebble into the lake. Its pale surface caught the dim moonlight enough to see it bounce once before plopping in and sinking.

"Not bad."

"How can there be so much of it?"

"The water? Flood runoff. But Dad says it's way smaller than it used to be." He skipped another pebble, more aggressively this time. "Like I said before, it's poisoned. That's why we don't eat the cattails here."

Cassie touched one and pulled back. "So you were a biter?"

"Yeah. I only had eyeteeth so it was like fang marks. My mom called me her little viper and it stuck. It's a joke. Everyone's pretty much laughing at me every time they say my name."

Cassie saw through the bravado. The nickname was a gift from his mom. "I like it."

He looked at her, then said, "Shh."

"What?"

"You don't hear them?"

"Who?"

But he jogged off with his ear cocked. When she caught up again, he held out a hand to stop her. "Hear them now?"

She did, a little whirring noise almost like the Dowser drone made. Viper crouched, so she did, too. "What is it?"

"Grasshoppers," he whispered.

"You're not gonna make us catch them for breakfast, are you?"

"Just this one." His arm shot out like a snake. He pulled it back with his hand cupped. "Here, open your hand." He put the critter in her palm and put his hand over hers so it wouldn't jump away. "You could have it as a snack now. Fresh."

She pushed his arm aside and stared at the insect on her skin. Maybe it felt like she did, scooped up out of its world into something totally unknown. She lowered her hand and let it hop away. She rolled back on her heels and lay on the ground looking up at the stars.

Viper lay beside her. Their pinky fingers brushed against each other. "Okay, but you're not winning any points with Lake. That's O for two in the exoskeleton food group."

"I'm gonna start hanging out with Cake instead."

Something tickled her bare foot. She squealed and kicked.

"Sorry! Sorry, it was me." He wasn't sorry. He was laughing hysterically. She punched him but laughed, too. Pals. *Or*...on an impulse, she rolled on top of him and kissed him hard. Her hand moved to the pecs she'd appreciated that day stealing fruit, then down his poky ribs and over his firm, shallow mound of belly and down some more. He squirmed but she pinned him with her hips.

As his rose to meet them, she paused. "I'm not going to have sex with you."

He blinked at her, his dark lashes meeting and parting like curtains over his big brown eyes. "Cool."

"It's just- I've had a longer relationship with a goldfish."

His eyebrows wrinkled. "You have?"

"It's an old expression. I think."

"Ah."

"Sure you're alright?"

"Definitely. Just gimme a sec—"

"We can still—"

"Oh. Good—"

"Just not—"

"I follow."

It still left plenty to discover about each other's bodies. Cassie found a spot and laughed.

"What?"

"You have a birthmark here."

"Yeah, so?"

"I was remembering when I first met you and your brother. I couldn't tell you apart."

"And now?"

"Still can't."

He pinched her.

"More research required." She did something and Viper moaned.

In stereo.

Nuts.

Cake.

They pulled apart.

"What do you want, dickweed?" Viper snarled.

Cake wasn't moaning. He was outright bawling. He plunged to the ground to clasp his brother, knocking Cassie out of the way.

"What? What is it?" Viper searched his face. One could never be sure with Cake.

Cake mumbled something hard to understand. But twin-sense made Viper shoot to his feet with a look of urgent dread. Cassie scrambled up beside him with prickling nerves.

Cake clung to Viper's shins. He got words out. "They're back."

Déjà vu came over Cassie in slow motion as if she knew what he was going to—

"Dad's dead."

PART 4

Stoikheîon (Gr.): (principal) element. The root of both metaphysical inquiry (stoichiology) and chemical measurement (stoichiometry), together the basis of thermosocial dynamics. Hydrologically, the efflorescence of water of crystallization pulverizes a mineral into salt. Biologically, dehydration dissipates the body (ultimately by decay, fossilization, etc.). Socially, the disappearance of one or more key individuals portends cataclysm (viz. secular or religious). These processes are mutual.

—Glossary of Alchemy

CHAPTER 23
INMA & TEDDY

THE TREK THROUGH the smoking forest had been treacherous. Trails wound up and down and wrapped around hills above valleys waiting to swallow anyone who slipped on a narrow pass. Day was often dark as night under a shroud of ash. When a gust of wind nudged the incessant flames in a new direction, even a vigilant traveler might not react in time to skirt them.

For all his urban survival skills, Teddy would have died without Inma, for the second time. The fires burned away the last of her cultivated meekness. She knew how to find the measliest spring or make a spile to tap a tree for water and she reminded him to use the urine filter every time he peed. The incinerated landscape harbored more life than first appeared and Inma knew what could be eaten and what indigestibles could be mixed in to make it more filling. When they reached desert, she repeated the trick in entirely different terrain, all while steering clear of places that might have more food and water but also Dowsers.

That Gray paid in kind to save Teddy's life made him

queasy. They barely knew each other. Teddy didn't ask for that ultimate favor. His gratitude was speckled with embarrassment. He avoided the subject with Inma by prying from her the tale behind her unexpected prowess. "I never knew Cassie had a ninja godmother."

Inma tested a shaky-looking splotch of pebbly dirt for stability before stepping through it. "Young people never know old ones have lives."

"Where'd you learn all this? I thought you were an office drone. No offense."

"I am. But I was something else a long time ago. Before you or Cassie were born."

"Which was—?" Teddy teetered for a second where the path narrowed to a ledge on the steep hillside. *Don't look down.* He already knew that lesson from thieving.

"You know the history."

"A fighter?"

"A lot of us were then."

"So why did you hide it? I mean, that whole kindly old aunt routine. No offense."

"What do you think the Dowsers, let alone the Judges, would do?"

"Yeah, but wasn't everyone fighting back then? They can't still be mad about it."

"The demand of peace was to put the past behind us. So I did. By then, I had a more important job to do."

Teddy looked around and thought about how far Inma had gotten him already. "Okay, but I don't think everyone who fought had skills like this. I think maybe you were a bigger deal than you're saying. In the rebellion."

Inma winced at Teddy's choice of words, then made a full squeeze of it. Her eyes were always burning from the cindered air and couldn't produce enough tears to wash themselves out. "Uprising. No," she lied. "I wasn't."

She might never have told him anything if the all-enveloping haze didn't shroud them like souls wandering the meadows of Asphodel—she conversed to confirm they were still alive. But she certainly wasn't going to tell him everything. As soon as they reached open desert, she clammed up again. And once they reached Vegas, there were other people to talk to.

It was less difficult than she had predicted to remain anonymous either at the border or in the city itself. Choppered-in tourists were scarce but the locals were nervous, causing a level of traffic unseen for decades and leaving the authorities too occupied to beat the bushes for travelers without papers. Something had happened since Inma and Teddy fled home, although it took a while to find someone willing to speak to this unlikely pair of strangers who were so scruffy and scraggly they must be either beggars and best avoided in case they were also pickpockets, or else Dowser agents in over-the-top disguise. The news, when they learned it, was that saboteurs had launched a concerted attack on several targets at once, an unheard-of act of boldness and coordination right under the nose of the Dowsers and clearly aimed at scaring off, if not maiming or killing, eastern tourists.

A crackdown was coming and it wasn't safe to stay. The trail was cold, besides. Even once Inma threw caution to the wind and inquired with more and more people, none provided a lead that sounded authentic. The best they could glean was that a Transcendent caravan had arrived in town within the right time frame and quickly left, seen heading east. That left northeast or southeast. With dread, Inma decided on the latter. It was the direction outlaws would most likely go. She tried not to think of all the kinds of outlaws: Transcendent weirdos, lawless bandits, organized smugglers, and, worst of all, traffickers—she buried the thought—of all kinds.

She spent one of the chips on which she'd squirreled away funds to buy provisions and another to hitch a ride with a peddler family who seemed as intent as she was to avoid encounters with authority on the road. Along the way, they heard the same story of haphazard but seemingly coordinated acts of revolt in the towns they passed through (or, preferably, by). Then the towns ceased.

Inma wanted to keep heading south but their ride wouldn't go anywhere near the Phoenix ghostopolis. If the evildoers who haunted its husk didn't enslave you, you'd be picked up—or off—by the patrolling drones that filled in where the natural mountainous barrier petered out. They drove into Tonto and there the family pitched up with friends of theirs who had staked out a plot near a pond. Inma and Teddy were on their own again.

She was torn. She was determined to check out Phoenix and face the worst if necessary. But she was loath to risk Teddy's so recently saved life to do so. Yet he couldn't be persuaded to stay behind and wait. In the end, she decided it was better to hang together. He had a right to this quest, too, if not as great a one as she.

On foot once again, they exited the wilderness and almost immediately came upon what would have been suburbs when such a thing existed. The low-slung, grey, wind-whipped homes might as well have been built five hundred years ago as fifty.

Trouble found them soon after they passed an outcropping of gigantic boulders dotted with smaller ones, as if imitating budding cacti. It came in the form of a posse of hard-bitten outlaws. Inma had the sense to walk straight into their clutches rather than try to run.

"This one," a turbaned woman pinched Teddy's chin and snarled, "can work." She pinched something else. "Maybe night work." Teddy glanced nervously at Inma but she kept her expression blank.

"This one's old," a man missing half an ear said, pulling Inma's dust mask from her face.

She squinted at him. "Coming from a man who looks like he bounced Moses on his knee."

The outlaws exclaimed a grab bag of misinformed slurs on the subject of genitals. Teddy gasped at Inma's brazenness. But Inma's eyes were twinkling.

The man she insulted side-eyed her. He started shaking his head. Then his body. Soon he was laughing full throated. "As the river flows," he said almost to himself. Then to her: "You don't exist anymore."

"And yet," Inma shrugged, her own smile growing on her face.

"This is a story I want to hear."

"Maybe over a meal?" she suggested hopefully.

"Gang," the man turned to his companions, "this here is a true endling—the last of a kind. She and her...son?"

"Uh huh," Inma said noncommittally. Best to be cautious, even if Axel was an old friend of sorts.

"They're our guests," Axel announced. "I shall explain shortly."

The woman let go of Teddy's arm grudgingly. He stepped closer to Inma.

A bit later, over dinner in an abandoned squat within sight of the downtown skyline, Inma and Axel revealed to the others that they had been companions in the war. With a mix of regret and pride, she noticed Teddy and Axel's companions absorb the respect he showed her and realize that she had been his superior. Inma was careful not to let Axel spill too many personal details, though, even if many references were to people and places Teddy would never have heard of.

When the story ended, Inma licked her lips and looked out at the fandango sky. Some of the skyscrapers in the distance were missing chunks, as if titans had stooped and taken a bite. So much for the old days. She braced herself. "Axel, I'm here because I'm looking for someone."

Her friend nodded. She wasn't the first. Most left disappointed, if they left at all.

"A girl, about his age." She nodded toward Teddy. "She was picked up by Transcendents and they might have come down this way. Or they might have...sold her to someone who did."

"Hm." Axel thought for a moment. "Whenabouts?"

She tried to reconstruct the timeline for him as accurately as possible. She choked up describing Cassie's physical attributes, remembering the girl on the cusp of womanhood and what a joy that was, as well as what a terrible risk it might pose in the wrong circumstances.

Axel looked around at his gang. They all shook their heads. "No one like that's come through. Or been brought through. We would know. Nothing comes down from the north side without us on top of it."

Inma gauged him. She had always trusted Axel but then again, it had been a long time. He was engaged in other activities now—she had been trying hard not to think about them because she needed him and because she felt partly responsible in the grand scheme—and might not tell her the truth. Even if he was honest, he might be lying to comfort her. "Do you promise me?"

Axel took out his pocketknife. He sliced a gash in his arm. "If I'm lying, may I lose it."

Inma blanched. That display of loyalty, that was an old thing, an unexpected thing. A liar wouldn't casually rehabilitate it. Neither would someone moved simply by charity. Impulsively, she leaned forward and hugged him. "Thank you," she whispered, fifteen years of pent-up disenchantment dissolving for an instant in their embrace.

The news left one route open: to make their way back north. Inma didn't want to lose precious time retracing their steps. But the road northeastward posed two obstacles. One was the military base at Flagstaff, which was the major drone control center for the Southwest. The other was the Navajo Nation. Axel mapped out how to skirt to the south of the former. They would have to chance the latter on their own.

≈

Chance brought them face-to-face with a Navajo officer not many miles into his territory. Inma had tried to stay discreetly in the scrubland rather than walk close to the road but she didn't know this land and worried that following the crow's path would lead them into pitfalls. Apparently, the officer didn't mind offroading his truck to catch up with a couple of unidentified nomads. Equally apparently, he did it often, because the truck was badly banged up.

"Perhaps I can escort you whence you came," he offered cheerfully when the dust from his tires settled.

"We're just passing through." Inma kept her head down and kept walking. Teddy followed.

"That's the thing." The officer released the brake to roll alongside them. "I can't let you do that." He pulled ahead and in front of them to make the point.

Inma walked up to the passenger window and looked straight at him. "Look, sir—"

"Siláo," he said and pointed to a tag: "Lee Toby."

"Siláo Toby, it's a very long story but so far a Judge, hangman, wildfires, Dowsers, and cutthroats haven't stopped me. Us." She pointed back at Teddy, who had decided to let her do her thing. "With all due respect, this boy and I are going north and the only way to do it is by crossing your land. I apologize but believe me, we have no interest in tarrying here."

"Tarrying, eh?" Lee scratched his cheek. "You might 'tarry' quite a while if you try to walk another couple miles without a clue where to find water and no one 't'll sell you any."

"Then maybe you can escort us to your northern border. Save everybody the hassle of dead bodies and guilty consciences."

Lee chuckled. "Why would I feel guilty?"

"I see." Inma put her hand to her nose to catch a drop of sweat. Tears would be next. She was on the verge. "Officer Toby—I assume that's the title you told me—I—we—have been trekking many days in search of someone we love. A child, sir. The Transcendents took her and the last clue we had was in Vegas. They could be anywhere now, given how those people operate, and I will do *anything*—" she glared threateningly "—to continue on our way unmolested."

"Transcendents." It was more a comment to himself than a question. "They're up to something, but I don't see what they would want with a stranger child." He glanced at Teddy as he said the last word. "Alright," he grumbled. "I got my own. I don't want to have to think about beetles picking over your bones. Get in."

Inma climbed into the middle seat and motioned Teddy to follow. "North?"

"North. I'll leave you at the Twins. There's a canteen under the seat there, boy."

No one talked much at first as they joggled along. Eventually, however, Lee broke the silence. "My cousin's one of those travelers. They're not bad people. She was headed to the same place you said to meet up with her caravan. So maybe that's where your girl is. Or was. They don't stay long in one place."

"That's why we're aiming east of it. Do you have any idea where they were going next?"

Lee shook his head. "She wouldn't tell me and I wouldn't ask."

Inma looked down at her hands in her lap.

Lee sighed. "Something's afoot, though."

"People are revolting against the Dowsers," Teddy spoke for the first time. Inma shot him a warning look.

"That could be it."

"The Transcendents don't cause that kind of trouble," Inma countered.

"Well, I don't know," Lee demurred. "It's always the quiet ones, don't people say."

"You think it's coordinated?"

"Could be. Could be. My native nose tells me war is in the air. Haha."

Inma wasn't sure how to read his sarcasm. Some tribes had reasserted sovereignty because the feds were unequipped to maintain the same footprint as earlier, which wasn't to say they hadn't suffered like everyone else. She didn't know how this man would view another uprising. "Let's hope it doesn't come to that." Silently, she thought: *only the senseless would fight again.*

Lee swerved as a jackrabbit sprang across the road. "Hope springs eternal. Unlike what we really need."

They continued the rest of the way without speaking until he dropped them off on the Utah side and waved off their thank yous. "You save those up. I have a feeling it's a long road ahead still and not many friends to shorten it," he said.

But soon luck struck again. Inma and Teddy came across a Transcendent caravan camped by a back road. They shouted for Cassie until a middle-aged man came to them. "We take new names," he explained grumpily. "Whoever you're looking for wouldn't answer to an old one. You're exposing her by using it. Best if you're on your way."

His secretiveness burned Inma's cool. "I'm not leaving without her. You can't just kidnap a child! Let us in or I'll be back with a marshal to make you." As soon as the empty threat left her mouth, she expected him to kill her and Teddy on the spot.

Instead, the man took pity. "We don't kidnap. There's no strangers new-come to this clan. Not a young one, for sure. Maybe she's with another but our hospitality expires. Most likely she was set on her way almost as soon as she found them." As a casual afterthought, he added, "Unless she tested."

"Tested?"

"And was initiated."

Inma had never considered that possibility before. Much as she distrusted this cult, it was something, if little more than tumbleweed, to hold onto in the otherwise purchaseless wilderness. "I'm sorry. Thank you." As he turned to go, she called out, "You must talk to the other groups sometimes, right?"

"We're not a relay server for outsiders."

"No- I understand. But if you hear of a sixteen-ye—"

"Stop! I can't hear this description."

"What about mine? You've seen me. I'm from Los Angeles." She saw his eye twitch the tiniest amount. "Please, if you know something—"

"I don't. But…" he sighed. Inma was sincerely looking her puppiest. The man finished his thought quickly, whispering, "Another caravan sent an unusual signal that way not long ago. Head north and you might catch them coming east from the salt lake. They won't take the old highways. That's all I'll say. Now leave." He hurried back into the thicket of vehicles.

Inma grabbed Teddy's arm and rushed away from the encampment. "It's her," she said. "It has to be."

"Where is she?" Teddy asked.

"That way." Inma pointed north. "Two, three hundred miles." She braced herself. So near, and yet.

〜

Teddy tightly held the chip containing the beggarly remains of Inma's cash stash. She might be the expert in everything else but water acquisition was his domain. Their drinking supply exhausted, they had found this makeshift market between tiny, nondescript mining towns that dotted the Old Spanish Trail. As smugglers came down with fresh liquid plunder from the nearby mountain, they drew scattered residents who had the funds or something else desirable to barter.

He shifted his feet to the familiar rhythm of the crowd's bovine restlessness. Jockeying for position and fraying tempers were normal behavior in the city markets, too. So was the fear of being turned away, the smugglers abruptly closing the tap, or being robbed on the way in—or worse, on the way out.

What shocked him, however, was the open political talk. A woman with a shaved head and scarred wrists cursed the Dowsers and Judges at ever greater volume. Others laughed and egged her on to preach it while cruelly calling her a crazy bat.

"You're all full of it," a man in a cowboy hat too holey to hold a gallon said. "Knowin' the law's out there's the only thing keeps those traders shellin' out the drip."

"No, old man, it's the money does that," someone called out.

The cowboy spat. "Money's polite. They could take our money and keep the water on top. Like the rustlers who jump you on the way home. Smugglers don't 'cause the system works and it works 'cause the lawmen and watermen confabulate to keep it that way."

"Judges're okay, maybe," a short young woman carrying a lidded bucket on her head said. "But Dowsers, they twist the tap left, right, left like a bit in the mouth."

"Other way around," a man wearing a shirt missing its sleeves and a smile missing its molars jumped in. "Dowsers come from our own kind. They're just trying to sort it all straight. The lawmen're outsiders. Imperialists."

"They both deserve what they're getting. Heard fourteen killed in San Jose four days ago." A bunch of cheers went up.

"How'd you hear anything out of Cali—"

Teddy stopped listening. Having newly escaped a noose by the skin of his teeth, traitorous talk jiggled his bladder.

K'hww. A gunshot echoed off the mountain. Teddy nearly pissed himself for real. Someone shouted "Rustlers!" The crowd broke like a panicked herd to escape the robbers. The attackers, though, came in full force and cinched everyone in a horseshoe up against the cliff wall. They weren't rustlers, after all, but Dowser cops on foot and, sprinkled among them, marshals on motorcycles. A raid.

"Inma…" Teddy trailed off.

She gripped his arm and led him deeper into the crowd, which was balling up defensively. "They'll only confiscate the water and scatter us. When I say so, we run."

"Okay." He trusted her.

They waited for their chance. Sometimes, at home, the cops would dump out a pail to make a point and rough someone up to make another. But now, while the Dowsers disarmed the guards and went for the smugglers' tanker, the marshals pulled up a bus and began pushing everyone onto it. Teddy and Inma were funneled inexorably to its door.

"Where are you taking us?" "We're buyin' a ration, no more." "Please…" the people around them pleaded.

"Shut up." A marshal pointed to a drone hovering nearby, recording everything. "We got it all. You're going to Topacio."

What was that? Teddy looked frantically to Inma. She shook her head "I don't know" and clamped his arm tighter as a marshal shoved them onto the bus.

CHAPTER 24
CASSIE

CASSIE HAD NUMBLY stopped counting days but it must have taken weeks to round back past the south side of the lake and then wind gently northeastward. The Transcendents were in a hurry to get away yet avoided the highway further south because it was still in use. Instead, they followed back roads, roads behind those roads, and offroads, where the occasional resident they encountered honored a code of mutual invisibility.

The caravan's composition was changing. A few people fell away on missions Cassie wasn't privy to and were sometimes replaced by people in the vein of David and Shadow. Vehicles that couldn't handle the mountains ahead were ditched. Cassie's work for Sierra intensified proportionately with the demands placed on the remaining transports. She learned how to replace a solenoid, jerry-rig a sensor, and repair a busted nanoconductive panel to optimal efficiency.

Range extension was the heaviest task. Just as the Transcendents eschewed auto-navi-chaining off a human lead driver in order to evade tracking, they avoided re-powering en route even where the roadway was still electrified. Sometimes, Castle could jam potential intercepts long enough to get a boost but it bought scant minutes to charge a few vehicles before the EM bubble itself might draw attention. Therefore, Sierra and Cassie were constantly attaching and detaching portable high-frequency generators to different vehicles and aligning the coils with those on the power-plant trucks so they could transfer charging energy. The worst part ought to have been collecting biofuel for the power plants but Cassie had practice from the pit back home.

Home. The thought was indelibly stained with guilt. No amount of work could stop her spiral of shame and remorse. Because Cassie had so singlemindedly, selfishly pined for home, she had allowed herself to be caught by the soldier, whom Clementine killed to save her, which led to Clementine's departure, which made Meskit volunteer for the Bumblehive mission where, trying to fulfill Cassie's fantasy of "home," he had stumbled onto a pulse mine.

Shadow had returned to camp that night long after David, Tesla, and Castle. He carried Meskit's body slumped over his shoulder. It took a while for information to reach Cassie piecemeal. Everything had gone according to plan inside the Bumblehive. On the way back out through the surrounding security zone, the team had spotted Dowser soldiers like the one Clementine killed. Stealth was critical so rather than engage they had split up. Shadow had teamed with Meskit to draw the soldiers away. Somehow those two had been separated as well. Eventually, Shadow found Meskit hiding in a long ditch. As Meskit moved to meet him, Shadow's detector went off. Too late, Shadow called out for him to stop. The mine detonated.

People said that Shadow was tormented because he was the one who sent Meskit off the planned route, and that Tesla was perplexed because Meskit shouldn't have been carrying any electronics at that point: the mine, a seizure-inducing pulser laid to fend off local malcontents or the merely curious, should have been fatal only if something on Meskit's body amplified its energy.

No one else could piece it together fully. Only Cassie knew it was her plan that killed him. Her first instinct was to flee. To where, she had no idea. Meskit's failure burned her ticket to join the farmers. That thought triggered her first pang of guilt and an urge to confess. She was halfway to the secret-keeper's yurt when bile scorched her esophagus. She ducked behind a bush and dry heaved until whatever words she meant to say mingled with the acid spittle in the dirt.

Dahlia found her there. Mistaking the cause of Cassie's anguish, she patted her back soothingly and, an arm around her shoulder, walked with her toward the elders' circle. They had to be on their way as quickly as possible, which meant they had to hurry through the Transcendent funeral rites.

First, there was the draining to take the precious water from Meskit's body. It was laid on a table on a platform high enough for everyone to witness. Dahlia inserted needles in various points until blood and fluid flowed through tubes into bags. Cassie retched and wanted to look away but Viper and Cake were intently watching, as was everyone else. Sierra saw her hesitation and whispered to her that to look was to honor Meskit's life and this last sacrifice. Understanding that last part more deeply than any of them knew, Cassie forced herself to watch. All the while, various Transcendents took turns recounting memories of Meskit's qualities and exploits.

Next, Shadow, David, and a few others lifted Meskit into a casket-sized chamber they brought from one of the vehicles. Cassie had never seen it before. It seemed like it was made of metal, although the outside was paneled or painted to look like oakwood. They sealed it and Dahlia worked its buttons. This was the disappearance. Over the continuing eulogies, Sierra explained that, inside the casket, Meskit's corpse was being acoustically disintegrated. The process was biochemically similar to cremation but ecologically sounder. This phase was even more important because only by evaporating the water trapped in his cells could they reclaim most of that which made a living person bloom. The water would be filtrated, purified, and used but it was also symbolically vital. The way Sierra spoke it was hard to tell which counted more.

Finally came the dispersal. Harv delivered last respects to their fallen comrade. When silence fell, without unsealing the chamber, Dahlia pulled a small inornate box from beneath it. She called forward the orphaned twins and handed it to them. Their voices steeled against the unbearable, the boys spoke the leader's lines of prayer in unison while the rest of the clan tearfully responded: *Ash to ash / so let us live / as water transpires / so I transcend.* They walked to the edge of the crowd and emptied the box into the wind, the particles of their father scattering westward into adumbral gloom as a lick of pink spread over the eastern sky.

Afterwards, time resumed at a quickened tempo as everyone packed and rolled out. Viper clutched Cassie's hand and wouldn't let go. No one, not even Dahlia, objected when she rode in the truck with him and Cake instead of with Sierra. He cried on her shoulder the whole journey to the next stop.

Every tear that touched her burned with his grievously misplaced trust.

$$\approx$$

After that first night, however, Viper had withdrawn from her. Cake, before he slipped deeper into his own personal weirdness, explained that Viper blamed himself. "He was having fun with you while Dad was getting zapped to death." There was nothing accusatory in Cake's voice, not toward her. But how Cassie wanted there to be. If only they would scream at her, rage at her, she could accept that flogging as penance.

But they didn't. And the moment to confess had passed somehow. She was afraid for herself but more afraid that knowing why Meskit really died would destroy the twins completely. This way, they believed it was for the greater good. They could share that bond with Shadow who, having lost both Meskit and Clementine, had taken up residence with them. They became a glum trio that stuck to themselves, or rather each to himself. Cassie returned to Sierra's hometruck and didn't ride with them again.

The one exception occurred for a few hours one night near what counted as the Colorado border for anyone who still kept track of such things. Shadow said the most words he had ever said to her: "Come with me."

She followed him to a borrowed car. Viper and Cake sat bundled up in the back. "What's going on?" she asked Shadow.

"Secret-keeper said you need this, too." Shadow got in the driver's seat.

Cassie climbed into the passenger seat. She turned around. "Hey." Neither answered but Viper at least met her eyes and nodded once. Cake stared at…whatever recess of his mind he usually stared into.

Shadow pulled away from the caravan and drove through the desert. Nobody spoke until he parked far enough away from a crumbling building to keep the car out of sight. There wasn't anyone else around, though. He got out and led the others with a beam of light. "Watch it," he warned. Rusting metal, jagged stones, and glass shards littered the floor.

"What is this?" Viper asked impatiently.

"A quarry."

Cassie tasted metal in the air, not sharp and hot like the metal she worked with daily, but musty and cold. It made her feel even more forlorn.

"You brought us here for rocks?" Viper persisted.

Shadow seemed about to berate him but didn't. He raised the light, shining it against a steep rockwall and sweeping it until he hit upon something.

"Whoa," Cake couldn't help exclaiming. "Is that…"

"Dinosaur fossil," Shadow confirmed. His light panned across the facade. There were more. Many more. Embedded everywhere in the rock face.

Legs, arms, pelvises—and skulls and even near-whole beasts that twisted and tucked in suspended animation. They leapt in the torchlight, cave paintings in motion, more awake now than they'd be in daylight. Cassie thought they might squeeze out of the rock, crack their necks, and lumber into the night to reconquer the world.

The wall was pocked in places as if hacked with a pickaxe. Shadow moved the light across the shambles of broken displays and toppled pedestals. "There used to be more," Shadow said. "Government took 'em for 'safekeeping.' More likely sold to rich people to put on their walls."

"They grind them up to eat, like they could become them." Viper's voice still had a petulant edge to it but his eyes were fixed on the wall, as mesmerized as Cassie and Cake.

She watched her bereaved friends gaze at the awesome sight. Cake reached out a tentative finger to stroke the ghosted tooth of some fearsome carnivore. Viper was looking all around and above as if this aeonic yawn in the earth might explain his father's death to him. Or maybe Cassie was projecting her own bewilderment.

She stepped closer to him. They hadn't said a word more than "hey" to each other in days. But now their puffs of breath intermingled in the frigid air. This place made her feel small and boundless at the same time. Knowing that she didn't matter at all in the cosmic scheme of things made her feel infinite. It gave her the strength to tell him the truth he deserved to know.

But Viper spoke first. "Dad was a builder. Before the war. When they were still trying to build houses that would work. He didn't do any Tesla stuff. Just actual building, he said, things the robots couldn't do." He paused and sniffed, maybe from the cold air. "He used to make these tiny models from scrap—tires you couldn't patch, rusty nails, whatever was past salvage. 'Which one are we gonna live in?' he'd ask, make a game of it, tease us about who'd get the bigger bedroom. That's all he wanted when this was over. To give us a home we didn't have to pick up and move every day." He swallowed. "I've thought a lot about who killed him—"

"Viper—"

"—and you know what it doesn't matter. The soldier or

whoever planted the mine. Or said where to. Or made it. I mean, I do hate all of them." Cassie winced at his vehemence, feeling her resolve dissipate as he went on. "I'd strangle them with my bare hands, I would do that. But they're like…ants. So are we." He pointed at the graveyard of splayed bones. "Stuck, stupid, helpless. We'll all die and it won't matter because it won't change anything." He stopped and looked at her with terrifying hopelessness. And something else. "Thank you."

"For what?"

"I know I've been—whatever. Quiet. I don't know how long it'll take me to…or if I.…" One hand scratched his scalp in frustration. "Just thank you." His other pinky brushed hers like it had that fateful night, then he abruptly turned and walked toward the entrance.

Cassie exhaled. Had she stopped breathing? His gratitude—and that desolate look—had pinned her in place. She no longer felt infinite. The feeling of responsibility she had felt for Teddy surged through her anew. It reacted with the disgrace that churned her insides, boiling until it all melted and cooled to a sharp and righteous lust for vengeance. The fault for Meskit's death was hers but it was also—more so—someone else's. What happened to him as he tried to help her, to Teddy, Bridget, Gray, so many others, and very nearly to Cassie herself on the calamitous night that her path crossed with Meskit's in the first place—what greater proof of the vicious cycle?—was someone else's doing. And she would make them pay: the Dowsers, the Judges, the marshals, all of them.

The next day, Cassie asked Sierra to ink the image from her sketch into her skin. The tattoo would be a reminder and a pledge. Sierra was reluctant, even frightened, which was a new look on her tigery face. She refused to do the large shoulder one Cassie proposed. Cassie wore her down to a small, inconspicuous tattoo behind the ear by promising to keep it covered by her hair. The pain drilling into her skull cemented her vow. When it was done, Cassie burned the paper. She would be her own message now.

CHAPTER 25
INMA & TEDDY

TOPACIO TURNED OUT to be a camp in the middle of the desert, which could have been anywhere else in the desert as far as Teddy could tell. This place, however, was cordoned by a chain link fence and patrolled by women and men who could only be described as irregular troops. Not quite marshals but not run-of-the-mill Dowser city cops, either. Something paramilitary in between. Inside the fence, hundreds of people sat or lay on the dusty ground, waiting.

Teddy had been waiting there with Inma for weeks. Each was allotted a mylar blanket for the night, a morning and evening ration, and two daily trips to the trench latrine. Scant shelter from the sun was a first-come-first-serve, free-for-all situation.

No one told them what they were waiting for. No one asked for their papers. Hardly anyone spoke at all except two competing doomsayers. One railed against the Dowsers and Judges alike. The other was the toothless man whose outspokenness at the water market had helped trigger the dragnet. He was still at it, preaching pro-Dowser propaganda against the Judges. He took beatings from the guards but the brutality seemed to trigger enough tender sympathy from a fellow inmate or two that he continued taking lumps for the cause.

At last, one of the meaner-looking guards stomped through the camp and yanked Teddy to his feet. "Come on."

Inma sprang up. "Where are you taking us?"

The guard pushed her to the ground. "Him. Not you."

"I'm coming, too," she insisted.

The guard pressed a dirty boot into Inma's stomach. "Not you."

"It's cool," Teddy lied as the guard shoved him forward, "I'll be right back."

He was marched to the edge of the camp to a canopy that was welcome relief after days in the sun. Beneath it sat a man with excellent hair and teeth. He seemed vaguely familiar. The man nodded at the guard, who left them alone. Then he flashed those teeth at Teddy. "Have a seat." He pointed at the folding chair beside him.

Teddy did.

"Drink?" The man offered him a cup of water.

Despite his initial determination to hold out for justice or at a minimum information, Teddy took it. He gulped it all at once. It poured down his throat into his belly like cool fluorescent light.

"Theodore Bergson," the man said. "It was difficult to find you."

Teddy froze.

"A drone got an image in Arizona but we lost track again for a while. Luckily, you were snagged in this roundup and a sharp-eyed agent holo'ed me your pic."

Teddy looked to one side, then the other, out at

the open desert. Suddenly, this shady spot was making him claustrophobic.

"Don't worry, I'm not one of them," the man tossed his head toward a couple of marshals standing at a distance and monitoring the lesser guards. He jutted his profile at Teddy. "You don't recognize me?"

"Yeah, you're uh from the tube, the, uh—"

"Owen McClarrick, Water Councilor for your home region." More of those teeth.

"—Dowser," Teddy finished his sentence.

McClarrick frowned slightly. "Yes, that's the term that stuck."

Teddy swallowed. He had only ever encountered Dowser cops before, not a stuffy suit. As far as he was concerned, Judge or Dowser "Councilor" was six of one and half a dozen of the other. Especially this Dowser. He recognized the man's name now. Boss Treviño had spoken of him as a friend—right before Treviño threw Teddy to the wolves.

"There's a term that's stuck to you, too, Teddy," McClarrick went on.

Teddy curled his cheek and scratched his ear. No point in offering up anything incriminating for free.

"Hero."

Teddy blinked. "What?"

"A lot of people were watching your case. A lot of them didn't like it. Sure, the Judges have executed children before, but you're extra sympathetic. Coming from a large, poor, close-knit family—"

Teddy couldn't help snorting. His family had done nothing for him.

McClarrick smirked. "It doesn't matter what you think.

It matters what the people think. And they think you're one of them. I'll be square with you: seeing you hang was my first choice." Teddy squirmed but McClarrick waved a hand. "Not anymore. We're past the need for spectacle. You're more valuable alive now. I hear the buzz about you even around here. You defied the hangman. You're killing a marshal a day and making it rain." Seeing Teddy's disbelief, he went on, "Yeah, I don't think they realize it's *you*. Still, that's from these sorry souls under boot and barrel. Imagine what's happening in the towns and cities. They're encouraged. But their actions have triggered a crackdown. The people are still no match for the powers that be."

"Isn't that you?"

McClarrick's glibness vanished. "No," he said earnestly. "I'm tired of being caught between the Judges' jackboot and the smugglers' venality. Aren't you? But the council can bring legitimate and lasting peace."

"What does this have to do with me?"

"You are the face of something, Teddy, or would be if you showed it again." McClarrick produced a document. "I don't have the power to pardon you, but that will come in due time if we succeed. For now, this is a warrant securing your person to my custody. I will take you back home—"

"No—"

"—and protect you. They're too worried you'll become a martyr to execute you now."

"What do you get in return?"

"Your face."

"You want me to work for the Dowsers."

The incredulity in Teddy's voice must have been obvious. McClarrick leaned back. "I might have misled you earlier.

Your sabotage became an act of resistance and your disappearance became a symbol of hope. But that doesn't mean you're not a criminal. You can still die quietly." McClarrick nodded again toward the marshals. "You have two choices."

The noose had finally tightened. Even Inma couldn't help him escape a place crawling with agents, into a hostile expanse. But if their mission ended now, what about Cassie? Teddy pondered. He had learned something from the debacle with Treviño. He looked McClarrick in the eye. "I'll come with you."

McClarrick beamed.

"But I need something, too."

≋

When they took Teddy, Inma stalked the camp, harrying any guard she could find, heedless of whatever treatment she received. She got nowhere. Taking a break in the shade of a pole ceded to her by a young woman, she caught the lilt of a Transcendent's way of speaking on the wind. She followed it to find a tall man of forty or so with dreadlocks. He was hawking clothes.

"Soft and comfy," he winked, seeing her double take. He held out a long-sleeved shirt. Inma rubbed the fabric between her hands. "A hundred-percent cotton," the trader added. "Washed, mended, and ironed for your maximum luxury."

"They didn't take these from you at the gate?" she asked.

"They're barbarians, but so, too, they have rules." He grinned. "And we have ways around them."

"You travelers always manage to get by, don't you?"

He stared intently at her. "You look like you get by okay."

Something in how he said it gave her pause. She leaned closer. "It's not clothes I'm looking for."

He matched her conspiratorial tone but kept his sly expression. "Transcendence, mayhaps?"

Inma shook her head. "Something very concrete. A person."

The man leaned back. "Ah. I offer only clothes and a path."

"To death?"

He raised his eyebrows.

"I recognize your voice. You preach around this camp as if you want people to revolt. How do you think that will end when all the weapons are in the other side's hands?"

"Are they?" His smile returned. "They cannot be everywhere. We are everywhere and everywhere are we fomenting."

It confirmed what the Navajo officer had implied. The sparks of revolt they had witnessed in the past few weeks weren't haphazard. She decided not to press that issue, not trusting herself to keep her tongue. "Please, I need to find this person. I know she was taken—" she corrected herself "—taken *in* by a caravan. If you're everywhere, can you tell me where this one went? It was by the salt lake but that was weeks ago now."

His face took on the same glassy, incommunicative expression his type always did when asked for details about their members. Inma was at the end of her tether. There was only one thing left to try. With a heavy heart, she reached into a pocket sewn into the inside of her underwear. She pulled out her hand and uncupped her palm ever so slightly so that only she and he could see what it held.

"I can pay you." She suddenly became aware of the

tremendous risk in displaying an object of such value, monetary and otherwise.

It had an effect, though she wasn't yet sure what. The trader blinked rapidly a few times. Wheels were turning. He held out the sweater. "Take this as if that's what you're buying." Inma obeyed. The man plucked the price from her hand. "Tell me who you seek."

Inma described Cassie and explained everything she knew of what happened to her. When the man told her she was likely at the Fence, Inma's alarm grew exponentially. She asked why the caravan would go there. "To hit them where it hurts," came the matter-of-fact reply.

While he spoke, something prompted Inma to look more closely at the garment. She checked its size, its buttons. It was torn in more than one place, but also expertly mended. She couldn't be absolutely sure but it looked very much like the sweater she gave Cassie for her birthday. Her hands started shaking. The man squeezed them compassionately. He grinned at her surprise to feel her payment reposited into them.

McClarrick's man eventually found her near the gate of the camp, where her feet had taken her automatically. She had no hope of exiting it. And yet he gave her travel papers and a satchel and whisked her through. Teddy was already on the other side, waiting twenty yards from a helicopter, clearly scared but beaming with pride, too, at having negotiated her release. She swallowed back the warning on her tongue that he was playing with fire. It was done, and the world was already ablaze again, and he had as much right to make decisions as she'd ever had. So she simply embraced him instead. Their good-bye was cruelly short after all they had been through together. Then she was on her way, back into the desert with a ration of food, a full canteen, and her screw nut silver ring with its sapphire jewel once more pressing reassuringly into her hip with every step she took.

CHAPTER 26
CASSIE

DEEP WINTER WAS beautiful. Driving through deep winter sucked. Thankfully, the clan had built up stores of tight-woven polyester clothing of the same undyed hue as their summer hemp. Acquiring it had meant relinquishing lighter wear like Inma's sweater to the stream of Transcendent trade but it was worth it. Someone remarked offhand that the new clothes would be good camouflage. Cassie only cared that they kept her from freezing to death. And that the stockpile of preserved foods staved off protein starvation. On the bright side, snowmelt was a liquid miracle. Deep winter might be survivable.

She asked Sierra why snow wasn't the answer to the whole world's problems, west of the Fence, anyway. Sierra shrugged: they were nearing the high point of a brief, fierce winter. What Cassie saw as mountains of snow were a thin shadow of how things used to be. Just like in Utah, it had to do with the water cycle. Hotter, drier conditions below deposited more dust up high, which quickened the pace of melt, sending it down-stream too early to benefit farmers and too fast for the ancient collection systems. As summer came (sooner and sooner), evaporation claimed an ever-greater share, too. In the highest elevations—not far from where they were headed—deeper snowpack actually made things worse by blanketing the earth beneath so that it warmed, reviving frozen microbes that farted carbon and nitrogen into the atmosphere. Listening to her, Cassie began to see the mountains as sleeping giants, poked awake and rampaging uncontrollably. Sierra almost said more, something about stealing, but bit her tongue. Cassie assumed it was to avoid insulting her but she didn't care. Not about any of it, in that moment. It was too marvelous to be in the middle of a fierce winter, however brief it might prove to be.

Taking advantage of the lengthening nights, the caravan logged steady miles, reached its destination, and finally hunkered down. For the first time since Cassie joined them, the Transcendents left their vehicles and moved indoors. They chose a spot flush against a mountainside.

Cassie wasn't sure what kind of ghost town it was at first. There were a lot of cabins and empty stores and some larger buildings in varying states of disrepair. What was confusing were the huge pylons posted in lines up the mountains, some with cables still hanging between them. She had heard of old telecoms systems that used poles and wires. Back in the city there were some defunct ones, although these were much larger. She thought it was an old army base until Dahlia called it a ski resort, a term that took more explaining until Cassie understood the basic idea of riding up the mountain in a suspended bench and rocketing down it. Now that Dahlia pointed them out, she could see where the trees were thinner in strips that once formed the lanes.

Cassie bunked with her boss and some other people in a

large cabin. She had spent almost every waking minute plotting her revenge on the authorities. The problem was what to do. Sabotage was within her skill set but felt too impersonal. The sneakier skills might transfer to assassination, though. She had snuck close to dangerous people and well-guarded places many times before. *Could she take a life in cold blood?* Every time she doubted it, she thought of everyone she cared about, everyone who'd suffered because of the people in charge. When she reached Meskit, Viper, and Cake, she knew she could do it—more than once.

When and where were another challenge. She was already battened down with the Transcendents, waiting for whatever was supposed to happen next in the scheme they wouldn't share with her. She remembered learning somewhere that wars paused during winter. Maybe that's what they were doing. She'd also read a book where this warrior monk meditated on retribution until the spring thaw.

Zen wasn't really Cassie's forte. Almost immediately, she started suffering from what Cake called "cabin fever." The twins hadn't recovered much, despite the crack in Viper's shell at the boneyard. Once, she almost cheered them up with a game she invented. She had found a square piece of scrap in Sierra's junk pile and walked up the mountain as far as she could, sliding down and weaving through the trees until a protruding root tipped her over. After dusting herself off, she found more metal sheets and persuaded Viper and Cake to join her. They all trudged even higher up to catch more snow and whooped through the plunge as icy wind ripped their faces.

But when they reached the bottom, Harv was waiting with a stern reprimand. No more "sledding." He spewed a list of other restrictions on time spent outdoors and disturbances of the landscape. They couldn't chance it with overhead surveillance, he warned. The boys took the scolding hard and immediately abandoned all frivolity. They began spending even more time with Shadow and with David.

Cassie was left with the dwindling amount of vehicle repairs. The transports were tucked away. Sierra said the break was their reward for getting everyone to winter camp safely. When there was work, it was mostly from new people. Other caravans wound their way to the hideout and the later they came, the more difficulty they had on the roads. Even so, Cassie spent a lot of time lying on her bedroll, staring at the ceiling and trying to catalog ways to kill someone and escape before anyone else found out.

"I need a spare tire." It was a youthful voice.

Cassie had earned her title as assistant mechanic by now and didn't bother to turn her head. "You know what kind? If you don't know exactly what kind, go back and check before I get up."

"LT three oh five seven oh—"

"Okay okay." Cassie lugged herself off the bedroll. In the doorway stood a stalk of sinewy muscle with short strawberry blonde hair and green eyes the color of the pine needles outside. She looked about the same age as Cassie.

"Come with me." Cassie led her to the supply room. "Those specs are pretty ancient." She grabbed a patch kit. "How far?"

"I need a tire," the girl repeated emphatically.

"We'll see. How far?"

"Two miles."

"Great." Cassie steeled herself against the cold and started walking down the road. The snow cover thinned to slush and mud filled the potholes. The girl's truck had bounced in one and struck a sharp rock. Cassie started working on it.

The girl leaned against a tree. "What's your name?"

"What's yours?"

"Aspen."

"Cassandra. Where's the rest of who rides in it?"

"Up there." Aspen indicated the cabins. "No one felt like waiting around. I got short end. Won't that make it worse?"

"What?"

"That thing you're twisting into the hole. Won't that make it worse?"

"It's a reamer. It's how you do it."

Aspen chortled. "I bet it is."

It wasn't super amusing to be risking frostbite doing manual labor while being laughed at. Cassie's concentration broke. The pick slipped from her hand and slid under the truck. She went to grab it and face-planted in the muck. Aspen lost it.

Cassie was prepared to designate her a nemesis, first class, but that evening Aspen came by with a few strips of dried fruit and an extra pair of wicking socks. After that, they got along fine. Better than that, because Cassie finally had a friend again.

〰

"Do you know what they're up to?" Cassie asked. She and Aspen were sorting kindling.

"Who?"

"Them- us. Are we holing up in this place all winter?"

"Seems like it. Why?"

"Exactly. Why?"

"You have somewhere better to be?"

Cassie did—out picking off Dowsers. "Come on. The

elders from my caravan are even more paranoid than usual. I know they did something back in Utah. And everyone coming together like this. You really don't know?"

"I really don't care. One place sucks as much as the next."

"We're near the Fence, right?"

"Yeah, I guess."

Cassie wasn't getting anywhere. She tried a different approach. "Does your brother know?" Aspen still hadn't introduced them and somehow he was never in the same place they were.

"He won't tell me."

"What about me?"

"What about you what?"

"What if I ask him?"

Aspen groaned. "Fine. If it'll make you shut up about it. Let's go and you ask him." She poked Cassie in the face with the twig she was moving to the dry side of the woodpile. "But that's all you do."

"What else would I do?"

Aspen waggled the wood. "Just keep it in your pants."

They found Thorn in a downstairs room of the main hotel, hanging half-naked from an exposed beam. He was a few years older than the twins. Definitely eye candy. As she watched his muscles hoist him above the bar, Cassie understood why Aspen had kept her away from him. But that was before he spoke.

"You don't need to know," he huffed in between pull-ups after Aspen mumbled an introduction and Cassie posed the question. "You're kids."

"You have nothing to worry about," Cassie told Aspen.

"Huh?" Thorn asked.

"Nothing," Cassie answered. "But please, we're here, aren't we? I mean, all of us are here in this place, including us." She pointed at Aspen and herself. "So it does concern us."

Thorn dropped and went straight into push-ups. Aspen rolled her eyes at Cassie and mimicked stomping on his back. Cassie snickered in solidarity but she didn't mind the side show. As long as they got answers.

"No one should be training," a man testing the bulbs in thin tubular lamps said. He was older than all of them, maybe thirty-something, with a receding hairline and full lips.

"Ignore him, he's an Alchy," Thorn huffed. He was doing the push-ups one-armed now.

"I'll sweep his elbow if you want," Aspen offered to the lamp man.

He added the one in his hand to the stack beside him and pulled apart his beautiful lips. "What kind of Alchy would that make me?"

"What do you think you're prepping those for?" Thorn demanded of him.

"'Cohesion precedes and exceeds friction in seeking,'" the man answered.

"That's Alchy-speak for 'we're along for the ride,'" Thorn smirked to Cassie.

She didn't care about their spat. "Training?" It hadn't slipped past her. "Is that what you're doing? For what? Does it have to do with the Fence?" she asked excitedly. Her nebulous notion of that looming totem was the only thing that could push aside thoughts of revenge. She looked from Thorn to the lamp man. The latter merely raised his eyebrows with a laconic smile.

Thorn was sitting on the floor now, his abs straining to

hold him in a shallow V. Aspen shot a glare at Cassie, who shot it right back. "She won't leave until you answer," Aspen said. "And I'd really like to leave, so…"

"Ask. One of. Your elders. Not. My problem," Thorn puffed. He eased to his back. "Can you grab my legs and push the stretch toward me?" he asked Cassie.

"No, she cannot," Aspen said. She dragged Cassie away before Cassie could protest that she had zero interest in actually touching Thorn's sweaty shins.

♒

"'S not a children's crusade," was David's rebuff when Cassie found him. David was the likeliest of her elders to be training like Thorn. He would never have told her anything so she started keeping track of his movements. When she figured it out, she dragged Aspen with her to one of those buildings called a lodge. This one was off the beaten path, on the far edge of the resort. Like everything else, it was mostly wood outside and in.

She could see Viper and Cake inside. She cocked her head at David—the days of fearing him were past. "If they can, I can."

David frowned. "Shadow said they earned it. With blood."

Cassie lost her nerve. That was a road she didn't want to go down.

She was turning to go when Gypsum came up the path behind her. "What're they doing here?" she asked David.

"Wanna train," he replied.

She seemed unfazed. "Might as well. It's for defense, too. Not like a shoulder claw's a state secret." She walked inside.

David looked at Cassie and Aspen for a second, then

shrugged. He went in. They followed. The training took place in a room large enough to host around twenty-five pairs with space to move, four hours a day in rotation with other groups. The ceiling timbers peaked in a triangle with arched beams criss-crossing it.

That first class, he made a painful example out of her. But he was a relentless instructor with everyone. He remained as spare as ever with words but one of the adults let slip to Cassie that he had been a marshal once, which was both shocking and not. It made more sense of David's demeanor, although Cassie couldn't wrap her mind around the idea of an ex-marshal living among Transcendents.

She regretted her intrusion from the start. David began with drills every time, with the repaired windows shut to warm up the room. By the time they were learning actual moves, the stench of fifty other people filled it.

The useful parts weren't any more heartening. Cassie was terrible at hand-to-hand, worse even than some of the adults she had assumed to be soft or meek all this time on the road. She saw that her fantasy of becoming an assassin was just that, the silly daydream of a child. The first time she tried to sneak up on an official, their bodyguards would tear her to pieces. After each session, Cassie slumped and screamed silent, raging frustration that she would never atone for Meskit's death.

At first, Aspen made things worse. She was a taller, stronger sparring partner. Cassie had a water thief's agility but was more easily winded. Finally, one of the women explained that it was the altitude and showed her breathing exercises to compensate.

But things really looked up only after David made everyone watch Gypsum and Truck spar. He wanted to prove that anyone could take on anyone with the right skill set and mindset. Cassie watched Gypsum flip Truck onto his back and fake a jugular slash. It gave her hope at last. She had all winter to improve.

Less burdened, she found the rhythm. The close, tactile contact was so unlike solitary thieving but it tapped into something Cassie had missed with a new blend of pleasure and pain, anticipation and fear. She loved the suspense of circling her opponent, sending and receiving intentions charged with primal emotion before the space between them snapped kinetically and they traded blows.

She longed to feel it with Viper but he always paired with Cake, pouring their rage and grief into hurting each other as badly as possible and then retreating to lick their wounds in separate corners. Cake was finally gaining weight despite the food at hand—or because there was no way to score up here. Viper had lost the bit of padding he had when Cassie met him. They both cropped their hair. Watching them pummel each other, she thought Viper remained stronger while Cake was more volatile. But soon they blurred together like they had the very first day she woke up in their care.

Only once, Viper agreed to spar with her, because Cake had a cold and Dahlia put him on bed rest. If he, too, felt sensuality behind the menace of squaring off and the sweaty slip of flesh on flesh, he didn't show it. His eyes had lost their humor. When her strikes landed, or his did, she realized that her own muscles had hardened as well and wondered what people saw in her eyes.

〜

"So were you two a thing?" Aspen asked the next day. They

had found random pieces of a bunch of different old games in a basement and combined them to make up their own.

"Why do you say that?"

"Because you don't look at me like that when we're sparring. You don't look at anyone like that except him."

Cassie threw a small sack of gravel at a mat stamped with colored circles. "Not really. Almost. It's complicated."

"Why? Someone else?"

Cassie thought of Teddy. How unskilled compared to her now he and Waldo had been, hammering at each other what seemed like years ago, before he was stabbed. After they kissed. "I don't know. What about you?"

Aspen rolled a die. She didn't answer for a long minute. "She's dead," she finally said without emotion.

"I'm sorry," Cassie said softly. By now, she knew that everyone had a story of death. It wouldn't help to exaggerate sympathy. "What happened?"

"She wasn't one of us. She was from a town we camped near for a while. They caught her thieving." Aspen bit her thumbnail. It was the first time Cassie had seen her display a nervous tic. "At least they didn't do it in public for the tubes. I heard they were doing it that way to people in Los Angeles. Even some guy our age. How can people watch that?"

The room started to close in on Cassie. *It couldn't be, right? She was only thinking it because she had been thinking of him before Aspen said it. Right?*

Aspen was still talking. "You know, I wasn't into it at first. I went along with you because what else am I gonna do around here. But I like it. I really like it. I don't care what they say. If we're old enough to die, we're old enough to fight. Hey—you okay?"

Cassie was kneeling on the floor, staring into space. "The guy they…hanged. Do you know his name?"

"I don't know. No. Why?" Aspen bent over her, starting to look worried.

"Was it Te- was it Theodore?"

"Maybe. Uh…yeah? Could be. Bronson or something. Cass, are you from- did you know this person?"

Cassie looked up at her. "Can I tell you something? Secret."

Aspen sat across from her and took her hand. "About Los Angeles?" The taboo on talking about the past-past had weakened during the lengthy confinement.

But Cassie shook her head. "No. I know they think you and I are training out of boredom or something. Whatever they're planning to do, we're not invited. But I have my own plan." As she had gotten better at fighting, her confidence had returned. She told Aspen how she would leave the Transcendents to exact justice for Meskit and everyone else like him. Teddy now, too. It wasn't so unlike Transcendent raiders. Speaking of whom, Clementine was out there on her own. Clementine had said Cassie wasn't ready to desert. But she would be when spring came.

She finished and waited for Aspen to respond. "Okay," Aspen drawled, "assuming you could—I know you could— would you really? Kill? I mean, it's murder, even if it's one of them."

"You just told me they murdered your girlfriend."

"It's different."

"How?"

"They had a reason—they thought they had a reason."

"So do I." Cassie pulled her hand away.

"I know. But- I don't know how to explain it, it's like *you* know better. Or, two wrongs don't make a right or something."

Cassie's irritation mounted. Aspen wasn't making any sense. Why couldn't she see Cassie was right? "I do know better. My reason is better because theirs is so messed up."

Aspen picked at the molding floor and shook her head. "I don't know. My whole life I've been raised to hate that idea."

Cassie wanted to shake her, to wake her up. "The Transcendents are going to start killing. They call themselves warriors. *Wars are about killing.*"

Aspen hunched her shoulders defensively. "So all this killing you're gonna do—how exactly? I mean, who winds up dead? Or is it just go out and randomly pick off anyone who's got the wrong job?"

Cassie was stumped. She hadn't gotten that far yet but there was time. "No, I'll- it's not random…"

Aspen seized on her hesitation. "The Transcendents are trying to change the world, not make themselves feel better."

Was there a difference? Aspen was stuck in her cultish mindset. Cassie gave up and stood up. "You don't know that."

"Yeah, I do. That's the balance between Warriors and Alchemists. Where are you going?"

Cassie was at the staircase. "I need to bandage my hand before session."

"Cass—"

But Cassie was already bounding up the stairs. She was seething. She had poured her heart out only to have Aspen shoot her down. Call her out. She felt raw and angry. Humiliated. And maybe—a tiny bit—wrong.

CHAPTER 27

DAHLIA

DAHLIA RETURNED TO the small room she had to herself in the suite that now housed her medical practice. She went straight to her personal cache and retrieved a tiny tin canister. She twisted its lid, put a dab of peppermint lotion on each middle finger, and massaged her temples. She remembered the man who gave her the lotion. It was a year or so ago in the San Joaquin. He was an outsider. The caravan passed through on his lucky day because Dahlia saved his life in the nick of time. Her entire reward was this dollop of herbal remedy.

But it worked on her headaches. Her duties had increased. She was working overtime as both a physician and an elder as the caravans rolled in. The patients were a pleasure compared to her colleagues. Each caravan had played its part so far, as hers had at the Bumblehive. Some were still scattered, instigating here, lying in wait there. Others, like hers, had gathered at the mountain. The plan had been set in motion long ago but there was nothing like a face-to-face reunion to rekindle old friendships and old grievances. And nowhere like a committee to air them in excruciating detail. Warriors and Alchemists, especially, had the time and opportunity to rehash everything all over again. Dahlia didn't care. She wanted to get it over with already. But she still had to sit through the meetings.

She reversed the little circles to counterclockwise. Although she husbanded it, the peppermint was almost gone. That wouldn't matter much longer—it would be over soon, one way or another. She nudged aside the canvas covering her window and peered at a distant summit. If she wanted it to be a good way, there was still that other thing to do. She wasn't entirely confident but today was the day. She began layering up. She had to leave enough time to get down the hill and meet the driver.

Her hand was on the door knob when there was a knock from the other side. She opened it with a start. Speak of the devil.

᛭

"That's a lot of swelling," Dahlia commented, inspecting the cuts and bruises on Cassie's hands. They were in the outer room where she kept clinic. Dahlia had shed her coat and gear. She bandaged Cassie's left hand, moving quickly because she was concerned about the time. But she was also worried by these injuries. The girl had emanated defiance from the start but there was something harder in her eyes today. "What happened?"

"I'm training with David."

"You are?" Dahlia was taken aback. She liked to keep tabs on Cassie but with her workload they obviously weren't close enough.

"Don't, Dahlia," Cassie warned.

Dahlia put her hands up. "Okay." It wasn't, though. She genuinely cared about her well-being. "Let's get some ointment for this scrape." She went to search one of the bins stacked on the floor. "Can I ask why?"

"Why is everyone else?" Cassie shot back.

A fair question and not one Dahlia was prepared to answer. "Not everyone."

"You mean alchemists? The secret-keeper told me he was one, when I met you all."

Dahlia made a sour face to herself. The secret-keeper was the worst of them as far as she was concerned.

Cassie went on, "I heard another one say, um, cohesion precedes…"

"Friction." Dahlia found the iodine tincture and came back to daub Cassie's leg.

"Yeah. It means they don't like to fight?"

Dahlia thought of her committee meetings. "They like to fight, believe me."

"But not like, say, David," Cassie insisted.

"The Transcendents have always had a Warrior streak in them, too. When you roam the wastes hoovering up the dregs of society, you end up with combative types as well, I suppose."

"Even though we don't believe in killing?" It was a challenge.

Dahlia stood and changed the subject. "There. I'm afraid I'm late for something. I'll walk out with you."

As Dahlia gathered her things, Cassie persisted, "You all keep saying Warriors like it has a capital W. Same with the others."

"They're two halves of a whole. Warriors and Alchemists.

Action and consideration. One to guide the other, depending on the situation." Dahlia paused at the door and looked earnestly at Cassie. "Promise me you'll stop—" she saw Cassie balk "—or take a break. Please."

Cassie stared back with equal frankness. "The situation now—is it another war?"

Dahlia chewed her tongue. She didn't like to be the cornered one. She started walking quickly down the hall toward the staircase. "Any creature, even an Alchemist, will fight to the death if she doesn't have a choice."

She glanced over her shoulder. Cassie, following her, looked like a weight came off her shoulders. That worried Dahlia all over again. She added, "But not you. If you're training because you want to fight...." They were outside now. A gust of wind whipped through the portico. "I don't want your broken bones on my conscience. Your hands—I'd've had to cut that ring of yours off you if you were wearing it."

"No jewelry at training," Cassie said dismissively, as if that were Dahlia's point. "It's with my stuff. So which are you?"

Dahlia had been distracted for a moment. "Which am I what?"

"A Warrior or an Alchemist?"

"Oh." Dahlia blinked. Her eyes were tearing up. Winter or summer, searing air was one thing that never changed. "I only try to survive." She'd never said anything truer.

"I guess that's what I'm doing, too," Cassie rejoined and took off down the path toward the training center.

Dahlia watched her for a second, then pulled her collar higher and went the other way, toward Cassie's cabin. She really was quite late now but the detour might actually prove helpful.

≋

The driver stopped the snowcruiser across the tracks from a train depot. A row of evergreens wearing epaulets of snow stood sentinel beside it like an honor guard. Dahlia grimaced wryly: not quite that. She stepped over the tracks and longingly traced the rails past the depot with her eyes. They led to the Unity Tunnel, the only unsealed overland portal across the continental divide through which a person (with clearance) might travel. It was a lifeline—and a conduit for pacifying troops.

She entered a small guardhouse attached to the depot. Inside, a young marshal stood at attention. Dahlia had thought there would be more but the only other person was a woman sitting by the fire with her back to the door. When a draft followed Dahlia in, the woman tucked a stray blond strand beneath her hat and tugged a scarf tighter around her neck.

Dahlia coughed. "Your Honor."

"I thought you were going to stand me up." The woman—the Judge—the Chief Justice—didn't turn around.

"I'm sorry. But the delay had everything to do with me coming to see you." The woman raised an arm and beckoned Dahlia to join her near the fire. The marshal remained still as a statue but Dahlia felt his wary glare track her movements. "My colleagues begged me not to go to Denver, even," the Chief Justice continued. "What would they think if they knew I crossed to the Western Slope to meet a traveler?"

Dahlia held her hand out to shake but the Chief Justice didn't reciprocate. Dahlia saw that her fingers were curled up inside her gloves. Since the only real chair was occupied,

Dahlia swallowed her pride and sat on a low stool. "What do they think?" she asked.

"That I'm inspecting the internal border. It doesn't matter. I said they begged, not questioned. Not openly." The Chief Justice's lip curled. She sized Dahlia up. "You're not what I expected."

Dahlia raised her eyebrows. She was quite unaccustomed to being the subordinate in a conversation. She was old enough to be this woman's mother, to boot.

The Chief Justice's laugh was surprisingly mirthful. "You look like a compliance officer at an electrodialysis plant. Who knows, maybe that's where you'll end up. Say, Chicago?"

"I'm a medical doctor, Your Honor."

"My apologies—" she clearly wasn't sorry "—Doctor—"

"Dahlia is the only name I use now," Dahlia said, trying to disguise her irritation. She had to keep her eye on the prize.

"You can call me Cybil, then, so we're even." Cybil's smile was false.

They were by no means even, although Dahlia did hold an exquisite piece of leverage. "I assume I'll get a new identity?"

"That depends. I've come a long way on the strength of your promises. Forgive my skepticism. She vanished from the city without a trace. So did her guardian, by the way. You expect me to believe you found her when the Dowsers couldn't."

Dahlia blushed but held her ground. "Call it fate. Or luck. Or—" Dahlia's thoughts flashed to Gray, news of whose execution had reached her through another caravan "—ingenuity."

Cybil brushed the empty fingertips of her gloves together. "Hm. You have a holo to prove it?"

"No. I couldn't for this."

"What, then?"

Dahlia pulled a glass tube from her pocket. There was a hair inside. "DNA."

Cybil took the vial and peered at the strand. "Easy to fake."

Dahlia couldn't help snorting. "So is a holo. If we had that kind of tech on this side of the Fence—"

"The plan—" Cybil emphasized the word as if it were Dahlia's fault it failed "—was to school her properly and bring her through official channels as a judicial apprentice. You know the laws." She waved a hand around the grimy, slushy building. "This improvisation is a grave risk to my reputation and position. Even searching for her was…. To become a laughingstock would be the best-case scenario. My authority would evaporate. Not to mention the circumstances under which you propose I do this. It's not unlikely you and I both end up with a rope around the neck. I need more convincing proof."

Dahlia was prepared. "You know how we choose names."

Cybil shrugged. "Vaguely."

"She chose 'Cassandra.'"

Cybil twitched a tiny bit. For the first time, Dahlia felt the balance tilt in her favor. But Cybil pressed, "It's a famous mythological name."

"She has a picture. I think an old one of you." Dahlia had been mulling the similarity between the young woman in the chip pic she spied Cassie looking at in the ambulance bus and the ruler whose holo'ed face bedeviled her dreams. The flesh-and-blood version before her confirmed her suspicion.

"Easier to fake than a holo," Cybil scoffed.

Dahlia had one more card up her sleeve. She reached into

her too-thin coat's pocket again. "She cherishes this. Does it mean something to you?"

Cybil seized the ring. Someone had attached it to a silken thread. She pulled off a glove to touch its cold silver edges. She rubbed her thumb over its ruby facet. Her cheeks flushed the same shade. Hastily, without even reading the inscription, she pocketed the ornament with a look that dared Dahlia to protest. Her reaction answered Dahlia's question, though. The accumulated evidence was formidable. With uncharacteristic quiescence, Cybil asked, "When will you bring her?"

Dahlia inclined her head meaningfully. "After. I'll have to improvise again."

"She won't come with you willingly?"

Even power must bend to pity, Dahlia thought with relish. "You have to understand, she doesn't know you're alive. Doesn't know you at all. She's one of us now. If I tell her, she'll despise you for what you are. I'll bring her to you but you'll have to convince her otherwise."

Dahlia held her breath while Cybil contemplated her words. Had she crossed a line? But Cybil seemed preoccupied by something else. "You know, I thought it would be thrilling to come back to this wild, white wonderland." She looked at Dahlia wearily. "But all I feel is cold."

❧

Dahlia asked to stay and watch Cybil's train glide toward the inky mouth of the tunnel. She resisted the urge to race in after it. She would have asylum, freedom, luxury soon enough.

CHAPTER 28
CASSIE

THE WAY WAS lit by the lustrous reflection of moonlight on snow. One foot filled the print in front of her. The other repeated. It had been an hour of this. With each step, a thousand others stepped with her, hundreds ahead, hundreds behind. Cassie felt the heat of the human chain threading its way through the trees, up the winding slope to...she wasn't sure what. It was New Year's Eve but even for a holiday it seemed like an extravagant expenditure of energy for the Transcendents. Despite the forest cover and their single-file stealth, perhaps folly as well.

Then she reached the summit. Even at nighttime she had a complete panoramic view.

"The Fence." Viper spoke softly near her ear, the closest to touching her since the day they sparred.

"What?"

He pointed at the chain of mountains to the east. "The Rockies." His breath smoked in the frigid air as it drifted over her shoulder.

"That's the Fence?" Her words frosted after his.

"What do they teach you in Los Angeles?" The tease was his old self but it came out hollow.

"We never talked about it," she answered, awestruck. "I thought it was, you know, sticks. Really high sticks. Maybe electric."

"A lot of it is. But that—" Viper pointed at the towering peaks "—is what keeps us in." His voice trembled. She wanted to tell him she felt the same, that she had a plan to make it right. She started to turn around—

"Move," someone barked and pushed Cassie. "Inside."

She stepped through the doors of a lodge and lost track of Viper as the crowd swept her into a vast hall. They swirled around grand tree trunk pillars and packed in, standing room only, along the walls. Some work crew had clearly spent time shoring up the place, sealing the windows and roof. The ceiling was criss-crossed with beams as big and round as the pillars. Someone jostled her and she squeezed farther into the crush.

It was dark inside, too. A handful of the congregants held thin lamps—the ones the Alchemist had been checking the day Cassie went with Aspen to ask Thorn what was going on. The lights barely penetrated the murk. It reminded Cassie of the secret-keeper's yurt.

Just when she thought the press of bodies would suffocate her, silence rippled through the assembly. Cassie craned to see why. Scattered throughout the crowd, Harv and leaders of other caravans stood on pedestals above the rest. Each held a book or scroll or—this surprised Cassie, given their general feelings on com tech—a holographic.

One of the other elders, a short woman whose beautiful red locks pierced the gloom, opened her book and began reading. Maybe it was from memory, because Cassie couldn't figure how she could see the words in the dimness. "'The mighty dismiss it as mystery,'" the woman intoned in a gravelly voice, "'while the vainglorious seek it in vain. For only a whole people united will find it. Such is its charm.'" She closed the book and gazed out at her audience. "So the Teacher taught of what he called the depth of the elements, the very geometry of the universe, whose charm is that of the crystal that blossoms in ignorance of our ignorance. Let us seek together."

On that cue, the room rumbled with the Transcendent catechism, a thousand voices that vibrated through the timber and to the roots of the mountain:

As friction frees the sacred element from bonds, does injustice spur the seeker from chains.

As it coheres even against gravity, so we unite even against law.

As beyond transition its crystal blossoms, beyond seeking we transcend.

Cassie had uttered the creed a dozen times by now in smaller services along the road. And she had felt the tribal synchrony bind her at her initiation. Never before had it all been amplified to this scale, though. It took her over as she spoke in unison with the others. Her mind was theirs, their bodies were hers. She caught Aspen's eye—they hadn't spoken since Aspen rebuked her plan—and held it for an instant. For that instant, Cassie understood without knowing. If she could hold onto that feeling....

The chant ended and the spell wavered. Cassie looked away. She still didn't know exactly what it meant, what they were seeking. *Death? Something else? What*, Inma's pragmatic voice in her head demanded, *was their purpose?*

It was too hard to think as the ceremony continued. Other head elders recited verses about the sacred element from Gilgamesh, Gautama, Genesis, Gibran, Le Guin. The assembly closed each with an affirmation. Each time, Cassie was swept along again until she almost grasped why they had risked so much to unite at this high place, only to be left asking: *for what purpose?*

Then Harv spoke. "Family," his intelligent eyes seemed to connect with each person in the room, "on this eve of a new year, let us reflect on the one that has past. But let us also reflect on the past era, the one in which our tribe was born. Sixteen years now." His gaze seemed to rest on Cassie. "Long enough for a generation to be born, to mature, to seek. To what end our work, our sacrifices, our belief?" *Yes,* thought Cassie, *please.* "A new year promises a new beginning," Harv continued. This year, we fulfill that promise." Cassie felt restlessness skip through the crowd.

"That's right," Harv seemed to sense it also. "The plan is in place. We have kept it hidden to shield it, though no doubt many of you who do not know have already guessed. Here, on the watershed they use to divide us, we accept the burden of bloodshed to reunite us, *all* of us, for otherwise we seek in vain. And so, in a few short days—" he pointed out the window at the range in the distance "—our army will breach the Fence and end this injustice once and for all."

Shouts of approval rose.

But so did dissent. Was Cassie the only one who'd been in the dark? Or maybe, like the man who argued with Thorn, many remained equivocal. Warriors and Alchemists—two halves of a whole—accused each other of hiding nefarious intent or backsliding on promises, of bloodlust or cowardice, of a death wish or slavish fatalism.

Eventually, Harv held up his hands until everyone was silent again. "This plan was agreed by the elders. All of them. Those of you called the Alchemists, you are our heart. Don't falter now. Those called the Warriors, you are our arm. Direct yourselves at our enemy. This is our purpose, our transcendence. Remember the reading we started with tonight." He gestured at the red-haired woman. "Plato showed the way, in it is the great charm of the universe. It can only be revealed through our wholeness, as one!" Others took up the last two words and chanted them until no one could resist, including Cassie.

❧

Cassie was too unsettled to sleep. The ritual reverberated through her, as did the questions it begged. She slipped back into the bracing air. She considered going to Dahlia but decided she needed a different kind of counsel.

The winter days were sunny but night brought an echoless promise of desolation. Until tonight. She looked up the mountain to where the ritual lodge would be if she could see it. Up there, she had looked west over everything that lay between this place and her home, then east to the Fence and whatever was beyond it.

If the secret-keeper was surprised to see her, he didn't show it. Probably, he was hosting a line after the evening's event. He gave Cassie the choice of speaking in a regular room or one outfitted like his questioning chamber. She chose the former. She wanted to see his face clearly and for him to see hers.

"You're an Alchemist, right?"

"Mm."

"Why do they call you that? I mean, that word."

"You know now about the connection between water and the universal essence."

Sort of. "It's...a spiritual thing."

"But also some believe that water can be made directly into energy and vice versa. I don't mean water simply as an input—that was demonstrated some time ago when reaching for the stars still seemed like the answer to all prayers. But...." He looked around and picked up a tiny glass jar with amber droplets rolling around in a finger's length of water, forming larger blobs, then breaking apart again. "Take oil. Oils provide energy for living organisms and for manmade technology. Living organisms are mostly water but give oil when they die. Yet oil and water do not mix. Somewhere in that cycle—some believe—lies a way to convert energy into water without the ratchet of death. If so, it might be possible to replenish our losses without the chemical—or social—byproducts that proved disastrous in the past. A frictionless universe." He smiled. "It's physical and metaphysical."

"You believe all that?"

"It's an idea."

"And the Warriors?"

"Their idea is more...purely physical. Although I suppose in the end our leader is correct that the ends converge."

Cassie processed what he was saying. It had to do with her feeling during the ceremony. And with what Aspen had tried to tell her. She couldn't quite put her finger on it yet, though.

He clocked her hesitation. "Are you trying to ask me what I think you should believe? I can't tell you."

"I'm not. It just feels like everything changed. Tonight, I mean. For everyone."

"Everything is always changing." He conceded, "Especially now."

"Will it work? Attacking the Fence. Attacking the Judges and marshals. No offense, but—" she indicated the surrounding ex-resort with its current ragtag occupants.

The secret-keeper scrunched his lips to one side. It was a strangely ordinary gesture coming from him. It pushed up his cheek so that his eye patch popped out a little and she could see the scar glisten underneath. "That depends. You are right that we cannot do it alone. Extreme deprivation is not conducive to revolution. It takes a feeling of having a little while others grab too much. The hope of our elders, I believe, is that our compatriots have recovered enough from the last war to feel the inequity of its settlement. They have taken measures to encourage it. So, fortuitously, have others. Even the Dowsers chafe against their masters."

That was too much to believe. "The Dowsers are the ones keeping everyone else down."

"Who says human beings are consistent?"

Cassie considered it. "Sometimes, I think about the Dowser who chased me the night you all found me. Her face. She hated me." She thought about how Aspen told her that Teddy had been executed. "You remember when I told you all my secrets—"

"Not all," the secret-keeper smiled.

She returned it. She liked him despite his oddity. "The one about how excited I was to apprentice to a Judge?"

"I do."

"I only kind of understood who they are then. But that's

who *I* hate now. The Fence is theirs. They come across it to control us but they'll never be the same as us."

"You talk like a true Transcendent." He sounded sad. "But Cassandra—" it sounded real for the first time in ages because he was the only one here who knew it was "—this isn't your battle. Not the actual battling."

"Harv said it's time to breach the Fence."

"But you'll be waiting here until it's over. As will I. Don't worry, there will be plenty of important work to do when we topple them. We all have our own purpose."

Cassie nodded. Again, she heard Inma's voice in her head asking about "purpose." Inma was like this man, like the Alchemists. She had gone along with the rules to keep them safe. But Cassie left safe behind a thousand miles ago. Even earlier: every time she thieved water, she had stood up to the Dowsers and Judges. What had Dahlia said? Alchemists and Warriors each took the lead when it was time. It was the Warriors' time. And yet the Alchemist prayers had moved her. Cassie had been thinking too small, too selfishly. *Two halves of a whole.* A haphazard assassin might prick the giant with a pin but a thousand soldiers could cut it down with swords. A pinprick would make her feel good. A just war would make the world—would make Inma, Mariah, Viper, all of them—safe. And Cassie had as much skin in the fight as anyone.

︀︀

"Hey."

Cassie bucked. She had been marching singlemindedly toward the main hotel. She looked to the side. She was passing Aspen's cabin. Aspen leaned against a pillar near the door. "Couldn't sleep, either?" she asked.

"No." Cassie stopped. Her anger had dissipated now that she had figured things out. Still, she was anxious to get to the lodge.

"I'm not gonna apologize," Aspen pushed off the pillar and came up to her.

"You don't—"

"And you don't have to, either. 'As one,' right?" Aspen stuck out her hand. "Good?"

Cassie clasped it. "Good."

"What's up?" Aspen asked with a nod in the direction Cassie was headed.

Cassie chipped at more of the ice between them. "I get what you were trying to tell me," she admitted. "I'm going to tell my elders I want to fight. To join the Warriors when they attack the Fence."

Aspen shrugged, or maybe hunched her shoulders against the blistering cold. "You know they won't let you."

It wouldn't be the first time she surprised the elders or vice versa. "We'll see." Cassie resumed her stride.

Aspen came after her. At Cassie's sidelong glance, she grinned, "If you can, I can."

The last of the ice fell away. Cassie bumped into Aspen playfully and raced to beat her there over the slick slush.

She had intended to find Harv, who could summon the other six if he wanted. But he wasn't in his room. Neither was Dahlia nor any of the rest, nor any elders from Aspen's caravan. A woman they passed in the hall said all the leaders were gathered in a meeting in an old restaurant building down the main street. As they approached it, however, Cassie put an arm out to hold Aspen back. There were people standing outside the doors guarding the building. The chance was slim they would let two girls in to present their demands. Instead, she led Aspen through a snowdrift shored against the side of the building.

As she'd suspected, no one watched the back entrance. They swept away the snow piled in front of it. Cassie tugged the door. It was stuck but unlocked. The two of them finally managed to yank it open. Cassie went first down the dark hall into a kitchen. Beyond a swinging door, they could hear voices. Aspen was ready to go in but Cassie motioned her down.

Among the voices, she discerned Harv, David, and the red-haired woman who read the text at the ritual. Aspen signaled that another voice was one of her elders. Cassie snuck toward the door and peeked above the ledge of its round window. Some tables had been gathered into a loose circle. The leaders sat around it. In the center hollow was another table onto which a holo projected a map. A man she didn't recognize was pointing a chip at it.

"The South Pass feint is ready to go," the man said. A stream of light emanated from the chip to draw a red line through a gap in the northern part of the mountain range. Cassie dropped her head down again to avoid being seen. She sat with her back to the door to keep listening.

"Your Oregon Trail again," a woman scoffed. "They know we know it's too heavily fortified. Why waste resources there?"

"We need the decoy to take the pressure off." That sounded like the redhead. "There's no cover in the actual southern route."

Cassie peeked again. The man with the chip painted a line across the Arizona desert. "We'll burn one way or another," he agreed.

"South Pass, then, it's settled," Cassie heard Harv say.

"What about the real attack?" the woman who had questioned that choice asked.

"C'mon." That was Lake's groan; Cassie knew it well. "We settled that, too."

"And I still say we should go for the Unity," the woman countered. "We need to force our way through in numbers."

"A frontal attack on the main tunnel would be lunacy," yet another stranger's voice chimed in. "Maybe we overpower the marshals on this side but they would seal the eastern gate. We get through that, they pick us off as we come through."

"And how do you propose we get through a water tunnel they already did seal?"

Water tunnel? A gear turned in Cassie's mind. She looked at Aspen, whose eyes went wide. But they were looking up, above Cassie, at the window in the door. It swung back. Cassie toppled and hit someone's shins. She looked up, too.

David stared down at her with his infuriatingly placid glower. "Get up." He pointed at Aspen, who crouched beneath a countertop. "You, too."

All heads swiveled as David escorted them into the meeting room. Most were unfamiliar but Cassie quickly found the ones she knew best: Lake, raising a skeptical eyebrow; Tesla, looking intrigued; Harv, perhaps a flicker of amusement crossing his taciturn expression; Gypsum, seeming unabashedly friendly; Dahlia, ready to tut-tut with maternal consternation; and—no, Meskit was no longer there, of course, to laugh and applaud her ingenuity. Shadow had taken his place. Stone-faced, he was almost as much a stranger to her as the rest of the crowd.

Before anyone else could speak, Cassie cleared her throat. She tried to resonate but it felt like she squeaked. "I'll do it."

No one reacted.

Aspen grabbed Cassie's arm. "We'll do it."

Dahlia found her tongue first. "No. Of course not." She addressed the elders. "They're children."

Shadow murmured, "Some children will fight."

"And that's a stupid decision I'd make you take back if I could," Dahlia snapped.

The table broke out in an argument. Cassie took Aspen's hand as each tried to listen to the section where her own people sat. Finally, as usual, Harv calmed them. "Aspen, Cassandra, I'm afraid—"

"She's a water thief," David interrupted. He said it so blandly that it took Cassie a moment to grasp he was arguing in her favor. The news spurred another rustle of hushed debate. Then one by one elders began speaking for their caravans. Cassie saw Dahlia's alarm grow. But she focused on Harv.

When everyone else had spoken, he took a deep breath and turned to Cassie. "Maybe it's meant to be." Dahlia rolled her eyes in exasperation. Harv held up an admonishing finger. "This task. Only this task. As soon as it's done you return. You do not step foot on the other side of the Fence."

Cassie squeezed Aspen's hand and nodded soberly despite her whomping heart. She had learned by now when to argue with these people and when to go with the flow.

CHAPTER 29
CLEMENTINE

CLEMENTINE RETCHED. ANYTHING that went down boomeranged back these days. It was just as well because not much was getting out the other way. She felt another wave coming and covered the cramp so her companions couldn't see how bad the pain was. Having mastered the prosthetic, she was earning her keep as muscle. Muscle was worthless if it kept doubling over with stomach pain.

Not for the first time, she reflected on the irony of falling in with a group of smugglers. Sometimes, she considered slitting their throats in their sleep, but they refrained from doing the same to her so she called it square. Not that they knew who she was or that she'd killed that driver. Besides, one man's death months ago was a drop in the bucket by now.

When she left the caravan and Shadow behind, Clementine went north. She had no clear plan, only vague inklings that north might get her to Canada and, if not, residents of the Bowl neither cared for nor received much outside attention, which suited her prickly, wounded mood. But the Bowl—so named for being surrounded by mountains on three sides and high desert on the fourth—was brimming over with violence. Clementine hoped she'd finally gotten away from Transcendents but they were everywhere, it seemed. Over and over in the hardscrabble towns they trundled through, Clementine saw the telltale signs of Transcendent provocation that stirred the residents to revolt and even put surreptitiously transported arms into their hands while the provocateurs melted away to repeat the trick at the next stop.

It was a remote but effective place to kindle revolution. The region was already fiercely divided and under-governed. Some places were practically oases and looked to the Judges for security and resources to keep it that way. Others were trapped in a naturally ringfenced cage of fire and flood. Once weapons and news of strife further south (the smugglers often brought it with them) were added to the mix, the Bowl exploded.

That was exactly what Clementine had never managed to make Shadow see. People like Harv were perfectly prepared to have people like that driver be killed. Only it had to happen on their timetable. Strategy, she knew Shadow would call it. But how long could strategy outrun the chaos of war? Not long, judging by events around her.

For their part, the Dowsers more often than not sat on their hands and let the marshals try their hand at whack-a-mole. The new leader of their council was a master of doublespeak, winking and nodding about calm obedience while sounding the call to defend inalienable rights (*whose, though?* was her latest question). Clandestine holos were going around with a fugitive boy water thief proclaiming Dowser solidarity with the people or some timeworn b.s. like that. Of course, none of it stopped them from policing water.

Even the smugglers were schisming. Free thinkers among them hated martial law above all else and split off to join the rebels. Some in her convoy asked Clementine to join them; even in such a short time, she had proved her worth as a fighter, especially in these harsher lands where locals weren't scared to challenge the smugglers if the price was wrong. But those were the potential allies Shadow had mentioned and she refused. Instead, she hewed to those pursuing a philosophy that, as the double-dealing Dowsers tightened the spigots to check the agitators, uncertainty would grow panic into yet more profit. That singleminded honesty struck a chord in her now that she was seeing things from the smugglers' point of view.

Besides, profit was crucial. Her daily priority was saving up her wages and sneaking off to find a doctor, nurse, or quack who could infuse her with chelation chemicals. It sickened her stomach even more to trust people who quite probably were cheating her but she had no choice. The lead poisoning symptoms Dahlia had warned her about were getting worse. Clementine didn't know any other way to cure them.

"Snow," she heard Daq call out from the ATV next to hers. He stuck out his gloved palm to catch the lightly falling flakes. Plump, tenacious Daq was a natural on the bike. He could have stuck out his tongue and both hands and still ridden circles around her.

Clementine nodded and pulled her collar tighter. If it picked up, the techs would try to catch it. For now, it was barely a dusting. She hoped it stayed that way. A short ride up the old 78 there was a town still large enough to maybe have a medic. She could discreetly ask a customer for directions, then make a plausible dinnertime excuse and check it out.

The weather held. By the time they stopped there was only a fairydust coating that lent the sagebrush an otherworldly air in the diminished light. The sparser the population, the quicker word seemed to spread. People were lined up and waiting with everything from time-etched plastic bottles to portable cisterns.

Clementine walked the line on one side, Daq on the other, making sure no one planned anything funny. Daq had warned her they might have to break up fights between people and only the occasional assault on the smugglers themselves. But lately that wasn't true, what with the proliferation of politics, anger, and guns. There was a near miss three days ago that nearly left her with a gouged-out socket like the secret-keeper.

"Four back, on your side," Daq called out.

Clementine interrupted her cursory dialogue with someone in the line and her eyes went to the spot. A man—a kid, really—was staring ahead, not with the normal jitters of impatience but a little too intently. He wasn't talking to anyone around him. As she got closer, she saw his foot tapping the ground. She frowned.

"Step out," she ordered.

"What? Why?" He turned big brown eyes on her.

"Just step out for a minute and let me look you over."

He did but took a fraction of a second too long. The muzzle came up. Clementine was already there, wrenching the rifle from his hand and knocking him in the face with its butt. She pulled the punch—he was a kid—and paid the price because instead of going down he drove his grown-up-sized body straight into her.

As she fell backwards, she heard a gunshot and Daq's signature battle grunt. Then more shots and yells. The civilians in line screamed and surged forward, either to get away from the fight or to get to the water before the dispenser shut off the tap. Someone kicked Clementine in the face.

She let it slide because the kid who tackled her was fumbling with his rifle. He tried to fire toward the tanker but the weapon jammed. Clementine took advantage of his confusion to punch him hard in the kidney and choke him down to the ground. She tied him up with standard-issue plastic wire. Then she looked around.

There were four other bodies bleeding in the dirt. All civilians, though one other had been armed as well. The rest of the crowd was gone or fleeing. The convoy guards had circled the tanker. Except for Daq, who came over to help her up.

"What do we do with him?" Clementine nudged her captive with her boot.

"Let the captain question him if he wants. Personally, I'd leave him hogtied here 'til someone who cares enough comes by." He looked more closely at her. "Let me see your face."

Clementine turned away. "It's fine. Just a knock. It'll bruise, that's all."

"Suit yourself." Daq grinned. "'D'you work up an appetite?"

They ate dinner in shifts in case anyone had the bright idea to attack again. Clementine sat on the ground next to her ATV. Daq always ate sitting on his. She was beginning to suspect he was part-centaur.

"Been thinking it's not worth it anymore," he said between bites of barley paste crunch, as the decidedly amateur cook in the crew called it.

"You told me combat pay's almost double what you used to get," she answered.

"Yeah, but so's the combat." He stared at a morsel for a second, then lowered his voice. "D'you ever think about doing something else?"

"Like what?" Clementine shook a fog off her head. It had been happening lately, although maybe this time it was from the kick she received earlier.

"Combat for a reason."

"Don't tell me you're an idealist now, Daquan."

"I'm not," he said hurriedly. "I mean, for a better reason."

"Like what?" Recycling responses to dangerous talk seemed like a good idea given her brain fuzz.

"I dunno. I was thinking family."

"You have family?"

"Don't you?"

Clementine didn't answer.

Daq went on, "Mine's south. I wouldn't mind checking up on them. If it's all going to hell, I'd rather die there than here."

Clementine still didn't respond but she thought bitterly that he had a point. Too bad it didn't matter to anyone where she died, least of all herself. She stood too quickly and took a step. Dizzy, she slipped. Daq sprang up to steady her.

"You okay?"

"It's a little icy there. From the snow, I guess."

"Uh huh."

Now was her chance. "Actually, I think I will to try to find a doc. Maybe I got concussed."

"Good idea. I'll come with."

She put a hand on his arm and smiled her most convincing smile. "No, thanks. I'm good."

Her smile turned inward to see him relent. Daq already

knew her well enough not to argue. When Clementine wanted to be alone, everyone left her alone. It was hard to be a convoy guard and not have demons, but hers hung on her like fleas on a rat.

⁂

Before the commotion at the spigot, Clementine had managed to get a name and vague directions to an old army medic long retired from the old army. The place lay beyond the end of the dirt road on the edge of town. She walked through the brush straight up to the shack and knocked.

The man who answered didn't seem scared or surprised by his visitor. He ushered her in on the spindly legs of someone aging quickly, although his straight back and the roll of his shoulders still hinted at a vet's physique.

"That's a nasty shiner you got," he said as he led her to the kitchen or, truth be told, the only real room in the place.

"That's not why I'm here."

"Oh?"

Clementine tersely explained the situation.

The medic stuck his tongue between his teeth and chewed it. "Lie on the table."

She obeyed. "You have what I need?"

He didn't answer that question. Instead, he insisted on examining her over her protests, asking frank questions about the symptoms she had taken great pains to hide these past few weeks. Finally, he shook his head and helped her sit up. "I'm sorry, miss, I can't help you."

"Where, then?"

He put a hand on her organic knee. "No one can."

The fog had rolled back in, filling the space between her synapses. "What do you mean?"

"I'm sorry, but this is too far along. No one for two hundred miles could help you. Even if you got somewhere out beyond where they could, it'll be too late. I learned in the service that you never sugarcoat a poisoned pill. You're dying, friend."

ൠ

The night was still, the streets deserted. The calm after the storm. Clementine took her time returning to camp. The snow had stopped, leaving a teasing void behind. That's what it was like all the time up here. When it rained, it flooded, and when it didn't, it taunted you. *Was this where she wanted to die?*

She made noise on the approach so as not to startle the guards.

"You're late for your shift," the woman on duty said.

Clementine didn't argue. "I'll go get Daq."

She found him curled in fetal position under a waterproof blanket. Only his eyes, nose, and spikes of black hair poked out. She shook him awake.

"'Sup?" he murmured.

"Watch shift."

"Efemefel," he groaned.

"What?"

"Coming."

She waited while the rest of him emerged from the covers. He didn't remind her of anyone she knew and yet—or maybe that was why, like the fresh-scented promise of first snowflakes—the question popped into her head and off her lips. "Hey, Daq?"

"Yeah."

"Where did you say your people were?"

His sleepy eyes lit up when he looked at her. "Colorado."

CHAPTER 30
CASSIE

CASSIE STAMPED HER feet and tried to warm up as quietly as possible behind the stand of trees. She and Aspen were waiting for a raiding squad from Aspen's clan to confirm an all-clear. There shouldn't be any maintenance crews shuttled in to check on the disused tunnel but there might still be old sensors. Once the scouts gave the signal, Cassie and Aspen would join them.

Water diversion pipes like this one criss-crossed beneath the Fence. They were the legacy of a pioneering era premised on taming everything but the appetite for expansion. Some still drained the Western Slope to feed the garrison city in the East—that's what Sierra had almost said about stealing when they first arrived at the winter camp. The Transcendent army planned to march through one large enough to speed their numbers along. But gravity and pumps ensured flowing water that could impede them. If a sudden surge came through, it would be catastrophic.

Nearby, however, was this other one, smaller, narrower, and disused. A team would crawl through, exit, disarm any guards stationed near the outlet of the main bore, and shut off its pumps so the brigade could infiltrate for the sneak attack on Denver. The problem was that obsolete tunnels were often broken, grown over, or blocked up. A Transcendent spy had gathered intelligence but had not tested its aperture. The advance team might come out into water, mud, or a wall of soil, or even end up entombed under an icy ceiling of frozen pond. That's where Cassie came in. A water thief had the skill to gauge the situation and work around it without panicking.

Of course, this water thief was a claustrophobe who hated tunnel jobs. Had sworn them out of her life forever. This would be her sixty-fifth job, divisible by thirteen, which was unlucky. Unless you counted the one with Gray, which made that the unlucky one and this a relapse. Why had she volunteered? She was glad Aspen would be with her.

Cassie stopped stomping. Now she was hot and sweating inside the water-resistant clothing someone had cooked up for them. She double-checked her gear: all the familiar implements were there. The only thing missing was her ring. She'd developed a habit of rubbing it for luck or simply comfort. But it had disappeared recently. The Transcendents lived by honor but somebody must have stolen it while she was at training. Catching them was next on her list.

The signal came. The girls removed their snowshoes and walked to the entrance of the tunnel. It lay near a creek bed patched with snow, rock, and dirt. A groove ran alongside it for a few yards before disappearing. Aspen said it was a wagon rut from way back. It was strange to think of people risking everything to come over the Fence in this direction.

They stepped forward and slipped from the open air of the wild country into the tunnel's gloomy maw. Cassie switched on the weak headlamp Tesla made for her. The tunnel was round. She felt its damp floor through her gloved hands—and knees, for its diameter wasn't large enough to stand in and they couldn't stoop the whole way through, so they crawled single file. It was lined with concrete or something similar, which made her feel a little better compared to the bosses' slapdash tunnels back home. The lining was smooth but chipped in places. Crumbled lumps of it dotted the ground. She hoped its erosion was moving at glacial speed. She breathed—not too deeply—and practiced her calming breaths. They had miles to go.

The way seemed flat but Cassie knew it sloped gently to take advantage of gravity. No one told her that; it was a thief's intuition. It meant slouching deeper beneath the mountain with every step. Way more than six feet under. She wasn't sure what physical law kept tons of rock from crushing the pipe but it all seemed quite implausible. Not to mention how old this thing must be. Or what else might be scurrying through it.

No one spoke. The air soon became asphyxiating. They each wore nose plugs connected to a central tube that extended all the way back to the tunnel entrance, where the lookouts pumped in oxygen. In through the nose, out through the mouth. Every now and then, someone's knee compressed the line and Cassie felt a hiccup of suffocation. With the walls closing in, she resisted the urge to pull out the plugs, inhale carbon dioxide, and fall into the long sleep. Or was that wrong—maybe she was thinking of a different gas. Someone ahead of her did remove the cannulas and refused to put them back. When he hyperventilated, the two nearest people restrained him and forced him to breathe from the tube. Cassie shuddered.

An eternity of hours and four miles in, they took a break. There was barely enough room to curl her back against the tunnel wall and look at something other than the butt in front of her for a change. Aspen sat beside her, pulled a snack from her pocket, and offered Cassie a bite. "You're gonna be so stoked if we end up in a reservoir," she said. Cassie had told her the fantasy of breaking through a cistern into a giant pool.

"Totally worth the hypothermia."

"Too bad we're not allowed all the way through, though. Gotta crawl aaalll the way back."

Cassie tried not to think of the literal mountain of dirt surrounding them. "Uh huh."

"What's the plan for breaking through?"

"I don't know." Cassie patted her pack. "I have a sounding tool so I can try to gauge if it's air, liquid, or solid on the other side."

Aspen was impressed. "You know how to do that?"

Cassie decided to lie for the sake of her friend's nerves. And her own. "Yeah. But I still won't know how much of whatever is there, necessarily." She sipped from her canteen. "Back home, on a tunnel job, they usually had good intel on the specs of a cistern and there was an engineer who would tell them where to dig so the thief—me—would get pretty much to the right spot. You still never knew exactly what was on the other side." She gazed up and immediately regretted it. Her voice seemed tiny when she continued. "But it was a lot smaller margin of error. You went by instinct."

"You okay?"

"Uh huh." She didn't sound convincing even to herself.

The line started to crawl again. *Only a couple more miles to go,* Cassie told herself. They felt like the longest ones of all.

The leader finally called a halt. "Thief. You're up." Cassie looked over her shoulder. Aspen nodded. Cassie squeezed past those ahead of her and slithered to the front. Her lamplight shined on a wall of dirt. Panic tingled her groin, gut, spine.

"Steady," the leader said. She put her hand on Cassie's arm and directed her lamp ahead, too. "We should be near the terminus. We might even be out of the mountain by now. There could just be an overhang above us."

"Or else they sealed it. Or a mudslide covered the entrance."

"That's what you're here for, right?" The leader turned to Cassie and blinded her with the light.

"Right." Cassie tried to sound confident.

"Okay, then." The leader helped her slip off the pack. "I'm right behind you." She slid back to give Cassie more space to work. It was a tight spot but, she reminded herself, no tighter than a thieving tunnel. *Make it small in your mind. A few square feet of world to manage, that's it.*

She took out the sounder. She had seen something similar once before, wielded by Boss Whittier's lieutenant, but never used one herself. Tesla had given it to her along with some instructions. You pressed it against a surface, making sure the level reading was at the right angle for the direction you were sounding. Cassie figured perpendicular to the tunnel floor was the right place to start, so that the sound waves would beam straight ahead toward where its entrance ought to be.

She hit a button. A ticking sound meant a wave was traveling through the dirt wall. More ticks came at intervals. Tesla had explained that with some sonar systems, you simply waited for the reflecting wave to ping back at you. But if you didn't know what you were aiming at, the succession of waves would create a chain. If, say, it was clear air for miles, then the waves would never interfere with one another. If you started with a solid like this dirt and then hit air, though, the refractions caused by the different wave speeds and intensities would generate feedback. The machine would calculate distances and, assuming its estimates of unknown variables were in the ballpark, give you a map of what you were dealing with. It was way beyond water thieving 101 or even thieving at Cassie's level, though she got the sense from Harv that he was relying on her gut feeling as much as Tesla's wizardry. Maybe more—the instrument couldn't make a judgment call.

"What the- what is she doing?" Cassie heard a fierce whisper-shout behind her. The ticking had increased. "She'll kill us all!"

"Shut up, Thorn," Aspen scolded her brother.

"No one asked you. You shouldn't even be here."

"I'm here to stop you from acting like a baby."

The leader called back, "It's the only way to figure out how to get out of here."

A rumble overhead emboldened Thorn. "If whatever's on top of us is unstable, what that girl's doing could bring it down."

"Thorn," the leader warned, "you're not an engineer."

"Is she?"

"Let her be." That was Firn. She was from Aspen's caravan. In an on-again, off-again thing with Thorn. She seemed a lot nicer than him.

Cassie tried to concentrate on the job at hand. Her hand slipped. She hoped it didn't mess up the calculations. She stared at the device's tiny holographic panel, silently willing it to project the promised 3D map. Although she wasn't sure she could read it even if it did.

Something cracked behind her. Everyone went dead silent. Something else thudded. A chorus of cursing went up.

"Holy flooding- I told you so!" Thorn shouted.

"You better hurry up," the leader hissed at Cassie. *As if she wasn't trying.* To the group, the leader called out, "This thing's ancient. We saw chunks lying around since the start. You all came this far. We have a job to do and there's no one else to do it. Steady."

Cassie kept her eyes fixed on the machine. At last, a hologram flickered to life. Tesla had tried to explain how to read its thicker and wispier patches as varying densities that corresponded to air, liquid, and solid. Down here, under all this rock and pressure, she couldn't make heads or tails of it. She wished Tesla was with her but the engineer was off jamming drones or something.

The distance reading was easier because the machine calculated it and scaled it to the tiny projection. The darkest patch—the dirt wall—wasn't thick. A few inches in it hit something else even more solid, according to a very dark line in the hologram. But that wasn't thick, either. Maybe more concrete. Beyond it was much lighter: either liquid or air. She gazed toward the upper corner of the blocked tunnel and put down the sounder.

"Got it?" the leader asked.

"Uh huh." Maybe. Time to go on intuition. If she was right, it was basically like a cistern. She pulled out a drill and aimed. What was behind the dirt didn't feel like concrete but close enough: a steel plate. Cassie punched the drill through and held her breath. A wisp of air tickled her nose.

She exhaled and put down the drill to pick up a hole saw. They needed a door big enough to shimmy through.

She put one hand on the dirt wall to steady the other. It slid a little. Water. Coming through the drill bore. She froze. If they were under water and she opened a door....

Another crack. *Thud.* The tunnel behind them was caving in. They had angered the mountain. The team started shouting at her. Thorn tried to force his way up. The leader blocked his way. Aspen yelled a word of encouragement.

There was only one option. Cassie closed her eyes. She controlled her diaphragm. She listened intently for the source of the wind and felt deftly for the source of the seeping water. Then she powered on the saw and started cutting as close to the former and as far from the latter as she could. She went wide for shoulders to fit, then curved down. The water streamed through the cut now. They weren't high enough. They were going to drown, actually drown. *Was that better than being crushed or running out of air?*

When she had gotten almost all the way around, a third crack reverberated behind her.

"It's collapsing!" came a shout. "We're trapped!"

"Everyone okay?" the leader called back.

"No!"

"Talk to me."

A howl went up, echoed instinctively by other cries of distress.

"That Firn?"

"She's crushed," Thorn wailed. "It's on her back. I can't pull her out!"

Another, louder round of swearing boomed through the amputated tunnel. Cassie worked furiously, her arms aching.

She was letting them down. They were all going to die down here because of her. The saw kept slipping. Water was gushing through the steel flap. The leader ducked underneath her and came up in front to throw her body against it. It took all her force to hold it in place while Cassie worked around her.

"Firn?" the leader called. What came back wasn't words. The leader cussed to herself and grabbed Cassie's shoulder. "Now."

She was done. But the pressure on the other side was strong. "I can't knock out the flap."

"NOW!" the leader screamed and hoisted her up, launching her at the opening. The bit of metal Cassie had cut fell back…slowly…resistant. She had only enough time to suck in a last breath through the cannulas and hold it before a rush of water smacked her in the face. The leader was pushing her legs, forcing Cassie to crawl through the door she made. But her body was now the plug in the system. She thought she was going to explode. She clawed and kicked as hard as she could.

And then she was free. As icy shock gripped her, she smiled. She did it. She was floating in a pool of water. Her wildest dream come true at last. At the last. Numbness warmed her, her body disconnecting, letting go, sinking….

Something tugged at her. Someone was yanking her out of her death dream. Her head broke the surface of a reservoir pond. She was dragged onto its muddy bank. She tried to protest: *let me go back in*. It was warm and cool and nothing mattered in there and no one would tell her what to do or chase her or blame her or love her. All that came out was a searing lungful of water.

"You're hurt." Aspen inspected Cassie's side. "You're bleeding."

Cassie tried to sit up. Aspen propped her head on her lap instead. "You did it. We're okay."

"We're not okay." Thorn's purple face loomed over her. "You—" he choked on choosing an expletive harsh enough.

"Shut up, Thorn."

"Tell her."

"Tell me what?" Talking brought on another coughing fit.

Aspen bit her lip and looked away. "Firn."

"Firn is back in there." Thorn pointed at the tunnel. His eyes filled with tears.

Cassie managed to sit up this time. The pond wasn't deep—that was probably how they managed to overcome the pressure. At one edge was a hillock. A small whirlpool on that side was, she guessed, where the water was still pouring into the opening she made in the blocked-up tunnel. She looked around. They were in a sparse forest not unlike the one on the other side. *The other side.* Miles away on the other side of the Fence. She did it. She got them through. Except..."She's...?"

"She's flooding dead, thief." Thorn crouched down beside her. His spit hit her face like daggers. "No, you know what? Probably not yet." He thrust his fingers into her shoulder, hard. "You broke her back, you suffocated her—"

"I'm sorry—" Cassie tried to say.

But Thorn kept sobbing and hitting her. "You drowned her. She's been dying for minutes, all alone, and she's going to rot in there because of you."

Aspen pushed him away. "Lay off. It was already falling apart."

Thorn stood and spat snot past Cassie's head. "Keep her away from me." He stalked off.

"I'm sorry," Cassie said again, to no one and everyone.

"It's not your fault," Aspen said.

The leader came up to them and looked down at Cassie. "Okay. You did okay. The terrain was a death trap but your aim bought enough time to get us out."

"Firn…" Cassie mumbled.

"Firn was the first casualty of the campaign. More to be expected." The leader looked over at the rest of her team. "But you should probably keep your distance." To Aspen, she added, "You know the deal. You shouldn't be on this side. Can't help that now, but the main portal's half a mile that way. Find a spot to hide. When it's safe, I'll send someone to get you."

Aspen pointed at the slice in Cassie's arm. "She needs a medic." The leader didn't say anything. She clicked her canines together rapidly a few times, thinking, then walked away.

Cassie looked at her body for the first time. Her clothes were shredded. Besides her arm, there was a nasty gash from her belly around to her back. She must have cut herself on the steel coming through. A delirious giggle burped out of her. Now she had a wound to match Teddy's. *Funny, she hadn't felt any pain. Until now. Now, it hurt like a....*

CHAPTER 31
MAELSTROM

CASSIE WOKE TO find Dahlia peering at her closely. Was she back on the other side? *No.* Even unconscious she would feel that trip. Besides, the air was somehow different here. That meant Dahlia had come through. *Dahlia—with the troops?*

"Can she walk now?" That was Aspen. *Right.* Cassie had taken too long getting them out of the tunnel and people were pissed off and left her and Aspen to wait for the cavalry. Which, apparently, was Dahlia. Searing pain knifed through her. *Oh.* Dahlia was a doctor.

"Don't try too hard, dear," Dahlia said.

Cassie realized she was scrambling to stand up. "I can't think straight."

"I gave you something for the pain. It will fog things up for a while."

"Am I…okay?"

"You're fine," Dahlia replied cheerfully. "Nothing a strong, healthy young person can't bounce back from."

"We should go." That was Aspen again. "Meet up with the others."

Dahlia straightened and looked up at Aspen. "You did your part. You're to go back through and wait until it's over."

"That's not gonna happen. Which way?"

"Those are orders, young lady," Dahlia held her ground. "Not mine. Your brother's."

"Like I've ever listened to him. Cass—"

"Coming." She tried to stand again.

"Oh no you're not." Dahlia placed a hand on her shoulder to keep her down.

"Well *you* can't stay here," Aspen protested. "If we get to the main tunnel, you two can walk back through."

"She can't yet. And I have to stay on this side. There will be casualties. You go," Dahlia said, shooing Aspen away. "I'll look after her." When Aspen still hesitated, she added, "If it makes you feel better, see if the medics can spare a transport to get us. That would be helpful."

Aspen nodded. "Right." She squatted down and kissed Cassie's cheek. "You were amazing. None of this would be happening without you. See you when we've won!"

Cassie grinned opiately and waved at Aspen's receding figure. She looked at Dahlia and mumbled, "Now what?"

Dahlia looked around the forest. "I don't think it will be entirely safe here. If we do run into anyone, they might see that pipe and realize we crossed from the other side. We should move. Hiding in plain sight might be the best thing to do. How about it? Ten more minutes, then you think you can walk? You can lean on me."

Cassie smiled again and nodded before nodding off.

≋

By the time Aspen reached the portal of the main tunnel, the forward team she and Cassie had been part of had taken out the paltry unit that manned it, shut the pumps, and sent a signal through to the Transcendent army waiting to cross under, which it was now doing in force. She found a medical team and told them where to find Cassie and Dahlia, then looked for her brother.

"Thorn."

"Hey." His eyes were puffy from mourning Firn but his expression was resolute. "Good. Where's the other one?"

"Still back there with their doctor."

"When the last of these people come through, go home."

"No flooding way. If you fight, I fight."

"I'm not arguing about this, Aspen. You're a kid."

She pointed at two boys her age passing by on their way out of the tunnel. Cassie's sort-of friends, the twins. "They're kids."

"They're not my responsibility. You are."

"I'm already here. I almost died ba—" she cut herself off with immediate regret.

But Thorn wasn't angry with her. "Exactly." He shouldered his pack, put his hands on Aspen's shoulders, and looked her square in the eye. "Look, I get it," he said with brotherly concern. "But think of it this way. There's almost no one left over there watching the fort. This thing could go torcher and the marshals and Dowsers come at us with a vengeance on our home turf. A lot of those other caravans aren't from the mountains. They won't know where to go. You can help them get out, hide, survive. It's not a kid's job." He looked over to where his squad leader was shouting orders to his mates. "I've gotta go. Promise. Do it for me, Ass." A tiny twinkle broke through as he teased her with the old nickname.

It worked. If she went to the battle, he'd worry about her, fairly or not, which could endanger him. And if she got hurt—or killed—he would have lost two people he loved in the same day. Besides, he wasn't wrong. And Cassie might show up by then and need help getting back. She nodded. "Okay."

Thorn nodded back and trotted off. She watched him go, a silent prayer on her lips, then turned to watch the troops pouring through the leak in the mountainside.

Cake saluted Aspen as they marched past her. He nudged his brother. "C's not with her."

"So?"

"Where is she?"

"How should I know?"

Cake punched him in the arm but there wasn't time to wrastle because their squad was gathering around David.

Shadow watched the twins horse around, then regain their composure as they joined him at the squad briefing. As soon as the forward team had sent the signal, Tesla fried the data center—the fruit of the Bumblehive mission what seemed aeons ago. With luck, the chaos would draw the enemy's eye away from the Fence and provide cover for the Transcendent cells that would rise up everywhere between it and the ocean.

As well as cover for the invaders crossing it. Hundreds of guerrillas might not easily conquer the frontier city but they could at least capture key assets and destroy the illusion that the Fence would keep trouble at bay in the wild West. It would force the Judges to talk rather than let the revolt burn itself out.

The others nodded along while David explained what came next. The army could only bring small vehicles like motorcycles through with them. But they had sympathizers on this side who were already pulling up with transports. The main targets were three and close by. One was the military installation to the south, near the highway that led both west to the Unity Tunnel and east to the city. A diehard band of Transcendent Warriors would tackle that suicide mission.

The second was the city itself. The least experienced fighters would fan through it sowing panic. This prong had caused the most queasiness among some of the elders. They were assuaged by a reaffirmation of the tribe's prohibition against unnecessary violence. Under no circumstances should civilians be harmed beyond what couldn't be absolutely avoided. It was a wishy-washy compromise. Shadow remembered Clementine's rebuke: this was war, and war was always total.

The third group—here the squad leaned in closer—would make straight for the courthouse. Symbols mattered. None would be more potent than raising their flag above the building that represented power and oppression. In fact, David carried one folded tightly in his pocket. A Transcendent tailor had stitched it from Castle's silk and tinged it with carefully amassed dye. One vivid color—the blue of the element of life—poured diagonally across it through the grip of a human fist. For the Warriors. In the far top corner, like a single guiding star, perched the interlocking green and blue—world and water—shapes. For the Alchemists.

If they also captured a Judge or two as a high-value prisoner, so much the better.

Shadow knew the plan because he helped develop it. He only half-listened to David as he watched the boys bounce with adrenaline. He had defended their participation because of Meskit but he was having serious doubts that this was the way to honor his fallen friend. As David led the team in a huzzah, Shadow made up his mind. This was as far as he would let them come. While the squad headed toward a nondescript van that would usher them discreetly to the city center, Shadow grabbed Cake and Viper each by the elbow. "You boys stay here. Guard the portal."

"No flooding way," Viper retorted.

They had already picked up slang from the other caravans. "Yes. What's ahead could be a one-way ticket." Shadow pointed to the tunnel entrance. "So I need you by the way back."

"You brought us here," Viper protested. "This is what we're here for. This is what Dad wan—"

"Your father wouldn't want this for you."

"You agreed."

"I was wrong."

"No, you weren't. You don't know. You didn't know him like we did." Cake was uncharacteristically vociferous.

"I knew him longer than you did. I know what he wanted for you. Stay here. It's important work. But you're not coming with us." He shoved them in the chests to make sure the point got across and jogged off to the van, where David was distributing extra weapons the sympathizers had stashed in it.

Viper, hot with anger and shame, tore off the suffocating

waterproof jacket and slammed it to the ground. He drew back a hand to punch something, anything. Cake gently stopped him. Viper turned his fury on his brother but Cake rolled his eyes and his neck with a weird look plastered on his face. Viper followed it past teams rushing around to a little tree standing alone off to the side as if it, too, was being left behind. Parked beneath it was a beat-up motorcycle. No one seemed to have claimed it yet. They rolled it out of sight, waited long enough to remain unseen, then sped toward the city behind the Warriors.

≈

Cassie jerked awake at the sound of a shot.

"Only a backfire, dear," Dahlia soothed.

Cassie shook off the daze and remembered. They were in a car, a two-seater. They had come across it outside a cabin. She had talked Dahlia through hotwiring it.

A siren dopplered back around with a piercing scream. She looked out the window. Piles of things were burning at the intersection ahead. She looked up. A swarm of drones flocked drunkenly overhead.

The siren blasted through them again. Cassie winced.

"Here." Dahlia handed her a pill. "You need to stay ahead of the pain."

Cassie looked down at her bandaged mid-section. She did hurt badly. She swallowed the pill, the bitter powder sticking to her dry palate and throat. She wanted to ask something. It was.... *To ask something about....*

As Cassie drifted off, Dahlia concentrated on maneuvering through the chaotic streets. She only hoped no one would stop them before she reached it—and there it was. The neoclassical temple came into view. The blocks around it had been razed. At each corner stood a guardhouse. Bollards shaped like miniature obelisks spiked the perimeter. On the north and south sides, almost as tall as the building itself, were statues of twin rams recumbent, one facing east, the other west.

The building was under attack already. Dahlia grew nervous. She wasn't sure how to make the connection. To buy a minute to think, she pulled into an alleyway near the southwestern corner and stopped the car.

≈

The road stayed rural for a long time, although Cake, shielding his face from the wind behind Viper's back, couldn't tell if it had always been that way or was emptier than it ought to be, like on their side of the Fence.

They passed a few homes that were aflame, their residents huddled safely but angrily outside under Transcendent guard. Further along, some of their compatriots lay siege to a building. Its occupants returned fire with gusto. Closer still to the center of town, they encountered a roadblock but Viper spoke to the Warriors manning it and they waved the bike through.

Viper didn't know exactly where to go but the courthouse had to be downtown, where homes and yards gave way to an even more spartan district. From there, he followed the sounds of battle. And then it loomed in front of them. He parked and they dismounted. Viper lowered his head and marched toward the building but Cake yanked his sleeve and pointed off to the side. Cake and his perpetual distractedness, although Viper had to admit it often led somewhere. He cast an anxious look at the battlefield, then begrudgingly followed his brother.

A rap on the passenger window startled Dahlia. A familiar grin came into view. She muttered an oath under her breath.

Cake opened the door. "What are you ladies doing here?" He helped Cassie out. "Whoa."

Dahlia hurried out from the driver's side. "What are you boys doing here?" she countered in the sternest tone she could muster. They ignored her.

Viper steadied Cassie by her shoulders. "What happened to you?"

"Twins," Cassie tittered vaguely. "With Teddy."

Viper exchanged a puzzled look with Cake. "What happened?" he asked Dahlia.

Dahlia removed his hand from Cassie. "She was injured, obviously. She'll be fine, if you don't exacerbate it. You can talk later."

"Injured where? At the tunnel? What's she doing here?" Viper was confused.

"That's my question to ask of you," Dahlia deflected.

"Shadow let us help," Cake replied. "You know that."

Dahlia turned hawkish eyes on him. "Then why aren't you with him?" She pointed toward the battle unfolding at the courthouse.

Viper followed her finger. The Transcendents had breached the perimeter. Someone lobbed a grenade that burst against a column. A crack team of marshals maintained their defensive position. He looked back at Cassie, peering earnestly into her eyes. She smiled but was out of it. "We'll talk later," he parroted, then, to Cake, "Come on."

Dahlia exhaled some of her tension seeing them go into the fray.

"I was afraid you disregarded my instruction to come alone," a voice said behind her.

Dahlia flinched but her eyes didn't leave the scene. "That looks like a real fight."

"It won't be," Cybil smirked, "thanks to your warning. We let it look that way to draw the transients deeper into the trap. The more we catch, the more we crush, and the quicker order can be restored once and for all."

Dahlia swallowed and said nothing.

"You said you'd bring her after your people attacked. How did you think we would respond? Because of you we were ready." Cybil turned her attention to the girl. "What's wrong with her?"

"I sedated her to keep her calm." Dahlia faced Cybil and added after a moment, "She's wounded."

Cybil arched an eyebrow.

"Not by me."

Cybil placed an elegant hand beneath Cassie's chin and lifted it. Dahlia saw the hand tremor. Cybil backed away and nodded to the guard behind her. He hoisted Cassie over his shoulder like a sack of seeds.

"What you promised me?" Dahlia inquired.

Cybil turned icy eyes to her. "Do you have children, Doctor?"

"Truckfuls."

"Well. I only had one. I didn't think of her for years. Then

I did. So I looked for her. And found her." Dahlia started to interject but Cybil made a motion as if snatching the words out of the air. "Exactly. Through sources. You were one, I know that. What a long game you played, waiting for your moment to pounce—"

"What?" Dahlia felt panic rising. "No! She came to me. I had no idea it was the same child, not until—"

"I admire it, truly," Cybil waved off the objection. "You stole what's mine and tried to sell it back to me. You are a gifted traitor."

"I didn't betray you, not you." Though frantic now, Dahlia's voice crumbled like chalk.

It was as if Cybil didn't hear her anyway. "Still, you did bring her to me. I'll show my gratitude by not killing you on the spot."

As all hope slipped away, Dahlia reached for her belt harness. "You promised."

Cybil followed the movement and warned her off with the slightest nod toward the guard. His free hand held a gun aimed straight at Dahlia. Cybil glanced at the courthouse, where her enemy had broken through the line but her soldiers had regained the flanks. "This will be over soon. I suggest you run while you still can."

Stunned, Dahlia turned to stare at the firefight and felt the hairs on her neck relax and knew Cybil was gone and she was entirely alone as she had not been for ages. The scene in front of her was something out of the propaganda tubes. Now that she was paying attention, she could pick out people from her own caravan.

There was Truck, the reluctant Warrior, his unmistakable bulk like a one-man siege machine.

And David, leaping, lunging, knives out, slashing through the best the Judges had to throw at him. Stopping, falling, bleeding, unmoving.

A gray-haired woman Dahlia didn't recognize ran to him, checked his pulse, and, without missing a beat, retrieved something from David's pocket. She—it was Gypsum, Dahlia realized, grayer than she remembered—strode onto the alabaster staircase between two smaller ram statues that guarded it. Her thalassic eyes flashed as she unfurled the flag to encourage her comrades.

A defiant fistful of water waved briefly between the columns of the palace of justice.

Bullets carved into Gypsum and she, too, fell.

A peculiar sensation of fellow-feeling washed over Dahlia as the magnitude of her treason hit her. She drew her weapon. She raised it, unsure whether to rush into the fray with it or turn it on herself.

The feeling passed. Either way, what would be the point? She let her arm drop. She looked around. Not far away, a fallen marshal lay in the street. Dahlia rushed to her, stripped off her coat, and swaddled herself in it. She ran back to the car and turned it around.

※

Shadow picked himself off the ground. He brushed shards of the shattered window from his hands and reached for another grenade. He was inside the building, enemy bodies lying around him. He turned to check who of his own was still with him. Not David. Not Gypsum. Not Griz. Sierra still bounded on, agile as a great cat, and solid Castle, but not many others.

Then he saw the twins, rushing through the melee toward

him. They had defied him. He was furious and proud at the same time. He shouted at them to go back but something exploded near him and muffled his cry.

He tossed the grenade to slow down the marshals filling the hallway. Half a dozen of his comrades sprang through the decimated windows. The boys, too. Shadow tried to keep an eye on them while fending off the defenders hand to hand.

He heard a scream. He knew—he had a knack for knowing what each of his soldiers would sound like in battle, though only battle called forth such sounds. He knew before he looked. One of the twins was down. *Right, twins*—he *didn't* know which fell, while the other threw himself over his brother, sheltering him, wailing.

More marshals flanked into the arcade, threatening to surround the surviving Warriors. The attack had failed. The building couldn't be taken. Shadow only hoped that the other battalions succeeded because this front was a lost cause.

He knelt beside the fallen boy. Now he knew. He checked his pulse, his youthful, peaceful face. Gone. A lost cause.

Shadow made a decision. Called out a command. Grabbed the living brother and dragged him back outside ahead of the retreating line of Transcendent fighters. He led them: Shadow, Warrior, patron saint of lost causes.

Cassie tried to call out but her mind, vision, tongue were all blurry. She'd tried to tell the man carrying her that she hated tunnels but he didn't stop so she thought maybe it was a nightmare and then they came out of the tunnel into a hallway with tall windows but then the windows exploded and there were only tall gaps and a rain of glass and a shower of humans jumping through them. And she knew one of them, his name was…Shadow. *Why was Shadow in her dream?*

Then she knew another one splayed on the ground.

Viper.

No: Cake.

No: Viper.

Agony. Relief…guilt. Despair.

Which one was it? She had to know. She hunted through soupy synapses for the way to know. Shadow dragged away the other, living, breathing, crying Viper-Cake. He resisted and the tussle scrunched his pants off his hip. That was the way. Was that the birthmark she'd kissed in the grass by the lake?

Wait! she tried to scream, to get away, to move, turn, plant, rotate, shift as David taught her but she was in mid-air and her muscles were fuzzy and Shadow didn't wait and the man carrying her didn't wait. He ducked into a doorway and suddenly it was quiet and Cassie fell deeper into her dream.

Cybil followed the guard carrying the girl into the chamber. She was breathing hard. That was a close call. The transients fought better than anticipated. She saw one of them move like—like in the old days. She forced back the thought. The present was what mattered. And the future.

Cassie's eyelids fluttered open. The dream was fading. She was lying on a bench in some kind of inner temple. Her head lay on something soft. Her eyes traced the temple columns upward. There was an inscription on the frieze they supported: "Peace Dependeth on Justice." A new dream, then. She closed her eyes again.

Cybil smoothed Cassie's hair. The long fingers of her other hand spun the ring she reclaimed from the traitor. Until that day at the train station on the far side, Cybil hadn't seen it in a very long time, or even thought of it. A relic of another life. This time around, the risk was equally great but the goals were better. Two birds killed with one stone: the restoration of order and of her family.

She gathered a strand behind Cassie's ear, uncovering a small tattoo on her neck. Cybil stared at it. Another relic. She pressed it with her thumb, covering it, hating it, herself. How could she have let it come to this mark—this permanent stain? She pressed harder. Cassie flinched. Cybil removed her finger. The skin beneath the tattoo reddened angrily. The symbol popped against it, vibrant like in the old days, as if the fist shook at her.

A homey melody surprised her on her own lips. One of those melodies passed down through an impossibly long chain of generations while other bits of culture fell away. Infinitely adaptable, from the crèche to the barracks to the sacristy, carried across continents by troubadours and mothers and conquistadors. She hadn't hummed it in ages. Not since giving it revolutionary airs and watching them evanesce. Now, here, it seemed small again, a mournful lullaby.

Cassie felt the music. She opened her eyes. The something soft her head lay on was a lap. The vibration resolved to a tune. She knew it. *Dahlia? Inma!?*

She arched her neck to see who cradled her. Her vision went astral. It cleared and she saw the ring dangling above her from another's neck. "That's mine."

The woman who wore it smiled upside down at her. A latch flipped open on the Pandora's box buried in Cassie's heart. The face was fleshed with age, wisdom, and fatigue. Yet clear in it were the same eyes that sparkled at someone unseen offscreen in the image on Cassie's old chip. The digital avatar never changed its sphinxy expression. But this face leaned down and opened its mouth.

Cybil placed a hand on Cassie's forehead and crooned softly in a voice she had only dreamed of all these years, "No, my baby girl, it's mine. And so are you."

EPILOGUE

THE PLACE HAD been practically deserted when Dahlia returned. She'd reached the portal entrance soon after the first casualties were brought in to the field hospital. Old habits died hard and she sought to avoid Aspen, who'd entrusted Cassie to her, but apparently Aspen had already gone back through the tunnel. Knowing what fate awaited anyone left on this side of the Fence, Dahlia finally, honorably, advised an evacuation. Desperate to cross back herself—how ironic, given all she had done to come this way—she accompanied the first group of walking wounded. It was a far cry from the march to battle. They slipped and slid, grabbing onto her, pulling her down, stumbling together through the tunnel and back to the camp. There, Dahlia had done what she could for them before crawling into her own bed, thinking she might never leave it again.

It dawned on her that the song in her dreams had been an appeal from her subconscious. A warning about the woman she handed the girl to, about dealing with a double-crosser. There had been a better way to use the girl—and help her, too, of course, in the bargain. Too late now.

She needed to confess. Dahlia was a woman of science.

She firmly believed the mind was a natural phenomenon. But she didn't feel equipped to tackle what ailed hers alone, not now that she understood a traitor's soul. Of all people, she needed the secret-keeper's help.

₩   ₩

The place seemed deserted but Clementine recognized the traces of her former fellows even on the approach. The lead was solid. She squeezed Daq's shoulder to let him know to continue. They'd left their ATVs miles back when she started losing control and swerving. Daq traded them in for a bike so Clementine could cling to him for dear life. She couldn't believe he did it; he practically slept on that machine. This was a friend of the kind she'd never had, not since her sister Martine. Not even Shadow.

They dismounted at the main building. It seemed as good a place to start as any. Daq helped her search the downstairs, then upstairs, opening every door. Each led to an empty room, except for one that revealed two elderly Transcendents and a terrified child looking after them. Clementine didn't recognize them. She shut the door and moved on.

She opened another door. This room had a bed. Someone was in it, wrapped in a blanket. Clementine looked around the room. Its contents seemed familiar. She stepped closer to the bed. A pair of eyes were watching her.

"You're alive."

"Dahlia. Not for long. I guess your diagnosis was spot on." Her bitter tone melted as she looked closer. Dahlia was shivering violently. Her hair was wild. Her eyes darted between Clementine, Daq, who stood behind her, and the floor. Clementine peeled back the blanket. Dahlia's clothes were covered in slick wet grime.

"I came back to..." Dahlia trailed off.

"Where is everyone?"

Dahlia rolled her eyes up past the head of the bed as if it held the answer. "Other side." She started again, "I came back to...."

"They got through." Clementine whispered it.

Dahlia nodded. "Under." Suddenly, she seemed to regain her old composure. "You're very ill, dear, I can see it."

Clementine sat beside the doctor. "And you're hypothermic. You were over there? What happened?"

Dahlia shook her head frantically and tried to pull the blanket up over her head. "I—let me—I came back—I...."

Clementine took her hands and tried to lock the older woman's eyes with her own. "Dahlia, what happened?"

"They're dead," Dahlia snapped.

"Who?"

"All of them."

Clementine swallowed. That simple act was more painful each day. She swayed. She wanted to lie down, too. Daq steadied her. She tried to find the question. "Sh- Shadow?"

"They're all dead, dear. I'm sorry." Dahlia wrenched the blanket free and covered her head. Her muffled voice came through it. "I'm sorry," she repeated. "I came back to...seek. Will you bring the secret-keeper?"

Clementine stood, swayed, and slumped into Daq's arms. "I'm okay," she said and planted her feet to prove it. She walked toward the door.

"Where are you going?"

"I have to look for some—thing," Clementine fudged the

end of the word. If what Dahlia said was true, it wasn't a who, but she didn't know what, either, only that she had to keep searching until she found it.

"Okay." Daq moved to join her.

"Stay with her, please," Clementine said, nodding at Dahlia. "I need to go alone." To the blanket she said, "If I find the secret-keeper, I'll send him."

Clementine wandered out of the lodge and crept at a snail's pace among the other buildings, pausing to catch her breath and opening doors until she found the room that had his scent about it. Not home, but the closest she would come. She smiled and lay down on the bedroll. It was time to let go of caveats like that, of being right, of the unclouded view of the void and of the solitude of reaching it before others (*before him*) and facing its eternity while they (*he, please, most especially he*) still hurtled through time toward it. Let go and be not alone anymore. She pulled Shadow's ring from her pocket and held it to the light and then closed her eyes while a girl's laughter chimed in the warm wind rustling through the mango leaves.

꙳   ꙳

The place wasn't deserted, after all. Only the slow, arduous climb on foot had spared Inma altitude sickness. Her feet were bleeding. She was out of food. Despite her fearlessness, the nights frightened her, its noises unfamiliar to a city girl. The days reminded her of the nights' peril; one morning she came across a chewed carcass not far from where she'd slept. She felt like a rescuer at the end of a failing tether that anchored her to promises made ages ago while she stretched as far as she could reach into the darkness to grab the hands of a little girl trapped somewhere in the wideness of the world.

So it came as something of a relief when someone—a child, really, about Cassie's age—accosted her brusquely at the outskirts with an order to halt on pain of death. Relief, indeed, when this Aspen confirmed that this was Cassie's last place of residence. Alarm that Cassie was on the other side of the Fence, wounded. But the child soldier reassured her that a doctor was escorting Cassie home personally.

Inma went into the ghost town and waited. She read the signs of defeat in the bedraggled remnants that trickled back from the other side. She waited some more. She'd waited this long. But she was moving most of that time. She needed to move while she waited. She moved among the defeated, helping and searching at the same time.

She heard that a captain of sorts from the caravan that took Cassie was back. She went to this Shadow's cabin. No one answered her knock. She went in anyway.

Inside, a boy Cassie's age rocked back and forth on the floor with his face twisted in pain and a guttural lament curling his lips.

Nearby, a man was on his knees, bent with his head resting on the breast of a supine woman. She lay on a bedroll, sick. No—in a place beyond sickness. The man stroked the curls that framed her forehead. His bearish hand caressed her unstirring cheek.

Clementine's expression was more peaceful than Shadow had ever seen it before, while his own cheeks dripped with tears enough for both of them. He drew a finger across the broad nose that always drove him wild for some reason, like she had done to tease him because she knew it. He took her hand in his, stroking her knuckles. On her finger was a ring. His ring.

Inma knew that ring.

"Robert," she whispered before her thundering heart throttled her.

Shadow lifted his face to her. Tearstains marred it. He opened his mouth. Closed it. Blinked. Opened his mouth again. He formed a name soundlessly. "Inmaculada."

They embraced fiercely until speech returned.

Inma pulled her thumb across the thin, soft skin above the apple of his cheek, the tip of her finger tickling his lashes. They had always been pretty, a starburst of youthfulness in his rugged face. Did eyelashes go gray? "Who is she?"

Robert-Shadow looked back at Clementine's body. "A prophet. The only one who understood. I failed her. Inma, I failed again."

She couldn't meet his eyes. She looked at the boy. "Is he… your son?"

Fresh grief deepened the lines of his face, if that were possible. "No. I never had a child."

Inma flicked her eyes back to his.

"What are you doing here?" Robert-Shadow asked.

"I came for my—" Inma stumbled, then knew she could say the word aloud, had earned it "—my daughter." She swallowed. "Robert, she—" Inma cut herself off. *Not yet.* Let him mourn this woman now. There would be plenty of time when Cassie returned.

$$\approx \qquad \approx \qquad \approx$$

*I hope you enjoyed reading this book
as much as I loved writing it.*

*If so, I'd be grateful if you spread the word
and considered leaving a review.*

Thank you!

*And sign up at www.fruitstonepress.com for
more from me and the WATERSHED world!*

ACKNOWLEDGMENTS

Many thanks to Lara Deeb, Tom Farrell, Lucy Keating, Erin La Rosa, Kiesha Minyard, Kathleen Nishimoto, and Jenny Walton-Wetzel for their thoughtful notes, especially Lara and Tom, who let me come to them often; Thomas DeTrinis and Erin La Rosa for helping me navigate the process; the wonderful team at Damonza for turning my manuscript into a beautiful book; David Carlson for making me look good; my parents, Hera and Ziad, for making books so central to my life; Lara, for leading me to so many great ones; and Tom, for making sure I wrote this little one.

ABOUT THE AUTHOR

HN Deeb lives in southern California, where the water crisis is real and growing, with his partner (and, fingers crossed, a soon-to-be-adopted dog). After professional forays into law and then anthropology, he now makes a living as a screenwriter and author. He's in it mostly for chocolate and cookies—Inma's agony in the bakery felt all too real to write.